D1398915

What the c ⌐ ⌐ ⌐⌐⌐...

"HEARTS ARE WILD is a sexy, sometimes saucy, always heart tugging mix of stories." ~ *Angela Camp, Romance Reviews Today*

"Emotional, highly erotic and sensual, HEARTS ARE WILD will definitely keep you warm on a cold winter night." ~ *Susan, Enchanted in Romance*

"Three exciting tales to heat up a reader's libido!" ~ *Alegria, Coffee Time Romance*

"[HEARTS ARE WILD] will definitely go on my keeper shelf along with my favorites from each of these three extremely talented writers." ~ Patrice, *The Romance Studio*

"HEARTS ARE WILD is a wonderful and exciting book by three incredible authors." ~ *Phyllis, Romance Junkies*

"The sexual content is hot and exciting and all three romances are, in their own way, heartwarming. It's hard to beat cowboys in heat." ~ *Page Traynor, Romantic Times BOOKlover's Magazine*

HEARTS AFIRE

"This one [HEARTS AFIRE] will make you gasp and make you cry but in the end say, in the words of a country tune, Hell Yeah...!" ~ *Patrice The Romance Studio*

"...She [Patrice Michelle] has a way of telling a sensual story plus adding all the great mystery elements. Kudos to a super work...!" ~ *Joyce Coffee Time Romance Reviews*

"...The humorous, always sexy, deep, and loving characters, and the suspenseful, intriguing, and masterfully written multi-layered plot had me guessing what would happen next, and wishing I had my very own cowboy to quench the blazing inferno of lust this story ignited..." ~ *Christine eCataromance Reviews*

WILD HEARTS

"I hope you're up for a little bareback, because I'm pretty sure that this fast-paced sexual romp is what they mean when they say "Save A Horse, Ride A Cowboy!" Nicole is a hardheaded spitfire, and Kev is a demanding, possessive, dominant to the core, 100% alpha-male cowboy. Together they absolutely sizzle off the pages, and that makes for a blisteringly hot erotic story with quick-witted, brazenly bold, and hilarious characters." ~ *Christine, eCataRomance Reviews*

"Cheyenne McCray never disappoints by giving hotter than hot sex, characters you can't help but love." ~ *Jennifer Ray, The Road to Romance*

HEARTS ARE WILD

Cheyenne McCray

Patrice Michelle

Nelissa Donovan

ELLORA'S CAVE
ROMANTICA PUBLISHING

An Ellora's Cave Romantica Publication

www.ellorascave.com

Hearts are Wild

ISBN # 1419952102
ALL RIGHTS RESERVED.
Hearts Afire Copyright © 2004 Patrice Michelle
Wild Hearts Copyright © 2004 Cheyenne McCray
Branded Hearts Copyright © 2004 Nelissa Donovan
Edited by: Sue-Ellen Gower, Heather Osborn, Briana St. James
Cover art by: Syneca

Electronic book Publication: December, 2004
Trade paperback Publication: October, 2005

Warning:

The following material contains graphic sexual content meant for mature readers. *Hearts Are Wild* has been rated *E-rotic* by a minimum of three independent reviewers.

Ellora's Cave Publishing offers three levels of Romantica™ reading entertainment: S (S-ensuous), E (E-rotic), and X (X-treme).

S-*ensuous* love scenes are explicit and leave nothing to the imagination.

E-*rotic* love scenes are explicit, leave nothing to the imagination, and are high in volume per the overall word count. In addition, some E-rated titles might contain fantasy material that some readers find objectionable, such as bondage, submission, same sex encounters, forced seductions, etc. E-rated titles are the most graphic titles we carry; it is common, for instance, for an author to use words such as "fucking", "cock", "pussy", etc., within their work of literature.

X-*treme* titles differ from E-rated titles only in plot premise and storyline execution. Unlike E-rated titles, stories designated with the letter X tend to contain controversial subject matter not for the faint of heart.

Contents

Prologue

"Bye, Aunt Viv," Nicole called out as she shut the door behind the last of their guests.

"Whew!" She plopped onto the soft red cushions of a nearby Queen Anne chair and tucked a strand of her shoulder-length, blonde hair behind her ear. "I'm glad we turned Aunt Viv's fifty-fifth birthday celebration into a family reunion, but I'm plain worn out. I'm used to hosting much smaller groups at my bed and breakfast, not one hundred and fifty family members bent on asking me when I plan to settle down and have a passel of kids."

"You could've just worn a sign around your neck that read, 'Remember, I'm the *wild one* in the bunch. I'll go down fightin'," Sabrina teased her cousin as she finished off her glass of wine and reclined back on the sofa.

"Hey, I heard you getting the third degree, too, Bri," Nicole shot back.

"Uh-uh, ladies." Their cousin Lily entered the family room, her long blonde hair already pulled back in a ponytail. Her violet eyes narrowed as she carried a roll of plastic trash bags in one hand and paper towels in the other. "Up and at 'em. Clean first, relax later."

Sabrina was once again struck by Lil's tall, willowy figure and striking blonde hair. Between Lil and Nicole, her cousins' fairer looks always brought to mind the stark contrast she made with her midnight hair, olive skin tone, and petite stature. She may not be voluptuous and buxom like Nicole or tall like Lily, but, she reminded herself, dynamite came in small packages with a sarcastic wit that just couldn't be contained.

Lil always was the sensible one in the bunch, but it didn't mean she had to like it. "All right, Lily White 'the good', can't you just relax for one minute?" Sabrina grumbled. Nicole's teasing reminder gnawed at her. It was true. She'd had her own fair share of comments about her "still" single status, which after the hundredth time, got old real fast. Now she remembered why she avoided huge family get-togethers.

Lily used the paper towels to point to each of her cousins, punctuating her words. "Oh, and as the oldest of the bunch, I don't want to hear any bitching about family asking you your marital status. I took the cake in that category today. Geez, you wouldn't think thirty-one was so over-the-hill."

Chuckling, Sabrina turned to Nicole. "Speaking of cake. How about Aunt Viv and that cowboy taking off for dinner together? The birthday cake was a nice touch, Nickster."

Nicole laughed and purposefully ignored the paper towels Lily tossed her way, letting the roll drop to the floor. "I thought Uncle Ted's eyes were going to pop out of his head when that sexy cowboy jumped out of the cake. You couldn't have picked a better birthday present for our always-wanna-stay-single-aunt, Bri."

"Me?" Sabrina gave her cousin a quizzical look. "I thought you set up the surprise birthday cake?"

"Nope." Nicole shook her head, her aqua eyes twinkling. They each turned their heads to look at Lily.

Lily snapped open a trash bag, her cheeks rosy with embarrassment, a wide-eyed innocent look on her face. "Don't look at me. You girls *know* better."

The cousins stared at each other for the beat of a moment and then burst into laughter, saying in unison, "Aunt Viv!"

Sabrina held her stomach and wiped the tears from her eyes, saying, "Leave it to Aunt Viv to one-up us on her own birthday present."

"But what a birthday present," Nicole said, bobbing her eyebrows up and down. "He may have been older, but I'd like to find a man who's going to look that sexy when he's in his fifties. He even seemed to enjoy hanging out with the family."

Lily joined Sabrina on the couch, still chuckling. "Well, now we know why Aunt Viv never joined a nunnery."

"With all the pranks she encouraged in us by telling us stories of her wild youth during our visits with her each summer?" Sabrina rolled her eyes. "Get real, Lil. She would've been kicked out of the nunnery her first week there."

"In all fairness, she did preface her stories with, 'Don't do this at home, girls'." Lily defended their aunt, a small smile on her lips.

"Yeah, but she always finished that up with, 'But you're not at home right now, are you?'" Sabrina countered, laughing.

"And you know that's akin to an I-double-dog-dare-you challenge to a bunch of teenage girls," Nicole chimed in.

When their laughter died, they lapsed into silence for a few moments.

"Hey, I've got an idea. How about a little friendly 'dare' for old times' sake?" Sabrina offered. She may be the middle-of-the-road kinda gal, but she was always the one that came up with the ideas. Nicole, being the wild one, was always the first one to take the plunge and Lily always went with the flow.

"Hmmm?" Her cousins turned curious gazes her way.

"Yeah, since we're all in the same boat, you know, being drilled on our single status, why don't we make a pact that for...hmmm, let's say, the next month we agree to let our hair down and go with the flow when it comes to men."

"Uh, just what terms are you talking about?" Lily looked wary.

"Remember Aunt Viv saying she was happy, but she wished she had someone special to celebrate her birthdays with? As much as I admire Aunt Viv's 'single status', I don't think any of us want to end up single at fifty-five, right?"

Nicole and Lily nodded their assent.

"Well, then I suggest a set of rules we follow for the next thirty days." Sabrina leaned forward, getting into the plan. "Here are the rules. Rule number one—Inhibitions? You no longer have any. Rule number two—The first man you meet that trips your trigger, go for it, even if your old rules about what kind of man you think is right for you rear their ugly heads, ignore them. Rule number three—Sex is your friend and you need lots of it to determine where this relationship is going. Rule number four—You don't have to marry the guy, just have fun. We can even check in at the halfway point to keep each other on track."

When she finished, Nicole piped in, "Sounds good to me."

"Okay, I can see where this pact might help me loosen up," Lily said, her cheeks stained bright red. She paused and cut her eyes over to Nicole before continuing, "But I don't see how these rules are a challenge for Nicole."

Nicole grinned unrepentantly at them.

Sabrina shook her head at Nicole. "Oh, you're not getting off scot-free, Nickster. I know your penchant for enjoying the buffet life has to offer. But this time, you have to stay for dessert and breakfast, too. You're in for the long haul, cuz."

Nicole narrowed her eyes and lifted her chin toward Sabrina. "And what about you, Miss I've-spent-my-whole-life-riding-the-fence?"

"Well, now I get to find out if riding something else is a lot more fun," Sabrina shot back.

As Sabrina sat back on the couch, a wicked grin tilted the corners of her lips. "Hearts are wild, ladies. Let's see if we can't do our best to tame a few."

Hearts Afire

Patrice Michelle

Acknowledgements

To my husband, my real life hero. Thank you for always supporting me.

And to my editor, Sue-Ellen Gower, who was literally my partner-in-crime on this book. Thank you, Suz!

Chapter One

Man, it's amazing what a nice ass can do for a pair of faded blue jeans, Sabrina thought as she stood in line at the airport waiting to pick up her rental car. Busy travelers walked past, their cologne and perfumes teasing her senses, not to mention the strong smell of coffee the man behind her held in a paper cup. The rich aroma made her stomach growl and reminded her she'd skipped lunch.

She leaned to the side, peering through the mass of people flooding to the conveyer belt to pick up their suitcases, to keep her line of vision clear to the tall, well-built, dark-haired man she'd caught a glimpse of. He had his back to her and a cell phone pressed to his ear as he leaned against the column right next to the conveyer belt. He shifted his black carryon bag over his shoulder and switched the phone to the other ear as he dug a piece of paper out of his back pocket.

Oh, yeah, to be *that* pair of jeans, she grinned at the concept.

"Miss? Um, Miss?"

Sabrina turned and realized the girl at the counter was calling her.

Pulling her suitcase behind her, she approached the clerk. "Oh, sorry. I was just checking out the great scenery Texas has to offer," she said with a smile.

Following her line of sight, the girl laughed and nodded her head in agreement before asking, "How can I help you?"

"I wanted to pick up my rental car."

She glanced to the side as the man she'd been checking out walked over to the counter near her and asked another rental agent for a pen.

"The name?" the girl asked.

"Sabrina Gentry," she answered as the guy scrawled something on the piece of crumpled up paper and spoke into his phone before he flipped it closed and clipped it to his belt.

"I don't have a reservation for a Sabrina Gentry," the clerk responded after checking her computer.

"But, I made a reservation—" Sabrina cut herself off and sighed. "Can you just set me up in a rental now please?"

"I wish I could, but we just had a large group come through and they took all the available cars we have. I can have a car for you by tomorrow," she offered, looking optimistic.

"How am I supposed to get to the Lonestar ranch? I'm wearing running shoes, but I don't think my suitcase wheels could keep up," she finished, irritated at the inconvenience Speedy Rental Car's lack of planning had put her in.

"We could have Robbie take you, but you'd have to wait until it slowed down a bit. Probably a couple of hours," the girl suggested.

A couple of hours? Sabrina's good mood began to evaporate.

"Or we could call a cab for you?" the girl replied.

"Ma'am?" a man said next to her. She turned and it was the guy she'd been ogling earlier.

"I couldn't help but overhear your dilemma. I'm on my way to Boone if you need a ride."

He was even better looking from the front side—dark wavy hair, high cheekbones and a full bottom lip completed his handsome face. Damn, she regretted that "ingrained" upbringing, the one that caused the "don't ever hitch a ride with a stranger" warning bell to clang its annoyingly loud sound inside her head.

She met his chocolate brown gaze with an appreciative smile. "Thank you for the offer, but I'll just call my friend Elise."

"You're talking about Elise Tanner, right?"

Sabrina gave him a puzzled look before the name sunk in. "Sorry. I've known her as Elise Hamilton since college. Yes, she recently married."

The stranger smiled, then nodded. "I met her briefly at a function a few weeks ago. She married Colt Tanner, a good man."

"Dirk Chavez," he said, extending his hand.

Her heart skipped a beat when she took his hand. She replied with a broad smile, "Sabrina Gentry. Nice to meet you." *Friend by association and therefore no longer a stranger, Bri*, she told herself with an inward, smug smile.

"If you're sure it won't be too much trouble?"

He reached down and grabbed the handle of her bag. "Not at all, Ms. Gentry." Glancing at the girl behind the counter, he said, "Call the Lonestar ranch when you've located a car for Ms. Gentry."

"Will do," the young girl called after them as he and Sabrina walked out the airport exit.

While Dirk stowed his bag in the back of his black pickup truck, Sabrina stood on the passenger side and called across the open bed, "I can't thank you enough for the lift."

"No problem, ma'am. I live to rescue damsels in distress," he replied with a grin.

"Call me Sabrina," she insisted as she returned his smile. Man, she so loved the respectful way these Texan men treated their women. Some women didn't like being called ma'am, but when it came accompanied by that sexy drawl, she just melted.

His biceps flexed underneath the short sleeves of his black shirt as he lifted her suitcase up and into the truck's cab. She couldn't help but think to herself, *Hmmm, niiiiice! This vacation is already starting to look up.*

"Only if you call me Dirk," he said, then asked as he pulled out of the parking lot, "Ever been to Texas before?"

Sabrina shook her head. "And I feel bad on the timing, to be honest."

When he gave her a curious look, she continued, "I totally forgot how newly married Elise and Colt were until after I'd called her." She rolled down her window and smiled as the hot wind whipped her long black hair all around her face.

Holding her hair down, she continued, "I don't want to intrude."

Dirk's eyes lit up with understanding. "Colt's a great guy. I don't think you'd feel at all like a third wheel around them." He chuckled, then finished as he turned the car north, "Plus Mace will be there to keep you entertained."

"Mace?"

"Yeah, Colt's little brother…the consummate ladies' man."

Sabrina chuckled. "Ah, now I see."

Maybe someone like Mace is exactly what I'm looking for. No strings attached, she thought even as she checked out Dirk's muscular forearms and the defined veins running down them. *But this Dirk guy…*

Her thoughts were interrupted by the sound of the CB on his dashboard crackling before a voice came through loud and clear.

"The chief has called a mandatory meeting. All firefighters, get your asses down to the firehouse."

Her high spirits plummeted at the announcement over the CB. Well, damn, why did he have to be a firefighter? she thought as Dirk gave her an apologetic smile and picked up the CB handset to respond to the call. Why couldn't he have been a police officer or an ambulance driver…anything but a firefighter? Unbidden, thoughts of her dad floated to the surface, but she pushed them to the back of her mind as she'd learned to do many years ago.

She managed a smile when he put the handset back on the CB holder and said, "Sorry, 'bout that. Duty calls. I can still drive you to the Lonestar since it's on my way."

* * * * *

Ten minutes later, Dirk pulled up the long drive to the Lonestar and stopped in front of the ranch house. She jumped out of the passenger side to grab her bag, but Dirk was already there, pulling down her suitcase and setting it on the ground. As he let the handle go, he gave her a wide grin and said, "If you do start feeling like a third wheel while you're here—"

Disappointment ran through her that she'd have to turn him down after he'd been so nice to her. Sabrina was saved from responding when the CB kicked off again, "Chavez? You there?"

Taking her suitcase, she nodded to the CB inside his truck and smiled. "Thanks for the lift. Now go to your meeting."

He nodded and rounded the truck to get back inside. As he drove off, he called out, "Take care, gorgeous."

* * * * *

Sabrina waved goodbye to Dirk and turned to take in the Lonestar ranch. A rambling white ranch house with hunter green shutters and a long front porch sat back from the long driveway. Ten feet away from the ranch house sat a smaller house painted with the same overall look. A barn and stables that led into gated wide open pastures completed the overall "ranch" look.

"Hi, Sabrina." Elise waved to her as she walked out of a screen door from the main ranch house. Skipping down the steps, she said, "I was getting worried about you." Looking around, she had a puzzled expression on her face. "Uh, where's your car? I heard one pull up."

Sabrina put down her suitcase and hugged her friend tight. "Speedy Rental Car didn't have a car available for me yet, so I hitched a ride into town with Dirk Chavez."

Releasing her, Elise pulled pack as she waggled her eyebrows up and down. "Oooh, Dirk, eh? How'd you manage that?"

"He had just arrived at the airport and was standing at the car rental counter using a pen he'd borrowed when he overheard where I was going," Sabrina said with a smirk.

Elise laughed. "And here I thought it was something more dramatic like you tripped him to get his attention or even better, dazzled him with that brilliant smile and that gorgeous body of yours."

Sabrina glanced down at her low-riding jean shorts and casual green tank top and looked back at her friend with a wry smile. "Somehow I don't think the outfit was what did it. I think it was the rescuer in him that made him have pity and offer me a ride."

"Ah," Elise said with an understanding nod.

When Sabrina stared off into the beautiful rolling pastures beyond the main ranch house, deep in thought, her friend continued, "Thinking about your dad again?"

Sabrina met Elise's green gaze. "Yeah, even though it's been seven years, it still hurts. When I heard the CB call in his truck and found out Dirk was a firefighter, it brought it all back."

Elise took her suitcase from her and set it on the porch. Wrapping her arm around Sabrina's shoulders, she started toward the stables. "Your dad wouldn't want you to be sad, Bri. He loved you with all his heart. Did I ever tell you he told me that?"

With a bewildered look, Sabrina shook her head.

"He told me while we were sitting in the dorm room your first day at college. Your mom and you had gone out shopping for food for the fridge."

Sabrina's heart lurched. Her dad wasn't a demonstrative person. She knew he loved her, but he rarely showed, much less expressed, his emotions.

Stopping mid-stride, she glanced at her friend. "He said that to you?"

Elise nodded. "Yeah. Maybe it was easier for him to talk to someone he didn't know very well. I think he was feeling sad that he was losing you to the next stage in your life and he didn't know how to express those emotions to you...so he told me."

"Why didn't you tell me?" Sabrina asked, upset her friend held back from her.

Elise squeezed her shoulder and continued walking her toward the stables. "Because you lost your dad that very next day. I thought I'd wait until you were over his death, but as time went on, it seemed you just became very sad whenever you thought of him. Remember? You'd be depressed for a couple of days if his name came up. I didn't want to contribute to that."

"Why tell me now?" Sabrina's chest felt heavy with the knowledge.

"Because I'm older and hopefully wiser and I realize that what you need to hear is just how much your dad loved you, how much he wanted you to be happy. He told me that's what he lived for...to make sure his little girl was the happiest she could be in life."

Tears gathered in Sabrina's eyes and she swiped them away. She missed her dad terribly, but Elise's words were like a balm to her frazzled, exposed emotions when it came to her dad's sudden death in that downtown building fire. The fact she didn't get the chance to say goodbye always tore at her heart.

Wrapping her arm around Elise's trim waist, she hugged her back. "Thanks for inviting me and for finally sharing what my dad said to you. It does help a little."

Her friend grinned. "See, that's just what I'm here for...to cheer you up."

As they entered the stables, Elise called out to a man who'd just ridden in from the pastures.

"Hi, honey. Come meet my college roommate, Sabrina Gentry."

A rugged-looking man wearing a black cowboy hat dismounted from his horse. His scuffed, dusty boots stirred the dirt floor as he walked over to meet her.

Putting out his hand, he said with a grin, "Colt Tanner. Nice to meet you, Sabrina."

When Sabrina smiled and took his hand, he glanced back and forth between the two women, his expression amazed. "Other than a slight difference in height, it's uncanny how much you two look alike."

Elise laughed and let go of her friend to step into her husband's embrace and wrap her arms around his waist. Hugging him, her expression happy, she replied, "Yeah, while we were in college, even though Sabrina's complexion is darker than mine, people mistook us all the time for sisters, and if they were drunk, twins."

Colt kissed his wife on the forehead, saying in a gruff tone, "Darlin', I could spot you in a crowd fifty feet away with your back to me."

Sabrina grinned at the love that reflected in his gaze when he looked at Elise.

"Oh, to be a newlywed," she sighed dramatically.

"That could be easily remedied," Elise shot back. "Dirk is available."

Unconsciously, Sabrina stiffened. "Uh, I'm not ready to settle down yet."

As she spoke, another man on horseback trotted into the stables, his brown cowboy hat pulled low over his face.

"Well, then *do* I have a man for you," Elise teased. Sweeping her arm toward the man as he approached, she said, "Sabrina, meet Mace Tanner."

Mace walked his horse close to them and pulled off his hat. Looking down at Sabrina, his gaze intrigued, he said, "Howdy, ma'am." His tousled, light brown hair, square jaw and beautiful green eyes caught her attention. She couldn't help but smile at the interested look in his gaze as he held hers.

Her smile turned into a grin as she remembered the "ladies' man" description Dirk had used to describe Mace.

He leaned on his saddle horn and winked at her. "You must be Elise's friend, Sabrina. I promised her I'd take you on a tour when you were ready. How about now?"

Sabrina shook her head as she looked up at him. "I've never ridden a horse before."

Mace put out his hand and she put hers in his, expecting him to shake it. Instead he held fast and looked at Colt. "Give her a boost, bro."

Before she could decline, Colt had grabbed her waist and lifted her up on the horse in front of Mace. "Enjoy your tour," he said with a grin. Then he looked at his brother with a meaningful gaze. "Behave, little brother."

Mace gave a deep laugh as he turned the horse around back the way he had entered the stables.

As Mace's horse trotted out of the stables, the unfamiliar, bouncing movement underneath her made her stiffen. Gripping the saddle horn for support, she said in a nervous voice, "Whoa there, horse."

When they emerged and headed toward the open fields, Mace wrapped an arm around her waist and said in an amused tone, "Relax, Sabrina. It's half the battle in learning to ride a horse."

Sabrina tried her best to relax when Mace urged his horse into a full gallop as they took off across the green pasture.

When they'd ridden for a while and Mace had pointed out different sections of the Lonestar ranch where the cattle and horses grazed, he slowed his horse to an easy walk.

As he started to pull his arm away from her waist, fear of falling made Sabrina clasp his hand and hold it in place.

Mace chuckled in her ear and wrapped his arm around her waist once more, this time pulling her against his chest. "Better?" he asked in a soft tone.

Sabrina laughed. "Yeah and why do I get the feeling you don't mind a bit?"

"'Cause I don't, darlin'. Not at all."

"So I've heard. Your reputation proceeds you, Mace Tanner."

"Ah, someone's been talking about me?" His tone dropped to a seductive whisper near her ear. "I hope it was all good."

"Considering my source was a man, er...I hope not," she teased.

"No worries there. Must've been jealous," came his amused, yet assured response.

"Are you always so sure of yourself?" she asked, both intrigued and entertained by his sexy confidence.

"Why not?" She felt his shoulders move behind her in a shrug. "I have nothing to lose."

"Now I like that attitude," she said, openly smiling.

"I think we're going to get along just fine, Sabrina." he replied with a chuckle. "Elise tells me you're here for a couple of weeks."

She nodded. "Yeah, I'm taking some time away from work to, um...find my inner self." She couldn't help but laugh at her own inside joke. Her cousins would be howling and rolling on the floor with laughter if they'd have heard her comment.

But Mace, being the type of man he appeared to be, drew his own conclusions. He spread his fingers across her rib cage saying, "Just let me know and I'll be glad to help you find out exactly what makes you purr."

Sabrina's heart raced at his words, but underneath that sexy confidence something about Mace felt like he was holding a part of himself back. She recognized that attribute well...she'd perfected it herself.

"I'll keep that in mind," she replied with a chuckle.

Sitting up straight, Mace gave her space as he said, "Ever been on a ranch before?"

She shook her head.

Turning his horse toward a different pasture, he said, "Come on, let's go meet some of the Lonestar ranch hands. They'd love to tell a beautiful woman all about what they do on a daily basis."

"And what do you do? Well, besides flirt outrageously with your female guests."

"You mean there's more to life?" he asked in a shocked tone. Sobering, he continued, "I help run the ranch, but I spend most of my time working on marketing for the rodeo side of the Lonestar. What about you? What do you do when you're not flirting with men you've just met?"

"Touché," she said with a grin. "When I'm not taking an overdue long vacation in the summer, I help run an advertising agency in Arizona."

"Darlin', we should definitely exchange notes," he commented, his tone more than a little suggestive.

"You are too much," she shot back at his double entendre.

"I'm a man and you're a gorgeous woman. You can't blame me for tryin'," came his unrepentant reply.

"I imagine it'd be so easy to fall under your spell." She gave a soft laugh at how much this man's attention boosted her ego.

The truth was this vacation was also about getting away. Her confidence had really taken a beating with Jeremy's rejection. When her boyfriend told her his career came first, she knew he wasn't the man for her. No man would say something so heartless to a woman, especially a woman he was sleeping with.

At least she didn't think so. Maybe that was her problem. Did she expect men to fit some ideal mold and they just never seemed to measure up?

"Won't know just how easy until you try..." Mace countered, his teasing suggestion drawing her out of her reverie.

Laughing and shaking her head at how skilled this man was at turning even the most mundane conversations into a flirtation, she parried, "I'm here for two weeks, Mace. The words 'take it slow' come to mind."

Chapter Two

"Sure you don't want me to help you with that?" Mace drawled from his leaning position against the stable door.

Sabrina tossed her long dark braid over her shoulder and blew her wispy bangs away from her eyes as she looked at him.

"I know exactly what you want to help me with, Mace Tanner, and the only one getting a rubdown is Lightning," she quipped, turning back to the horse as she unbuckled the saddle.

"I'm good with my hands. How long you gonna keep me at bay, darlin'?" he cajoled.

"'Til the cows come home," she teased.

After several seconds of total silence, the sound of a cowbell ringing and fake mooing coming from the stall doorway had her laughing out loud while she pulled the saddle off the horse and put it away. "Go back to work, Mace. I'll join you for dinner later."

"You know you're breakin' my heart, don't ya?" he asked, sounding wounded.

Sabrina cut her gaze back to him to see a cowbell hanging from his neck as he put his hands over his heart, the expression on his face as if he were in real pain.

"The only thing I'm breaking is your string of successful seductions."

Elise's laughter floated from behind Mace before she appeared beside him. Looping her arm around his, she tugged on her brother-in-law's arm. "She's got ya there. Come on, Mace. You've played constant host since Bri arrived. Let's give Bri a few moments alone." She looked at her friend and finished with a laugh, "Even if she wants to spend them working."

"I find grooming a horse relaxing somehow, strange as that sounds," Sabrina said as Elise pulled Mace away. "See you guys in a half hour," she called after them.

Turning back to Lightning, Sabrina looked around for the grooming brush until she spotted it up on a wood shelf on the wall. Standing on tiptoe, which probably gave an additional three inches to her five-foot five height, she tried to reach the horse brush that some too-tall moron had put on a high shelf. Didn't they realize not everyone in this world was over six feet tall?

She lowered her arm and looked around the horse's stall. Nope. No stepstool in sight, darn it. Sighing, she stood on her toes again, straining her calf muscles as her fingers brushed the bristles and pushed the brush back away from the edge of the shelf.

Lightning neighed behind her, apparently impatient for her to get on with the grooming. After being on the ranch for over a week, Sabrina still hadn't gotten up the nerve to ride a horse by herself, but she'd asked Elise to show her how to groom one and found she really enjoyed the task.

Eventually she'd work her way up to riding on a horse on her own, but in the meantime, she convinced Elise to let her give Lightning a good rubdown when her friend arrived back from a ride with Colt.

Mace had been a gracious host and constant companion, all the while never giving up on seducing her. And as much as she had fun joining in their outrageous flirtation, she didn't let it go any further.

She liked Mace, found him very attractive, but a part of her held back and she wasn't sure why. She didn't feel guilty not indulging with Mace because the rule between her and her cousins was "If he trips your trigger, go for it". Mace made her laugh and her ego soar but something was missing…oh yeah, the tripping of the trigger part, she thought with a smirk as she put one hand against the wall while reaching with the other in one last attempt to retrieve the grooming brush.

"Here, let me help ya." Strong hands came around her waist at the same time the man spoke. His hard chest pressed against her back, causing her to freeze and her heart race.

He smelled so good, like faint cologne and leather. God, he smelled of *leather*, she thought as he easily lifted her so she could retrieve the brush. The smell of leather was the ultimate turn-on for her. Sabrina quickly grabbed the brush and waited for the stranger to set her down so she could see his face.

Instead, he lowered her slowly to the ground as he said in a low, husky voice, its deep timbre skidding down her spine, "I don't think I'd ever be allowed on this property again..." He paused and let go of her waist with one hand so he could push her heavy braid away from her neck as he finished with a whisper in her ear, "if Colt knew the impure thoughts running through my head right now."

Sabrina's heart slammed in her chest at her reaction to this man, a man she'd yet to see, a man who had the hots for Elise, big time!

As she started to speak, the man set her away from him saying in a gruff tone, "I'm sorry, Elise. I shouldn't have said that."

Sabrina turned around, saying, "Well, I guess it's a good thing I'm not Elise, so those impure thoughts can just stay between you and me."

When she let her gaze scan the man's six-foot tall form, the first thing that came to mind was definitely impure thoughts... Did he ever trip her trigger...wow!

Trim, jean-clad hips, a silver and gold buckle, a black T-shirt that fit his muscular physique very well, broad shoulders and the sexiest, square jaw she'd ever seen. But what made her body jerk to attention was the intense look in his arresting teal green eyes, before his expression shifted to surprise. Man, she'd love to have him look at her like that! Well, technically he did, but he thought *she* was someone else.

His straw cowboy hat hid his hair color, but from the color of his eyebrows, she'd say his hair was dark blond.

He quickly swiped his hat off his head as an embarrassed expression crossed his face. "I'm sorry, ma'am. Please forgive—"

Ohmigod, he had the sexiest wavy dirty blond hair she'd ever seen! She interrupted him before he could finish. "Impure thoughts are only bad if they aren't returned." She followed her comment with a devilish grin.

His regretful look changed to surprise at her statement. Then a broad smile spread across his face as he put his hat back on his head and held out his hand. "I'm Josh Kelly. My family owns the neighboring Double K property next to the Lonestar."

Sabrina shook his hand. "Nice to meet you, Josh. My name is Sabrina Gentry. I'm a college friend of Elise's visiting for a couple weeks."

Josh's grip was firm and once he shook her hand, he didn't let go, but instead ran his thumb slowly across the soft flesh between her thumb and forefinger as he spoke. "Are you from Virginia, too?"

She looked down at their hands, mesmerized by the seductive movement of his finger across her skin and the tingling sensation it caused to slide up her arm. Blinking to clear her head, she met his gaze once more.

"No, I live in Arizona."

"Ah, so you're used to the heat, then." His Texas drawl coupled with his arresting gaze as he let it slowly roam over her lavender cotton T-shirt to her breasts before slowly returning to her face, made shivers course through her body. Damn, but the man just made her feel as if he undressed and caressed her. All with just one seductive, sweeping look.

Her heart racing, she let go of his hand and turned to begin brushing Lightning. *Boy, was it getting hot in here or what?* "Yes, I'm very used to the heat."

Josh's hand landed on hers and his chest pressed against her back as he said in a low tone, "Here, this is how you do it," as he slowed her movements down, guiding her hand across the horse's back, showing her the best way to stroke the hair.

His cologne tickled her nose again as she let him show her his technique. When his chest brushed against her back, she resisted the urge to lean against him, but she couldn't help closing her eyes and inhaling his arousing, masculine scent.

"See," he said above her, his voice soothing and calm as Lightning pawed the ground. "She likes the strokes slow and easy."

Lurid thoughts filled Sabrina's mind at his mention of "slow and easy" strokes. Man, but she liked a man that took the time to understand what a woman wants, even if that "woman" was an animal. That just meant he'd be even better with the human variety.

Lightning neighed again and turned her head, causing Sabrina to open her eyes. When she saw Josh put his hand out and the horse turn to try to rub her nose in his palm, she chuckled.

"You sure have a way with women, Josh Kelly."

He chuckled in her ear, the sound sexy and husky. "I try my best to please the women in my life."

"I'll just bet you do. How sorry were you that Colt snagged Elise?" she quipped as he let go of her hand and moved to stand in front of Lightning to rub the horse's nose.

Josh gave her a wide grin. "Elise who?"

She laughed out loud at how deftly he'd avoided answering her question.

"Josh?" she heard Elise call out as she rounded the corner and entered the stall. "There you are. I saw your horse and wondered where you went off to."

"Hey, Elise. I came looking for you and ran into Sabrina."

Sabrina watched Josh's reaction to Elise with interest. His relaxed stance had changed to an alert one. Interesting.

"Thanks for coming," her friend replied. "I wanted to show you another bull. We're hoping to trade for one more pleasure horse, like Colt did with Lightning. Interested?"

"Yeah."

"Lightning was your horse?" Sabrina teased, amused that he'd led her to believe Lightning had taken to him that quickly.

Josh winked at her as an unrepentant grin spread across his face. "She misses me sorely."

"Yes, Lightning was Josh's horse. Colt traded a bull for her as a gift to me."

"Yeah, he one-upped me on that one," Josh grumbled.

"You got the bull you wanted," Elise teased.

At the look in Josh's eyes, Sabrina thought, *That's not the only thing he wanted, Elise.*

"Come on, Josh." Elise beckoned as she started to exit the stall. "I'll show you our bull."

Turning to Sabrina, she said, "Hurry it up, slowpoke. Dinner's almost ready and Nan's cooking a special one tonight just for our guest."

Sabrina grinned. "Just for me?"

"Yep." Elise nodded. "So get a move on and head over to the kitchen. Nan always likes company while she's cooking. I'll meet you there once I finish up with Josh."

Josh pulled on the front of his hat as he faced Sabrina. "Nice to meet you, ma'am. Hopefully I'll see you again."

There he went with that sexy drawl. She melted and thought with an inward smirk, *You can bet on it, cowboy.*

Nodding, she said with a smile, "Nice to meet you, too. I'm sure I'll see you around." *Even if I have to show up on your doorstep, Mr. Hunky Neighbor.*

Once Elise and Josh walked off, Sabrina finished up with Lightning and after washing up, made her way over to the kitchen.

"Hi, Sabrina," the older lady called out from her position near the stove. Her stark white teeth made a striking contrast against her dark skin as she gave Sabrina a broad, friendly smile.

"Come on in and sit down a spell. Tell me how you're enjoying your vacation so far."

"Oh, no, you don't," Sabrina said as she picked up an apron and tied it around her waist. "I might be a guest but I like to do my fair share. How can I help?"

"I like you, child." Nan laughed as she turned over a piece of chicken to let the other side brown. Nodding toward the cooked whole potatoes sitting in a blue and white bowl on the table, she said, "Why don't you mash those up and then add some butter, milk, and salt and pepper for mashed potatoes?"

"Will do," Sabrina answered as she picked up the bowl and turned toward the sink to mash them up with the utensil Nan had stuck in the bowl.

As she began to mash the potatoes, voices outside drew her gaze to the open window. Elise and Josh walked up and stood talking outside. Josh put his hand on Elise's shoulder as he said something to her, then laughed at her response. That smile on his face as he listened to Elise…yep, he definitely still had feelings for her friend. The knowledge made her a little sad for Josh. He must really feel torn to be so attracted to someone and not be able to have her.

* * * * *

Having dinner with Mace, Colt, Elise and Nan was a real treat. Her first few nights at the ranch she and Elise had gone out to eat and the other nights it was usually Colt, Elise and her eating together and sometimes Mace, but tonight they all enjoyed a special home-cooked meal with Nan, complete with her own homemade mashed potatoes.

At the end of the meal, Colt had turned quiet as he picked up Elise's hand and kissed the palm. "The next two weeks won't go by fast enough," he said, the look in his gaze earnest and totally engrossed in his wife.

Elise smiled and kissed him on the cheek. "These two weeks will go by faster than you expect, I imagine, since you'll be so busy following the rodeo to a few towns."

"Yeah, but you've got a distraction," he grumbled with a half smile, nodding to Sabrina.

"I've got to make sure the online store is working properly," she reminded him.

"Ooh, to have a man say that I was a 'distraction' and mean it in an entirely different way," Sabrina chimed in wistfully with a swooning look on her face.

"Elise, have you noticed what a *distraction* it is for me to have your friend here? I'm not gettin' a lick of work done," Mace piped in at her comment.

Sabrina laughed heartily at the man. He really was a card at times.

The phone rang and Elise got up to answer it while Colt said in a stern tone, "You'd better, little brother. You're running the ranch while I'm gone."

"Ah, man, do I have ta?" Mace mock complained. He gave Sabrina a heated look and finished, "I was planning on playing chase."

"You mean that's not what you have *been* doing?" Sabrina shot him a shocked look.

"Nah, darlin', I was just warming up," he said with a wink as he pretended to tuck his denim shirt into his Wranglers as if trying to look good for a date. "Ah, but I still have my nights free." He waggled his eyebrows up and down as he addressed her. "Wanna go out with me tomorrow to Rockin' Joe's? It's my usual hangout on Thursday nights."

"Mace Tanner, you really are a piece of work," Sabrina said, shaking her head.

"Don't encourage him. He just gets worse," Colt warned in a dry tone.

Elise hung up the phone and walked over to pick up hers and Colt's plates as she said to her husband, "That was Josh. He's going to come by tomorrow with the horse we wanted."

Turning to Nan, she smiled and said, "Go on in the living room with the guys and relax. Sabrina will help me with the dishes. Thank you for another wonderful meal."

"But she's the guest," Nan said in surprise.

"Who's very grateful to be here and would happily do her part," Sabrina said as she stood and moved her hands in a shooing motion. "Now go take a break."

Nan grinned. "It's always nice to see the boys at the table." She cut her gaze between the two men and finished in an admonishing tone, "It doesn't happen near often enough."

"Hmmm, I think we're being asked to make up for quality time. What do you think, big brother?" Mace asked with an innocent look.

Colt stood. "Break out the Scrabble board. I don't believe Nan's delivered her special dose of whoopass on us in quite a while."

Nan gave a deep belly laugh, her large breasts bouncing against her full–figured frame. "Come on, boys. Let the master show you how it's done."

Elise laughed as the men and Nan exited the room. She picked up the plates and began to scrape off the leftover food into the trash can.

"They're very close, aren't they?" Sabrina asked as she opened the dishwasher and began to rinse the dirty dishes.

"Yes, Nan helped raise Colt and his brothers when his mother left."

"Ah, now I get it." Sabrina nodded her understanding at the family-like atmosphere she'd seen between Nan and the men.

They worked in silence for a while until the dishes were all done. While Elise was making a fresh pot of coffee, Sabrina dried her hands with a towel and leaned against the counter. "Want to hear the little bet about men my cousins and I made?"

Elise laughed as she finished pouring the water in the coffee machine and slid the pot in its holder before turning it on. "Knowing the stories you've told me about your cousins, especially Nicole, this ought to be good."

Pulling the chair out, she sat down at the empty table again, her green eyes alight. "Have a seat and do tell."

Sabrina sat down with a wide grin on her face. "Yep, you've got Nicole pegged all right but this time...the idea was mine."

"Now I'm *really* intrigued. Go on."

"Well, after we attended our aunt's birthday party and were bombarded with constant questions by relatives as to why we're not married yet, we girls decided to make a pact. For the next month, we decided we would disregard our normal reservations and apprehensions concerning men and 'let ourselves go' with the first man who tripped our trigger."

Elise chuckled. "Ah, now I know why you came to Texas." She winked, then teased, "Going to catch yourself a cowboy, Bri?"

Sabrina grinned. "Seems *you* did all right." She shrugged, then brushed her long braid over her shoulder. "I'm not looking for Mr. Right to come from this adventure, but we made a promise to let go and not get caught in our normal hang-ups about men. So I'm bound and determined to stick with the plan. I can't let my cousins show me up," she finished with a challenging tilt of her chin.

"Look out Texas men," Elise said with a laugh, then leaned in and teased in a conspiratorial whisper, "Is Mace your 'project'?"

Sabrina shook her head. "I just *love* flirting with that man, but as good-looking as he is, he doesn't 'trip my trigger', not like that tall, hunk-of-burnin'-love Josh Kelly does."

Sabrina held her breath and waited to see what kind of reaction she'd get from Elise with her revelation.

Elise looked surprised, then her expression turned serious. "Josh is a wonderful man. He's definitely a sweetheart who is also very sexy—"

"But?" Sabrina interrupted her. "Why do I hear a 'but' coming?"

A cell phone sitting on the counter started to ring, distracting them both. Colt walked in the kitchen and answered his phone.

Before Elise could reply, Sabrina continued in a lowered voice while Colt walked out in the hall to talk. "I know Josh has a thing for you, Elise. I've seen the way he looks at you."

Her friend put her hand on her arm and said, "No, it's not that, it's—"

Colt walked back into the kitchen with the cell phone in his hand, a serious look on his face. "Elise, it's your mom, honey. Since our line rang busy earlier she called my cell phone. You need to take this call."

"Excuse me for a second," Elise said as she rose and walked over to take the phone from her husband.

Sabrina watched her friend's face grow pale as her mother spoke to her. "Is he all right?"

Colt put his hands on his wife's shoulders and pulled her close as she listened to her mother talk.

"When's the surgery? I'll be on the next plane out. I know he doesn't want me to worry, but I'll be there when he wakes up." Her voice broke when she finished, "Mom, just in case… Tell Dad I love him very much."

Tears fell as she closed the cell phone. Colt immediately turned her in his arms and pulled her close. Kissing her forehead, he said, "I'm going with you, darlin'."

"But you can't go. You've got all your travel plans made," she insisted between sniffling.

"Mace can go in my place," Colt insisted. "You're not going there alone. Just in case, I want to be there with you."

Elise hugged him tight and kissed him on the jaw saying, "I love you very much, Colt Tanner."

Sabrina's heart swelled for her friend and the obvious love she and her husband shared. She stood up from the table when Elise let go of her husband, handed him the phone, and walked over to her.

Hugging her, Elise said, "My dad had some heart pains and when he went to his doctor, they wouldn't let him leave for fear he'd have a heart attack. He was on the verge of one with clogged arteries. He's scheduled for emergency angioplasty surgery tomorrow."

Pulling back, Sabrina felt tears in her eyes. "Oh, Elise. I'm so sorry. I hope the surgery goes well. I'll get out of your hair."

Elise held her hands and with a bright smile said, "Absolutely not! I'm only going to be gone for a couple of days. My dad's as tough as nails. He'll pull through this and I know him, he'll love the fact I'm there, but I'll be ready to come back when I know he's out of the woods."

"Are you sure?" Sabrina asked, feeling like her friend was trying to accommodate her.

Elise smiled and squeezed her hands. "Very much so."

While Colt used his cell phone to call and make airline reservations, Sabrina asked in a low voice, "You started to say something about Josh…"

"Yes, I did…" Elise began, then paused. She met her gaze, then gave her a broad smile. Hugging her tight, she whispered in her ear, "Go for it, Bri. You only live once and life can be way too short."

Leaning away once more, she said with a wink, "I'm sure Josh would be happy to keep you company while I'm gone. I'll call him in the morning before I leave and let him know to hold onto the horse until I get back. Then I'll tell him, 'but I do have this guest who might be bored out of her mind for a few days…'"

"Um, I'd prefer not to look so obvious," Sabrina replied with a chuckle.

Elise laughed as she let go of her hands and moved over to the cabinets. Pulling down some mugs, she suggested, "Josh was supposed to come by tomorrow anyway. How about I don't tell him that I'm going to be gone and when he arrives you can explain the situation? That work better for you?"

"Much. What time was he supposed to stop by?"

"He just said late afternoon. Are you going to get all spiffed up for Josh?" she asked with a grin.

Sabrina batted her eyelashes innocently, then grinned. "What do you think?"

Chapter Three

"Well, I'll be damned," Sabrina grumbled as she looked at her watch. "Leave it to me to pick a man who can't even show up on time on the very first date." With the Texas sun beating down on her, its heat making her skin sticky and wet, she must've uncrossed and recrossed her legs for the hundredth time while she sat on the front porch top step. Leaning against the railing, she'd hoped she appeared to be just resting and not the wilted-flower-waiting-impatiently-for-Josh-to-show-up person that she was.

Granted, Josh didn't know it was their first date, but damn it, it was six o'clock and the man still hadn't shown. Remembering she'd heard the phone ring fifteen minutes ago, she called across the porch through the screen door, "Hey, Nan, was that Josh that called?"

The screen creaked as Nan walked out, tugging her large denim purse over her shoulder. "No, hon, he hasn't called. That was my sister confirming our dinner plans."

Her chocolate brown eyes held an apology as she pulled her keys out of her purse. "I feel bad leaving, but I'm meeting my sister to celebrate her sixtieth birthday."

Sabrina laughed and shooed Nan on. "Go on, enjoy yourself. Don't worry about me."

"I'm sure it'll seem quiet around here without Mace," Nan said in a teasing tone.

"The man does have a certain charm about him. I already miss his banter," she replied with a smile.

Nan walked down the stairs saying, "That's Mace...always the one who knows just what to say to the ladies."

"He's got it down to a science, I believe," Sabrina agreed.

Nan nodded to the screen door. "I left you a dinner plate in the fridge. Just pull it out and heat it up when you're ready."

"Thank you, Nan. Now go have a blast with your sister. You only turn sixty once."

"I've turned sixty for the past five years. It's called 'sixty and holding'," Nan said as she shot her a wide grin, then winked before walking away to her car.

After the older woman drove off, Sabrina waited another half hour for Josh. The wind kicked up, blowing her long hair around her and giving her a break from the oppressive heat. That was another reason she was so hot. She'd left her hair unbound. Glancing at her cream linen miniskirt and baby pink linen top, she frowned at all the wrinkles.

As evening approached and the wind whipped around her again, she glanced up to see dark clouds rolling in the night sky. Sighing, she decided she'd better go eat some dinner. When she shut the screen door behind her, the wind howled, causing the door to swing wide open and slam against the main door. Sabrina shivered at the loud sound and decided it might be best to close the main door, too.

Opening the refrigerator, she pulled out her plate and stuck it in the microwave. As the smell of fried chicken and baked beans wafted from the microwave, she watched the trees bend back and forth in the wind and wondered why Josh hadn't shown or at least called.

Turning off the kitchen lights, she walked into the casual living room and flipped on the TV while she set the plate on the coffee table and sat down on the couch to eat. The TV's sound in the background made her feel less alone. Nan was right. She did miss Mace and everyone else. The house seemed so quiet now that Elise, Colt, Mace and Nan were gone. When she thought of the reason for Elise's absence, Sabrina said a little prayer for her friend's father before she began to eat her meal. She hoped he made it through his surgery without any complications.

A warning flashed up on the TV screen, making her turn up the volume out of curiosity.

Earlier today, Eddie Clayton, convicted for the murder of his longtime live-in girlfriend, escaped the bus that was transferring him from his temporary cell to his permanent twenty-year stay in the state penitentiary. If you see this man, don't go near him, please call 911. He was last seen heading south on foot as he ran into the woods off Highway 17.

Sabrina shivered at the picture that flashed up on the screen of the menacing man with his long black hair, full beard and beady black eyes. Highway 17 was only a few miles from the Lonestar ranch. What part of Highway 17? she wanted to scream at the TV. When the news flash ended, she clicked off the TV and turned on the side table lamp to light up the entire room.

Walking into the kitchen, she turned on the light and cleaned her plate and glass, dried them and put them away. She'd just turned off the light in the kitchen and started to walk into the living room when she thought she heard a knock at the door.

Apprehension washed over her and her heart rate slammed in her chest as she peeked out the kitchen window. No one appeared to be standing at the back door, but she noticed a glow that drew her gaze. An oil lantern sat on the railing holding down a piece of white paper that fluttered in the wind.

No way would an escaped murderer take time to write a note, let alone find a lantern. Feeling better, she opened the door, walked outside and lifted the lantern to retrieve the paper. She set the lantern back down as she read the note.

Elise,

Meet me at the stables. I've got a couple of things to go over with you.

Josh

With a smile, Sabrina crumpled the note and set it on the railing beside the lantern. That news flash on TV had really spooked her. In more ways than one she was thankful for Josh's company. Grabbing the lantern, she carefully walked down the stairs in her high-heeled sandals.

She didn't care about the wind slamming into her or the thunder off in the distance, announcing an impending storm. She just wanted to see Josh again. Hmmm, he might be disappointed that it wasn't Elise meeting him concerning the horse, but as her heart raced in anticipation of seeing him again, she hoped her appearance in the stables would make him glad he came by anyway.

The wind had apparently blown the large stable doors closed. She had to pull hard to open one of the heavy wood panels against the wind. Once she'd opened it enough for her body to squeeze through, she slid inside.

As the door slammed closed behind her, a couple of horses neighed, drawing her attention. Holding up the lantern, her heels sank into the dirt floor as she turned in the direction of the agitated horses and called out in a loud whisper, "Josh, are you there?" *Why the heck am I whispering?* she wondered.

Maybe it was because, with the main doors closed, the stables were almost pitch-black. The darkness combined with the sound of the wind buffeting the stable walls outside made knots form in her stomach. Hearing that story on TV and knowing some psycho-killer was running around free didn't help either, she thought with a smirk.

As she walked toward the neighing horses' stalls, she realized Josh never answered her. She held the lantern higher and found herself hissing out in a whisper once more, "Josh Kelly, I'm spooked enough as it is tonight. I don't need you goofing around. You'd better show yourself or…or I'm going to tell Colt what you said to me yesterday."

When Josh didn't answer her joking threat, the knots in the pit of her stomach turned to queasiness and then a cold feeling shot down her spine as fear caused the hairs on her arms to stand up. Something definitely didn't feel right.

"Colt can't have what belongs to me," a man said from behind her, his low voice dripping with hatred.

As Sabrina started to whirl around to shine the light on the man, a sharp pain flashed through the back of her skull. She fell to the dirt floor, felt the bits of scratchy hay underneath her cheek and then nothing.

* * * * *

Sabrina awoke feeling like someone had beaten her with a baseball bat. When she tried to turn her head to see around the room in order to determine where she was, she moaned at the pain the small action caused in the back of her head.

Lifting her hand to her head, a sharp sting in her hand caused her to gasp. Josh leaned over her and grabbed the IV pole that had tilted with her swift movement, righting it. Apparently that's what had caused the pain. She had an IV needle stuck in her hand.

"Hi there," Josh said softly as he pushed her hair back from her forehead. Concern lined his brow as he looked down at her, worry and relief paramount in his gaze. He smelled of smoke and he had dirt on his face. Smudged with soot and crumpled, his white T-shirt looked as if he'd pulled it out of the "to be bleached" pile of laundry.

"You look about as bad as I feel," she croaked out.

The corner of his lips tilted in amusement and his teal green eyes twinkled. "You must not be too bad off then, or do you always wake up handing out compliments?"

She managed a smile. "I'm not a morning person. That's for sure. Uh, is it morning?" she asked, confused once again.

"No, it's almost midnight. But as far as your comment on not being a morning person," he paused and ran his thumb down her jaw, his gaze following its path as he finished in a husky tone, "I'll keep that in mind."

"Where am I? What happened?"

Josh's brows drew together and he took her hand. "You don't remember what happened?"

Her heart thudded against her chest and her stomach tensed that she couldn't recall how she got there or why her head hurt so damn bad. His warm hand on hers helped calm her frazzled nerves. At least the fuzzy feeling spreading from his contact with her hand to the rest of her body was comforting.

"Why were you so late?" she asked, trying to remember when he finally showed up at Elise's house. Staring at his tousled hair and five o'clock shadow on his sexy jaw, she wondered how the hell she could forget him finally putting in an appearance.

"Sabrina, Josh saved your life." Nan's upbeat voice came from the other side of the bed.

She turned her head as Nan entered her room. Taking in the sparsely decorated room, the IV pole, the hard twin bed she was residing in and the cotton gown with a blue floral print on her body, Sabrina realized she was in a hospital.

Nan patted her other hand then picked it up and squeezed it. "I'm so thankful you're okay. When I got back and saw all the fire trucks—"

"Fire trucks?" Sabrina interrupted, her voice raising an octave as panic started to take over. "What fire trucks?" Even as she asked, she realized the mention of the fire trucks explained Josh's bedraggled appearance.

"The stables were on fire and you were unconscious inside," Josh explained.

"Oh my God," Sabrina said as she raised a trembling hand to her mouth in horror, afraid to ask. But she needed to know. "The horses?"

"Are fine, my dear," Nan answered with a calming smile.

"What *do* you remember?" Josh asked, his question urgent.

Sabrina met his intense gaze, frustrated that she couldn't recall. "I waited for you to come to…to tell you that Elise had to go out of town suddenly." She furrowed her brow, hoping the rest would come back to her.

Nan took her hand back and squeezed it, concern on her lined face as she glanced at Josh. "I know you're rattled, Sabrina. What else do you remember?"

"All I remember was hearing a sound and walking outside to see what caused it. And...and..." She struggled, trying to remember. Fear slammed into her and she blurted out, "I do remember someone or something hitting me in the back of the head but...but who and how, I just don't know."

"You don't remember anything else?" Josh asked her, his expression insistent as he came around to stand beside Nan.

She slowly shook her head. "No, I'm sorry. That's all I remember."

Josh gave a heavy sigh. Then he said to Nan, "The doc won't let her talk to the police until he's checked her out himself."

"The police?"

Josh nodded. "I stopped by to apologize to Elise for missing our appointment when I saw the smoke coming out of the stables."

He met her gaze, his serious, concerned. "Here are the facts as I know them for now. The stables were on fire and the doors were locked from the outside. You were inside the stables and you have a knot on your head as if you were hit from behind. We're not sure yet if the fire was intentional or not but whoever hit you must've also locked you in."

Looking at Nan, he said, "Go ahead and get the doc so the police can leave."

As Nan rushed out, fear set in, making her chest tighten and her breathing increase as she said, "But that doesn't make any sense. No one knows me here. Certainly not enough to wish me harm."

"Maybe it wasn't you they were after." His green eyes darkened, churning with unfathomable intensity. "I wouldn't want anything or anyone to harm you," he said, sounding serious, almost possessive.

She tilted her head to the side and said with a half smile, "I *do* remember what you said to me in the stall the day before when you thought I was Elise. I guess the fire doused your plans to meet with her." When she realized what she'd said, she quickly added, "About the horse, I mean." Well, crap! Why couldn't she leave well enough alone? Why did it bother her so much that he cared about Elise? She'd just met the man.

"Er, sorry. I didn't mean to imply...well, it's just that... I didn't imagine your attraction to Elise yesterday in the stables—" she started to say, but he cut her off as he moved closer and put his hands on the bed on either side of her, his statement low and rumbling.

"Once upon a time...maybe...but that was the first time I'd ever been attracted to Elise's backside."

He paused and ran his finger along her jaw, his intimate touch taking her breath away despite the incessant pounding in her head.

Then he continued, "If you had any idea what I thought about doing with you all day after I'd laid eyes on you, you wouldn't be questioning what woman I wanted 'cause I sure as hell don't."

The heated look in his intense gaze, mixed with the conviction in his words, made her heart skip a beat. Unsure how to respond to his revelation, she started to speak when Nan walked into the room followed by an older, silver-haired man with gold-rimmed glasses. Josh straightened but stayed close to the bed as the doctor approached.

Pulling his stethoscope out of his coat, the doctor said in an upbeat tone, "Hi there, young lady. I'm Amos Shelton. You gave us quite a scare tonight." Glancing at Josh, he said, "Stand back, Josh, and let me have a look at my patient."

When Josh moved back to the other side of the bed to allow the doctor room to work on her, the doctor checked her out thoroughly. Once the doc was finished, Josh asked him, "Is she up to going home tonight?"

The physician nodded. "I'd like to evaluate her for another half hour, but she doesn't appear to have a concussion. As long as she's going to have someone to watch out for her over the next couple of hours, then I'll release her."

The older man looked at her and asked, "There are two police officers who want to ask you some questions. Are you feeling up to it? I told them to be brief."

Sabrina nodded and the doc left the room to get the police officers. It seemed within seconds he was back with two officers in tow.

"Hi, Miss," the young, blond male police officer said as he entered the room and pulled out a pad and a pen. "I'm Tom Jenkins and this is my partner Renee O'Hara. We're the investigating officers on this case. Are you feeling well enough to give us a statement?"

Sabrina nodded and ran through the exact same scenario she gave Josh and Nan.

"Are you sure there's nothing else you can remember?" the female police officer asked as she tucked a stray lock of red hair that had escaped her ponytail behind her ear.

Sabrina shook her head.

The woman looked at her partner. "It's possible she could've stumbled on the escaped convict trying to hide in the stables. I just heard over the radio he was picked up a couple of miles from the Lonestar. They're questioning him as we speak."

Sabrina's heart jerked at the news her assailant could've been a convicted felon. Either way…someone tried to hurt her. As a shiver passed through her, she said in a shaky voice, "Thank goodness you caught him."

"When we hear back from the arresting officers, we'll give you a call," Renee said. "Where will you be staying?"

"She'll stay with me," Josh interjected.

Sabrina turned a surprised expression his way. "Um…"

Josh met her gaze and held it as he said, "Elise would never forgive me if something happened to her friend. I'm taking a personal interest in your well-being, and I think, at least for tonight, you'd feel better staying somewhere else."

"Pshaw," Nan said. "Sabrina, you're welcome to stay with my sister. She's a bit crotchety at times, but she wouldn't mind the company."

"I'm…I'm not sure…" Sabrina started to say, not at all sure whom she wanted to stay with.

"What are your wishes, my dear?" the doctor asked her.

"She'll stay with me," Josh insisted, his tone broking no argument. "Nan, I'll bring her back to the Lonestar tomorrow."

"Josh," the doc said in a warning tone. "I don't want my patient upset."

"Josh Kelly, I've never seen you so argumentative," Nan said in a shocked voice.

Sabrina turned to her to say, "It's all right, Nan. I'll let Josh watch over me." That's when she noticed the amused look on Nan's face. Hmmm, why did she feel she'd just been hoodwinked into staying with Josh? Better yet, why didn't it bother her one bit? Because he tripped her trigger. That's why.

"Have Colt and Elise been informed of the situation?" Tom asked Josh.

"I have a call in to Colt's cell."

"Good. Let us know when you reach him," he said, closing his notepad.

"And until we know for certain Sabrina's assailant was the escaped prisoner, no one beyond the people in this room should know where Sabrina is staying tonight," Renee suggested to everyone.

"That's enough questions and people for now," the doc said, ushering the police officers out of the room.

As the physician followed the police officers out the door, Renee called over her shoulder, "We'll be in touch."

"Are you hungry?" Nan asked when the door closed behind them. As she spoke, she pulled out a sealed plastic bag of biscuits with a sideways look at the closed door. "Hospital food is never good," she whispered.

Sabrina smiled when the doctor reentered the room and Nan quickly shoved the biscuits back in her oversized purse.

"Okay, Nan Marie," he said, rubbing his hands together. "Let's see what goodies you've got stowed away in your purse. Did you really think I couldn't smell your good cookin' a mile away?"

As Nan chuckled and pulled out the bag of food, the phone beside her bed rang.

Josh answered it. "Kelly here."

Sabrina listened intently to Josh while the doc negotiated Nan's biscuit recipe in exchange for lenience on the hospital food rules.

"Hey, Colt.

"Yeah, she's a bit bumped and bruised but she's fine. All the horses made it out okay but the stables are a total loss." Josh met her gaze as he continued talking.

"The police think Sabrina might have surprised an escaped convict who may have been hiding out in the stables. Whoever it was, he knocked her out and possibly was the one who set the stables afire. No, right now she doesn't remember what happened. I understand you can't be here for a couple of days." Josh nodded and he reached for Sabrina's hand as he sat on the bed beside her. Lacing his fingers with hers, he rubbed his thumb across her palm in a slow, rhythmic motion, his gaze on hers. "Don't worry. I'll keep an eye on Sabrina."

Sabrina's heart raced as Josh held her hand as if it was the most natural thing for him to do. The intimate way he looked at her, as if they'd known each other for years, made a shiver of sensual awareness run down her spine.

Josh handed her the phone, drawing her out of her reverie.

"Elise wants to speak with you."

Sabrina took the phone. "Hello?"

"Ohmigod, Bri, are you all right?"

"I'll be fine," Sabrina answered. "How's your father?"

"There was a small complication after the surgery, so I won't be able to come home for a couple more days. I'm so sorry, Sabrina."

Sabrina heard the fear and regret in her friend's voice. She squeezed Josh's hand. "Don't worry. Josh said he'll take good care of me."

"Oooh, he did, did he?" Elise chuckled despite the worry in her voice. "Sounds like you've got him right where you want him."

Sabrina laughed when Josh began massaging her hand. "You have no idea."

"I want to hear all about it when I get back," Elise insisted. "In the meantime, stick to Josh like glue."

Sabrina looked up at Josh's handsome face, felt the tender touch of his work- roughened hand on hers, the heat of his thigh against her hip and smiled. "You don't have to tell me that twice."

Hanging up the phone, she asked, "When do we leave?"

Chapter Four

The irony that she almost died in a fire when that same fate happened to her father didn't escape her. Riding beside Josh in his red dual-cab truck, Sabrina took a deep breath then smiled at her rescuer. Her head still felt tender but at least it wasn't pounding any longer thanks to the painkiller the doc had given her.

Josh pulled up to a large ranch house. Even though the lights were off, she could see its overall size in the dim starlit night. He quickly walked around to her side of the truck and opened the door for her, saying, "We're here."

Clasping her hand in his to help her out of the truck, he didn't let go when he shut the door behind her. His cowboy hat hid his expression, but she knew he was looking down at her because instead of letting go of her hand, he laced his fingers with hers and stepped closer to her body until his thighs brushed against hers.

He literally towered over her. With his broad, muscular shoulders, she felt very petite and protected standing in front of him.

Josh lifted her chin until she looked up toward his face. "Welcome to the Double K, Sabrina," he said in a serious tone, his voice filled with pride.

It was almost as if he were saying "Welcome home", he had such sincerity in his voice. Regardless of how he meant it, that's how Sabrina took his sentiment. A feeling of rightness settled over her as she wrapped her arms around his waist.

Laying her head on his chest, she inhaled his smoky, masculine scent and breathed out. "Thank you for rescuing me and for taking care of me."

Josh started to wrap his arms around her when the porch lights came on behind him.

The screen door squeaked as an older woman wearing casual gray lounge pants and a matching top stepped outside. "Hi, Josh. Nan called me and told me you'd be bringing Sabrina here. I've put her in your old room since the guest bedroom is in a shambles while we're remodeling it. Your room is next on the to-be-renovated list," she finished with a grin.

Josh addressed his mom, "Well, it's about time you're finally getting around to my old room. You're up really late." Putting his arm around Sabrina's waist, he said, "I planned to take Sabrina to my place."

"No, sir. Not tonight," his mother insisted while she stepped off the porch and walked toward them. Placing her arm around Sabrina's shoulders, she pulled her out of Josh's embrace and gave her son a meaningful look. "You can sleep on the couch if you don't want to go to your place."

Turning to Sabrina, she said, "Hi, Sabrina, I'm Julia Kelly. Come with me, dear. I know you must be exhausted."

With Julia's expressive eyes and short blonde hair, Sabrina saw where Josh got his good looks from. As Julia led her away, she asked his mother, "Would it be possible for me to take a quick shower?" Looking at her dirt-smudged skirt and top that held a strong smoky smell, then down to her muddy sandals, she finished with a grimace, "I feel so grimy."

Julia's smile reminded her of Josh's genuine grin. "Sure you can. I'll give you a change of clothes for you to sleep in and to wear back to the Lonestar tomorrow.

"How awful what happened tonight. I'm just thankful Josh was there to save you," Julia rambled on as she walked Sabrina into the house, steering her through the warm kitchen with its pale yellow walls and decorative navy blue accents. Once they walked through the kitchen, she turned down a long hall to the last door on the right.

Opening the door, she looked over her shoulder at her son who had followed them and gave him a stern look.

"Josh, Sabrina needs her rest after what she's been through. I'll let you say good night while I get her some clothes and then it's off to the couch with you."

Sabrina watched his mother walk down the hall, her steps assured and steady as she opened a door and disappeared into one of the bedrooms.

Despite how tired she felt, she turned in the doorway and met Josh's gaze. Winking at him, she said, "Your mother's a lovely woman. I see you get your smile from her."

Josh leaned his arm on the doorjamb and used his thumb to push back the brim of his hat. "Why, thank you, ma'am," he said with a grin, purposefully drawing out his Texan drawl.

Sabrina's stomach tensed and her heart hammered in her chest when he leaned close, his five o'clock shadow brushing against her cheek as he whispered in her ear, "Sweet dreams, good lookin'."

As she watched him walk down the hall, those faded jeans fitting his nice ass to perfection, her stomach flip-flopped. Instead of following him down the hall like she wanted to, she had to force herself to walk into the bedroom and await his mother to return with some clothes.

Julia returned within a minute, handing her towels, soap, shampoo, and a hairdryer along with a pair of jeans, some tennis shoes, and a T-shirt for the next day. She'd also included a soft cotton, lavender nightgown...one that buttoned all the way to her neck and went all the way to her calves.

Sabrina suppressed her amusement at the *prim* nightgown and gave Josh's mother a smile of thanks before she headed for the bathroom.

When she'd finished showering and drying her hair, she looked around Josh's childhood room for a few minutes. Sports trophies lined the desk and certificates of achievements in sports and academics covered the walls. She glanced down at a picture of a young blond-haired boy around seven or eight wearing fireman's gear. He had his arm around another boy with dark brown hair who was wearing a police officer's uniform. Halloween costumes, perhaps? she thought with a grin.

Either way, the smile gave the blond boy away. It was Josh's smile.

When she looked down at the twin bed, she noticed the man's white T-shirt neatly folded on the end of the bed. Picking it up, she put the material to her nose and inhaled. Josh. He must've left it for her while she showered.

The shirt smelled like him...the way he'd smelled yesterday when she'd met him for the first time in the stables. Had she really just met him for the first time such a short time ago? It seemed like she'd known him so much longer. Then again, tragedies had a way of bringing people closer together, right?

Pulling off the nightgown Josh's mom had given her, she slipped into his T-shirt, which fell almost to her knees she noticed with a chuckle, and turned off the light.

The house wasn't overly cool, so she pulled off the quilted comforter and slid in between the cotton sheets.

Lying down on the pillow, her mind shifted back to Josh. All she knew was their first meeting wasn't the most common for two people to have, nor was their second for that matter, she thought with a wry smile. No wonder they seemed to have known each other for ages. That had to explain the instant chemistry she felt whenever he was around.

She thought of his warm hand on hers, remembered his hard chest against her back as he'd helped her groom Lightning. Closing her eyes, she pictured his handsome face and sexy smile, imagined him pulling her close, how he would kiss. Would he be an aggressive kisser? Or would he let her take the lead? She let out a low moan at her wandering thoughts.

"I hope that sound is for me," came a man's whisper next to her bed.

Sabrina started to let out a gasp of surprise, but Josh put his finger over her lips and sat down next to her on the bed saying, "Shhhh, it's just me. Everyone's in bed, but I promised I'd keep an eye on you for at least another half hour."

The outside lights gave off some illumination in his room, allowing Sabrina to see the slow smile that spread across his face as he let his gaze roam over her form under the sheet. He smelled like soap. He must've taken a shower too.

Sabrina allowed her gaze to drop to his bare chest and felt her own chest tighten at the sight of the sprinkle of blond hair across his muscular pecs—gorgeous, sexy hair that vee'd its way down his hard abs before disappearing into his jeans. With his belt gone and the top button unbuttoned on his jeans, damn, a man had never looked sexier to her than Josh Kelly did as he leaned over her next to his childhood bed, staring down at her as if he wanted to devour her.

Sabrina smiled, drew back the sheet, and scooted over on the narrow bed to give him room. "Looks like there's only one place to sit."

Josh flashed her a quick grin and crawled into bed beside her. Leaning back against the headboard, he pulled her into his arms and said quietly, "Somehow this just seems the right way to end a day like today."

"Amen," she replied as she snuggled against his bare chest and wrapped her arm around his trim waist.

"Do you have any family?" Josh asked in a quiet voice.

She nodded against his chest. "I have two older brothers and my mom. My...my dad passed away." She was glad she was able to get that out without dwelling on the subject.

"I'm sorry, Sabrina," he commented in a genuine tone as he lifted her long hair and put it to his nose.

"He died a few years ago," she replied, ready to talk about something else. As he inhaled her hair's shampooed scent, she asked, "Tell me about the boy who used to live in this room."

She wanted to learn about the man who had saved her life and held her in his arms as if he'd known her forever.

She felt him shift under her cheek and realized he was looking at the wall of trophies and achievement awards she'd noticed earlier.

"He was a good kid. He's got a brother and a wonderful mom and dad. He was always happy with his lot in life, even if he was the competitive type, hence the sports trophies," Josh said and she felt, rather than saw, his amused smile.

"You mean you never gave your parents a bit of trouble?" she asked, surprise in her voice as she glanced up at him.

His chest rumbled with low laughter. "I didn't say that. My brother and I gave our parents hell growing up. I'm just highlighting the good parts." As he laced his fingers with the hand she'd had on his chest, Josh ran his other hand down her spine, spreading his fingers to cup her hip in an intimate manner. "How else am I going to impress you?"

Heat radiated from his hand on her hip as she laughed up at him and said with a grin, "How indeed?"

Snuggling against him once more, she asked, "So tell me about you and the little boy in the picture you were playing 'dress up' with."

Josh's entire body tensed when she asked the question and Sabrina instinctively knew she'd hit a nerve.

After a few seconds, he relaxed and ran his fingers through her hair in a rhythmic manner as he spoke, "Nick was my best friend growing up. We got into all kinds of trouble as kids. Who knows how much more mischief we'd have gotten into if… Well, he's gone now…"

He trailed off and she thought she'd heard a hitch in his voice as if he didn't want to speak of it or couldn't speak of the past with his friend. Apparently, it wasn't easy for Josh to talk about.

Sabrina hugged him tight and whispered, "I'm sorry, Josh…for whatever happened."

Josh put his finger under her chin and lifted it. Their gazes met and locked and he leaned closer, his lips a breath away from hers.

"I've wanted to know ever since I held your sweet body against mine while you retrieved that damn brush," he said, his voice full of desire, his gaze hungry and intense.

She raised an eyebrow and smiled. "Impure thoughts?" she whispered, letting her gaze drop to his mouth. If he didn't kiss her, she thought she'd die. Her heart rammed in her chest and her breasts ached for his touch.

"Very impure thoughts," he responded.

She really, really wanted him to kiss her, but if she let him, she knew she wouldn't want him to stop. For that matter, she'd kill him if he did stop. But tonight, in his parents' house, she wanted to respect his mother's moral standards.

Placing a finger on his lips as he had done hers earlier, she stopped his mouth's descent to hers.

"Josh, it's important for me to respect your mother's home and her wishes."

Josh's gaze flared for a second before he playfully bit her finger. "You need your rest tonight anyway, but there's no reason I can't *tell* you what I want to do to you," he finished as he pulled her hand from his mouth and laid a kiss on her open palm.

Liquid heat flowed south as he then kissed her wrist and growled low in his throat.

"You smell so damn good, I want to taste you everywhere."

He met her gaze once more and continued with a heated look, "And I do mean *everywhere*."

Tapping her nose, he said, "I'd kiss you here." Then he slid his finger down to her lips and said, "And here—" before he slowly drew a line down her throat to her rapid pulse and continued, "—and here, so I could feel how much you wanted me to continue down the rest of your body."

Sabrina's heart thudded against her chest and her sex throbbed as he ran his finger down her chest, stopping at the peak of one of her hard nipples through the thin cotton shirt.

"I'd tease your nipples with my mouth through this shirt, making it wet so I could see the pink color through the material. Then I'd nip them just to hear you moan a little deeper."

She felt her sex pulsing to the beat of his words and the lowering descent of his hand. Unconsciously she rubbed against his jean-clad thigh to assuage the sexual tension building inside her.

Josh took advantage of her movement and grasped her bare thigh, pulling her leg over his until she was wrapped around his thick, hard thigh.

Sabrina gasped in pleasure when he raised his leg slightly, purposefully rubbing the hard length of his thigh against her mons. God, she'd never survive this.

"I'd want to hear your breath hitch just like that when I touch you," he said, satisfaction lacing his calm tone.

Two could play at this game. Sabrina put her hand over his hard erection through his jeans and used her other hand on the bed for leverage as she slid up the length of his body until her mouth was close to his once more. She smiled at his own hissing intake of breath when she squeezed his cock.

"Be careful, Josh Kelly. You might be the one to start this fire, but I can assure you I'll be the one to make it burn fierce and bright."

Josh slid his hands past her shirt and clasped her buttocks in his big hands, his touch possessive and sure as he pulled her fully on top of him until her sex laid right against the head of his cock through his jeans. The feel of his rough jeans through her thin silk underwear made it seem as if she were wearing nothing at all.

His eyes glittered, full of challenge and desire as he pushed her hips down while he thrust upward, fitting himself inside her through their clothes.

"I know a good bit about putting out fires, Brina," he countered in a low, dark tone while his hands slid down to her rear end to cup her buttocks once more. With a firm grip, he moved her body just enough to rub her clit against the fly of his jeans.

Sabrina clasped his shoulders and bit her lip against the arousing friction he created. "Damn you," she hissed out as she pounded one of his shoulders with her fist in sexual frustration.

"She's all fire...just what I wanted to know," he said as a tight, satisfied smile tilted the corners of his lips.

His hands dropped to her bare thighs, cupped the back of her legs and pulled her knees forward until she sat atop his hips.

Then he surprised her by swiftly sitting up and changing positions until he was leaning over her and her back was on the bed. Her breathing came out in short pants as he held her hands pinned to the bed above her head, his hips spreading her thighs. He pressed her body against the soft bed with his weight. "I think you like me holding you down," he teased before his expression turned serious once more. "What ironic justice, that the kind of woman from every single adolescent wet dream I've ever had will sleep in my childhood bed tonight."

He leaned close, his breath warm on her cheek as he finished with a heated whisper in her ear, "Because I'll be dreaming of all the adult ways I *will* have you in the near future while I sleep tonight."

Before she could respond, he stood and scooped her in his arms. Settling her back on the pillow, he pulled the sheet over her and said in a controlled tone, "Good night, Sabrina. I'll see you in the morning."

Sabrina watched him leave the room, her sex aching and throbbing as he shut the door. The promise in his words, the steady regard in his gaze when he told her they would be together echoed in her head, making her heart hammer in her chest in anticipation. Never had she felt so aroused and sexually frustrated in her life.

She considered satisfying her own needs, but decided against it. She "wanted" to anticipate, wanted to let the sexual tension build between them—to let it simmer and burn. Because deep down she knew when they finally came together, the explosion would be well worth the wait.

Chapter Five

"Hiya, girl," Sabrina crooned as she patted the horse's nose over the stall door. "One of these days I'll get up the courage to ride one like you on my own," she continued as the horse neighed and raised her head up and down as if in agreement.

Sabrina had wandered outside after having breakfast with Josh's family. When she'd gotten dressed and walked downstairs this morning, her growling stomach followed the smell of bacon and eggs and coffee. The fact Josh wasn't present made her a little unsure what to do once she made it down the hall. But Julia met her in the living room with a sunny smile, saying, "Come eat breakfast, Sabrina. Everyone wants to meet you.

"Everyone, meet Sabrina. Sabrina, meet the Kelly family," Julia said as they entered the kitchen and approached the table.

"Hi, I'm Ben," the little blond-haired boy at the far end of the table piped up. He looked to be around ten years old. "If you're a friend of Josh's, you must be all right," he said. His child's logic broke the ice and made her nervousness completely disappear as he decided to play host.

"That's my dad, Ben senior," he continued, pointing to a tall, sandy blond-haired man pouring himself coffee by the sink. "And this is my mom, Lacey." He nodded to a woman with short auburn hair sitting next to him. "My grandpa, his name's Kenneth. He's outside already since he's a real early riser."

"Good morning, Ben, and thank you for the welcome," Sabrina had replied with a laugh before she sat down and enjoyed a wonderful breakfast with Josh's family...well, minus Josh.

Just where was the man? she wondered as she turned to walk out of the stables and head back toward the house.

Josh came riding up, his straw cowboy hat pulled low on his head. Sabrina noticed his thigh muscles flex through his soft, worn, well-fitted jeans as he turned his horse sideways so he could step next to her.

"Good morning, beautiful. Ready to go?" he asked, his sexy smile making the butterflies in her stomach multiply tenfold as he rested his forearms on his saddle horn and met her gaze with his arresting teal one.

"Out and about early this morning?" she quipped, still a little put out that he'd deserted her.

Josh's smile turned to a grin as he pushed his hat back a bit. "Why yes, ma'am, I was. I had to take care of a few things. I'm sorry if I left you hanging, but I knew you were with my family so you'd have been well taken care of."

She looked down at her borrowed baby-blue cotton T-shirt and jeans a couple sizes too big, then let her gaze move to her bare feet—she'd foregone the tennis shoes that were a size too small—and laughed as she met his gaze once more.

"Yes, but I'll be glad to get back into some of my own clothes."

Josh lifted his gaze and called out to his brother entering the stables, "Ben, how about saddling Dusty for Sabrina for me?"

"Will do." His brother waved his hand in response.

Sabrina put her hand on Josh's knee, her stomach knotting in fear. "Where are we going, Josh? I've not gotten up the nerve to ride a horse, yet. I was working my way up to that by grooming Lightning."

"Really?" Surprise flickered through his expression, then he called out to his brother, "Ben, never mind. Just give Sabrina a foot up. She's going to ride on Ace with me."

Even though the idea of riding with Josh made her fear lessen somewhat, Sabrina's stomach still remained a mass of nerves while Ben helped her mount Josh's horse. As she settled on the saddle in front of Josh, she tensed all over, grabbing onto the saddle horn for dear life.

Josh's arms came around her waist and he chuckled low in her ear. "Relax, Brina," he said as he pulled on the reins and nudged his horse so he would turn around and walk out of the stables.

"Where are we going?" she asked again, thankful to finally be alone with Josh, even if it was up on a horse's back.

Ace exited the stables and headed for the back of the Tanners' house. Once the horse reached the edge of the woods, Josh said as he entered the woods, his tone intimate and full of promise, "I thought you might like to see my place." He paused and continued, "I've taken a couple of days off. As much as I'd like to say I'm doing this to watch over you, the truth is... I'm hoping that you'll decide to stay and spend some time with me."

"Oh," was all Sabrina got out before Ace began to climb a slight incline. The fact that Josh wanted her to stay with him made her heart hammer in her chest while the horse's movement upward forced her body to lean back against Josh. Her head settled in the cradle of his shoulder and her rear end rubbed against his crotch as she slid back in the saddle.

Josh tightened his arm around her waist and growled low against her neck saying, "This ride is going to be pure torture."

"Which is exactly the state you left me in last night," she countered, purposefully grinding her butt against his obvious erection pressed against her backside.

"We both suffered, Brina," he said in a husky tone while he splayed a hand across her belly. As the horse walked at a slow pace up the slope, he rubbed his thumb on the underside curve of her breast in the same rhythmic movement.

"What do you do when you're not visiting friends on vacation?" he asked conversationally as if he weren't arousing her body with his tantalizing touch.

"I work in an advertising firm."

"Travel much with your job?" he asked as he began to pull her tucked-in shirt from her pants.

Her heart sped up at his slow, purposeful seduction. Rational thoughts were fading fast. "Uh...um...no. Actually most of my job is done via email and phone with travel only to a couple of meetings a year. Marketing isn't always as glamorous as it sounds," she finished with a chuckle.

"I was hoping you traveled to Texas a *lot*," he emphasized the last word as his fingers brushed against the bare skin on her belly. Warmth began to spread through her body competing with the Texas heat that clung to her skin even in the shade-covered trail.

"Technically my job could be done from a home office for the most part," she laughed, warmed by the idea that he hoped to see more of her.

Josh's touch made it hard to focus on her surroundings as it was, but she realized a moment's panic when he knotted the ends of the reins together then suddenly dropped them to put his palms on her thighs.

"Josh, the reins," she gasped in alarm as she used her grip on the saddle horn to lean forward to grab the reins lying across Ace's neck.

She sucked in her breath when his hands encircled her waist and quickly pulled her back against his chest.

"Ace knows the way," he replied with confidence. "I need both hands to learn every inch of this new territory that's before me," he whispered in a seductive tone before he planted a tender kiss on the sensitive spot behind her ear.

The gentle brush of his lips on her skin caused shivers to course through her.

As his hands moved higher, her stomach tightened in arousing anticipation while blood rushed to her sex in pulsing tension.

When his hands cupped her breasts, Sabrina gripped the saddle horn tighter and closed her eyes, waiting with bated breath as her heartbeat thrummed in response.

The first brush of his thumbs across her nipples through the fabric of her bra made her gasp at the pleasure that shot straight down her thighs and lower belly.

"Put your hands on my thighs," he ordered in a gruff voice.

Sabrina's eyes flew open. "No," she breathed out in fear, clinging to the saddle horn even more.

Josh's fingers slid down to her nipples. "Trust me, Sabrina," he said, this time pinching the hard nubs.

The slight pain heightened her arousal, making her moan in sheer carnal bliss.

Slowly, she let go of her "lifeline" and put her hands on his thighs.

"That's my girl," he said, then continued in a calm tone, "Now lean your body fully against mine, close your eyes and feel."

She did as he requested and closed her eyes.

When Josh's lips touched her neck, nuzzling her at the same time his hands cupped her breasts fully, she purred her pleasure.

"Do you feel the horse moving under you, Brina? Feel his movements? Can you anticipate with your body and move with him, instead of against him?" he asked as he slid one hand down her bare belly.

Oh, God, he was going to kill her with this slow sexual torture, she thought before she answered with a nod. Even his scent, a mixture of fresh outdoors, faint aftershave and leather worked to ignite her senses.

"Leaning against you, I can feel how you move with him." And she did notice the difference. Slowly her body had begun to relax, following the horse's motion.

When she started to put her hands back on the saddle horn, his grip on her breast and belly tightened and his body tensed behind her.

"No, keep your hands on my thighs." His tone lowered, darkened as his hand landed on her knee.

Her eyes opened once more. "What are you planning—" she started to ask.

She didn't get to finish her question because her breath caught in her throat when his hand slid up her inner thigh.

"There's a lot I'm planning to do, darlin'," he drawled, feathering his lips down her throat as he cupped the inside of her other thigh as well and applied pressure to both, pushing her legs further apart.

"Josh," she hissed out as she gripped his hard thighs and tightened her own against the horse. The anticipation was almost her undoing.

Then he found the closure on the front of her bra and unsnapped it, rasping, "Feel for me, Brina," as he pushed the cotton material out of the way and rolled her bare nipple between his fingers.

She let out a low moan at the jolts of desire that radiated from her breast straight down her body. Her moan turned into a loud gasp when Josh's hold on her inner thigh tightened before his touch skimmed higher until he reached her mound.

Just when she hoped he would begin to move his hand, he whispered against her ear, "When I touch you for the first time, I want to see your expression, the pupils in your eyes change." His grip on her breast tightened as he continued, "Do you want to know what I thought about last night while I lay on the damned couch?"

She could only nod her head when he brushed his thumb across her nipple once more.

"I thought about pulling all your clothes off, taking my time so I could discover every inch of your sweet flesh," he said as he unbuttoned the top button on her jeans, then unzipped her pants.

Her body heated all over at his words.

His hand slid down her belly beyond her underwear until his fingers teased the curls below. Sabrina bit her lip to keep the whimper that threatened to escape her lips inside.

"Then I'd lay you down and run my hands all over your body. I'd want to touch you *everywhere*. You'd arch your back, silently begging me to touch your breasts, then you'd lose control and tell me exactly what you wanted."

Her heart hammered in her chest at the visual he painted and the stimulation his teasing caused.

"But I'd want to taste them instead," he continued in a seductive whisper, his breath hot against her ear as he withdrew his hand from her pants and cupped both breasts fully, his grip firm and possessive.

"I'd suck long and hard on your nipples, until you twisted and whimpered and pushed my head between your gorgeous thighs."

Sabrina's pulse thrummed at the sexy image he described. When his thumbs just barely brushed across her nipples, she squirmed against the hard saddle, trying to assuage the painful ache that had settled between her legs.

"I'd put my hands on your thighs and spread them wide while my thumbs massaged your pink flesh. It'd turn me on to see just how wet you were for me, and I'd be unable to resist taking a long, leisurely taste with my tongue."

He's killing me, she thought.

Josh moved a hand to cup her sex through her jeans. He applied pressure as he continued in a husky tone, "But one taste wouldn't be enough and I'd go back for more and more." His voice took on a relentless tone as he continued, "I'd trace every fold, every bit of your sensitive skin, making you so horny you'd beg me to make you come."

Sabrina's breathing turned choppy and her heart hammered in her chest at the wanton scenario he painted. Perched atop a horse, holding on to this sexy man's rock-hard thighs, his muscular chest and hard-as-marble erection pressed against her backside—all this while his words and teasing touches built a fire burning inside her—she'd never been more turned on in her life.

"I hear you panting," he continued in a determined voice as his grip on her sex tightened. At the same time he plucked at one of her nipples, saying in an intense, insistent tone, "I can't wait to hear you scream for me when you come, Brina. I know you're a screamer and fuckin' hell…all last night I thought of nothing else but hearing it."

Sabrina closed her eyes and moaned at the intensity in his voice as the need for physical release engulfed her body, causing a sensual burn to build inside her, spiraling out of control.

While she unconsciously rocked against his hand, she heard his pleased comment near her ear, "That's it, baby. Damn, I can't wait to feel your sweet body wrapped around me."

When he stopped speaking and wrapped his arms around her waist, saying, "We're here," she realized his horse had stopped walking and she opened her eyes, shaking herself out of the sexual web of desire he'd woven around her.

With her body still quaking, Sabrina managed a shaky smile at the quaint house before her. His two-story wood-sided home with a bench swing off to the left of the front door and a couple of pale wood rocking chairs to the right created a homey look that surprised her considering he was a bachelor.

She noted that there wasn't a big front yard and practically no backyard since the woods backed almost all the way up to the house. Nodding to indicate the front yard that blended right into the woods, she said, "Now I know why you didn't drive me up here. Is there even a road to get to your place?"

Josh chuckled as he slid off the horse onto the ground. "Yeah, I guess the grass driveway you see appears to lead to nowhere. We used the road to bring up the materials to build my house and on the day I moved my stuff in. But I prefer riding my horse up here, so the driveway has grown over by forest underbrush over time." Nodding to the back of the house, he said, "There are open pastures beyond the woods behind my house. I just haven't cut a path to them yet."

As he finished speaking, he reached up and clasped her around the waist. When he effortlessly lifted her off of Ace and set her on the ground, Sabrina's unbuttoned pants must've decided they'd spent enough time hanging around her hips because they immediately fell to her ankles.

Despite the fact Josh had just had his hand in her underwear, heat infused her face. There's just something totally mortifying about being caught with one's pants down.

Josh didn't miss a beat as he bent down and pulled her pants back up, saying with a grin, "I'd planned to get you out of your pants as soon as possible, darlin', but this wasn't quite how I envisioned it."

His humor at the situation soothed her embarrassment, making her laugh as she zipped up and buttoned her loose pants then resnapped her bra.

Josh took off his hat and ran a hand through his hair, his penetrating teal green gaze searching her face as he visually connected with her. Her heart hammered at the long, sexually charged moment that passed between them.

"Why don't you go change into your own clothes while I put Ace away?"

Sabrina's spirits perked up. "You have my clothes?" She was too thankful to have her own clothes to be peeved that Josh "assumed" she'd stay with him.

He nodded. "Yep, that's where I was this morning— retrieving your belongings. Nan wouldn't let me leave until I had assured her I would bring you to the ranch today so she could see for herself you were okay."

Sabrina grabbed hold of the waistband of her pants, just in case, as she turned and walked up the steps to enter Josh's house. She chose to ignore his good-humored chuckle as she closed the door behind her.

The contemporary design inside surprised her. Raised up on a couple of wooden steps, the kitchen and dining room sat on an "island" in the center of the room. Josh must put a large importance on cooking if his kitchen held the center of attention, she thought.

Geez, she sure hoped he didn't expect her to cook. Eggs and toast were about all she'd learned to do. She'd always been in awe of her cousin Nicole's ability to just "whip" up a meal from practically nothing. Sabrina's creativity came in the form of advertising slogans and "understanding" the target market.

Even though Josh's choice for where to place his kitchen seemed very modern and contemporary, he'd kept it warm with rich leather and polished wood barstools against the tall wood and slate counters. Spindle back chairs graced the oval oak dining table. Everywhere she looked, wood floors graced the house from wall to wall.

To her left was apparently a living room with its well-worn leather sofa and matching smaller sofa for two sitting on top of a rug with an Aztec design. Very few pictures graced the walls but the ones that did depicted horses. Oils and watercolor pictures decorated the living room while black and white photos of horses running decorated his office off to her right.

Once again, Josh had added an Aztec designed rug in deep maroons and blues in the center of his "office" room. A single mission style desk in a rich cherry wood and a tall black leather chair made up his office. A laptop, a printer/fax machine, and a telephone sat atop the desk.

Sheesh, except for the few papers she'd seen scattered on his desk, Sabrina just realized how utterly immaculate Josh's place was.

The whole other back side of the main room in his house held a foosball table and a poker table. Must be the recreation room, she thought with a grin as her gaze followed the wrought iron spiral staircase against the wall in the center of the far back wall of the house. The staircase led to a small sitting area landing that overlooked the whole house and had a huge picture window that must have a gorgeous view of the woods behind the house.

On the far wall of the main floor, two doors led off on either side of the room, presumably to Josh's bedroom and a guest bedroom.

She bit her lip, wondering where Josh had put her stuff. When her gaze landed on her small suitcase sticking out beside the sofa, she let out a sigh of relief. At least she wouldn't be rifling through Josh's bedroom looking for her belongings. Despite their instantaneous sexual attraction, she'd rather be invited into his room first.

Grabbing her suitcase, Sabrina went to find the bathroom and change clothes.

* * * * *

His cock throbbing and anticipation coursing through him, Josh forced himself to a slower pace as he walked Ace to the barn and opened the stall door.

After he pulled his horse inside, he rifled through the pouch in his saddle and retrieved his cell phone.

Dialing the police department, he asked for Officer O'Hara.

"O'Hara here."

"Renee, this is Josh. Just wondering how the interrogation went on the escaped convict who was caught last night. Did he confess to attacking Sabrina?"

"Nothing yet," she hedged.

Her evasive tone irked him. He had to know the answer for sure. "So are you saying you still think it was him but he just hasn't confessed yet?"

"No," came her concise reply.

"Wow, you're just a fount of information, aren't you?"

She sighed on the other end. "It's an investigation, Josh. I shouldn't even be talking to you about it. So I'm hanging up now."

"Wait!" he called out, then cajoled, "C'mon, Renee. You can tell me."

"I'm not at liberty to say," she replied, her tone curt.

"Do you still skinny dip in the lake on the far side of the Masterson's estate? Oh, I think that you do," he said with a grin.

"That's really low, Josh," she hissed, then lowered her voice. "How do you know that?"

"I'll tell you, if you tell me," he replied as he leaned against the stall's doorway.

Another big sigh came across the line and Renee said in a low voice, "We have to look at all scenarios, all motives. Considering the fire occurred while Colt and Elise were out of town… Well, we have to investigate all possibilities."

"Such as?" he prompted, anxious for her to get to the point.

"We checked to make sure their homeowners' insurance hadn't been increased on the Lonestar property, up to and including a rider for their fire hazard insurance."

"You're investigating insurance fraud?" he asked, incredulous. "I know we've determined that the fire was set by the lantern, but that could've happened by accident when Sabrina was attacked."

"It could've been an accident," she agreed. "But as I said, we have to look at the possibility the person who attacked Sabrina wasn't the man we have in custody. The locking of the stable door begs the 'premeditated' question. Based on our inquiries, Colt and Elise are clean on any recent changes to their homeowners' insurance, but we're still probing to rule any other scenarios out."

"You're barking up the wrong tree, Renee," Josh warned. "Keep me posted when the convict confesses," he finished, letting her know just what he thought of her current turn of the investigation.

She chuckled. "I wouldn't hold my breath. He's not talking. Okay, Josh, your turn. Who knows I skinny dip?" she asked in an expectant tone.

"Dirk," he replied, a grin riding his face.

"Dirk Chavez! Oh my god, has he been watching me?" she asked, her tone horrified.

"I dunno. You'll have to ask him," Josh shot back, trying to keep the laughter out of his voice. Renee had always been known as a prude in school, so the discovery she had a somewhat "freer spirit" side to her personality made him want to chuckle. Sobering, he continued, "Keep in touch with me on the investigation. I may be able to help."

"Will do," she said, her tone turning all business before she hung up.

Josh ended the call and left the stables, heading back to his house. As he mounted the porch stairs, his cell phone began to vibrate. Thinking it was Renee calling back, he was surprised to see Colt's name on the caller ID. He flipped open the cell phone and put it to his ear.

"Heya, Colt. How's it going? Nan told me about Elise's dad. How's he doing?"

"Hey, Josh," came Colt's deep, Texan drawl across the line before he chuckled. "He's a tough bull. Elise and I wanted to see how Sabrina was doing."

"She appears to be doing fine," Josh replied, thinking Sabrina was more than fine. She was the best damn looking woman he'd ever laid eyes on.

"Actually, she's staying with me for a couple of days. So if Elise needs to reach her, tell her to call my cell phone."

"Got it," Colt acknowledged. "Elise will be glad to know Sabrina has a protector watching over her. Tell her we'll be home in a couple of days. Oh, and Josh, do me a favor and keep an eye on the ranch, will ya? I don't like being gone with no one there watching the place. You know Jackson's ways."

"Sure thing, Colt," he promised before hanging up.

Chapter Six

Sabrina slipped into her rayon miniskirt. Smoothing her hands over the black and white floral pattern, she then pulled on a white fitted v-neck sleeveless summer sweater. The cropped hem showed a hint of her lower belly, and the vee plunged quite low, revealing her cleavage, small as it was. She inhaled, turned sideways and shrugged at her less-than-voluptuous silhouette. If the man wanted large boobs, he'd have to look elsewhere. With her petite stature, nothing on her body fell in the "supersize" category.

Checking her image in the mirror once more, she slid the rubber band out of her long braid and shook out her hair. As she ran her brush through the thick, black-as-midnight mass, she smiled at the sensation of her hair flowing behind her. Because her hair was waist-length, she usually pulled it back to keep it out of the way. Running her fingers all the way to the tip ends of her hair caused her mind to shift to one of the last conversations she had with her old boyfriend.

"Why don't you just cut it all off?" Jeremy had asked while she pulled her hair up one day.

She'd shrugged as she let the clip lock onto the hair piled atop her head. "I just can't bring myself to part with it, I suppose."

"Seems like a nuisance to me," Jeremy had grumbled.

Shaking herself out of her reverie and the memory of just how irritated his comment had made her, she met her own green gaze in the bathroom mirror and said, "Ready to go headlong, Bri? No reservations, no hang-ups. Just you and Mr. Sex-on-Wheels...doing well, sex-on-a-horse and wherever else we can think of." Which wasn't such a bad idea, she thought with a grin as she turned and walked out of the bathroom.

The pep in her steps slowed as she made her way back into the main living area of Josh's home. With its rich earth tones, deep blues and shades of maroon, it really was a very homey house—the kind of house she could see herself living in. *Don't even go there, sister,* she told herself. But somehow thinking about having guilt-free sex with Josh would make more sense in a hotel room, not his warm, cozy home.

She almost turned around in her high-heeled sandals and hightailed it back to the bathroom to change clothes to something less revealing until she spotted Josh leaning against the fireplace. *Whoa baby!*

His elbow rested on the wood mantel and he was staring out the large picture window when she walked into the room.

Josh turned his head and his teal green gaze burned a slow, lingering path down her chest to her legs and then back up. As his gaze met hers once more, he lowered his arm, pulled off his hat and tossed it on the coffee table. Then he started walking toward her, his pace sure, unhurried. He looked entirely too sexy for his own good with his chambray shirt untucked and unbuttoned.

With each step he took, the open flaps of his shirt revealed glimpses of his sculpted chest and the fine blond hair that swirled all the way to a seductive vee into his jeans. His belt's large gold and silver buckle brushed against his tanned washboard stomach with his movements, making her mouth water.

Sabrina swallowed and her heart rammed in her chest at the sight. God, was she in trouble.

Josh's expression shifted from determined to intense as he closed the distance between them, stepping right up to her. Sabrina took a few steps back, enjoying the out-of-control feeling of being stalked by this too-delicious-for-words man.

When the backs of her shoes hit the wooden baseboard, she put her hands against the wall and tried her best to control her rapid breathing.

Josh put a hand on the wall above her head and pressed up against her body, sliding his jean-clad thigh right between hers as if he had every right to put it there.

Sabrina stared at his rock-hard chest until his finger lifted her chin so she had to meet his gaze.

As his thumb traced her lips, her chest rose and fell to her rapid heartbeat. But when his fingers slowly feathered down her chin and then her throat, continuing to descend lower, she held back the urge to pant, but damn it that's exactly what he made her do. Pant!

The sensation of his work-roughened finger tracing the vee of her sweater, touching her bare skin while his gaze held hers, made her weak in the knees.

"Touch me, Brina," he said, his tone gruff and full of desire, the teal green shade of his eyes turning the color of a churning, stormy ocean.

Sabrina lifted her hands from the wall and slid them under the flaps of his shirt until her palms rested on his pectorals. The muscles flexed underneath her palms, the power behind his hard working-man's body more than intoxicating. It was addictive, she thought as she explored his corded chest and ab muscles.

At the same time she slid her hands around his waist, Josh's finger brushed the swell of her breast, then slowly dipped in between the cleavage her bra created.

Sabrina sucked in her breath at his intimate touch and saw the corner of his lip quirk upward as he added another finger. He moved them in and out of her cleavage in a slow, rhythmic movement…letting her know exactly what he planned to do to her.

Unconsciously, her hands on his waist lowered to his belt loops and she held on as she lifted her lips to his descending mouth.

Josh's lips brushed over hers once, twice, three times in a teasing, sexual dance before his mouth claimed hers in a hot, passionate, possessive kiss. While his tongue slid against hers, his hand spread over her breast, cupping it. She sighed at his touch and he took advantage of the break in their kiss, biting at her lower lip as his thumb rubbed across the hardened bud, teasing her, taunting her, making her want him more.

Desire swirled from her breast down to her sex and Sabrina gripped his hips, pulling him closer, moaning against his mouth. Josh obliged her by dropping his hands to her rear and cupping the cheeks. Sliding his thigh harder against her mound, he yanked her against him, breasts to chest, hips to hips.

She cried out when he pushed her against the wall and replaced his thigh with his cock. He rubbed his erection against her entrance through their clothes, rocking his hips in a slow, erotic thrust as his lips lowered to her throat.

"Damn, I've never wanted a woman as much as I want you," he groaned against her throat, his fingers flexing on her rear as he lifted her body off the ground so he could fit himself fully against her mound. She gasped in pleasure as he ground against her, buckle, jeans and all.

When his waist and hips connected with hers, the cold metal of his buckle pressed against her lower belly. The cool pressure of the buckle against her skin, the roughness of his jeans rubbing against her while his knowing hands slid over her…ohmigod! The tactile sensations combined with the smell of leather to create an ultimate sensory aphrodisiac for Sabrina. Her sex throbbed and her breasts ached as she moved her hands to clutch his shoulders. Wrapping her legs around his trim waist, she met each jerk of his hips with counter pressure ones of her own.

"Oh God, Josh, I'm going to come," she moaned out as her body tightened with her impending climax.

"It'll be the first of many today," he said, his voice husky, dark and promising. She felt his hot breath on her neck as his own breathing increased.

When he bit lightly on her throat, Sabrina clung to his shoulders as her orgasm slammed through her. Never before had having sex with her clothes on been more erotic and sensual in her life. Josh didn't stop thrusting until her gasps of delight stopped and the only sound in the room was their heavy breathing.

Sabrina laid her head back against the wall while Josh put his head on her heaving chest. She ran her hands through his thick, wavy hair, holding him close. He'd surprised her in that he didn't immediately want her naked and in his bed. Instead, he'd taken her against the wall, giving her what she desired without taking what he obviously needed. The unselfish gesture melted her heart. Without thinking, she bent and kissed him on the top of his head.

Josh pressed his lips against the swell of one of her breasts and lifted his head with an intense look on his face. Straightening, he walked with her over to the sofa, his hands clasping her buttocks to hold her against him. He kissed her on the jaw before he put his knee on the couch and lowered her body onto the cushions.

Standing up, he held her gaze as he yanked off his shirt. Sabrina's breathing kicked up at her first sight of his fully naked chest in the light of day. Wide-shouldered and lean-hipped, the man just made her drool. There was no way around it. As he started to lower his body over hers, she put her foot up, pressing her sandal's heel against his chest. She said with a grin and a lift of her eyebrow, "Aren't you forgetting something?"

Josh looked down at her shoe and with a sexy smile ran his fingers up her leg until he reached the buckle of her sandal. Removing it, he worked on her other shoe. While he did so, Sabrina put her bare foot back on his chest.

There was something so sensual about her foot resting on his chest—skin to skin. She wiggled her toes against the hard surface and smiled when he winked at her.

Once he'd removed her shoes, Josh encircled her ankles with his fingers, easily encasing them. His action reminded her just how much larger he was than her. His teasing expression turned serious as he slid his hands back down her legs. When he reached her thighs, a hungry look crossed his face as he cupped the insides of her legs and slowly pulled them apart.

Sabrina saw his nostrils flare as he stared down at her panties. She held her breath and her heart began to hammer in her chest as his fingers brushed against her damp underwear. The expression on his face, one full of desire and thoroughly focused as he touched her clit through her underwear, made her pulse thunder in her ears. When his thumb rubbed the highly sensitized flesh in small circles, her stomach tensed in anticipation.

But she wanted him to feel as out of control as she felt, so she lifted herself up by pulling on his belt buckle with one hand while she clasped his sac through his jeans with the other hand. Josh's breath came out in a ragged hiss at her aggressive action. Closing his eyes for a brief second, he placed his hand over hers, moving it to slide over his rock-hard erection.

When she applied pressure to his erection through his jeans, he opened his eyes and bit out, "No, not yet." He pulled her hand away from him, then reached around her hips, saying in a gruff tone, "Lift your hips, baby. I have to taste you."

"Josh," she said while she complied with his request. Touching his hair as he slid her underwear down her legs, she finished, "You've got to be ready to explode. Enough. You've proven how easily you can make me fly apart."

Taking his hand, she pressed his fingers against her naked flesh, then slid one of them inside her channel and finished with a breathless whisper, "I'm ready for you, Cowboy."

Josh's head snapped up and a muscle ticked in his jaw as he withdrew his finger from her body and quickly unbuckled his belt, pulling it through the loops then tossed it on the floor.

When the belt's buckle clattered against the hardwood, her stomach tensed and blood rushed to her sex at his I've-got-to-have-her-now jerky actions. As he leaned over her, the muscles in his arms flexed and she couldn't resist touching them before she reached a hand between their bodies to unbutton his jeans.

The phone rang, causing her to pause.

Josh shook his head, silently telling her to ignore it. His expression took on a tortured, ravenous look as he glanced at her lips. He leaned closer, his mouth a breath away from hers and said, "You'll never know the benefits of taking it slow if you don't let me show you, darlin'."

He moved away from her lips and instead planted a kiss on the curve of her breast. The phone continued its incessant noise, each ring seeming to punctuate his seductive descent down her body as he lifted her shirt and kissed her belly, then moved to brush his lips against her navel before he slid lower to nuzzle the dark hair between her legs.

Before he lowered his head to taste her, his gaze met hers once more. "I want to enjoy you before I lose total control. God knows once I'm inside this warm, sweet body of yours, it'll take all the concentration I have to take it slow with you, Brina."

His answering machine picked up, but Sabrina was too caught up in his make-me-melt declaration to pay much attention to it. She nodded as she relaxed her thighs, giving him full access to her body.

Josh didn't say another word as he slid his hands behind her naked cheeks and clasped the firm flesh. Lifting her hips slightly, he lowered his mouth to her damp flesh.

Just when Josh's tongue made a long swipe from her opening all the way to her clitoris, a voice came across his answering machine, interrupting the sexual tension between them.

Josh lifted his head and listened as a man's voice came across the line. "Kelly, get your lazy, good-for-nothin' ass over to answer the damn phone so I can chew it off. Why the hell did you tell Renee I've seen her skinny-dipping? I just got this phone call from her…" His friend then proceeded to mimic an upset female voice.

"Dirk Chavez, keep your peeping-Tom eyes to yourself. I can arrest your sorry ass, you know."

Switching back to his own voice, Dirk continued, "Thanks for rattin' me out. Just because you pull all kinds of extra hours at the station doesn't mean I can't convince the chief to give you hose cleaning duty the next time you're at the firehouse."

Once he'd finished his rant, Dirk sighed and said with a low chuckle, "Better get that bristle brush ready. Call me, ya freakin' turncoat." Then he hung up.

Sabrina's eyebrows shot up and her heart jerked in disappointment at the information she just learned. She recognized Dirk's name. And the fact he was a firefighter, coupled with his comments on the answering machine made her think…ah, damn.

Josh must've misunderstood her raised eyebrows — as if she were questioning what he'd done to his buddy. He said with a grin, "It was for a good cause," before he started to kiss her body again.

But Sabrina put her hand on his head, stopping his descent as she tried to scoot back on the couch.

His gaze questioning, Josh held firm, tightening his grip on her butt.

"Please don't tell me you're a firefighter," she managed to squeak out as she felt her entire body break out into a cold sweat.

He nodded, his expression turning concerned. "What's wrong, Sabrina?"

She couldn't do it — couldn't let him start something that she wouldn't allow herself to finish. The magnetic pull he seemed to hold over her...damn, she liked him too much already.

"Maybe this wasn't such a good idea," she said in a flat tone.

Why the hell didn't Elise tell her? she wondered frantically as Josh continued to stare at her. *I'm going to kick her ass*, she thought with conviction as self-preservation kicked in and she shoved with all her might at Josh's chest.

Taken by surprise, Josh let go of her as he slid off the couch onto his knees.

Sabrina took advantage of the reprieve, quickly stood and turned on her heel to walk away.

Before she knew what happened, she was flat on her stomach laying half on the hardwood floor and half on the area rug. Josh held her arms stretched over her head with one strong hand while he laid his body across her back, his thigh pressed between hers.

He shifted slightly and his hand slid under her skirt, cupping her ass as he bit out next to her ear, "I damn well know you want me, Brina. So when the hell did my being a firefighter fall in rank next to being just a plain old cowboy?"

She heard the anger in his voice and couldn't believe how turned on she was by his aggressiveness.

His fingers grasped her butt cheek as he continued, his whiskers tickling her cheek. "If you've had a change of heart about us," he said as he slid his fingers closer to her entrance, not touching her mound but hovering very close. "Then I can accept that, but if you're pushing me away because of what I do..." He paused as he brushed his fingers across her labia, the barest of touches, but oh-so intentional, then continued, his voice, low, angry, intense, "now *that* I won't accept."

She gasped at his fine-tuned playing of her body, at how, with the slightest touch, he made her want him to touch her, to slide his fingers inside her. Even as she struggled to free her wrists, she couldn't help involuntarily arching, spreading her legs, or the thrill that zipped through her body at being held while he touched her as intimately as he wanted.

He slid his finger down her slit, then paused. Circling her entrance in a slow methodical movement, he kissed her neck and said in husky tone, "I'm waiting for your answer."

Her own words to her cousins came back to her... *No inhibitions, don't hold back no matter if he wouldn't normally be a man you'd date. If he trips your trigger, go for it!*

"Oh, God," she managed to gasp between pants when he slid two fingers inside her, then pulled out. His movements, slow and sure, initiated a wave of pure pleasure.

He moved his body off hers and let go of her wrists at the same time he withdrew his fingers from her body. Laying down beside her, he clasped her thigh in a firm hold and said in a husky tone, "I want to finish what we started. Will you let me, Brina?"

Sabrina sobbed at the intense throbbing that had commenced in her body since he'd pulled his fingers away. Josh loosened his hold on her while she rolled over to her back to lay fully on the carpet.

As she met his deep teal gaze, she lifted to pull her shirt off and tossed it on the floor. His gaze followed hers as she moved his hand from her thigh to cup his palm against her sex, saying, "Finish what you started."

She felt Josh's body relax a little at her response but as his gaze locked on her white lace bra, his eyes darkened and a different kind of tension flowed through him as his hand flexed against her body.

Lifting his hand, he reached for the waistband of her skirt. As he slid the smooth material down and off her body, he rasped, "Take off your bra, baby. I want to see every inch of your bare flesh."

Sabrina's heart raced as she reached up to unsnap the front of her bra. Biting her lip in anticipation, she shrugged out of the lacy material and tossed it on her discarded sweater.

The morning sun shone through the large picture window across the room, bathing Josh's blond hair and sculpted torso in a golden glow. She wanted to run her hands all over the hard planes and cut angles that made up his chest and broad shoulders.

Josh leaned up on his arm while he put the flat of his other hand between her breasts. Slowly he slid his palm down the middle of her body until he reached her lower belly. The primal look on his face as his gaze trailed down her body, as if he could devour her whole, made her insides turn to mush.

During his descent, he turned his hand sideways at her waist and spread his fingers wide, saying in surprise, "You're so tiny I could literally span your body with my hand."

"Don't let the small package fool you, Kelly," she replied in a playful yet stern voice. "I'm made of sturdy stock."

Before she could say another word, Josh was laying across her body, his hands holding hers above her head once more.

With his mouth a breath away from hers, he replied, "I'm counting on it, darlin'."

Chapter Seven

Josh's kiss was deep and thorough as his tongue sparred with hers. Kissing him back, Sabrina tried to tug her hands free, to hold him close, but he held firm. His lips trailed a burning path to her jaw and then her throat while his hands slid down her arms even as he continued to hold them above her head.

Sabrina arched her back when he flicked his tongue across her hard nipple, then moaned deep in her throat as he sucked hard on the sensitive nub. The tug of his mouth caused an aching throb to shoot straight to her sex and goose bumps to form on her skin.

She sighed in pleasure and tried once again to free her arms to touch him.

"Not yet, Brina," he said against the curve of her breast before he moved to her other breast and lavished the nub with the same attention.

"Bend your knees," he ordered in a husky voice as he released her arms so he could trail his lips down her abdomen.

Sabrina started to pull her arms down to thread her fingers through his blond wavy hair, but as she bent her knees, Josh surprised her when his big hands slid down her chest and cupped her breasts.

He gave her a devilish grin as he twirled her nipples between his fingers. She could only gasp and close her eyes as desire swirled in her belly.

She jerked in surprise when she felt him laving at her entrance with his tongue.

Josh said in a calm tone, "Easy, baby, I just want to love on you."

She'd bet her last dollar he'd used that gentled tone a million times on the horses he'd helped his family raise. No wonder Lightning reacted the way she did with him, putting her nose in his hand, seeking his attention. Sabrina tried not to think about the women he must've used the same technique on as he nuzzled her mound, then found her clit with his tongue.

Letting the tension ease out of her body, she gave in to feeling as Josh took long leisurely swipes of his tongue against her sex. When his tongue slid inside her and he pinched her nipples at the same time, she keened her excitement at the dual combination.

Panting, she slid her fingers in his hair, arching her back. Then Josh kissed his way to her clit and mumbled, "You're so sweet. I love the way you taste." Right before he sucked hard on the swollen bit of flesh.

Her entire body shook with the pent-up sexual anticipation his actions caused. When Josh let go of one of her breasts then slid two fingers deep inside her and began stroking her hot spot, Sabrina gasped and dug her toes in the carpet underneath her.

"Oh, God, Josh, yes...but," she panted, then laughed.

"What, Brina? Let me guess. You feel like you want to pee?"

She nodded and bit her lip.

He lifted his head and chuckled as he continued to stroke inside her body. "Looks like I hit the right spot. You're going to come. Let go, baby, and feel," he rasped before he lowered his head to her body and laved at her clit once more.

Her sex aching for release, Sabrina's body shuddered with the feelings rocking through her. Damn he was making her feel things she'd never experienced before and it felt good with a capital "G".

Josh let go of her breast and moved a hand to cup her buttock, pulling her closer. He briefly lifted his head and said in a rough voice, "Give in, Brina. Come for me, darlin'. This sexy body of yours was made for lovin'. Show me just how much."

When he finished, he kissed her inner thigh, then pressed his thumb on her clitoris while he continued to heighten the tension, his thrusts harder, deeper, more aggressive with each stroke.

Sabrina rocked against him, her heart racing. When her orgasm slammed through her, each wave more intense than the last, she pressed closer to him, her keening scream of pleasure slicing through the silence in the room.

After she quit moving, Josh leaned over her, holding himself above her as his mouth covered hers in a scorching kiss. She tasted the salty sweetness of herself on him and accepted the aggressive thrust of his tongue against hers, knowing the action told her just how ready he was to be inside her.

Reaching between them, she pulled at the buttons on his jeans until they were all undone. Pushing at his waistband, she kissed his neck, telling him without words that she was more than ready for him.

Josh quickly stood and shrugged out of his jeans and underwear. Before he tossed his jeans aside, he pulled a condom out of the pocket. Sabrina sighed inwardly at the perfectly corded thighs and calf muscles the man had, but when her gaze landed on his impressive erection as he rolled on the condom, she felt her lower stomach tense in anticipation.

As he knelt between her legs and she got a much closer view of his shaft, she realized he was wider than any man she'd ever been with, if not longer, and a bit of apprehension gripped her. When he used his knees to nudge her thighs further apart, she noted the expression on his face—the intensity and sheer concentration—and she realized just how on-the-edge-of-control he was.

Sabrina put her hands on his shoulders and tried to relax as Josh pressed his erection against her. As he entered her body, she felt the corded tension in his shoulders, noted a muscle ticing in his jaw, heard his breathing turn shallow as he pushed further inside her.

She tensed at his width, surprised at how much he stretched her.

"Relax..." he tried to say, then paused, closed his eyes and took a deep breath. After a couple of moments, he locked his sexy teal gaze with hers once more and finished in a ragged tone, "You're so tight. You've got to relax for me, baby, or I'm going to hurt you."

Sabrina took a deep breath and gave a small laugh saying, "This is one time when being petite in stature might be a *real* pain in the ass."

Josh chuckled at her humor, despite the intense sexual tension between them. Then he withdrew and pressed back in once, twice, three times, rocking at her entrance, priming her.

"You can take me, Brina. I know you can," he encouraged as he continued to shaft her body in a slow, rhythmic glide.

She closed her eyes and arched her back at the amazing sensations rippling through her. Liquid heat flowed with each tantalizing thrust, easing his entrance. As his penetration moved deeper, Josh laid his chest on hers and ground out, "You feel so good." At the same time he thrust hard, seating himself fully inside her sheath.

Sabrina gasped at the breadth and depth with which he filled her body.

Josh stopped moving and whispered, concern in his voice, "Are you okay?"

She nodded and gripped his shoulders, wrapping her legs around his trim waist. "Give me what you got, sexy. Hard and fast will do."

Josh let out a deep growl, withdrew and slammed into her, giving her exactly what she asked for.

"Yes!" she screamed out and dug her nails into his shoulders as his body continued to brush against her clitoris, setting off a series of small tremors deep inside her.

Josh dipped his head and nuzzled her neck, saying close to her ear, "See, we're a perfect fit. I feel every little tremble, every muscle clench against my cock and it's making me crazy. Come, baby, and scream while you're doing it. Make my fantasy as real as it can get."

When he finished talking, his strokes turned more dominant and aggressive. After a particularly forceful downward thrust, he ground his body against hers and that was all it took.

Sabrina whimpered when her orgasm started, then couldn't hold back her scream any longer. She wrapped her arms tight around his neck and pulled him as close as she could get while she lifted her hips against his body, hoping to drag out the body-rocking sensations as long as possible.

Josh cupped the back of her head and gave a low groan as he came. Once he stopped moving against her and his heart rate slowed, he met her gaze and said, "No words can describe—"

Sabrina interrupted him, saying quickly, "So let's not try." She didn't want it to mean more. Already she knew she'd be pining after Josh when she left Texas. She didn't want to be reminded just how spectacular they were together sexually.

Josh gave her a puzzled look, then supported his weight on his forearms so he could meet her gaze.

Searching her face, he asked, "Why was my being a firefighter a problem?"

She shook her head, saying in a light tone, "It's not a problem."

"Not buying it," he countered as his blond brows slashed downward.

She raised her eyebrows at his adamancy, then tried to move him off of her. "Really, it's fine, Josh."

He didn't budge. "I'm not letting you up until you tell me, Sabrina."

His expression had turned serious and she realized he meant what he said.

She sighed. "My father was a firefighter. He died fighting a fire. It happened while I was…away at college." She tried to say the last as unemotionally as possible, but instead, she choked on the last few words.

When she finished speaking, all the color had drained from Josh's face. "God, I'm such an ass. I'm sorry, Sabrina."

Her chest constricted at his look of concern. "It's okay. You didn't know."

Josh rolled over, pulling her close to him. Kissing the top of her head, he said, "Do you want to talk about it?"

She shook her head, then rubbed her nose against his chest, enjoying his masculine smell. "There's nothing to tell."

When she met his gaze, he gave her a doubtful look, then he smiled. "You'll tell me when you're ready."

Slowly running his fingers through her hair, he said in an appreciative tone, "I love your hair, Brina. How the sun reflects off the blue highlights in it. I like it best flowing down your back."

She tried to turn her head and winced because the ends of her hair were caught under her shoulder. Shifting, she pushed it out from under her and gave a wry smile. "Sometimes it can get in the way. I've considered cutting it."

Josh grasped the tip ends of her hair. "It's gorgeous long."

She sighed at his knowing touch as he ran his fingers from the top of her head all the way to the ends of her hair.

"Thank you for the compliment. I wear it braided or in a ponytail, but I just can't bring myself to cut it."

"Don't cut it off," came his vehement reply. "I love it long." He fisted his hand in her hair, grasping the mass near her head and gently pulled her head around until he could look into her face.

The seductive look in his gaze made her breasts ache and her sex throb all over again.

"The length has definite advantages," he finished in a husky voice as he stole a kiss.

She kissed him, smiling at the sexiness the man exuded without conscious effort before she laid her head back on his chest.

After a few minutes of quiet, peaceful silence, he said, "I told Nan I'd bring you back to the Lonestar so she could see how you're doing. Why don't we do that now and then we can spend the afternoon together back here? Alone."

His voice went husky with that last word, making her smile. Sabina glanced up at him, grinning, and said, "I like your way of thinking."

* * * * *

While Ace followed the path through the woods that led to the Lonestar, Josh was thankful for the shade the trees provided so he didn't have to put a hat on Sabrina's head to protect her from the heat. Selfishly, he wanted her as close as he could get her and her hat's brim would just get in the way.

Pulling Sabrina close against him, he breathed in the floral scent of her shampoo and her natural sweet smell and was surprised at the way the scent made him feel. He felt content, happy and horny—in that order. Sabrina seemed more at ease riding this time and he was sure the fact she had changed into a comfortable pair of jeans for their ride helped.

As Ace walked down the wooded path, the underbrush crunching under his hooves, Sabrina laid back against his chest, sighing in contentment. With the flashes of sunlight streaking through the trees, adding to the beautiful silence in the forest, Josh couldn't resist kissing her temple as a feeling of rightness settled over him. Sabrina was everything he wanted in a woman—sexy, uninhibited, responsive, strong of heart and challenging.

When she told him about her dad, he felt a familiar stab in his chest. The memory of Nick came rushing back as if it were yesterday, making his heart ache and his gut knot in regret.

They'd had so much fun that late fall day, pretending to be a policeman and a firefighter. He and Nick had played into the early evening until their parents had called them home. Promising to meet at their fort the next day, they'd gone home.

Nick never made it to the fort the next day. A faulty floor lamp caught his house on fire in the middle of the night and Nick and his entire family were killed in the blaze.

Josh shrugged off the melancholy memory. Instead he focused on the sweet woman in front of him and just how much she'd come to mean to him in such a short time. When he was with Sabrina, the guilt driving him to be at the fire station at all hours, the warped sense of duty that had driven him since Nick's death, moved to the back of his mind.

What he felt for Sabrina went far beyond anyone he'd ever been with. He couldn't believe how quickly he fell into feeling protective and possessive of her and...damn, he knew he was jumping the gun. For all he knew she didn't feel the same about him. Yeah, he knew they were sexually compatible, but he wanted to give them a try. One thing he knew for certain...he had a helluva hurdle to jump with her own loss of her father.

How could he overcome her reservations to dating firemen? The loss of her firefighter father to a fire was a damned hard memory to forget. And at the same time, he knew he couldn't give up what he "needed" to do. Firefighting meant a lot to him.

He wrapped his arm tight around her waist, hugging her close as they entered the Lonestar property.

Just then a black truck drove past them, kicking up dust behind its wheels as it sped down the driveway. Josh tensed at the sight of Jackson Riley's truck. His presence on the Lonestar only spelled trouble. He said in a low voice, "Hold on," to Sabrina as he kicked his heels in his horse's side and Ace picked up his pace.

* * * * *

"Isn't that the officer from last night speaking to Nan? What was her name? Officer O'Hara?" Sabrina asked as they approached the ranch.

"There they are," Nan called out from the porch as Josh stopped Ace and slid off his back. He kept an eye on Jackson as he wrapped the reins around the porch post, then helped Sabrina off his horse's back.

The older man with salt and pepper hair climbed out of his truck and put on his black Stetson. "Hey, Josh." He nodded to Josh as he walked past them and stood at the bottom of the stairs staring up at Nan.

"What are you doing here, Jackson?" Nan asked as a frown replaced the smile that had been on her face.

"Why, Nan, is that any way to treat a neighbor?" Jackson asked, a mock hurt expression on his face.

"When the neighbors are like you, yes," she snorted.

"I came by to see what all the commotion was about last night," Jackson said, ignoring her rude comment. He slid his gaze over to the burned-out stables and met hers with a raised eyebrow. "I heard the fire trucks. What happened?"

"Someone attacked Miss Gentry last night and set the stables on fire," Renee answered in a matter-of-fact tone before she turned to Sabrina. "How are you feeling today? Have you remembered anything?"

Sabrina touched her head and shook it, saying, "I'm still a bit sore back there but I'm sorry to say, I don't remember what happened."

"You were attacked last night?" Jackson turned to them, his expression surprised.

Sabrina nodded. "Yes, I was."

"Who attacked you?" he asked.

She shook her head. "I don't know. It all happened so fast."

Putting out her hand, she smiled. "I'm sorry. I don't believe we've met. I'm Sabrina Gentry, here visiting my friend Elise."

Jackson stared at her for a second, his brown eyes assessing her before he grasped her hand and shook it. "Jackson Riley. My property neighbors the Lonestar land." Looking around, his brow furrowed as he shrugged his stocky shoulders and dug his hands deep in his back pockets. "Speaking of the Lonestar land... Where's Colt?"

"He and Elise are due back tomorrow," Josh lied. He knew Jackson didn't have a sincere bone in his body. He didn't trust the man, nor—with all the stunts Colt believed Jackson had pulled to sabotage the Lonestar ranch in the past—did he want him to think the owner of the Lonestar was going to be absent for long.

Acknowledging Josh's answer with a curt nod, Jackson looked at Sabrina once more, squinting against the bright afternoon sun. "You look a lot like Colt's new wife. You two could be sisters."

Sabrina laughed at his comment. "Yes, people mistook us for each other all the time when we were in college."

"As Josh said, Colt isn't here, Jackson. If you wish to speak with him, call ahead next time. It'll save you a trip, I'll bet," Nan interrupted in a dry tone, letting him know she wanted him to leave.

While Jackson's lips tightened at the abrupt dismissal, Josh had a hard time holding back the grin that threatened at Nan's blatant dislike of the man. The older woman never was one to mince words.

Jackson stared at her for a second, then turned on his booted heel and headed for his truck. As he got in his vehicle and drove off, Nan mumbled, "Pain-in-the-ass, good-for-nothing old coot."

Renee nodded with an understanding laugh. "There's always one in the bunch."

Josh turned to Renee and noted the thoughtful look on her face as she glanced over at Sabrina.

"Did the escapee confess yet?" he asked the detective.

Shaking herself out of the daze she seemed to be in, she pulled a notepad out of her back pocket and said cryptically, "No. But I have a few more ideas to follow up on. By the way, what time is Colt due back tomorrow? I'd like to ask him a couple of questions."

"They aren't due back until day after tomorrow."

When she gave him a questioning look, he shrugged and said, "I figured it was none of Jackson's business."

She glanced at Sabrina as she pulled the pen from the spiral part of the notepad and jotted down a number. "If you remember anything, anything at all, call me, okay?" When she finished, Renee tore off the piece of paper and handed it to her.

Sabrina took the paper and said, "I will, Officer O'Hara." As she started to shove it in her pocket, the note fell out of her hand and the wind blew it across the porch's floorboards. The paper skidded and came to a halt as it hit a railing, spun and fell off the edge right behind the bushes that butted up against the porch.

When Josh started to go after the note for her, Sabrina said, "No, I'll get it," as she quickly took the stairs down to the ground and went around to the front of the bushes. "It'll be easier to reach from under here, I think."

Stretching her arm under the thick hedge, she felt for the crumpled paper and stood up smiling as she shoved it in her jeans pocket. As she stared up at Renee on the porch, she rubbed her temples and said with a sigh, "I just wish I could help more."

Renee smiled, one of her rare smiles. It made her look much younger than her thirty-one years. The kindhearted smile she gave Sabrina certainly didn't mesh with the tough investigative officer exterior she'd built her reputation on, Josh thought. But it made him realize just what an attractive woman she was. No wonder Dirk was pissed at him.

Renee walked down the stairs and put a hand on Sabrina's shoulder. "It'll come to you. Don't push it."

After Renee left, Josh and Sabrina had lunch with Nan. While they ate, she entertained them with stories of Colt and his brothers' antics as children. Her tales made Josh grin from ear to ear. That was blackmail material for sure.

When lunch was over and he and Sabrina walked back outside on the porch, she put her small hand in his and looked up at him with a smile on her face. Damn, she tugged at his heart already.

"Ready to go back home? Uh, I mean to my home?" he asked, feeling like an idiot for what was apparently a Freudian slip of the tongue.

Without skipping a beat, she said, "Yes."

Yep, he was a goner.

Chapter Eight

"So what's the deal with Nan's dislike of Jackson Riley?" Sabrina asked as Josh pulled himself up behind her on Ace's saddle.

He put his arm around her waist and nudged the horse into a walk back down the driveway toward Double K land. The warm Texas sun beat down on them, making her squint and appreciate the fact she'd braided her hair to keep it off her neck. He pulled her closer and said in a low, husky tone, "I'm glad I didn't put a hat on you. Gives me an excuse to pull you close so my hat can offer some protection from the sun."

Sabrina grinned at his excuse to hold her close, but appreciated the bit of shade his cowboy hat provided.

"In answer to your question, Jackson has spent a good portion of his life trying to figure out how to get back the land his father lost in a poker game."

"What land?" she asked, her curiosity piqued.

"Colt's land. Colt's uncle and dad bought the land from the winner of the poker game that Jackson's dad lost. That land is where the Lonestar ranch is now located. For years Jackson has tried in various ways to drive Colt's daddy and uncle apart. See, the two brothers each owned half of the land. Then there's the unexplained batches of bad water for the horses, maimed bulls and cattle, and several downed fences that have occurred over the years."

"Um, I'm no rancher, but doesn't all that stuff happen sometimes on a ranch?"

She felt him shake his head behind her as he urged Ace into the woods back toward his property. "True, but not with the frequency that Colt has experienced it over the years.

"When Colt's uncle died, I understand Elise inherited his half of the Lonestar land."

Sabrina nodded. "Yeah, Elise told me how Colt wasn't too happy when his uncle didn't give the land to him as he'd promised he would."

Josh chuckled. "I heard Jackson had tried to buy the land from Elise, so I'll bet it ate at him that Colt and Elise fell in love and married. Yep, that union took away his chance to at least get half the land back."

Sabrina grinned then her brow furrowed as she considered Jackson Riley. Leaning back against Josh as Ace started to climb uphill, she asked, "Why hasn't Jackson been arrested for his unscrupulous deeds?"

Josh snorted out, "His name should've been Wiley instead."

At Sabrina's laugh, he continued, "No, I'm serious. For all the mischief he's caused, he's never been caught doing any of the things I mentioned. So it's just Colt's word against his."

"Man, that's got to suck for Colt," she sighed.

"Yeah, and even though he might have come across to you as a curious neighbor, I can guarantee you Jackson was more than thrilled to see Colt's stables in their burned-out condition."

"That's such a shame to have a neighbor like that. To never feel like he won't ever give up."

"He hasn't done much in a while," he responded. "Maybe he did finally give up once Elise married Colt. Because by doing so, she finally brought the two halves of ownership of the land back together after all these years."

Josh's hand slid up her waist, then grazed the side of her breast before his thumb traced her nipple lightly through her clothes as he said, "Enough talk about Colt. There's only one man I want you thinkin' about," he said, his voice husky, insistent.

Applying pressure to her nipple, he continued, "You see, there's only one woman I've been thinking about. I want to see her lying naked in my bed, her gorgeous black hair spread out over my pillows. That's my fantasy," he rasped, his aroused tone washing over her in a wave of tempting seduction. "Care to make it a reality?"

* * * * *

Sabrina awoke the next morning to see Josh staring at her. He was lying on his side with his head propped up in his hand. She let her gaze skim every part of his gorgeous body she could see. His blond hair looked windblown and his morning beard made him look sexier and even more like the bad boy she knew he could be.

"Hey," he said, his chest muscles flexing as he trailed a finger down her collarbone to the curve of her breast peeking out from underneath the white sheets and quilted comforter.

"Hey," she said back, rolling over in the bed to face him. Noticing the time on the clock, she said, "Ohmigod, is it really 10:30 a.m.?"

Josh nodded with a grin. "Yeah, I've been up since dawn. Fed and exercised Ace and came back to bed to wait for you to wake up."

She wasn't sure what to say after the afternoon and evening they'd just spent together. Never had she been so physically in tune with another in her life and the realization pretty much blew her away. Josh seemed to have this ability to make the wild woman come out in her whenever he touched her. That's the only way she could explain how uninhibited she'd been with him.

"Sleep good?" He cupped the back of her head and pulled her up against his hard, naked chest as he leaned down and nuzzled her neck.

"Hmmm, hmmm," she responded, enjoying the smell of outdoors and leather mixed with his own masculine scent. The rough feel of his whiskers on her neck and jaw made her heart race. "Though I am a bit sore from all the *extra* exercise I got yesterday."

"Daily exercise is good for your heart," he said with a wink as he lifted his head. "I recommend at least three times a day to keep you in shape."

She reached up and rubbed her hand across his scruff. "You mean three would be enough for you?" she teased.

He shook his head, an adamant expression on his face. "Uh-uh, darlin', that's just to get us start—"

The phone rang, interrupting him. Josh sighed and answered, his tone brisk, "Josh Kelly."

Sabrina half listened as she looked around his bedroom.

"I took the day off, Sam."

The surprisingly large room held very little furniture—a queen-sized bed with a mission-style wood headboard and a chest of drawers.

What she did like about the room was the extra-wide French doors that led to a brick patio facing the woods. She'd seen deer outside last night and a few rabbits. She loved being so close to nature.

"Okay, I'm on my way."

She turned to Josh with a questioning look as he hung up the phone.

"I'm sorry, Sabrina. There's a huge fire on the outskirts of town and they need all available firefighters on site."

As she watched Josh climb out of bed and make his way over to the walk-in closet, panic set in. Her heart raced, feeling as if it were going to burst from her chest. He couldn't have delivered more upsetting news to her. She rubbed her suddenly damp palms on the sheets and then gripped the cloth against her naked chest as she sat up.

"Do—do you really have to go?" She tried her best to keep the pleading out of her voice, but it seemed to creep in despite her efforts to suppress it.

Josh poked his head out of the closet, pulling on a white T-shirt. "Yeah. When the chief himself calls, you know it's got to be important."

"But you did take the day off." She knew she must be coming off sounding like she were the most selfish woman in the world while people's lives were in peril, but damn it, Josh's life was more important to her. Fear for his safety was uppermost in her mind. That combined with the realization of just how attached she'd grown to this man in such a short time hit her hard.

Josh came out of the closet pulling on a pair of firefighter pants, his brow furrowed as he looked at her.

"I'm sorry that I have to leave you. I'll be back as soon as I can." He walked out of the room and came back in. Handing her a cell phone, he said, "Here's my cell. Keep it with you and call me if you need anything." He grinned as he touched her upturned chin. "And it even has a built-in GPS. That way I can keep track of your whereabouts so I can immediately know which room I'll be ravishing you in when I get home," he finished with a devilish smile.

She flipped open the cell phone and stared at the lit-up display. "Is it really that precise?"

He chuckled. "Nah, but I like to think about the possibilities of certain rooms we've yet to christen."

"What are you doing with a cell phone that has GPS tracking in it anyway?"

He sat down on the bed and put on his shoes as he answered her. "It was a gift from the guys at the firehouse. I'm…um…notorious for losing my cell phone." Glancing at her, his expression turned sheepish. "Keys I can seem to keep up with but my cells…" He trailed off, then shrugged before he continued, "The guys got me this cell phone for my birthday last year as a kind of joke. The truth is I actually have used the 'locator' feature via the web several times. So far this year I haven't had to buy a new cell phone. Last year, I had to buy three new phones."

Despite how upset she was, Sabrina managed a smile at this endearing look into Josh's foibles.

He leaned over and kissed her on her lips, lingering as if he really didn't want to go. When she lifted a hand to hold onto his shoulder, Josh pulled himself away, a regretful expression on his face.

He walked back over to his closet, grabbed his jacket and said as he turned her way, "There's sandwich meat and cheese in the fridge, fruit, whatever you'd like for lunch. I'll be back before you know it."

It won't be soon enough, she thought as he walked out of the bedroom and left the house.

At the sound of the door shutting behind him, she climbed out of bed and headed for the shower. As she stood under the hard spray, rubbing Josh's spice-scented soap over her body, all she could think about was losing her father and how difficult it had been for her to adjust to that loss.

She finished her shower and dried off, standing in front of the mirror. Wiping away the fog on the glass, she stared at her reflection. She saw fear and worry in her own deep green gaze.

How can you let yourself get so upset over this? she asked herself as she combed through the long, dark hair. *It's not like you and Josh are in a committed relationship.* For that matter, Josh certainly didn't say anything beyond this weekend together.

While she ran the hair dryer, she realized that the fact of the matter was she did care about Josh, cared what happened to him. She couldn't just stand by and watch the same thing happen to him that happened to her father even if they were just sleeping together.

Once she was dressed in a casual floral sundress, Sabrina smoothed the short skirt's cotton material across her thighs as she walked into the living room. Standing in the center of the large open house, she heard every single sound the house made, from the creaking of a floorboard as she walked across it, to the ticking of the standup pendulum clock on the fireplace mantel. She opened the window, hoping the forest sounds would drain out the sounds of sheer emptiness she heard in the house everywhere she turned.

Hugging herself as she stared into the woods, Sabrina wished she could talk to someone about her fears. Elise always knew how to make her feel better but she had enough on her mind without Sabrina adding to the burden. Then she remembered she was supposed to check in with her cousins, to let them know how she was doing on her part of their bet.

Once she walked back into the bedroom, she picked up Josh's cell phone. She knew he had long distance on his phone since he'd called Colt. Best to use his cell instead of his landline just in case. She'd purposely left her own cell phone behind in Arizona. Otherwise she'd have never really *gone* on vacation from work. People always had a way of finding you if you carried your cell phone around.

Thinking about something happening to Josh had her stomach in painful knots. She really needed to talk to someone. "Please be home," she whispered as she dialed Nicole's number. What if her cousin wasn't home? When Nic answered, she breathed a silent prayer of thanks before she spoke.

"Hey, Nic. How's it going?"

"Heya, Bri! Checking in halfway through your month of sanctioned wild-'n-crazy monkey sex?" her cousin teased.

Sabrina gave a dull laugh. "Ha. I wish my feelings weren't so hard to separate from the oh-so fun actions."

"Say it ain't so, Bri! Men aren't worth that much emotion. They certainly don't expend it on us."

"Oh, Nic," Sabrina sighed.

"What's wrong, Sabrina?" Nicole asked, her voice taking on a note of concern.

"I-I guess I need some moral support," she replied in a shaky tone.

"You know I'm the last person you should be asking any serious relationship questions to. Hey, I've got an idea," Nicole replied in an upbeat tone. "I'll call Lily and we can all talk. Sound good?"

"Yeah, sounds perfect," Sabrina replied with half a smile.

"Hold a second and let me try and see if I can get a hold of Lily."

Sabrina waited, her stomach tensing as the seconds ticked by.

"Hey, Bri. Lily said she could get online with us. Are you able to get online? It'll be just like the old days when we were in college and we'd do a group chat."

"No..." Sabrina started to say, when she turned and saw Josh's laptop in his office. "Oh, wait, I think I might be able to get online. You guys have the same IM sign-on names?"

"Yep. See you in cyberspace in a couple of minutes. We're here for you," Nicole said before she hung up.

Sabrina walked behind Josh's desk and turned on his laptop. She clicked on the Internet icon and signed into the instant messaging system she and her cousins had used throughout college to keep in touch with one another.

BREEZY: Hey guys! Thanks for being here. Gives new meaning to a three-way, doesn't it? Hahahahha.

NIC_LOVES_EM_ALL: But only if there's at least ONE man involved, cuz. LOL! See, hanging with us brings out your sense of humor, no matter the problems you've got going on.

LILY_WHITE: Yey, glad you're here, Bri. And Nic...your handle never ceases to crack me up. Must be pure hell right now sticking with just one man. You *are* living up to your end of the bargain, right?

NIC_LOVES_EM_ALL: *I* never kiss and tell.

BREEZY: Sheyah, right. Have you at least met someone, ladies?

LILY_WHITE: I have. ::dreamy sigh::

NIC_LOVES_EM_ALL: Yes and I'm having the world's most amazing sex...grrrrrowl.

LILY_WHITE: So much for not kissing and telling. Hehehehe.

BREEZY: Knowing Nic, she's not telling how she *really* feels about this guy.

NIC_LOVES_EM_ALL: No comment.

LILY_WHITE: Hahahhaha. I think you got her, Bri! Hey, Nic, just don't kick him out while his pants are still down, okay?

NIC_LOVES_EM_ALL: Verra funny. I think you should change your handle, Lily. Somehow, I don't think you're so *pure* any longer. ;o)

BREEZY: Hopefully that means she's living it up as we'd all promised we would.

NIC_LOVES_EM_ALL: Speaking of living it up...tell us what's going on, Bri.

BREEZY: You guys know about my dad and how I swore I'd never date a fireman. Weeeell...

NIC_LOVES_EM_ALL: No way! Your *stud* is a fireman? Is the problem that you like sliding up and down his pole a little too much?

BREEZY: ::cracking up:: Nic, yes the sex is beyond fabulous, but my feelings for Josh run a lot deeper. In other words, it's going to be hard to imagine walking away from him when my vacation is over, but at the same time I don't think I can handle dating a fireman. He's fighting a fire as we speak and I feel like I'm going to throw up.

LILY_WHITE: Oh, no, Bri! Of all the irony...but if this guy makes you feel better than you've ever felt with anyone else, don't push him away. Give him a chance, give the relationship a chance first.

NIC_LOVES_EM_ALL: Yeah, for all you know, it might not work out after a month of dating anyway.

LILY_WHITE: ::rolling eyes at Nic:: No, what I meant was…sometimes you just have to believe things were meant to be. I know I'm starting to.

BREEZY: I know, I know. It's just really hard to separate my feelings on this issue. I know I need to come to terms with it and in my heart I hope I eventually will, but I can't imagine feeling this way every time Josh goes to work.

LILY_WHITE: No one says this will happen overnight, but if you really care about Josh, your feelings for him will eventually overrule your fears of being with a firefighter over time. The fear of losing him in the line of duty may never go away, but if it means being with him or not being with him, then only you can decide what you can handle.

NIC_LOVES_EM_ALL: All sappy stuff aside, I do agree with one thing Lily has said. In my humble opinion, whether this guy is worth it or not, I believe you should live your life as if tomorrow will never come. That way you have no regrets and can look back on your past with a smile on your face.

LILY_WHITE: Hence the reason Nic constantly has a wide grin on hers. :o) Bri, give Josh a chance. He may be the one you've been looking for all your life.

BREEZY: The problem is, even after only a couple of days with this man, that's what I'm afraid of. He's the ONE. Thanks for talking to me, girls. You've given me some food for thought and I appreciate it!

BREEZY: What about you, Lily? How's your love life going?

LILY_WHITE: I don't think "love" life is the right word. Maybe "lust" life. :o)

NIC_LOVES_EM_ALL: Oooh, more power to ya, babe! Enjoy, enjoy, enjoy!

BREEZY: Listen to Nic…she's definitely in her element now! ::grin::

LILY_WHITE: You both need to give me hints on how to think of something besides S-E-X! It's very distracting.

NIC_LOVES_EM_ALL: That's the whole point, remember? Bwahahahaha.

BREEZY: Well, Nic's right. Just enjoy your time with your man, cuz. Something may come from it but in the meantime…at least you're getting your exercise in. ;o)

LILY_WHITE: ::rolling in laughter:: You two are making my sides hurt! Well, I gotta go. Take care, girls, and see you in a couple of weeks.

Sabrina logged off the instant messaging system feeling a bit better. No, she wasn't one hundred per cent but she could cope. Work was always a good outlet when one had too much time to ponder things too much. She logged into her email and checked it via the web. Yep, there were several messages waiting to be answered.

She spent the next few hours responding to emails, only pausing to rummage through Josh's fridge and make herself some lunch. When her shoulders started to feel sore from sitting so long working on his laptop, Sabrina decided she'd worked long enough. She shut down the computer and looked at her watch. Frowning as worry crept into her consciousness once more, she realized four hours had passed and she still hadn't heard from Josh. She moved to stand by the big picture window and stared out at the darkening sky and the trees blowing in the wind.

He could've called to reassure her he was okay and he didn't. Man, she was going to rail at him as soon as he walked in the door, damn it. Well, after she held him close and gave him a welcome home kiss. The thought of something happening to him…her heart sped up and suddenly her rib cage felt too small for the wild beating that hammered against it. She put her hand on her chest, the sense of panic setting in as her breathing turned to short, choppy pants.

God, Josh better come home soon, or at this rate I'm going to pass out, she thought with dread.

Chapter Nine

Sonofabitch, he ached all over. Josh stood under the hot stream of water in the firehouse's shower, washing away the sweat, soot and general grime from the fire. After they'd put the fire completely out, he didn't have a choice but to hitch a ride back to the fire station on the fire truck since his truck was gone. To save time, he'd driven his truck directly to the fire's location and parked away from the burning building. But while he did his civic duty, putting out a five-alarm fire, his damn truck had been towed.

Josh poured the fire station's antiseptic-smelling shampoo into his hair and winced as the soap ran over the cut on his cheek. He thought about Sabrina while he lathered the suds. Hell, for that matter he'd thought about her all the way to the fire. Only while he fought the raging inferno was he able to disengage his thoughts about the woman he'd fallen in love with. Yeah, he'd admitted it to himself on his way to the fire, but how the hell was he going to convince her living with a fireman wasn't so bad, especially when he had a gouge on the side of his face and—thanks to Dirk—a nice shiner on his eye, both physical reminders of his career choice?

"Sorry," his buddy had said as he accidentally elbowed him in the eye while they were pulling down the hoses. "See why it's important to have all your gear on. Accidents happen." Dirk had mock-scolded him as Josh rubbed his injured eye.

"Screw you," he'd grumbled.

"Nah, you already took care of that," Dirk tossed over his shoulder. Flashing him an unrepentant smile, Dirk continued, "Look at it this way…now we're even."

Josh shut off the shower and after he toweled dry, he touched his sore eye, chuckling even as he winced. Since the tow truck place closed at three, he had at least guilted Dirk into giving him a lift back to the Double K after he took a shower.

"Hey, *little* man," Dirk smirked, purposefully glancing at Josh's naked lower body as he poked his head into the locker room. "You've got a phone call."

Josh grabbed his larger than average cock and faced his friend with an eat-shit-and-die grin saying, "Bite me."

After he'd quickly dressed, he made his way to the front of the station house.

When he passed Dirk on his way to the phone, his buddy warned, nodding to his bruised eye, "I hope the reason she's calling you is strictly business or I'll have to give you a matching set."

"It's Renee?" Josh asked.

"None other," his buddy replied in a dry tone before he walked away.

Josh picked up the receiver from the front desk. "Hello."

"Josh, hey, it's Renee. Listen, I need to get a hold of Colt. You know where he is, right?"

"What's this about?" he asked, his stomach tensing.

"I just need to talk to him, that's all."

He didn't like the evasiveness in her tone. "This has to do with your investigation, doesn't it? You still suspect Colt?"

When she didn't reply, he ground out, "You going to tell me or not?"

"No."

"Suddenly, my memory isn't so good. I'm hanging up now," he said as he pulled the phone away from his ear, ready to hang up.

"Wait!"

"Yes?" he replied into the phone in a calm tone.

"Time is of the essence here." She sighed and said, "I got a call yesterday from a concerned woman. She'd heard about the fire at the Lonestar Ranch and that someone had been in the fire. She said she wanted to make sure it wasn't Elise Tanner. She went on to say that she was out for dinner one night and overheard Colt tease his wife, saying that if he was ever really that hard up for cash, he could always bump her off and collect the life insurance money.

"Out of curiosity, I checked all the life insurance companies in town and a representative from the Oracle life insurance company confirmed Colt and Elise had recently taken out life insurance polices with their company."

Josh snorted. "So. They recently just got married. Makes sense to me."

"Maybe you're right and I'm barking up the wrong tree, but several people have made the comment that Sabrina looks a lot like Elise, and from my notes the night of the accident, I know Elise leaving town was a last-minute decision. The fact that the barn was locked from the outside while an unconscious woman lay in danger of burning to death inside sounds pretty intentional to me. Even if the attack on Sabrina was intentional, at the very least, I'd say she was in the wrong place at the wrong time. Maybe whoever did this meant to attack Elise and not Sabrina."

"Are you implying what I think you're implying?" he fairly yelled into the phone as his anger rose.

"Josh—"

"Colt is with Elise right now. You know that from our conversation yesterday."

"Wasn't he originally planning to be out of town, though? Nice alibi," Renee countered, leaving the implication dangling between them.

He took a couple of deep breaths. He might know Renee personally but she was still an investigating officer and she took her job very seriously. He decided to go in another direction.

"What about that escaped convict?"

"No dice. When we pressured him with an attempted murder rap on top of his other offences, he finally confessed he'd broken into an empty house and stole some food around the time Sabrina was attacked. The house he broke into was two miles away from the Tanner ranch. The homeowner confirmed the timing of the break-in because they arrived home to see him running away from the house. There wasn't enough time for him to have been in both places at the same time."

Josh sighed, feeling like he'd been beat up twice today. He grudgingly gave her Colt's cell phone number then said, "You're way off base, Renee. Colt will set you straight."

When he hung up the phone, he realized just how tense the ongoing investigation was making him. Sabrina meant everything to him. The need to be by her side rocked through him.

"Dirk, we've got to go!" he called out in an urgent tone.

* * * * *

Josh left Ace in his stable while he dashed through the pouring rain to his porch. He'd rub his horse down after he saw Sabrina. He had to see her, to hold her close.

Opening the door, he walked inside and quickly surveyed his place. Relief washed over him when he spied Sabrina curled up in the window seat, leaning against the glass. He shut the door against the gusting wind then turned, tossing his hat on the chair and started to say, "Man it's raining like crazy out there—" when he was jolted back a step as Sabrina launched herself into his arms.

As she squeezed his neck tight and wrapped her legs around his waist, he held her close and closed his eyes, breathing in her arousing scent.

"Thank God, you're okay," she breathed out as she kissed his cheek, then his jaw and moved to his mouth.

Josh wrapped his arms around her and kissed her back before he said with a chuckle, "Now that's a helluva welcome home. I could get used to this."

Sabrina tensed in his arms and lowered her legs to the ground. Still holding onto him, she put her head on his chest and asked in a worried voice, "Why didn't you call me to let me know you were okay?"

His brow furrowed at her other question. "What do you mean 'why didn't I call you?' Didn't you get my text message?"

She glanced up at him with a confused look. "What message?"

Spying his cell phone on the coffee table, he let her go and walked over to it, picking it up. As he looked at the settings, he said, "That's right. I forgot I left it on vibrate mode. You wouldn't have heard it ring."

He set down the phone as she approached, saying in a suggestive tone, "I just asked you to meet me in the stables. I figured that was one place we hadn't christened yet. Plus, I just wanted you to know I was thinking about you," he finished with a wink as he faced her.

"Ohmigod, look at your eye and that gash on your cheek! What happened?" she asked as she put a shaky hand to her mouth.

"The cut was dumb luck at the fire and the black eye was Dirk deciding I needed a little payback for my transgressions against him," he joked, but then he saw all the color drain from her face and he tried to reach for her. "What's wrong, Sabrina?"

She backed away saying to herself, her gaze glazed over, "I thought I could handle…but I just can't."

"Sabrina?" Before he could reach her, she'd turned on her bare feet and dashed to the front door. Pulling it open, she ran out into the pouring rain.

"Sabrina," he called out again as he took off after her.

* * * * *

Sabrina's heart rammed in her chest as she ran down the steps into the rain. Her dress was immediately soaked through while she tried to decide where to run. Her heart hurt as if someone had tried to rip it from her chest. She couldn't put herself through another loss. Losing her father was enough. Not another man she cared for. She knew it was crazy to run out into the rain, but she just needed to get the hell out of there…away from Josh. If she reacted this way to something as simple as a black eye and the ragged cut on his face… God, she felt so sick to her stomach.

She fought through the cramps gripping her belly as she heard Josh call her name from the porch. Thankful she was barefoot, she dug her toes in the grass and bolted toward the woods. Twenty-five feet. If she could just get there, she could have some time to herself. Get away from Josh and every deep-seated emotion his handsome face and endearing ways caused to churn within her.

Sabrina's heart broke at the realization of just how much she cared for Josh and just how wrong they were for each other. Warm tears streamed down her face only to be washed away by the unrelenting cool rain.

Her breathing turned choppy and her lungs felt like they were on fire as she pushed herself to the limit to get to her destination as fast as she possibly could. Josh's heavy footfalls sounded not far behind her. The noise both comforted and scared her.

When she was within ten feet of the entrance to the woods, she felt a hand around her ankle and she went down, hard on her stomach.

Sobbing, she clawed at the grass, trying to free her ankle from Josh's grasp, but he was too fast and before she could move another inch, he'd rolled her over on her back and had pinned her to the ground with his body.

"No," she wailed as she swung her arm, doing her best to free herself from his touch, his attentiveness, his damned sexy heat. Her arm accidentally hit his jaw, causing his head to snap sideways.

"Sonofabitch, Brina," he hissed out as he grabbed her arms and slammed them to the ground above her head, his teal gaze narrowing on her. "Why are you running and why the fuck are you trying to break my jaw?"

"I'm sorry, Josh. I didn't mean to hit you," she replied, feeling suddenly hemmed in and vulnerable, her heart out there flailing in the wind. The knowledge had self-preservation kicking in full-force.

"Let me up," she panted, resuming her struggles as she bucked to get him off of her. God, she needed to get away from this man before she had a complete breakdown.

"You're not going anywhere until you tell me what's wrong," Josh insisted as he pressed his hips to hers, holding her firmly to the ground. Her heart raced at his deep concern for her while at the same time she couldn't mistake the hard flesh that nudged against her mound.

She jerked her surprised gaze his way and he ground out, "Hell yeah, I still want you even when we're fighting...*over God knows what*!

"What's wrong?" he asked again, a look of utter confusion and frustration crossing his face.

"I guess I need some space," she mumbled as she looked away from him, her chest constricting.

Josh cupped the back of her head, turning her to face him once more. Water ran in rivulets down his ticcing jaw as his piercing teal gaze met hers, willing her to listen. "Why? So you can run from us? Run from what you know is right?"

She blinked away the pouring rain, thankful the pounding water made it harder for her to meet his intense gaze.

His grip on her head tightened as he rasped out, "I love you, Sabrina. I won't let you shut me out."

Surprise jolted through her at his words. Sabrina raised her hand to hold onto his wrist. Her heart hammered out of control, in complete disregard for her earlier worries over her feelings for Josh. "Wha-what did you just say?"

His expression softened and he let go of her arm and then rubbed his thumbs along her jawline, saying in a husky voice, "I said I'm hopelessly, madly, deeply in love with you."

Emotions swirled within her...emotions she hadn't acknowledged and refused to identify. She didn't know how to respond to his declaration—to tell him his mere touch made her melt like no other man's did, but she couldn't handle being with a fireman.

"Josh, I—"

Josh didn't give her a chance to reply. He pulled her close and covered her mouth with his lips, his kiss tender yet dominant.

As his tongue brushed against hers, Sabrina wondered why all rational thoughts fled her brain every time the man's lips met hers. She kissed him back with all the passion she felt but couldn't express in words.

Thunder rumbled overhead, then lightning slashed, splintering the dark sky above her half-closed eyes.

Josh broke their kiss, glancing up at the sky. He quickly pulled her to her feet, saying as he put his arm around her shoulders, "That lightning was a little too close for comfort with us near these trees. Come on, we're closer to the stables. We'll wait out the storm there."

Sabrina followed him inside the structure. The smell of rain, hay, horseflesh, and the faint aroma of manure assailed her nostrils.

Ace neighed as Josh shut the stable doors against the driving rain. Sabrina smiled and walked over to calm the horse, noting all the empty stalls. Rubbing her hand down the animal's neck, she spoke to him in a soothing tone, "It's okay, boy. We're here to wait out the storm with you."

The horse snorted and pawed the ground as if in agreement. She smiled as she patted his jaw.

"You're got the touch with horses," Josh commented right behind her as he pressed his chest against her back.

"So do you," she commented as his heat radiated, seeping into her pores and warming her, despite the wet clothes on his body. She inwardly acknowledged her desire to push thoughts of walking away from Josh out of her mind for the time being. Why did he have to feel so right standing behind her, protecting her, loving her and damn it, seeming to understand her better than she understood herself?

"As much as you love horses, I'm surprised you don't have more on your own land. You've certainly got the room for them," she said, trying to get her tumultuous emotions under control.

"Right now I work too many hours to give them the attention they would need."

Josh pushed her wet hair out of the way, then trailed his lips down her throat. "Hmmm, the way you smell makes me so horny, I can't think straight," he ground out as he nipped at her neck.

Heated and hungry were the only two words she could think of to describe the intensity in his voice. And the sound caused her body to react in swift unadulterated arousal. Her nipples hardened, her stomach tensed and her sex pulsed while she turned to face him with bated breath. Josh had taken off his shirt and now stood there in front of her in his wet jeans. His biceps flexed while he kept his hands down by his side—as if it took supreme effort to do so. Man, did he know how to make her feel like the most desirable woman in the world.

His jaw ticced as he reached out and ran his finger across a nipple through her thin dress. Soaking wet, the material clung to her skin and without a bra, the combination did nothing to hide her pink nipples underneath.

"I've never seen a more beautiful sight in my life, Brina," he whispered as he clasped her around her upper back and pulled her to him to clamp his mouth over the hardened bud he'd just touched.

Sabrina arched her back and dug her fingers into his shoulders as he bit down on the cloth-covered dark pink bud and sucked it into his mouth.

After he'd managed to arouse her even further by sliding his thigh between hers and moving his lips to her jaw, she relished the feel of his hands unzipping the zipper on the back of her dress. The distinctive sound only seemed to accentuate the heated silence in the stables.

As Josh's lips found hers once more, he pushed the straps of her sundress down her arms, then to her waist.

While she shrugged out of her dress, Josh rubbed his thumbs across the taut peaks. The hard-working, rough surface of his fingers grazing across her sensitive nipples distracted her, setting her on a ragged edge.

Sabrina moved close to his chest and wrapped her arms around his neck, purposefully rubbing her breasts against the hard surface. The warm, taut skin, stretched over well-defined muscles and covered with fine hair only made her want more. Clasping his neck tight, she lifted herself and wrapped her legs around his waist.

Josh grabbed her ass through her underwear and squeezed while his teal green gaze seemed to penetrate straight to her soul. "I want to be inside you so bad, baby."

In answer to his comment, she threaded her fingers through his thick, wet, blond hair and kissed him.

Josh returned her kiss, then breathing heavily, he set her down beside Ace and ordered, his tone tight, "Turn around."

Excited by the barely controlled tone his voice had taken on, Sabrina turned around.

When Josh lifted her hands and clasped them around the horse's saddle horn, she wondered what he was doing as she elevated her heels off the ground a bit to get a full grip. Expecting Josh to slide her underwear down, she was surprised to see him slowly unwind Ace's reins from the post. As he began to wind the leather straps around her hands on the saddle, her heart rate kicked up to a thunderous rhythm.

"What are you doing?" she asked, looking over her shoulder as he leaned over her to complete his task. She'd tried to keep her tone calm, even though she felt far from it.

After he'd cinched the reins into a knot around her hands, Josh gave her a devilish smile as he patted Ace on the neck and said, "Hold boy," in a commanding tone.

"Josh!" she said, getting a bit miffed. "I'm not—"

He pressed his chest to her back once more and reached around, cupping her breasts in his hands while he kissed her neck saying, "Shhh, baby." His tone was dark, aroused and determined as he slid a hand down her hip and gave a hard tug on her underwear, ripping the wispy material right off her body.

Goose bumps formed on her arms and her nipples tightened as hard as diamonds at the evidence the man had very little hold on his desire. She couldn't help but squirm when he skimmed his fingers up her spine and said in a knowing tone, "You like it when you don't have all the control, don't you." It wasn't a question. It was an assured statement.

She felt the brush of his knuckles against her ass as he unbuttoned his pants and bit back a moan as blood rushed straight to her sex.

"I've seen the way you react when I've held your arms while I thrust inside you. It turns you on."

In the dimness, Sabrina stared at the stable's far wall, not wanting to admit he was right. Hell, for that matter, she didn't even know if he was right. "No, I—"

Josh clasped her hips and rasped against her ear as he easily nudged her stance further apart with his booted foot. "I want to feel every part of you, Brina. Do I need a condom?" he finished as he pressed his erection against her wet entrance.

She shook her head. "No, I'm on the pill. Trust goes both ways—"

He entered her as she spoke, a swift, hard, deep thrust. The decadent sensation of being taken from behind caused her to scream out in pure pleasure. The fact she didn't have a sure-footed hold while Josh had to bend his knees slightly to accommodate the differences in their heights made her feel protected and cherished. Her suspended-in-the-air position, where their bodies were joined, felt seductively erotic and so very intimate.

Josh stayed buried deep within her as he moved his hands up to cup her breasts then roll her nipples between his fingers, applying pressure.

"I can touch you anywhere I want," he murmured as he slid his palm slowly down her stomach. Once he'd reached her curls, he rubbed a finger against her labia until he found her clit. Circling the hard bit of skin, he finished with a satisfied tone, "And all you can do is come."

As much as she loved what he was doing to her body, Sabrina couldn't help but give him some of his own medicine. "If my hands weren't tied, I'd grab that nice ass of yours and pull you deeper, darlin'," she mocked.

Josh groaned at her words and in response tilted her pelvis as he ground his hips against hers, thrusting upward even deeper. "Like this?"

Sabrina could've sworn she saw stars with his last aggressive move, but she was determined to let him know how much control she still did have. "No, like this," she said in a smug, seductive voice as she clenched her inner muscles, contracting her walls around his cock.

He tensed behind her, then lowered his head to her shoulder. He didn't move or say a word. All she could hear was his shallow breathing and the rain hammering the roof above their heads. Seconds ticked by as she waited for him to move.

Then his fingers flexed on her hips, letting her know…she'd gotten to him.

Her last action made him shudder and his body break out in a heated sweat despite his wet skin. Josh had a hard time keeping his cool. He'd never felt these bone-deep, body-jarring sensations with anyone like he did with Sabrina. Loving someone as fiercely as he loved her must somehow intensify the pleasure. He wanted to take his time with her, bring her to peak with his hands first, but seeing her gorgeous naked body, discovering more about her responsive nature and feeling her wet, warm sheath wrapped around his cock holding him tight…damn, it was taking all his willpower not to just fuck her senseless like he wanted to.

Finally he gritted out, "I wanted this to last, to draw it out…" He stopped speaking and took a calming breath before he continued, "I've never wanted to just *take* someone so bad in my life."

She sucked in her breath at his comment, then arched her spine, pushing herself back against him. "Go for it, lover. I'm more than ready to *take* all you're willing to give."

Josh clenched his jaw as her warm body pressed further into his as if she somehow hoped to physically fuse her body with his. He'd never felt more connected to another. The softness of her skin, her sweet ass rubbing against him, the smell of sex all around them…she was so wet and ready. He held her hips while he withdrew and slammed back inside.

As pleasurable sensations ricocheted throughout his body, he pulled out and thrust in once more, clenching his jaw at the coiled sexual build-up slamming into his groin and balls.

He dropped one hand from her hip to rub her clit while he slid inside her body again and held himself deep inside her. When she screamed out and he felt her warm core contracting around his cock with her orgasm, fisting him in a tight glove of renewed wetness, he groaned in pent-up relief.

"Damn, Brina," he breathed out as he came, rocking his hips as his entire frame shook with a fire that burned straight down to his toes. Never had a sexual partner's orgasm caused such a heightened, satisfying response within him, a response that went way beyond a physical level.

After they both stopped moving, their breathing still ragged, he cupped her breasts and leaned his chest flush against her back as he kissed her shoulder.

"I'm never letting you go."

"Well, eventually you'll have to," she chuckled as she tugged on the reins around her hands.

He moved his hands to cup her butt checks and squeezed. "Or I could just put you up on the saddle just as you are, tied and naked and give you a ride to the house."

She heard, rather than saw, the devilish grin on his face. "You wouldn't dare!" came her fast reply as she tugged hard on her bonds.

"Why bother putting your clothes back on, darlin'? They're soaking wet. Plus, you'll just end up without them again once I get you inside," he finished as he reached over her and untied the reins.

"And here I thought taking off my clothes and ripping my underwear from my body was half the fun," she teased as she cast him a saucy grin over her shoulder.

"Never doubt it," came his fast reply as he turned her in his arms and pulled her close. He kissed her neck and said, "The storm's fury seems to be letting up. We'd better get you into some warm, dry clothes."

Chapter Ten

Sabrina lay in Josh's bed with his arms wrapped around her as they listened to the rain outside. They'd had a sexually charged dinner, amid many interruptions as Josh dabbed beef gravy on her nose just so he could kiss if off, which led to a heated kiss and finally they'd ended up in his bedroom.

The room was completely dark except for the occasional flash of lightning that lit up the entire room. Josh created a soothing rhythm as he ran his fingers through her hair from her scalp to the ends and then back again.

She moaned and said without conscious thought, "I could get used to this."

Josh never stopped stroking her hair as he replied, his voice quiet yet strong, "Then why not make this a permanent deal? Stay in Texas with me, Sabrina."

Sabrina jerked her gaze to his in the dark, thankful for the brief flash of lightning that lit up his face so she knew for sure he wasn't joking. A sincere expression greeted her questioning look before the room doused in darkness once more. She'd assumed he'd told her he loved her in the heat of the moment. Even though it had made her heart jerk to hear the words, she wasn't sure he'd meant it in a committed way.

"We—we barely know each other," she argued, trying to keep a calm on her rioting senses and thudding heart. *He wanted her to stay permanently?*

Josh shifted, pulling her underneath him, his response calm, assured as he spoke. "I've waited a lifetime to feel the way I do when I'm with you, Brina. God knows I've had some inner demons to face along the way, but since you've come into my life, I've been able to find a sense of balance I'd never been able to before. I'm not just going to let you go."

Surprised by his cryptic comment about his past and thrilled—more than she cared to admit—by the possessive nature of his words, she realized with a heavy heart that she needed to set him straight. She should've done so when he first told her he loved her. Putting her hands on his chest, she started to reply, "Josh, I'm here for now but—"

The phone rang, interrupting her. "Who the hell could be calling at this hour?" Josh cursed at the interruption as he picked up the cordless phone from its receiver on his nightstand.

"Hello?"

Sabrina waited as her entire body tensed and a lump formed in her throat at the possibility the phone call meant Josh would have to go fight yet another fire.

"Yeah, see you then. Thanks."

Josh hung up the phone and turned back to her, answering her unspoken question. "That was Dirk calling to tell me when he planned to pick me up."

"Pick you up? Not to fight another fire?" she asked, her voice unconsciously going up an octave.

Josh rolled over and pulled her across his chest. His hands flexed as he rubbed up and down her arms. "I meant, pick *us* up and no, there's no fire this time. I promise."

"Pick us up?" she repeated, curious as to where they were going.

"Yeah, my truck got towed while I was fighting that fire. Tomorrow morning Dirk's going to take us to get it."

He ran his hand up her shoulder and lifted her hair to cup the back of her neck. Rubbing his thumb across her jaw and throat, he said, "And yes, I meant us. I don't want you out of my sight any longer than necessary. Your memory could come back at any time. By my side is where you belong."

Warmed by the protective nature of his words, yet scared by the you're-here-to-stay undertones they held, she said, "I'm sure you can handle it without me."

Josh sighed. "I was hoping to avoid telling you this...to keep you from worrying, but the escaped prisoner has an alibi. It seems he was busy breaking and entering in another house while you were attacked. So that means whoever attacked you is still out there.

"At this point, he has to know you didn't die in that fire, which could make you a target. He doesn't know you don't remember the details. And since the details are still fuzzy to you, for all you know, you might have seen his face and could identify him."

"Oh God, I hadn't thought of that." Fear raced through her at the possibility Josh could be right. "Okay, I'll go with you tomorrow."

"After we pick up my truck, I'll give Colt a call. I'm hoping he was able to get Renee off his back."

"What are you talking about?" she asked, confusion reflected in her gaze.

"Renee's checking 'all angles' on the stable fire and your attack. She received a phone call from a 'concerned citizen' about the attack at the Tanner ranch. The lady who called in mentioned overhearing Colt tease Elise at dinner that if he were really in dire need for money, he could just bump her off and collect the life insurance money," he replied in an irritated tone.

"That's crazy!" Sabrina said, feeling pure outrage that anyone would even consider Colt a suspect. "Anyway, *I* was attacked, not Elise."

"Yeah, but everyone agrees you and Elise could easily be mistaken for one another and you *were* attacked at night, so for all those reasons, Renee is looking into it." His arms around her tightened before he continued, "Of course, I don't agree with it. Regardless, I'm sure Colt will set her straight."

Once they'd finished discussing the case and the silence stretched out between them, Sabrina felt the tension build in Josh's chest and arms, as if he were a tightly coiled spring, ready to snap. Wondering what current thoughts would cause him to tense up, her own stomach began to knot in response.

Why couldn't she pretend he'd never said, "I love you" or asked her to stay in Texas with him?

"Are you planning to answer my question?" he finally spoke, his voice tight as he placed his hands on her arms once more.

She let out a sigh and replied, "I'm sorry, Josh. There can't be more between us. I can't stay." Well, damn, didn't she just feel like the scum at the bottom of the ocean.

His hands gripped her arms in a firm hold. "Why?"

"As I said, we barely know each other. Plus I work in Arizona—" she started to respond, using any excuse she could think of, but he cut her off, anger evident in his tone.

"Bullshit! You said yourself that your job could be done anywhere. What you and I share is rare. I don't want to just walk away from that. Give it to me straight or not at all," he said in a clipped tone.

Her body stiffened in response to his anger. "Fine. You want it straight? I can't deal with you being a fireman. That's why I ran earlier. I felt physically ill while you were gone all day today, Josh. Then seeing you'd gotten hurt today threw me over the edge. I can't go through that every day, hoping you won't end up like my dad."

"That was just a scratch, baby," he cajoled. When she didn't respond, he said in a subdued voice, "You asked me about Nick the other night. Nick was my childhood friend. That picture you saw was taken the day we'd played all day long, pretending to be a fireman and a police officer. That day I'd told Nick I was going to be a fireman. He agreed I was the best fire starter and extinguisher on the planet."

Josh chuckled before his tone turned melancholy once more. "We'd planned to meet in our fort the next day, but Nick never made it. A faulty lamp caught his house on fire that night, killing Nick and his entire family in the process."

Sabrina sucked in her breath at Josh's sad story and her heart contracted for the loss he'd suffered in his childhood. She laid her head on his chest and listened as he took a deep, steadying breath and finished his tale.

"Ever since then, I've wanted to be a firefighter." He lifted his shoulders, shrugging underneath her. "I know it's irrational, but I guess deep down every time I've fought a fire, I've felt I was fighting that fire I never could for Nick, in some kind of atonement for not being there for him when he needed me the most."

She blinked back the hot tears that stung her eyes and felt the stirrings of deep love and appreciation tug on her heart. Sabrina fought the emotion that flooded her mind and heart, but how, in good conscience, could she ever ask him to give up firefighting after that sad story? She couldn't. "See what I mean. Fires and firefighting cause nothing but pain and heartache."

He hooked her chin and turned her face toward his. The sky lit up once more and Sabrina briefly saw his down-turned eyebrows and serious expression before he spoke, his voice turning urgent, "You waltzed into my life and forced me to sit up and take notice. You've made me realize that I shouldn't see an invisible ghost in every fire I fight, nor should I set unrealistic expectations for myself as a firefighter."

Rubbing his thumb across the tip of her chin, he then said in a tone asking her to understand, "The need to fight fires will always burn within me, Sabrina. I can't explain it any better than that."

"Just as my own experiences have colored what decisions I make," she replied. "After losing my father to such a violent death, I vowed I would never have a relationship with a firefighter…especially not one that could lead to a deeper commitment."

"I understand your pain and your motivation behind your decision, but I could just as easily die in a car accident tomorrow," he countered.

Damn if he didn't come up with a convincing argument, but she knew herself well enough to know…she'd make herself sick with worry every time he walked out the door, regardless of how many valid rebuttals he threw her way.

"Yes, you could," she replied, her heart sad. "But being a firefighter, the nature of the risks you take are beyond everyday life stuff. They're beyond what I know I can handle."

"So that's it? In a few days, you'll just walk away from me, from us, as if we'd never met, never connected, never meant more to each other than spectacular fuck partners?"

She gulped at how callous and cold he made her sound, even if unintentionally. She knew he was hurt by her rejection. Hearing that hurt in his gruff tone was bad enough. She was thankful for the darkness so she didn't have to see his teal gaze shift to a deep sea green as it churned with turmoil.

Slowly she nodded, knowing he could feel her answer since his hand was still on her chin. "I will."

Without a word, he swiftly flipped her over on her back, pulling her arms above her head as he thrust his thigh between hers. "Then I have very little time left to convince you that staying with me is far preferable than living without me," he said in a determined voice.

"Josh, I know you're upset—" she started to say, her heart breaking at their irreconcilable situation.

"I don't want your sympathy, Brina," he ground out as he pressed his shaft against her entrance and thrust deep.

Sabrina screamed at the satisfying completeness she felt when he was seated inside her—every time she felt that way, damn it. Sad tears streamed down her face as he began to move within her in measured, deliberately slow, tantalizing strokes. Her heart hammered in her chest and desire swirled in her belly as her body temperature rose.

When she moaned in ecstasy, his breathing turned choppy but his tone remained unwavering as he vowed, "I *know* I have your body, but I won't give up until I have your heart and soul."

His words stabbed at her heart, making their lovemaking the most bittersweet and emotionally intense she'd experienced with him. His heartfelt words, his knowing touch, the way they perfectly moved in tune with one another... Sabrina silently acknowledged to herself that Josh did have her body. He even had her heart, but she couldn't allow her soul to burn up in that white-blue flame only he seemed to be able to ignite within her.

Chapter Eleven

The next morning, Sabrina and Josh shared a quiet breakfast of bacon and pancakes, thanks to Josh's fabulous cooking. The mutual silence between them was almost as if they didn't want to break the peaceful spell that had settled over them. But Sabrina saw the heat, every time Josh looked at her across the table with his penetrating teal gaze. It was as if he thought he could *will* her to say, "Yes, I'll stay."

When they were done with their meal, he stood then walked around the table to hold his hand out to her. He looked so sexy standing there in his black T-shirt, faded jeans and black cowboy boots. Even the bruised black eye and cut on his cheek worked in his favor with his rugged good looks. All this "certified" cowboy was missing was his Stetson, but she was glad he didn't have one on at the moment because the hat would only hide his gorgeous wavy blond hair. Man, she loved to run her fingers through that head of silk.

She put her hand in his and allowed him to pull her into his arms. As she wrapped her arms around his waist, she'd never felt more secure and loved than she did when Josh's strong arms surrounded her. The spicy aroma of his aftershave teased her nostrils and she buried her nose in his shirt, enjoying the smells of laundry soap, aftershave and all male that commingled into an arousing cocktail for her senses.

"Look at me," he quietly commanded.

Sabrina lifted her chin and elevated her gaze to meet his serious one. He searched her face before he spoke. "I meant what I said last night. I love you too much to let you go."

She closed her eyes, unable to meet his gaze. When he laid a gentle kiss on each eyelid, she let out a tortured sob. The man just made her heart turn to sheer mush and her knees literally threaten to give out from underneath her. *Good thing he had her locked in a bear hug or she'd be a melted puddle on the floor at his feet.*

"I'd just pick you up and make you melt all over again," he chuckled.

Her eyes flew open at his comment as heat rode up her checks. "Did I just say that out loud?" she asked, already afraid of his answer.

"Yes, you did," came his satisfied reply as amusement danced in his eyes. He slid his hands down to cup her rear through her jeans, pulling her full against his body. "And don't think for one minute I'll let you forget it, darlin'. I'll use every advantage I've got when it comes to convincing you that you belong with me."

The ruthless look in his gaze belied the lightheartedness in his tone. Sabrina resisted the shiver of anticipation that threatened to shimmy up her spine at the promise his eyes, even more than his words, conveyed.

A distinctive, high-pitched beep-beep sound outside, interrupted the arcs of sexual energy and dual displays of willpower that seemed to flow unspoken between them.

Josh frowned at the horn's sound, then walked over to open the door. Sabrina followed him to see Dirk pulling his helmet off as he sat there in front of the house on his motorcycle, a wide grin on his face.

"Well, I'll be damned," Dirk said as his eyes lit up. "Aren't you just the luckiest dog around?" he said to Josh as he looked at Sabrina standing next to his friend. Nodding to her, he grinned, "Hello again, gorgeous."

"Hi, Dirk," she replied and held back a laugh as Josh jerked his gaze to her, jealousy and surprise evident on his face.

"You two know each other?"

She laughed. "Dirk gave me a ride to the Lonestar when I first arrived in Boone."

"Got your rental car?" Dirk asked.

She nodded. "Yep, the very next day. Not that I've used it much," she smirked. "But thanks again for your help."

Josh walked out onto the porch, his entire stance tense. "Why did you bring your bike? I wanted Sabrina to go with me to get my truck."

"Might've helped if you had mentioned that bit of information," Dirk shot back. "Plus, I just thought it'd be fun to take my bike up the hills to get to your place."

Feeling the tension flowing between the men, Sabrina jumped in, "It's okay, Josh. Didn't you say the towing place wasn't that far away? I'll wait here for you to get back. No big deal."

He turned his worried gaze her way. "I'd prefer not to leave you alone."

"No one even knows where I am. Remember we kept it a secret," she replied with a laugh.

Sighing, Josh nodded in agreement and walked inside to retrieve his keys and his wallet. When he came back outside, he said, "I'll be back in a half hour."

She smiled up at him as he bent to kiss her before he walked down the stairs toward Dirk's bike.

"Let's go, stud," Dirk teased as he tossed a spare helmet Josh's way and laughed when his friend grunted with the helmet's impact against his chest.

Once Josh put his helmet on and got on behind him, Dirk revved the motorcycle's engine and turned the bike around. Before he left, he gave Sabrina a rakish grin. "Don't worry, he'll be back in record time. I can guarantee it."

"I'd prefer in one piece," she called after the loud motorcycle as the men took off.

Sabrina went inside and closed and locked the door. What could she do to occupy her time while she waited for Josh? After she cleaned their breakfast dishes, she picked up the remote and clicked on the TV for background noise as she continued to scan the house. When her gaze landed on his laptop sitting on the desk, she decided to see if she had any responses to the emails she'd sent out yesterday.

She sat down at the desk and watched the last few minutes of an old sitcom rerun while she waited for his computer to boot up. Sifting through her email, she found a few that needed immediate attention and once she'd responded to those mails, her gaze was drawn to the news update that flashed across the screen.

Eddie Clayton, the escaped convict who was recently apprehended after four hours of freedom, was just transferred to a maximum security prison today to await his trial where they will determine the additional sentencing for his latest transgressions.

When the picture of the convict popped up on the TV screen, recognition dawned and suddenly that night came flooding back to her. She'd watched the news report, saw the convict's photo, heard the noise outside, then picked up the lantern and...and...there was a note and she'd set it down on the railing when she picked up the lantern. What did it say? Damn why couldn't she remember more? she berated herself as she tried to recall the rest.

An idea struck her. Maybe if she could find that note, it would jog the rest of her memory. Picking up Josh's cell phone, she flipped it open and quickly dialed the Tanners' residence.

"Hello?" Nan answered.

"Nan? Hi, it's Sabrina. A bit of my memory has come back but I'm hoping you can help me."

"Oh, that's great news! I'd be glad to help if I can. What can I do?"

"That night I was attacked, someone left a lantern sitting on top of a note on the porch. I remember picking up the note, but I can't remember what it said. I'm hoping that maybe the note might still be there, that maybe it fell off the porch and is in the yard somewhere. Can you look for me?"

"Sure thing, child," came Nan's indulgent response. "Let me go look around. I'll call you back. Are you calling from Josh's?"

"Yes, I am, but I'm calling from his cell phone…er…which I don't know the number," she apologized.

"No problem. I've got Josh's number. I'll call that one back."

"Okay." Sabrina breathed out in relief that she might finally be helpful in discovering her attacker. She hoped Nan found that note. Of course, after that hard rain yesterday, it might very well be ruined even if she did find it.

Once she hit the "end" button on the phone, she was about to close it when she saw the "text message waiting" indicator flashing. She smiled as she pressed the button to retrieve the message. That had been sweet of Josh to think about her yesterday.

When Josh's message popped up, she felt all the blood drain from her face.

Thinking about you. Meet me in the stables. Josh.

The familiar phrase flashed through her memory and came jolting back… *Meet me in the stables. Josh.* The exact same words that were on the note the night she was attacked. *God no!* she thought, goose bumps breaking out all over her as a shiver shot down her spine. *I went to the stables to meet with Josh. And then…* Her stomach churned. *…then I was knocked out and left unconscious while the stables were set on fire.*

Why would Josh do such a thing? Her mind frantically fought to sort through the confused and erratic thoughts tumbling through it. While her heart raced, she grabbed her belly, fighting off the waves of nausea. She felt physically ill…as if someone had just punched her hard in the gut when she wasn't prepared for the impact.

He did pretty much admit he had a thing for Elise when she'd asked him about it in the hospital…

"Once upon a time…maybe…" he'd said.

Maybe he hadn't gotten over Elise like he'd led her to believe. Leaning forward, she put her hands on her knees for support as she forced her rapid breathing to slow, even breaths. She'd never felt so bereft and betrayed in her life. *No, no, no! He said he loved me,* she argued with herself as she squeezed her eyes shut. But try as she might to keep her whirling mind at bay, snippets of things that Josh had said and done to keep her sequestered, to keep tabs on her whereabouts came slamming back to her.

"You don't remember anything else?" he'd asked her in the hospital, an urgent look on his face. *"She'll stay with me,"* he'd insisted... *"I'm taking a personal interest in your well-being."*

Was his initial worry for her insincere? Had he really just been trying to protect himself initially, to cover his tracks once he realized his plan had backfired?

"...I was hoping to avoid telling you this...to keep you from worrying, but the escaped prisoner has an alibi. It seems he was busy breaking and entering in another house while you were attacked. So that means whoever attacked you is still out there... I don't want you out of my sight any longer than necessary. Your memory could come back at any time."

Did he say those things to evoke fear in her? To keep her with him so he'd be the first one to know if and when her memory came back? She opened her eyes, trying to rationalize it out. But he'd seemed upset to think Colt was being blamed.

"Maybe it wasn't you they were after." He'd said to her in the hospital.

Yet his declaration of love for her had appeared so sincere during the storm. Could it be he regretted what he had done? Had he unintentionally fallen in love with her throughout this whole mess?

Damn, I'm so confused. Her body shook all over as she took gulps of air and silently prayed, *Please don't let me hyperventilate. I can't pass out now.*

Josh's phone rang, the sudden sound wringing a gasp of surprise out of her. She quickly stood up straight and almost passed out as her vision blurred. Blinking to regain her equilibrium, she shoved the cell phone in her back pocket and walked over to pick up Josh's cordless phone, pushing the "talk" button.

"Hello?"

"It's me," came Nan's familiar voice. "Well, I found a note but the note I found looks like a phone number. This must've been the phone number that police officer give you yesterday. Her name was Renee O'Hara, right?"

"Yes, that was her name." Sabrina frowned in confusion. "Hmmm, that's very strange because I know I picked up her note after I dropped it..."

She trailed off as realization dawned as to what might have happened. Sabrina ran over to Josh's bedroom and rummaged in her suitcase for her dirty clothes from the day before.

"You there?" Nan asked, her voice sounding worried.

When Sabrina pulled out the note she'd stuck in her jeans' pocket yesterday she slowly opened up the crisp paper and then called out in a shocked voice, "Oh my god, I had the note from the person who attacked me in my pocket all along. That must've been the note I picked up from underneath the bushes instead of the one from Officer O'Hara."

"What did the note say?" Nan asked, sounding excited.

Sabrina's voice trembled and she responded with a sob, "Oh, Nan...the note said *Elise, meet me in the stables. Josh.* I went to the stables to let him know Elise wasn't home. Josh must've been the one who attacked me."

"Lord, child! Josh? I can't believe it! Are you saying that he attacked you thinking you were Elise?" she asked, sounding incredulous.

"I know it sounds crazy, Nan. I can't remember being attacked. All I can remember is reading the note and heading for the stables and now I have proof as to the only other person who was in the stables that night right here in my hand," she finished with conviction as she tucked the note in her pocket.

Sniffing back the tears that threatened to fall, she straightened her spine, trying to put on a strong front. "I need to call Officer O'Hara right away. Can you please read her number to me?"

"Where's Josh now?" Nan asked.

"He's gone to pick up his truck that was towed yesterday while he fought a fire in town." With her memory partially returned, her fear spiked at the thought of Josh returning home. She wouldn't be able to pretend nothing was wrong. "I need to get out of here," she said, her voice frantic.

"Colt will be home any minute. I'm going to send him to get you, Sabrina," came the older woman's worried response. "After I give you Officer O'Hara's phone number, hang up and immediately call the police."

She'd just disconnected the call when someone knocked at the front door. Relief flooded through her. Josh had his keys so there was no way it was him. Setting the cordless phone down on the desk, she walked to the front door and peered around the side windowpane.

The sight of a black pickup truck in the yard and Colt's neighbor Jackson Riley standing at the door made her draw her brows together in surprise. She didn't get the impression from Josh that Jackson was the kind of person he'd expect a visit from, but then who the hell knows that anything that Josh told her was the full truth. Jackson might be able to give her a lift back to the Lonestar.

Opening the door, she said, "Hello Mr. Riley. I'm sorry, but Josh isn't home at the moment."

"It's about damn time you called the Tanner house. I've been waiting to find out where you were," came a very familiar deadly sounding response.

Chapter Twelve

Sabrina sucked in her breath at the look of determination on Jackson Riley's face. She glanced at the rope gripped in his hands, shock and disbelief rolling through her as her full memory of the night she was attacked came flooding back.

The *tone* of his words...the exact same inflection she'd heard that night. He'd sounded full of bitterness, lethal and deadly when he'd said, "*Colt can't have what belongs to me*," right before he knocked her out cold. Her heart jerked in her chest and her gaze flew back to his dark, narrowed one. Self-preservation caused her to react on instinct.

She tried to slam the door shut, but before she could shut it all the way, he jammed his booted foot between the door and the frame. Gritting her teeth, she put all her weight behind the door, shouldering it as she frantically tried to decide what her next course of action would be.

"I want that note. Where is it?" Jackson said through a howl of pain as the door crushed his foot. A second later she felt the door give behind his own shouldering efforts, the door jerking behind his weight. When she felt the door jump a second time, she knew she couldn't hold him off for long. Sabrina waited a brief second, then let the door go completely as she turned and ran as if the very hounds of hell were on her heels.

While she ran, she couldn't help but quickly glance back at her efforts. As she'd hoped, she hit the timing just right. Jackson must've been in the process of ramming the door with his shoulder again when she let it go. He slid across the wood floor while the door slammed open, splintering on its hinges and banging into the wall behind it.

"Take the note," she shrieked as she struggled to pull it out of her pocket and then threw it on the floor, hoping the prize he was after would buy her precious seconds of time. She let out a scream worthy of a banshee at the sight of Jackson's ferocity as he barreled across the room. The swiftness with which he recovered from his fall and was now heading across the hardwood floor, didn't bode well for her.

As he snatched up the note and then continued to come after her, a maniacal look still on his face, she picked up her speed. Dashing through the house, she clawed at a kitchen chair, then tugged on a standing lamp, knocking each piece over to try and slow him down as she made her way to the far side of the house.

The back door.

She had to get to the back door. Just a few more feet, she thought frantically as she heard his footfalls not far behind her, his heavy breathing as he hissed, "Get back here, you little whore. No one is going to get in the way of what I've worked my whole life for."

The man was clearly insane! When she made it to the door, her fingers fumbled with the latch. Relief flooded through her as she finally unlocked it. Pulling the door open, she ran across the deck and down the few stairs to the grass.

A rumbling thud sounded behind her as she started for the woods, spurring her to push herself harder. She'd only taken a couple of steps when he shoved her between the shoulder blades and she lost her balance.

Sabrina grunted as she hit the ground hard, the action bruising her rib cage. She screamed as she felt his hand pulling on the waist of her jeans and she quickly rolled onto her back, kicking at him with all she was worth.

Jackson bellowed in anger when she connected with his stomach, knocking him off of her. A sob of relief escaped her as she got up as quickly as she could and took off toward the front of the house. With the head start she'd gained, she hoped the house would hide where she entered the woods. She could hide in there until Josh came home.

Josh! Oh no! If something happened to her, everyone would think it was him. Guilt over thinking him capable of harming her, along with worry that people would believe he was her assailant, gave her a burst of speed. Just ten more feet, she thought as she started to pass Jackson's truck.

The sound of Jackson yelling her name when he came around the house had her glancing back for a second. She'd just turned to face her destination again when she saw someone step out from behind the truck as she rounded the vehicle. She was going too fast to stop as the woman reached out and used her arm to clothesline her.

Sabrina slammed down to the ground, the breath knocked out of her. As she wheezed to catch her breath, fighting to stay conscious, the voluptuous woman with long blonde hair leaned over her and tsked with a smirk, "Ah, did ya really think you could get away?"

When starbursts flashed before her eyes, her last thoughts were of Josh and her regret over the fact she'd never told him she loved him. In agonizing slow motion, her vision faded until even the tiny pinpricks of light left behind scattered into nothingness.

* * * * *

Just as Dirk had promised, Josh arrived home in record time. He frowned at the set of tire tracks that crushed the taller grass and seemed to lead right up to his front door!

Josh's heart jerked in his chest at the sight of his front door standing wide open. He dashed out of his truck, his pulse thundering in his ears as he took a flying leap over the four steps to the porch.

"Sabrina!" he yelled as he stepped into his house and faced his worst nightmare.

Taking in the broken door and the shambles his house was in, he hoped and prayed he wouldn't find Sabrina had been hurt or, God forbid, worse. Once he'd searched every inch of his home and couldn't find her, he stood in the living room, his entire body tense in fear for her safety.

His hands shook as he pushed them through his hair, trying to calm himself into thinking rationally. God, how the fuck was he going to find her and *who* the hell was after Sabrina in the first place?

His phone rang, jerking him out of his tumultuous thoughts. Josh picked it up, snarling, "What!

When there was a pause on the line, all he could think about was the unknown attacker torturing him with a silent call. "If this is you, you fucking sonofabitch, you'd better not hurt a hair on her head."

"Whoa!" Colt said, his voice calm. "What's going on, Josh?"

At the sound of Colt's voice, Josh shook his head to clear out the enraged thoughts rambling through it.

He took a steadying breath and ran his hand through his hair again as he said, "God, Colt, I'm sorry. I'm so fucking sorry."

"Hold on there. Take a deep breath and tell me what's going on," he replied in a soothing tone.

"She's gone," Josh's tone lowered. He sat down and put his head in his hand, trying desperately not to lose it. Sabrina needed him now more than ever.

"Sabrina?" Colt asked, his voice lowering as if he didn't want someone—more than likely Elise—to overhear their conversation.

"Yes," Josh answered, closing his eyes to keep the tears stinging behind them at bay. Pushing his eyelids hard with his fingers, he opened them and finished, "And I wish to God I knew where to start looking for her."

"Are you sure she didn't leave on her own?" Colt asked.

"What's that supposed to mean?" Josh growled, his head jerking up.

"Calm down, Josh. Nan just received an upsetting call from Sabrina. She found a note that implied you were the person who lured her to the stables the night of the fire."

"What!" Josh yelled into the phone. "I was fuckin' fighting a fire around the time she was attacked."

"After today's developments, I have no doubt of your innocence, Josh. I'll be there in two minutes," came Colt's firm reply.

"Huh? You're here?"

"Hell yeah, I'm home. Someone's trying to fuck with my life and it sounds like yours, too. I've got a pretty damn good idea who'd want to frame me for my own wife's murder," Colt ground out. "No matter what it takes, I'm going to nail the sonofabitch."

"Am I in *The Twilight Zone*? What the hell are you talking about?" Josh asked, his brow furrowing.

"Long story," Colt sighed. "Hang tight. Be at your place in two."

Josh hung up the phone, thankful for Colt's steadying words. Right now, he needed the voice of reason whispering in his ear because he wasn't going to get there on his own in his current, riled up, ready to commit murder state. And the thought that Sabrina could think he'd want to do her harm...he felt physically ill.

While he waited, he realized he needed to call the police and let them know Sabrina had been kidnapped. He didn't have time to deal with paperwork, waiting for the police and all that bullshit. Renee. He'd call her and she'd get the ball rolling so he wouldn't have to stop looking for Sabrina on his end.

Standing up, he glanced around the room, looking for his cell phone, which had Renee's number stored in it. He moved quickly, pushing overturned furniture out of the way, looking underneath couch cushions to see if it had fallen between them. He knew he'd left it at home.

Turning on the cordless phone, he dialed his cell phone at the same time he vowed to always keep the damn thing in the same spot so he didn't lose the phone every five seconds.

The phone rang and rang and that's when he remembered he had left it on vibrate mode. Then a thought struck him, the idea lifting his spirits. Did Sabrina have it with her? Could he get that lucky? He did ask her to keep it with her.

A steely determination settled over him as he headed for his laptop and pulled up his cell phone provider's website. Clicking on the GPS "locator" link, he punched in his access code and then his phone number and held his breath as the system's "verifying position" icon popped up.

He glanced out the large picture window and saw Colt's truck drive up and then heard his boots on his porch as the website finally completed its search.

When Colt entered his house, his gaze moved throughout the house, taking in the shambles Josh's home was in. Once Colt's blue eyes met his, Josh gave him a humorless, cold smile. He turned his laptop so his neighbor could see the results. "My cell phone locater program." He pointed to an area on the screen. "Sabrina's somewhere in this area." Glancing up at Colt, he continued, "I'm ready to help you fry his ass."

Colt looked at the computer screen, then jerked his knowing gaze back to Josh's as he bit out, "Not at all surprised. Jackson Riley."

* * * * *

Sabrina awoke to the smell of stale manure and the sensation of something rough yet cushioned underneath her. Realizing she was unable to move her hands and feet, she panicked as her eyes flew open. Rough ropes bound her wrists and ankles and as she shifted she heard the rustle of hay move underneath her.

Even though fear shot through her, rolling over her in alternating waves of cold sweat and hair-raising goose bumps, she did her best to remain calm as she took in the room surrounding her.

She saw the roof's rafters overhead and a quick scan of the room with its empty stables told her she was in an abandoned barn. Sunlight streamed through an open window in one of the stalls, nearly blinding her. Tilting her head away from the light, she squirmed, trying to sit up. The hay slid around underneath her and she lost her balance then fell onto her side once more. Damn ropes. The way they were tied around her—a short rope connecting her tied wrists to her tied ankles—made it near impossible for her to sit up.

"I see you're awake," she heard Jackson's comment off to her left.

She shifted her gaze to see the older man standing by a rough-hewn table against the wall, then quickly surveyed the room for his blonde partner.

"You won't find her here," he spat, his lip curling in disdain.

"Who?" she asked.

"May. The bitch who stopped you, then decided to take off, leaving me to clean up this fucking mess," he bit out.

"It's too bad," he continued while he lifted a hammer from the table and turned her way. "I was hoping you'd stay unconscious while I finished you off." Looking at the hammer, he examined the metal, turning it in the sunlight. He snorted, twitching his lips. "Shooting you would be easiest, but the noise would draw attention and a knife across the throat is just too messy." He offered a satisfied smile as he let the hammer fall in his palm. "A good knock or two or *three* in your skull should do the trick. Nasty work, but it must be done."

Her gaze widened and her heart raced at his words. When she glanced at the hammer in his hand and then back to his impassive face, sheer terror gripped her. "Heeeeeeeeelp!" Sabrina let out a scream that would wake the dead.

"No one will hear you way out here."

He seemed unruffled as she continued to yell at the top of her lungs until her voice went hoarse. When she finally ran out of steam, he lifted the hammer up and let it fall once more. "You think I'm happy with how this has turned out?"

"I *think* you're a lunatic," she croaked as anger began to overrule her fear. If she was going to die, she wouldn't die begging.

"Damn women. The whole lot of ya," he hissed out in disgust as he set the hammer down on the table and patted his plaid shirt.

"Yeah, but you didn't do this by yourself, did you?" she needled him. God, if she could just keep him talking, maybe someone would've heard her screaming as if she were *about to be murdered*!

"You referring to May?" he asked, glancing sharply at her. Pulling a pack of cigarettes from his front pocket, he continued, "May only helped at the tail end of my plan. But once again, like all the damn women in my life, she skipped out at the last minute, just like my mole at the insurance agency did when the police started sniffing around. *Which was the whole fucking point*," he bit out as he stabbed his finger in the air for effect. "They were *supposed* to come asking questions. She didn't seem to mind taking my five thousand dollars to manipulate records and falsify medical reports. Noooo! But when the heat got too close, 'I'm afraid I'm gonna get caught'," he mimicked in his version of a high-pitched, female voice.

He grumbled a few more disparaging obscenities then continued, "The dumb bitch skipped town on me yesterday. Then May, that good-for-nothing whore, the one woman I thought saw eye to eye with me on this whole deal says, 'See ya on the flip side,' when we arrived back on my property. If I hadn't had you in tow, I'd have taken her out myself just for sheer principle."

He clenched his fist and his face mottled in anger. Hope filled her as her will to survive overrode her fear. Maybe the old coot would die of a heart attack. She could only hope. But instead he picked up the hammer and slammed it down on the table, cracking the old wood. Her entire body tensed at the violence behind his action. After he struck the table a couple more times, he took a couple of deep breaths that seemed to calm him down enough to set down the hammer and pull a cigarette out of the pack before he returned the box to his pocket. Digging in his jeans pocket he withdrew a lighter and lit the end.

Taking a long draw from it, he closed his eyes for a second as if the nicotine truly settled him, then dropped the lighter back in his pants' pocket.

While he appeared to relax, her own nerves put her on the edge of hysteria. *I don't want to die. Keep him talking, whatever you do. Don't let him have too much time to think.*

"And then there's you," he bit out as he used his cigarette to point to her, his gray eyebrows slashing downward as he narrowed his gaze on her. Smoke came out of his nose and mouth in streams of curling plumes, reminding her of an old, angry dragon.

"If you hadn't shown up, I wouldn't have mistaken you for Elise that night. I'd have held off, bided my time a bit longer. My tap on Colt's phone line would've allowed me another chance to find another perfect time to frame Colt for his wife's murder."

"That's what this is all about? Your need to set Colt up?" she asked, incredulous.

"It was so much more than that," he said as he started to pace puffing on his cigarette. Then he paused and continued, smugness in his tone, "I had it perfectly planned. With his wife dead, the police would learn of the high-dollar life insurance policies he and his wife had taken out on each other—courtesy of May and me—" He stopped and looked at her with an I'm-so-clever smirk, before he continued, "In the end, Colt would get the murder rap and lose his land."

His face took on a faraway look as if he were picturing the entire scenario he'd just described in his head. Shaking himself out of his dream-state, he continued, "Once Colt was behind bars, if I couldn't find a way to get the land, at least I would know he was suffering."

Her eyebrows drew together in reluctant understanding as he told her his plan…almost as if he wanted someone to acknowledge all his plotting. The man was clearly mad. But now everything that had happened to her—being knocked out, the burned stables, the police's speculation on Colt's life insurance…it all made sense.

A smug smile tilted the corners of his lips at her expression. "Tell me how brilliant I am. How clever and devious. Aren't you impressed?"

"How can I be impressed with a man who had to depend on women to help initiate his master plan?" she said with sarcasm. "Hell, you couldn't even remember to retrieve your note that was supposed to lure Elise to the stables."

Scowling at her, he stuck the cigarette in the corner of his lips as he pulled the note he'd written out of his pocket along with his lighter.

Flicking the lighter open once more, he lit one corner of the paper, smiling a crooked smirk while the cigarette dangled from his lips and dropped bits of burned ash.

"No more evidence," he mumbled as the paper burned in a matter of seconds. He dropped the ball of fire before it reached his fingers, stomping the burning, charred remains out on the dirt floor beneath his boot.

Her stomach clenched as he dug his boot toe deep in the earth. She had no doubt he planned to "rub" her out of the picture just as easily as he did that paper.

"You talk too much," he said as he took another drag on his cigarette. He turned and picked up the hammer and let the heavy metal head hit the palm of his hand as he met her worried gaze. "But I can take care of that," he finished as he started toward her with a determined look on his face, the hammer raised, ready to strike.

Her fear skyrocketed and she tried to jerk herself out of his reach. *It's not my time to die*, she thought, her mind frantic as primal fear shot through her. "Get the hell away from me," she screamed, her voice fading out.

Jackson squatted beside her and set the hammer down. Taking the cigarette out of his mouth, he grabbed a fistful of her hair and jerked her onto her back.

"Going somewhere?" he asked, his laughter evil, higher pitched, maniacal.

The fine hairs stood up on her arms at the unbalanced sound of his laugh while tears stung her eyes from the pain his abusive action caused.

Slowly he wound the fistful of her hair up around his hand, then he seemed to relax as he smoothed the black mass across the hay above her head. "It's a shame I'll have to mar such a pretty face when I bash your skull in," he said in a conversational tone as if he wasn't brutally threatening her.

He picked up the hammer with one hand as he held the cigarette with the other and said in a cold tone, "But, pretty or not, women aren't worth shit." He raised the hammer.

"I knew you had a screw or two loose, but had no idea you were such a stupid sonofabitch," came a calm, controlled voice from the direction of the doorway to the barn.

Jackson immediately stood and glanced toward the doorway at the same time Sabrina jerked her frightened gaze toward the voice. She let out a sob of relief to see Colt standing there holding a shotgun trained on Jackson.

"Do you really think I'm that dumb, Colt? That I wouldn't have a backup plan?" Jackson answered, his tone deadly and focused as he took a leisurely puff of his cigarette.

"Put down the hammer, Jackson, or I'll shoot you where you stand," Colt bit out. "Give me any flimsy excuse to blow a hole in your sorry ass and I'll take it."

Jackson hissed in anger as he dropped the hammer at his feet. Folding one hand behind his back, he growled, "Don't think this is over. I'll never give up."

As he spoke, he tossed his cigarette behind him, right above Sabrina's head.

Her heart rate skyrocketed as she saw flames begin to dance above her head on the dry hay. She made an effort to move away from the flames and that's when she saw Jackson wrap his fingers on the grip of the handgun he had stuck in his belt behind his back. She tried to scream to warn Colt, but her hoarse voice just cracked instead. When she realized Colt's gaze was on the flames behind her and he didn't see Jackson draw his weapon, Sabrina did the only thing she could to help.

With all her might she flipped away and then rolled back, kicking Jackson behind the knees as hard as she could.

Jackson's knees buckled and his gun went off toward the ceiling at the same time Josh rammed the older man in the chest with his shoulder, knocking him flat on his back.

"You fucking maniac!" Josh yelled as he hit Jackson's hand with his fist, making him drop the weapon. He knocked the gun away as Jackson roared in anger, attacking him.

While the men scuffled, Sabrina smelled more than just the hay burning. She felt the heat all around her. She knew she needed to get out of the raging fire's way, but the bonds around her made rolling away difficult. A bit at a time was all she could manage while laying on her side.

When Jackson tried to hit Josh with his other fist, Colt was there, leaning over the man. "Stay down, you sorry bastard," he ordered as he slammed his fist square in Jackson's jaw, knocking the man out cold.

"Sabrina," Josh yelled as he scrambled over to her, concern and fear etched on his face. He didn't stop to think, just reacted as he used his hands to put the fire out that had just made its way to her hair.

Quickly picking her up, he rushed her out of the barn. Colt followed behind them as he carried Jackson's unconscious body away from the fire.

Once they reached a safe distance from the building, Colt dumped Jackson's limp frame on the ground with a hard thud. "Lunatic bastard," he mumbled, as he looked back up at the burning stables and shook his head.

Walking over to Sabrina and Josh, he brushed a strand of her hair away from her face, noted the burned ends, and asked with a concerned look, "Are you okay?"

She nodded, her heart still racing as she whispered with a trembling half smile, "I guess I'll be getting that haircut I've been putting off, but other than that, I'm fine."

"You're hoarse. God, Sabrina. I'm so sorry this happened," Josh said as he sat down on the ground with her in his arms and pulled his pocketknife out of the holder on his belt. Quickly cutting through the ropes around her wrists and ankles, he gathered her close.

"How did you find me?" she asked while she rubbed her sore wrists.

Josh shook his head in wonder. "My cell phone's GPS tracker."

She gave a shaky, scratchy laugh as she pulled the cell phone from her back pocket. "I'd forgotten all about it."

Josh took the cell phone and tossed it to Colt. "Do the honors. I'm sure you'll enjoy this."

As Colt walked away to call the police, Josh rocked her in his arms and said, "Thank God we got here in time. I don't know what I would've done if I had lost you, Brina."

She wrapped her arms around his neck, hugging him back. As she breathed in the scents that were all Josh, she whispered back as tears streamed down her face, "I'm sorry I thought for even one second you had a hand in attacking me."

He shook his head, his tone understanding. "Colt told me about your call to Nan. She was worried for you until Colt set her straight. Apparently Jackson had someone working for him at the insurance company, working to set Colt up. She's been arrested. There's no reason to apologize. Jackson surprised us all at how well he'd set us up."

She hugged him tighter. "I love you, Josh Kelly. I thought I'd never have the chance to tell you that."

When she spoke, Josh quickly looked at her then cupped her face in his hands, wincing as he did so.

She grabbed his wrists and gasped at the reddened flesh on the tips of his fingers. "Oh, no, your fingers."

"I've had worse. They'll heal." He shrugged the pain away as his serious teal gaze searched her face. "We've got what matters the most. The rest we'll figure out, okay?" When he finished speaking, he gave her a reassuring smile.

She knew he referred to his firefighting. She smiled back, nodding in agreement, then rubbed her nose against his chest, thankful to be in his arms once more.

* * * * *

Later that afternoon, Josh drove up in his truck as Sabrina walked out of the Tanners' ranch house waving goodbye to Elise. After the police had taken her statement and arrested Jackson, Josh and Colt had gone on to the police station to talk to Renee while Elise brought her back to the Lonestar.

"I have a rental car I've yet to use, you know. I can drive myself back to the Double K," she said with a smile as she stood on the passenger side of his truck, looking through the open window.

He grinned as he leaned over and opened the truck door for her from the inside. "I know, but I like having you with me. Get in, good lookin'."

"How'd the talk with Renee go? Any news?" she asked as she climbed into his truck.

"As I mentioned earlier, the woman from the insurance agency was arrested, but the police have yet to locate May Winston."

"Who *is* this May woman anyway? As whacked as he was, I understood Jackson's motivation, but why did she get involved in this?" she asked.

"She's a disgruntled ex-employee from the Lonestar rodeo who apparently had some major issues with Colt for firing her."

"Ah, now I see," she said as she smiled at him and flipped her shoulder-length hair. "Well, what do you think? Elise cried as she cut off the burned ends for me. Tomorrow she said she'll take me to get it shaped up at a salon."

His teal gaze turned serious as he reached over and threaded his fingers through the shorter strands, then he frowned. "Every time I think about how close I came to losing you…" He paused, his jaw ticcing before he continued in a controlled voice, "It's a good thing Jackson's in jail and out of my reach."

Charmed by his protective tone and gentle touch, she reached up and grabbed his wrist. Lacing her fingers with his, careful to avoid his burns, she lowered their hands and kissed the back of his hand with a happy smile. "I'm fine. My very own hero was there to save me."

"About that…" Josh put his other hand on the steering wheel and let his gaze scan the open prairie for a second.

When his gaze met hers once more, the heat and love behind it made her heart melt.

"I've decided to go to part-time firefighting status, Brina."

Surprised by his announcement, she squeezed his hand but couldn't help the guilt that washed over her at the feeling of elation that rushed through her. "Are you sure that's what you want to do, Josh?"

He raised her hand to his lips and kissed her palm. "There's one thing I learned today is that when it comes to you, I'm not willing to take too many risks. Every time I fight a fire, I'll still be fighting for Nick, but now I'm fighting for my own happiness. I've put it off for too long. Those empty stables you saw at my house? They will soon be full. My father's jumping up and down with glee that I'll be joining the family business of raising horses."

Tears shone in her eyes. "What you've always wanted to do?" she repeated, needing to know his decision was his and his alone.

He nodded. "Yeah."

Lowering their hands to the seat between them, he slid a huge sapphire flanked by two trillion cut diamonds on her finger. His teal gaze rose to meet hers. "I guessed at your size... Will you marry me, Brina? You don't have to say yes right away," he interrupted before she could speak, then finished, "Just say you'll wear my ring and think about it."

Sabrina's heart thudded in her chest as he settled the ring at the base of her finger. She threw her arms around his neck, then kissed him saying, "There's nothing to think about. I love you, Josh. It doesn't matter to me if I'd known you for years or just met you two days ago, my answer would still be 'yes, I'll marry you'."

Josh wrapped his arm around her waist and pulled her close, his kiss full of passion and love as his lips covered hers. Trailing his lips down her neck, he said, "I'll order any additional office equipment you need for your office. I promise you'll have the space you need to get your work done from home."

She sighed at his arousing touch. "I think my boss would go for a proposal for me to work out of my house if I promised to come back to Arizona a few times a year. Plus, it'd be a central place to meet up with Nic and Lily, too. It would probably take me a week or so to relocate my office."

He pulled her tighter, growling against her neck, "Hell, for that matter, you don't have to work at all."

She laughed and rubbed the tension in his shoulders. "It's only a week, Josh. I think we can handle being apart for a week or so."

"Speak for yourself," he grumbled as his lips made their way down the vee opening in her shirt.

Sabrina gasped as he cupped one of her breasts through her clothes. Regretfully, she pushed away from him, saying as she cast a sheepish glance up to the Tanners' ranch house, "I think we'd better take this home."

Josh gave her a devilish grin as he started the engine. "I couldn't agree more. Home sounds pretty good to me."

About the author:

Born and raised in the southeast, Patrice has been a fan of romance novels since she was thirteen years old. While she reads many types of books, romance novels will always be her mainstay, saying, "I guess it's the idea of a happy ever after that draws me in."

Patrice welcomes mail from readers. You can write to her c/o Ellora's Cave Publishing at 1056 Home Avenue, Akron OH 44310-3502.

Also by Patrice Michelle:

Wild Hearts

Cheyenne McCray

Chapter One

"Damn it." Nicole Landford propped her hands on her full hips and scowled. "You have some nerve up and dying on me out here in the middle of fucking nowhere."

With all her pent-up frustration, Nicole kicked the tire of her red '63 Corvette with the toe of her four-inch heel and winced. She had only managed to hurt her big toe, not to mention scuffing the bluish-green shoe that matched her mini-dress and the unusual shade of her eyes.

The 'vette ignored her tirade as steam continued to hiss from beneath the hood. An acrid burnt rubber stench rose up in the air, along with the smell of radiator fluid. Heat rolled over Nicole in waves, adding to the perspiration already beading on her face. Why couldn't the damn thing have died in Douglas, or even Bisbee? At least then she'd have been near a phone. And of course, actually bringing her cell phone would have been a stroke of genius.

With an irritated sigh, Nicole shoved her long blonde hair out of her face with one hand and looked around at the endless miles of ranch land. If she had been on a highway, she could have stuck out one bare leg, hitched up the miniskirt of her backless fuck-me dress, and flagged down some gorgeous man. Oh, hell, any man would do, so long as she could get to Dee MacLeod's house.

But here she was on a dirt road and she'd taken one hell of a wrong turn. That's what she got for not paying attention. Instead of ending up at least on the road to the Flying M, the MacLeod Ranch, she was stuck out here with nothing around her but dirt, grass, barbed wire fences, and cattle. It was a hot, muggy, and overcast late August afternoon, and more sweat dripped down the side of her face. Thunderclouds were building up to the south and she could smell the promise of a monsoon storm that could come out of nowhere in a hurry.

That would be the icing on her cake.

Off in the distance Nicole could see Kev Grand's ranch, but she was in no mood to mess with that cowboy, no matter how sexy the man was. She and Kev had been butting heads since elementary school, and all she needed was another confrontation with him. They never had seen eye to eye on anything, and the man always seemed amused by their arguing. No, she didn't have time for him.

Especially not when she was a woman on a mission.

A few days ago, Nicole and her cousins Lily and Sabrina had made a pact. The first man who "tripped her trigger", as Sabrina had said, was the man Nicole had to go all-out for, no matter what or who. Wild and crazy sex, and as much of it as possible. For one month and one month only.

They had made a bet and damned if Nicole was going to be the one to lose out on it. Out of all three cousins, Nicole was the one who had no reservations about enjoying sex with the men she chose to date. She was a free spirit—no emotional ties. All she ever looked for was a good time. Her cousins were more reserved—especially Lily, who probably hadn't been laid for years.

Nicole intended to make good on the bet. Only problem was, she had yet to find a single man who even interested her enough to cause her nipples to rise, much less make her panties wet. It had been a few days since they'd made the pact after Aunt Viv's fifty-fifth birthday celebration, and Nicole had no prospects that interested her on the horizon.

To try and stir up some action, before her damn car had died on her, Nicole had been on her way to the MacLeod Ranch where her friend Trace was visiting from Texas. Trace was happily married now to a sexy cowboy named Jess Lawless, but she was going to buddy up with Nicole, along with the sheriff's wife, Catie Savage. The three planned to head over to Sierra Vista to one of the local hot spots so that Nicole could find a man who turned her on enough to pursue a romp in the hay with. There were plenty of hot Border Patrol and Customs agents in the area, as well as sexy military men from Ft. Huachuca, not to mention some damn fine ranchers. All Nicole had to do was find one who made her hot and go for it.

But first she had to get there.

"Okay, you piece of—of…" Nicole went around to the front of the car, tried to pop the hood, and snatched back her hand. The damn thing was boiling hot.

She gave another frustrated sigh, but this time in deference to her pride and joy. "I'm sorry, baby. I love you and I shouldn't get so mad." Hell, she and her cherry red 'vette had been through a lot together, so what was a little breakdown now and again?

The low of a cow from the other side of the barbed wire fence drew Nicole's attention and wrath instead. "Beat it, you slobber-mouthed beast."

The white-faced Hereford just chewed her cud as she studied Nicole with her big brown eyes, and then turned away. The muggy Arizona summer afternoon intensified the smell of the cow and the dust her hooves kicked up. More cattle plodded by at a slow and easy pace, eating snatches of grass, green from recent monsoon rains. Occasionally, they gave a loud "moo". Two calves bawled and poked their faces through the fence, before their mothers nudged them along.

Nicole glanced to the south again. It would be her luck for the storm to rain on her parade. Not that it would matter now. Her blonde hair was wilting fast, her makeup running down her face, and her dress rumpling in the humidity.

So much for "dry heat".

After a few moments, the steam lessened. Nicole used a cloth from the backseat of her car to pop the hood and then prop it up. She tossed the cloth on the fender, folded her arms beneath her generous cleavage and glared at the radiator, which probably needed to be replaced. It wasn't easy finding parts for a car over forty years old.

She stomped away, as best she could in those four-inch heels she used to love —

And felt something warm and wet squish around her foot.

With a groan she looked down, knowing what she'd see. She had managed to step into a nice, big, smelly, fresh pile of cow shit.

Great. Just fucking great.

Nicole almost ripped both her heels off and threw them over the fence at the cattle and said to hell with it. Instead she took a deep breath and turned her gaze to the cloudy sky. "Are you out to get me?"

Thunder rumbled in the distance. Wind picked up and lifted her damp hair from her shoulders. Well, there was her answer.

She groaned and wiped off the cow shit on a clump of grass. So much for those heels.

When her shoe was mostly de-crapified, she leaned in the 'vette's open window and snatched the keys out of the ignition. She rounded the car, opened the trunk, and grabbed a new jug of radiator fluid. As she started to shut the lid, her keys slipped out of her hand and into the trunk.

"No!" she shouted, dropping the jug and leaping to stop the trunk lid.

Her keys clanked at the bottom of the trunk. The lid thunked shut.

Nicole groaned and flattened her palms against the sun-warmed car. "*Shit*. Shitshitshitshitshit!"

Before she realized what was happening, large male hands were on either side of hers, braced on the trunk lid, and a very big male body virtually surrounded her.

Nicole froze. Her heart started to pound like a cattle

stampede.

"Now, hon—" came Kev Grand's low drawl, "—you really ought to watch your language."

For a moment her body sagged, she was so thankful it wasn't some rapist who had snuck up on her. But in the next second she gritted her teeth, pissed it was Kev and that he had scared her like he had.

She tried to twist away but he had her blocked with his powerful arms. She clenched her hands into fists. "I'm in no mood for your bullshit, Kev Grand."

Just as she was about to try to push back and shove him off, he leaned in close, his body pressed against hers. She could feel his heat, the rough denim of his shirt against her bare back, his jeans through the thin material covering her ass. She could smell his masculine scent of sweat, horse, and summer wind.

"Now what *are* you in the mood for, Nicole Landford?" he asked in a low rumble that vibrated throughout her body and made the hairs on her nape stand on end.

Nicole's nipples tightened. A thrill zipped straight from her belly to her pussy and her thong was instantly damp.

Kev Grand had tripped her trigger.

"Not you." She slumped forward, buried her face in her arms on the trunk lid, and her words came out muffled. "I don't care. Not you. Not in a million years. *Oh, shit.*"

Chapter Two

Kev gave a low chuckle that caused Nicole to shiver beneath him. "Finally got you where I want you," he murmured close to her ear, causing the fine hairs to rise on her neck again.

Nothing doing. She was *not* going to have anything to do with Kev, no matter that she'd made the bet. Not that her cousins would even know.

Nicole rose up and pushed him away from her. "You just back off, Kev Grand."

She twisted around—and found his face just inches from hers, his arms on either side of her, still braced on the trunk. For a moment she couldn't move, couldn't think. He'd shaved off his mustache, but he looked just as hard-edged and weathered, and just as much of a bad boy as ever.

His straw Stetson shaded his hazel eyes so that all she could see was his angular jaw, his firm lips, and his tanned face. Damn, but a man in a Stetson turned her on. With one finger he pushed up the brim of his hat. She caught her breath as his gaze settled on her lips, then slowly traveled down to her full cleavage, her breasts nearly spilling out of her tight little dress. Her eyes followed his to her nipples, which were hard and oh-so obvious through the thin material.

His gaze returned to hers and his mouth quirked into a sexy grin. "Why, Nicole Landford, I do believe you've got the hots for me."

"You wish." She tossed her hair over her shoulder. "Cocky sonofabitch."

Kev's eyes fixed on her breasts again. He raised his hand and brushed his knuckles across her nipples in a slow movement.

Nicole's knees went weak. In that instant, she could picture him hiking up her dress and placing her bare ass on the trunk of her 'vette. He'd drive his cock into her pussy and fuck her like there was no tomorrow.

His gaze met hers again, and there was definitely smugness mixed with desire in his eyes. He knew exactly what he was doing to her, exactly what she was thinking.

And that pissed her off.

"Bastard." Nicole slammed her fist into Kev's gut, her knuckles coming into contact with his solid abs.

He didn't even flinch. Instead he grabbed her hand and drew her tight against him, so tight she could feel his erection against her belly, right through his Wranglers.

"Like it hard and rough, do you, hon?" He blocked her arms against her sides, grabbed her ass and pressed her tighter against his cock. "I always knew you would."

Nicole swallowed. Kev was talking like he knew all her fantasies—how she wanted a man to take control rather than always being the one to push things to the limit. And that limit had never been enough.

Thunder boomed closer now, the sky darkening as clouds rolled in. A horse whinnied behind Kev and Nicole startled. Earlier she'd been so wrapped up in her car that she hadn't even heard Kev ride up on the horse.

Nicole eyed Kev square on and leaned further back against her car so that his face wasn't quite as close. "It's not like you're gonna find out just how hard I like it."

Kev's lips hovered above Nicole's and she caught his spicy scent of pure male that made her body ache. "I think maybe you're wrong about that."

She sucked in her breath. Maybe Kev *would* be the perfect candidate to fuck for a month and then ditch like a bronc bucking off its rider. After all, Kev was the first man to come close to interesting her since she'd made the bet with her cousins.

No, no, no!

Nicole could feel his breath on her lips. "You'll just have to keep on wondering."

Lightning cracked the sky and thunder rolled across the desert. Quarter-sized drops plopped on Nicole's and Kev's faces. He raised his head and looked over his shoulder to the south.

"We'd best get to shelter." His gaze moved to rest on Nicole's. "We'll head to my ranch. You and I have some unfinished business."

"Like hell." Nicole never let a man tell her what to do, especially not Kev. She freed her arms and pushed against his chest. Raindrops splattered freely over her face and hair, and she blinked away the water on her lashes. "I'm going to the MacLeod ranch."

Kev glanced to the 'vette and back to Nicole. "Looks like you'll have a long walk ahead of you."

She glared at him and he gave a soft laugh. "Come on. Let's get out of here."

Nicole sighed. Even though she didn't want to admit it, she knew he was right.

After she grabbed her purse, rolled up the windows on her car, and put down the hood, Kev grabbed her upper arm and led her toward the big bay gelding several feet away. Clutching her purse, Nicole's heels sank into the now muddy ground and rain plastered the thin material of her outfit to her body, outlining every curve.

Kev's hands were hot through her dress as he grasped her waist and helped her mount the horse. Just as she swung her leg over, her dress rode up high on her thighs. Kev palmed her ass as he settled her in the saddle. She shot him a look and he gave her an unrepentant grin before swinging up behind her in a fluid motion. He wrapped his arms around her waist to grab the reins and scooted himself up so that he was firmly against her ass.

Nicole's pussy tingled at the feel of his erection. His hard male body felt good next to her bare back and she found herself relaxing despite herself. She wasn't about to let Kev into her pants, but she wasn't above a good dose of teasing.

Another crack of lightning and boom of thunder filled the air. Kev clicked his tongue, tugged on the reins, and the horse started off at a quick trot down the edge of the dirt road, toward his ranch.

Kev had wanted to get some serious time alone with Nicole for years. The two had never seen eye to eye, but Kev had always liked Nicole's spunk and her fire. He'd known it would only be a matter of time before he'd have a chance to show her just exactly how hot the fire could burn between the two of them.

He pulled Nicole tighter between his thighs, and as her ass rubbed against his cock with every jar of the horse, the tightness in his Wranglers became almost unbearable. He flicked Sport's reins, casually brushing the insides of his wrists against Nicole's breasts. The woman wasn't wearing a bra, and he'd enjoyed the view before he mounted the horse.

Right now he wanted nothing more than to mount Nicole and fuck her like she'd never been fucked before.

He let his wrists rub against her nipples again and he was sure he heard a soft moan.

"Damn it." Nicole tossed her long, wet hair over her shoulder, slapping strands across his face. "You'd better keep your hands to yourself."

He leaned close to her ear and nuzzled her hair. The soft scent of rain, musk, and woman flowed over him and his cock hardened even more.

Nicole shivered. "Knock it off, Grand." She reached back with one hand and pushed his face away from her, nearly knocking his Stetson off in the process.

Kev grinned. She wanted him all right.

Rain continued to pound the desert and the two of them were good and drenched by the time they reached his ranch and rode into the barn. His nephew Brad was there, brushing down his mare.

Brad raised an eyebrow at the sight of Nicole on the horse in front of Kev. His gaze rested on her lap, where her dress hiked up her thighs, barely covering her. "Why, 'Cole. What brings you out here?" he asked as his gaze traveled up to her generous cleavage before meeting her eyes.

"Thought I'd come and visit you, good lookin'," Nicole said with a sugary sweet note in her voice.

Kev scowled and Brad grinned as he hooked his thumbs in his belt loops. "Never thought I'd get so lucky."

Nicole laughed.

Kev's scowl deepened.

Brad had a reputation with the women around the valley and Kev was none too pleased to see the man's obvious interest in Nicole.

Kev dismounted his gelding. "Brush down Sport," Kev ordered as he put his hands at Nicole's waist to help her down.

Brad raised an eyebrow. "Sure thing." He caught Sport's reins and gave a good-natured grin. "I can see you've got your hands full."

Nicole braced her hands on Kev's shoulders as he slid her off the horse. Her little dress was hiked up so high that he caught sight of the thin strip of her blue thong covering her pussy, and this time he couldn't help a low groan from escaping.

When her heels hit the ground, Nicole tried to push away from Kev, but his grip was firm. The bastard had a possessive look in his eyes that made her panties wet, but she wasn't about to let him get to her.

Of course she wasn't.

Brad chuckled and led the bay gelding away. Kev slid his hands from her waist to her ass and squeezed. "Come on in the house and get dry."

Her hands were still braced on his shoulders, and this time she succeeded in pushing him away. He let go and she stumbled back. Just before she fell, he caught her by her wrist and brought her close to him again. "Careful, hon." His voice was low and sensual, making her nipples tighten. "Wouldn't want you to fall on that pretty ass of yours."

"You can just go to hell, Kev." Nicole jerked her hand away. "I need a phone to call Trace so she can pick me up."

He pivoted on his booted heel and headed out the barn door, back into the rain. He paused just outside the doorway, rain dripping from the brim of his Stetson. "Are you planning on staying out with the horses, or coming into the house?"

Nicole would have stomped after him if she hadn't been wearing those damn shoes. Instead, the spiked heels sank into the straw and dirt floor of the barn, and her ankles wobbled as she followed him out and into the pouring rain. She sighed and glanced at her purse. Even it was drenched.

Lightning flashed and thunder followed, closer now, and rain pounded her and Kev. She left the barn smells of hay, sweet oats, and manure for the scent of summer rain as she trailed after Kev the best she could in those fucking heels.

While she followed him, she couldn't help but notice how fine his tight ass looked in his Wranglers. The rain had molded his denim shirt to his hard-packed body. Broad shoulders and a muscular back to dig her nails into, tapered hips to wrap her thighs around...

Mentally, Nicole shook herself. Shit. No way was she fucking Kev Grand. No matter how badly her body wanted to at that moment. Hell, in high school he'd punched her prom date, dumped her best friend, and she and Kev had always argued about everything as long as she could remember. Nothing doing.

When they reached the front porch, Kev held the door open for her. Despite the fact he was as soaked as she was, heat emanated from him as she walked past him and into the ranch house.

The door shut behind them with a bang. She didn't have time to do much looking around. Before she had the chance to take a breath, Kev whirled her around and practically slammed her up against the wall.

Chapter Three

Kev braced his hands to either side of Nicole's head, pinning her up against the wall beneath his hard male body. She gasped at the force he'd used. He hadn't hurt her at all, just caught her by surprise.

"What the hell do you think you're doing?" she managed to say despite the fact that his dominance and the desire in his eyes made her pussy wet.

"What I should have done a long time ago." Kev pressed his full length tighter against Nicole, her back flat against the wall. "I'm going to fuck you, Nicole Landford, like you've never been fucked before."

Her belly pitched and she dropped her purse. Oh, God, how that statement turned her on.

"Like hell," she said, ignoring the part of her that wanted to jump him. Her voice was hoarse and unconvincing even to herself.

"I'm through with talking." His mouth came down hard on hers in a punishing kiss that took her breath away. She braced her hands against his chest and pushed, struggling to get free, but she really didn't want him to stop. She couldn't have stopped if she'd truly tried.

His Stetson bumped the top of her head and it fell away with a soft thud on the floor. He bit her lower lip, just hard enough to make her groan with desire, long enough for him to thrust his tongue into her mouth. His stubble chafed her skin, burning her, branding her with his mark.

The kiss was deep and fierce, unlike anything she'd experienced before. His erection pressed against her belly through her thin dress. She could feel every masculine inch of him, as if she was wearing nothing at all.

She couldn't help it. She kissed him as hard and fiercely as he was kissing her, with all the pent-up desire that had been building like the thunderstorm since he first tripped her trigger. Damn but she wanted the man. Maybe she'd always wanted him.

What was she thinking?

Their kiss grew unbelievably wilder yet, and Nicole's mind literally spun. His hands moved from the wall, down her arms, his touch making goose bumps prickle her skin. He palmed her ass while he thrust his hips against hers.

Nicole dug her nails into his powerful shoulders. His denim shirt rubbed against her sensitive nipples, and she longed to be free of the constraining material.

As if reading her thoughts, Kev tore his mouth from hers. His breathing was heavy and his normally hazel eyes burned a deep and passionate green.

He released her ass and brought his hands up to her breasts. With a movement so fast it caught her by surprise, he gripped the flimsy material and tore the neckline until her large breasts spilled out.

"My dress!" Despite her shock and the fact he'd ruined her favorite outfit, she gripped his shoulders tighter and arched her back, raising her chest up higher, offering herself to him.

"I'll buy you a new one." Her breasts overflowed his large palms and he lowered his head. "Hell, I'll buy you two."

And then his tongue flicked over one nipple and Nicole nearly screamed from the wild sensations that zipped from her breasts to her belly to her pussy.

He squeezed and fondled her breasts while moving his hot mouth from one nipple to the other. Nicole slid her hands into his blond hair and hung on for dear life. If he didn't have her pressed up against the wall, she would have slid down to the floor, her knees were so weak.

Kev groaned and brought his mouth back to hers and his solid chest and denim shirt rubbed against her nipples. He bit at her lower lip and she nipped back at his, their kisses wild and passionate.

"I always knew it would be like this." He kissed a wet trail to her ear. "You and I making fire together."

"Oil and water," she said with a gasp.

He gave a low chuckle. "Oil burns on water, hon."

She had to give him that.

While he traced her jaw with his mouth, Nicole's fingers slid from his shoulders, down his hard chest to his taut abs, and to his belt buckle. It didn't take her long to undo it and the top button of his Wrangler jeans. She unzipped them, yanked down his briefs, and his hot erection filled her hand.

"Damn you're big." Nicole stroked his cock and he groaned. She couldn't believe it when she said, "I can't wait for you to fuck me." But then a part of her told her she'd been denying what she really wanted all along.

Kev brought his hands down to the hem of her wet mini-dress and yanked it up so that the material was around her waist. "Woman, I'm going to fuck you so hard you'll be begging me for mercy."

Nicole groaned as his hands found the sides of her thong. "Never."

"We'll see about that." Kev shredded her thong in one sharp movement so that all she had on was her torn dress around her waist and her spiked heels.

Kev grabbed her thighs and hiked her up so that her legs were wrapped around his waist and her breasts were at his mouth. She clung to his shoulders and tilted her head, her long wet hair trailing across her back.

He rubbed the head of his cock against her pussy and she moaned. "Fuck me. Now," she demanded.

He spun her around. Before she knew it, he'd taken her down to the floor so that his jean-clad hips were between her thighs and she was flat on her back on a rough braided rug. She looked up at him and shivered at the intense desire in those sexy hazel-green eyes of his.

Mesmerized, she watched him as he rose up and ripped apart the snaps of his western shirt and flung it aside, where it landed on a lampshade. He pulled off his belt and threw it over his shoulder. The buckle clattered over the wooden floor. He stood and stripped off his jeans and briefs, and all she could do was stare at that lean muscular body, conditioned from years of ranching, and early on when he competed in calf-roping on the rodeo circuit. He was one fine man.

"Damn you're beautiful, Nicole." He knelt at her feet and his gaze met hers. "I always knew one day you'd come to me."

Heat rose to her cheeks at his statement that she was beautiful—Kev Grand may be a lot of things, but he wasn't a liar. She had confidence in herself, knew what she wanted, and went after it, but she'd never thought of herself as beautiful.

Nicole scraped her long nails down his chest. "You're not so bad yourself, you arrogant sonofabitch."

Kev gave her that sexy breath-stealing grin of his while he slipped off one of her shoes. He tossed it over his shoulder and she heard a crash and the sound of breaking glass. Kev never paused. He yanked off her other heel and disposed of it the same way, and something hit the floor with a loud thump. He reached for her then, grasped her dress and ripped it completely away from her body, flinging the ruined material aside.

By the time Kev settled between her thighs, she was ready to scream. She could smell her own juices mixing with his scent of sun, wind and intoxicating male musk.

Naked body to naked body, Kev braced himself so that part of his weight was against her, then brought his face close to hers.

"Kiss me," he demanded.

Nicole raised her head and fastened her lips to his, thrusting her tongue into his mouth. He pressed against her mound and she could feel his cock and balls rubbing her pussy. She wrapped her legs around his thighs, begging him with her body to take her now.

Instead he rolled onto his back, bringing her with him so that she was on top. He filled his palms with her breasts and she leaned back, her drying hair caressing her bare skin, almost to her waist. She moved her pussy along his cock, rubbing her clit and building up the fire already burning inside her.

Nicole brought her face to his and kissed him, her hair dropping over her shoulder to hang like a curtain around their faces. Their mouths mated and their kiss was wild and crazy, and she could feel her head spinning more than ever.

Kev moved in an athletic movement that must have come from years of calf-roping. One second she was on top of him, and in the next she was beneath him again, his face above hers.

He crushed his mouth to Nicole's, dying to get inside her. He wanted her so bad he could barely rein himself in. But he wanted this first time to rock Nicole's world. If he could hold back just a little longer…

Nicole moaned and kissed him back just as fiercely. She grabbed for his cock but he caught her hand, holding her back.

Her chest rose and fell beneath him. Her lips were red from his kisses and her skin pink wherever his mouth and hands had been.

"What are you waiting for, cowboy?" She squirmed beneath him.

"Are you protected?" he asked.

Nicole nodded. "Definitely. Now, come on."

"You want it hard, hon?" He pumped his hips against hers. "I think you do."

"Real hard." Her voice was low, husky. "Let's see what you've got."

Kev hooked his arms under her knees, spreading her wide open to him. He placed his erection at the entrance to her pussy, his gaze focused on her beautiful blue-green eyes. With one swift thrust, he buried his cock deep within her core.

Nicole cried out and arched her back. Oh, *God*, he felt good inside her. He moved her legs so that her ankles were around his neck and he began thrusting hard and fast, and oh-so deep.

"Damn, Kev." She reached up and dug her nails into his back. "Yeah, just like that, cowboy. Ride me."

He pumped harder into her, the sound of flesh smacking flesh filling the room. She looked between them and watched him moving in and out of her core. His cock glistened with her juices, and her scent mixed with his male musk was intoxicating. She loved the smell of their sex, loved the feel of him pounding into her so hard it made her breasts bounce and her head bump against a piece of furniture.

Rain pounded on the roof as Kev pounded into her. Thunder boomed, or maybe it was the blood rushing in her ears.

Her climax built up inside her, so wild that her vision blurred and she could barely focus on Kev's face above hers. He was gritting his teeth, sweat dripping down the side of his face. His balls slapped her pussy and he banged against her with the force of his powerful thrusts. She'd never been fucked so hard or so good.

Nicole grew dizzy with the intensity of her need to come and she thrashed beneath Kev. She raked her nails across his back and bit her lip so hard she tasted blood. Everything was spiraling out of control. Closer and closer and closer—

"Fuck me harder." Nicole dug her nails deeper into Kev's back. "I'm gonna come."

He rammed into her so hard, her hips rose high off the floor.

All hell broke loose inside her. Nicole screamed as the most powerful orgasm she'd ever had slammed into her.

Sparks flared behind her eyes. She screamed again as a second orgasm rocked her body right after the first. It felt like the Fourth of July, the way fireworks were exploding in her head.

Kev thrust into her several times more, drawing out her multiple orgasms, and then he came with a shout. His thick cock pulsed inside her pussy, his hot semen flooding her core.

Nicole's body continued to tremble with aftershocks as she stared up at Kev. His breathing was heavy and sweat dripped from his face onto her skin.

"Now that I've had you," he said in his deep, sexy voice, in between heavy breaths, "I'm not about to let you go."

Chapter Four

"Nothing doing." Nicole pushed at his chest at the same time she shook her head. "Sex doesn't make me yours any more than I've ever been. Which is not at all."

Kev grinned down at the woman he'd wanted for so damn long. Since elementary school when he'd stolen her dancing doll and strung the thing up by its crown. Nicole had chased him around the schoolyard for that bit of mischief. He'd been chasing after her ever since. He just hadn't been able to catch her until now.

She was so damn full of fire he knew she'd be work to convince, but he had no doubt he would. He wasn't normally a patient man, but with Nicole he'd just been biding his time. At one point over the years, when he'd thought he didn't have a chance in hell with Nicole, he'd thought Dee MacLeod would help him forget the spunky blonde, but it wasn't really what either of them had wanted. He was definitely glad things had turned out the way they had.

"Come on now. Get off." Nicole pushed at his chest, harder this time.

He rolled onto his back, taking her with him, keeping his cock deep within her core. She cried out, her eyes wide with surprise. His cock returned to its full hardness and he thrust his hips.

"Damn, Kev," Nicole groaned at the feel of his erection within her pussy. She braced her hands on his shoulders, his skin slick with sweat beneath her palms.

He thrust his hips again. "Ready to be fucked?"

"Like they say," she murmured as she rocked against him. "Save a horse. Ride a cowboy."

Kev chuckled and gripped her hips tighter, keeping his cock inside her. "Who says?"

"Catie Savage—" Nicole's eyes went from heavy-lidded to wide open. "Crap. I've got to call Trace and Catie. They'll be worried."

For the first time since coming into Kev's home, she glanced around at the masculine interior. Leather and wood furniture, bookcases, and a wide-screen TV occupied the room. It smelled of leather and wood, and a musky male scent. On the bookcase were Kev's football trophies from high school and college, along with countless rodeo awards.

And then there was the lamp, now shattered on the wooden floor, broken during their wild lovemaking, one of her high heels sitting in the middle of the shards. The remnants of her dress draped over the back of a chair, her other shoe perched on the coffee table, and Kev's boots beside the table leg. Right in front of her, his underwear hung over the telephone.

Nicole laughed and tossed the underwear aside, grabbing the portable phone. "Some decorating job, Grand."

His gaze followed hers and he grinned. "I think I'll keep it this way. Has a woman's touch."

She rolled her eyes then dialed the number to the MacLeod Ranch, where Trace was visiting her sister Dee. Ringing started on the other end at the same time Kev began fondling her nipples, his cock still inside her pussy.

Nicole bit back a moan as her best friend answered the phone, "MacLeod Ranch."

"Heya, Trace." It was all Nicole could do to maintain her concentration as Kev pinched her nipples. "Sorry I didn't make it."

"I'm so glad to hear your voice. I was worried." Relief filled Trace's tone. "Although I really should know better. You'd kick anyone's ass who tried to mess with you."

Like she had with Kev—*riiiiight*. "Don't you know it, MacLeod. Or should I say Lawless now?"

Kev took that moment to raise his head and start suckling one of her nipples. Nicole's pussy grew even wetter around Kev's cock, and she shuddered from the sensations of his hot, wet mouth on her.

Trace laughed. "My maid of honor isn't likely to have forgotten that." She paused as Kev suckled loudly at Nicole's other nipple. "What's that noise?"

"Ah, must be the connection." Nicole tried to squirm away from Kev, but he had a tight hold on her.

"What happened, anyway?" Trace asked as Kev lightly bit Nicole's nipple, and she bit her lip to keep from crying out from the pain and pleasure of it.

"Long story." Nicole couldn't hold back a moan fast enough as Kev started thrusting his hips, his big cock driving deep into her core.

There was a moment of silence on the other end of the line, and then Trace said, "Um, I bet it's a good one. I think there may not be any need for a trip to the nightclubs after all."

Despite the fact that Kev was fucking her while she was on the telephone, and she was about to come, Nicole managed to keep her voice steady. "Yeah. Well..."

She glanced down at Kev's blond head as he continued to suckle her nipples, from one to the other. "I'll explain later."

Trace laughed. "Oh, you bet you will, girlfriend. Catie and I will be waiting."

Nicole barely had the chance to say "Bye," and punch the off button before an orgasm broke over her in multiple waves. She cried out, her body trembling against Kev's with each crest. Thank God she hadn't screamed her release into the telephone for Trace to hear.

Nicole rocked against Kev, riding out the waves, her head light from the strength of her climax. "You are one devil of a man."

"You don't know the half of it, hon." Kev pushed himself up so that they faced one another with her astride his lap. He brought his mouth to hers in a deep and passionate kiss that made her mind whirl and her pussy throb around his cock.

When he pulled away, he said, "On your knees, woman."

Again, Nicole found herself turned on by his dominance, something that surprised her. She gave him a wicked grin and slipped from his lap. She positioned herself on her hands and knees on the braided rug.

Kev grabbed a couple of thick pillows from the couch and propped them under Nicole's hips, forcing her ass up higher and spreading her wide open to him. He lightly stroked her folds with one finger and she groaned. "I've never seen a prettier pussy."

"You all talk, cowboy?" Nicole looked over her shoulder. "Or are you going to put your money where your mouth is?"

"I've got a better idea where to put my mouth." Kev grasped her thighs with his big hands, lowered his head and swiped his tongue over her folds.

Nicole groaned, louder this time. "God, that feels good."

"And hell, if you're not the sweetest thing I've ever tasted," he murmured before licking and sucking at her pussy some more.

Kev not only enjoyed her taste, but her female musk and the way she moaned. The noises she made when he licked her pussy and when he fucked her made him harder than ever. She was a screamer, and that turned him on to no end.

"Fuck me." She rocked her hips back and forth. "I want that big cock of yours back inside my pussy."

A guy couldn't say no to that. Kev rose up, grasped his erection in his hand and placed it at the entrance to her core. He grabbed her hips with both hands and thrust fast and deep.

Nicole gave a loud cry and pushed back against him. "Damn, you're good, Grand."

"You ain't seen nothing yet, hon." Kev began thrusting in and out of Nicole's pussy. The sound of flesh against flesh echoed in the room along with the scent of her juices and his come.

Nicole couldn't believe how good sex was with Kev. She'd never imagined it would be anything like this. She'd have fucked him long ago if she'd realized how wild it would be, just to have a good ride now and again.

Her large breasts swung with every thrust of his hips and her nipples scraped the rug, making them even more sensitized. The feel of his hard body slapping against hers and his cock driving in and out of her was almost too much.

Nicole's orgasm came out of nowhere, just like that thunderstorm. She screamed, letting the strength of her climax power her cry.

Kev rammed her harder, her scream damn near making him come. "Wouldn't be surprised if the ranch hands heard that one all the way to the bunkhouse."

He could still feel the aftershocks of Nicole's orgasm gripping his cock. "Bet they wish they were getting some."

Just the thought of any other man touching her made him fighting mad. "And not a one of them will," he said through gritted teeth.

Nicole just moaned louder as he pounded into her harder. She took all he gave her, and he knew she'd take even more. Heat rushed his body, burning him like wildfire. His balls drew up tight and his cock jerked. His climax powered through him and he shouted from the strength of it. He pumped in and out of her sweet pussy a few times more, then tilted his head back as the last of his come emptied into her channel.

With a groan of satisfaction, he relaxed against Nicole's back. He wrapped his arms around her waist and said, "You belong to me now, Landford."

She pushed back against him. Kev rolled onto his side taking her with him, and his cock slid out of her pussy. He allowed her to turn around in his arms so that she was facing him. Her blonde hair was mussed and fire lit her eyes. Her breasts pressed against his chest and he draped his leg over her hip so that their bodies were flush. Their skin was slick with sweat and the musk of their sex was thick in the air.

Nicole didn't know what to make of the man. "Are you always this possessive after a good fuck?"

The corner of his mouth quirked. He raised his hand and tweaked her nipple. "Only when it's you I'm fucking. I'm staking my claim."

A strange thrill skipped through her belly, but she did her best to ignore it. She was a free spirit, she reminded herself. No ties, no commitments.

She studied him for a moment. She'd truly never realized just what a fine-looking cowboy Kev was. He had a strong jaw, firm lips and a day's stubble on his jaw. His skin was tanned and weatherworn and the corners of his eyes crinkled when he smiled. Right now he had a serious expression on his rugged face and she tried to make out what it was all about.

She tilted her head and met his hazel gaze head-on. "I don't know what to make of you." She shifted and felt his semi-hard cock against her belly. "We've been fighting since we were in elementary school."

Kev moved his hand from her nipple to a strand of her blonde hair. "I've wanted you just as long." His expression went from serious to amused. "Although then I didn't want you the same way I've wanted you once I was a teenager and started jacking off to porn magazines."

Heat rushed Nicole and she felt a tingle in her pussy. "You've fantasized about me while you've masturbated?"

His finger trailed along her jaw to her lips. "Yep."

Now, if that wasn't a turn-on, she didn't know what was. At least he'd said he'd *wanted* her, as in wanted to fuck her, not anything more serious than that. But he was getting way deeper than she wanted to go.

"So, you got anything for me to wear in this place?" She jerked her finger in the direction of the ruined blue cloth. "Seems someone ripped the hell out of my dress."

"It was damned good, wasn't it, hon," he said as a statement, not a question.

"Yeah." Her voice was softer than she liked it. "I can't say I've ever been fucked so hard in all my life."

"I know." He ground his hips against hers. "And I'll be the last man you ever fuck again."

Chapter Five

"Give me a break, Grand." Irritated, Nicole rolled out of his embrace and pushed herself to her feet. "You're so full of shit."

Kev propped himself on one elbow and gave her an unrepentant grin. "Just telling it like it is."

Why did he have to look so damn sexy? His blond hair mussed, his hazel eyes dark and mysterious, and that body. Lord a-mighty but he was fine. Lean and fit, and built like a cowboy should be.

Nicole crossed her arms beneath her breasts, which naturally raised them up, and she almost grinned at the way his cock went from semi-hard to rigid just like that. "Listen, cowboy. After all that wild sex, I'm hungry, so why don't you feed me? After I take a shower and you give me something to wear."

Kev got to his feet in a lithe movement and reached her in a single stride. He gripped her arms then ran his hands from her elbows to her shoulders and back, making goose bumps roughen her skin. "You're sexy as hell in what you're wearing now."

She looked up at the white ceiling and then back to Kev. "Men. All you want to see are my boobs bouncing as I walk around, and maybe to bend me over the kitchen table and fuck me again."

His eyes darkened. "Don't tempt me." He released her and turned toward a hallway leading from the large living room. "Come on. I'll show you where the shower is and find you something to wear."

Nicole followed him, enjoying the view. The muscles in his tight ass flexed as he walked. She wanted to bite that ass in the worst way. She remembered a bumper sticker she'd seen recently, *Cowboy Butts Drive Me Nuts.*

Damn straight.

He took her to what was obviously the master bedroom, and it definitely had that "lived in" look to it. Clothes were draped over a chair, boots kicked off in a corner, a belt curled up on bureau, a gray felt Stetson hanging on a hat rack.

"Some bachelor pad you've got here." Nicole sidestepped a pair of Wranglers lying in a crumpled heap.

"Maid's day off." He stopped in front of a closet, pulled out one of his large denim shirts, and tossed it to her. "Hope this'll do."

"It'll be fine." Nicole caught the shirt and held it to her chest. "Now about that shower?"

Kev gestured to the doorway behind him, which she had already assumed led to the bathroom. "Help yourself to whatever you need."

She moved within inches of him and ran her fingers along his cock. "What if I need this again?"

His hazel eyes grew greener yet. "Woman, you're asking for it."

She laughed as she passed him, then yelped when he swatted her ass.

After a nice, hot shower, Nicole toweled off, slipped on Kev's shirt, and snapped it up. She was a full-figured gal with large breasts, but his shirt still hung loose on her. It reached just below her ass and she also had to roll up the sleeves.

After she towel-dried her hair, she paused to look at herself in the mirror. A flush tinged her cheeks pink and her eyes were even more blue-green than normal. Apparently sex with Kev agreed with her.

She shook her head. "Who'd have thought I'd end up getting laid by Kev Grand?" Not that he hadn't tried to get her attention over the years. But she'd never thought they could do anything more than fight. Whenever they were in the same room they always ended up arguing about something—politics, sports, you name it. When she thought about it, he had seemed to get great pleasure out of stirring her up and making her flaming mad.

Well, one thing for sure—if he fucked her like that for the next month, she'd likely not walk straight for a good long time.

Feeling nicely sore and well-sated, Nicole slipped through the bedroom, back to the living room, and followed her nose to the kitchen. Smells of fresh brewed coffee, frying bacon and eggs, and even the smell of burnt toast, made her stomach growl like mad.

Nicole grinned when she saw Kev shoveling almost black bacon and extremely overcooked eggs onto a couple of plates. Blackened toast popped up out of the toaster and the coffee smelled thick and strong. He was wearing only his Wranglers, which molded his tight ass to perfection. What a sexy sight he was.

"Whatcha doing there, cowboy?" Nicole said as she peered over his shoulder.

He tossed a look to her and gave a quirky grin. "It's not much, but it's grub."

Nicole tried not to laugh at his cooking skills. "Well, let's eat then."

Kev grabbed an almost empty container of margarine and a half-full jar of strawberry jam, and set them on the table. Then they carried plates of food to the round oak table in the kitchen. He left to grab a couple of mugs and the coffee, returned and poured them each a cup before settling in one of the oak chairs.

She cocked an eyebrow. "Planning to be up all night?"

His gaze met hers and a sexy smile curved his lips. "What do you think?"

She couldn't help the thrill that tingled from her nipples to her pussy. "Only if you're lucky."

Kev smiled and picked up a strip of the charred bacon. "It's decaf. Drink up."

Nicole had never had worse-tasting food, but for some reason she found herself enjoying it thoroughly. The back and forth banter between them during the meal had her going from red-hot mad over what he thought of the president, to laughing at the stories he told. She especially liked the one about the greenhorn cowboy who managed to bind himself to the calf he was trying to hogtie for branding. She laughed so hard she almost choked on a mouthful of burnt toast and Kev had to pat her back. He obviously didn't know his own strength because he darn near caused her face to end up in her eggs.

Rain continued to patter on the roof and Nicole heard steady drips from the eaves onto the patio. The night was ink black, but through the sliding glass doors leading from the kitchen to the backyard she could see the bunkhouse lights in the distance. Just the thought of Kev taking her at the kitchen table and the cowboys watching sent a thrill through her belly. She'd never considered herself an exhibitionist, but there was a first time for everything. And she was a woman who unabashedly enjoyed sex.

Kev could hardly keep his mind on his meal. From the moment she'd walked into the kitchen with that just-got-fucked look, wearing his denim shirt, he'd wanted her all over again. It was damned hard trying to eat while his cock was making his jeans too tight to breathe.

He purposefully baited her with topics he knew she felt strongly about, just to see the fire in her eyes. And God, how he loved the way she laughed, a strong healthy laugh, not some simpering girlish giggle.

When they were finished eating, Nicole insisted on washing the dishes, including the ones he had let stack up. He wasn't much of a cook or a housekeeper, but he did know a good woman when he found her.

While she filled the sink with soapy water, he came up behind her and nuzzled her neck and ran his hands along the curve of her waist.

She shivered beneath his touch. "You can rinse off and dry."

He moved his hands over her hips to the bottom of the shirt and rubbed her thighs. "What if I'd rather take you right here and now?"

Nicole turned in his arms, wielding a handful of bubbles. "Don't make me use these."

Kev chuckled and scooped up some of the bubbles on his finger and touched them to her nose. "You're so damn cute when you're mad."

"Hmph." Nicole rubbed her nose with the back of her hand. "You just get busy."

He had to search the laundry room but found a clean dishtowel crumpled in a basket of laundry he'd just done. When he returned, Nicole already had a sink full of dishes washed and was rinsing and putting them in the drying rack. Kev made short work of the clean dishes, drying them as quickly as possible and putting them into his cupboards.

"How's the bed-and-breakfast these days?" Kev put another plate into the cabinet.

"Keeping me busy." Nicole washed a couple of forks, rinsed them off and put them into the rack. She pulled the stopper out of the sink and let the dirty water flow down the drain. "Joshua is taking care of business while I'm out for the night."

Kev dried off the silverware and slid it into a drawer. Without drying off his hands, he took Nicole by the waist and brought her close to him, so that her body was flush with his. "Better call Josh and let him know you'll be gone for the weekend."

Nicole placed her hands against Kev's chest. "I don't *think* so."

"Uh-huh." He lowered his mouth and brushed her lips with his. "You're mine until I let you go."

Nicole shivered at the promise in Kev's voice. Despite the fact that she'd never let any man tell her what to do, again his dominance was turning her on. It was like he was making her his prisoner for the weekend.

The bet, that was it. He was helping her fulfill the bet with her cousins.

Yeah. Right.

She moved her palms up his smooth chest to his shoulders. "You planning to make me your sex slave or something?"

"Sex slave." Kev's voice rumbled with desire. "I like the sound of that."

"Then what's holding you back...*Master.*"

Kev growled, his eyes flaring with obvious lust. He grasped her waist and in an effortless movement lifted her and placed her ass on the wet countertop. It was the perfect height.

He ripped open the snaps on the denim shirt she was wearing and undid the fastening on his Wranglers in just seconds. And he wasn't wearing any underwear this time.

His luscious cock sprang out and Nicole licked her lips. She didn't have time to even think before he thrust into her, burying himself deep inside.

Nicole gripped the edge of the countertop as she watched his length, slick with her juices, moving in and out of her pussy.

"You feel so good, cowboy." Nicole's eyes met his. "Don't know why we didn't do this before."

Kev braced his hands on either side of her. "Wasn't for a lack of trying on my part." He kissed her so hard and so fiercely her pussy flooded with more moisture. "Just took you awhile to figure it out."

"Shut up and fuck me." Nicole wrapped her legs around Kev, her thighs gripping his hips tight. "God, yes. That's it."

Sweat beaded on his upper lip and rolled down the side of his face. He moved one hand between her thighs and rubbed her clit, and that was all it took. Nicole's orgasm flared within her and she shouted with the strength of it.

Kev followed her moments later, his growl reverberating through her and causing her pussy to spasm even more.

Chapter Six

Nicole snuggled in the blankets, feeling sore all over like she'd had a good workout. The sheets smelled of Kev's masculine essence and the lusty scent of their sex.

She opened her eyes to early morning sunlight spilling through wooden blinds shading windows to either side of the oak bed. She rolled over, expecting to find Kev asleep beside her, but the bed was empty.

Well, duh. He was a rancher, and ranchers tended to get up at the crack of dawn to do whatever it was that ranchers did.

She eased out of bed, cotton sheets sliding over her bare skin and rasping her nipples. With a satisfied yawn, she stretched and caught sight of her reflection in a mirror over the bureau. She looked like a well-fucked woman, and she also looked like hell.

Fifteen minutes later, Nicole had showered and was standing before Kev's closet, trying to find something to wear. She finally pulled on a pair of old Levi's and cinched them around her waist by tying a braided belt in a knot, the buckle dangling down her abdomen. Despite her efforts, the Levi's kept sliding down her hips, but it was the best she could do. Of course the jeans were too long, even though she was a fairly tall woman, so she had to roll them up a few times just to reach the tops of her feet. She slipped on the same shirt he'd given her last night and let it fall over her jeans and down to her thighs.

For shoes, she was just plain out of luck. She'd have to go barefoot for now. After she tied her hair back in a ponytail, using a scrap of cloth she tore off her ruined dress, she went in search of Kev by heading out the back door.

Outside the rain-washed sky was a clear blue, reminding her of the color of her grandmother's favorite mixing bowl, the one she used to make cakes in when Nicole was a little girl. The air smelled clean and fresh from the rain. The back lawn was soft and wet beneath her bare feet and a cool breeze brushed her cheeks.

Not too far from the house were the corrals with a herd of white-faced Herefords. To the right was the bunkhouse and just to the side of the house stood the huge weathered barn.

In the distance she heard the sound of male voices. Nicole shoved her hands beneath the shirt, in the front pockets of the Levi's, and the jeans almost slid over her hips. She had to wrangle them back up around her waist while she walked toward one of the corrals behind the barn.

When she ran out of lawn, she walked across damp earth, avoiding puddles and mud the best she could, but it still squished through her toes. She laughed. The water did feel good over her toes and the mud made her feel like a kid again. Like she'd been when she'd first met Kev.

She could still remember his mischievous grin and the spark in his hazel eyes every time he teased her. Once in third grade he had pulled up her dress during recess and she'd started wearing shorts under her dresses to avoid the embarrassment of showing her underwear to everyone in elementary school again. In fifth grade he'd teased her about her first boyfriend, Greg Davis, who happened to be the smartest kid in the class. Then there was her freshman year, when he'd decked her prom date. She'd been so mad at Kev she could have spit fire. She never did find out why he'd given Ryan a bloody nose.

She stared up at the sky and watched a hawk circle over the corrals. Kev's teasing had started when she was in first grade and he was a couple of grades ahead of her. What was it? Oh, yeah. The Dancerina doll incident. Or was it the time he stole the cupcake her grandmother had made for her? No, it had to be the time he spread mud all over her face.

Nicole had to grin. Kev Grand had been a real pain in the ass. Hell, he still was.

She reached the wooden railing of one of the corrals and climbed up on it, the wood rough under her bare feet. Her gaze took in cowboys on horseback working cattle in the east pasture. Was Kev out there? She squinted, trying to make out his form, but she didn't see those broad shoulders and lean hips that she now knew intimately. The mere thought of just how intimately made her body flush with desire and her pussy wet.

Big hands grabbed her waist from behind, startling her, and causing her to yelp.

"Looking for me, hon?" Kev's deep voice rumbled in her ear.

"Admiring the view." She held onto the top rail and leaned back against his broad chest, confident he wouldn't let her fall.

She shivered as his lips moved close to her ear. "How would you like me to make you come now, while you watch my men at work?"

Liquid heat rushed between her thighs. "You wouldn't dare."

He slipped his hand beneath the huge shirt she was wearing, and around to the baggy waistband of the Levi's. "Want to bet on it, sweetheart?"

A low moan was Nicole's answer as he slipped his fingers into her wet folds. She knew his men wouldn't be able to tell what he was doing to her under that shirt, but it heightened her arousal beyond belief.

"You are one wicked man," she managed to get out, despite the fact he was fingering her clit, bringing her to the brink of orgasm in just a few strokes. She gripped the railing tighter, but at the same time her body sagged against Kev's muscular chest.

In the distance she saw the men riding their horses, rounding up cattle. She heard their whistles and shouts. But her vision began to blur and her hearing faded, and all she could do was feel. A violent orgasm took her and a cry left her lips before she could hold it back.

Dimly she became aware of her surroundings and Kev's low laughter. Heat rushed to her cheeks and her body gave a jerk as he gave her clit another tweak.

"*Kev*," she said under her breath as a couple of the cowboys turned their heads. "Get your hand out of my pants."

He slid his fingers up her belly and she felt the trail of moisture he left behind. She was afraid he was going to go for her breasts and that the cowboys would see, but he slipped his hand from beneath her shirt.

He brought his palms up to her shoulders and began kneading them through the shirt and she relaxed into the massage. "Anything else you'd like to bet me?" he said close to her ear.

She shook her head and felt her ponytail brush his face. "Not on your life."

Kev slipped his right hand from her shoulder, up her neck and to her nose. "Smell your desire for me. Even after all the times I've already fucked you since last night, you want more."

She breathed in the sweet and salty scent of her own juices on his fingers and her belly flipped. He moved his hand from her nose and she turned just enough to see him slip his finger into his mouth.

"Damn fine tasting, too," he murmured.

Nicole's stomach was doing some major somersaults now.

He lifted her off the railing and turned her so that her chest was flush against his. "Let's go have breakfast."

This time Nicole cooked for the two of them. She didn't have much to work with as far as Kev's supplies, but she was the owner of a bed-and-breakfast and an excellent cook. She could make do.

Kev took a shower while Nicole whipped up a potato, egg, and cheese breakfast casserole. While it was baking, he came back into the kitchen and sniffed the air like a man who hadn't eaten in a month of Sundays.

"Something smells damn good." He came up to Nicole and wrapped his arms around her waist. "You look terrific in my kitchen."

"I'll just bet." She pushed him away and snatched up a couple of potholders she'd dug out of a drawer earlier. "You'd like having someone around to cook for you."

Kev winked and grabbed a couple of mismatched plates from a cabinet, along with a pair of forks out of a drawer. "Can you blame a guy who can't cook worth crap?"

Nicole never saw a man eat so much so fast in all her life. She had a decent-sized portion that was enough to fill her up, but Kev had at least five times as much and she swore he would have licked the pan clean if she hadn't been sitting there watching him eat.

After his last mouthful, Kev settled back in his chair looking like a man who'd just had the best blowjob of his life.

The corner of Nicole's mouth quirked. "Had enough?"

He shook his head. "Still hungry."

When she raised an eyebrow he stood and drew her up out of her chair. "I've a mind for a little something more."

With a quick movement that caught her totally by surprise, he picked her up so that his arms were wrapped around her legs and her hands were braced on his shoulders.

She couldn't help it. She laughed. "What do you think you're doing, Kev Grand?"

He gave her a dark and sensual look. "Finishing off breakfast."

Kev carried her into his bedroom and tossed her on the bed. She laughed again as she bounced on the mattress, but her laughter turned into a groan as he shucked off his jeans and underwear, and stood in front of her. His cock was erect and her mouth watered at the thought of slipping her lips over his length and taking him deep.

He jerked her jeans off, which slid easily over her hips. Next went her shirt, and then he was braced over her, his hot male body pressed to her. Again he caught her by surprise when he grabbed her and rolled so that she was on top. Her long blonde hair spilled over her shoulders and he ran his fingers through the length of it.

"Sixty-nine, hon." Kev's voice was a low rumble. "I want to taste you."

Fire licked Nicole's insides and she eased around so that her mouth was over his cock, and her pussy against his mouth.

She cried out the moment his tongue swiped her folds and he thrust two fingers inside her. With the way he was licking her pussy and finger-fucking her, it was all she could do to concentrate on slipping her mouth over his delicious cock. He smelled so good as she took him deep. She worked his erection with her hand, from the wiry curls around the base of his shaft to her mouth, and back again.

Nicole moaned around his cock and squirmed as Kev devoured her folds. Damn, but he was good. He licked, he sucked, pounded her pussy with his fingers—shit. So close to orgasm, so close—

And then he stopped. She slipped his wet cock from her mouth, "Goddamn it, Grand, don't stop now, you bastard."

He gave a low growl, and in a fast movement flipped her over again and in a smooth movement rearranged himself so that his face was now over hers.

Whoa. "You're a man of many talents," she murmured. And she wasn't talking about the way he'd just turned her around. "Now, show me what else you've got."

Kev kissed her. He still tasted her juices on his tongue that mingled with the flavor of her sweet mouth. He'd never get enough of her sweetness. No doubt in his mind that she was becoming just as addicted to him as he was to her.

His tongue probed the depths of her mouth and she made those moaning sounds that he loved. Her pebble-hard nipples rubbed against his chest and the curls of her pussy caressed his balls.

Nicole grabbed his cock as they kissed and brought it to the opening of her wet channel. She arched up at the same time he drove into her.

Gasping, Nicole broke away from his kiss and her eyes nearly rolled back in her head. "So deep. So damn good."

"Your tight pussy feels like heaven around my cock," he said as he thrust into her. "I could just fuck you all day."

She raised her hips to meet his. "God, it turns me on when you talk dirty."

Kev hooked his arms around her knees and moved her legs so that her ankles were around his neck. "Do you want me to tell you what beautiful tits you have, hon? And your pussy. So hot and so wet, just for me."

Nicole's cries became louder the harder he thrust into her.

"I like the feel of your ankles around my neck." He pounded into her and the headboard banged against the wall. "And I love how deep you take me when I fuck you like this."

"I'm going to come." Nicole's voice trembled as her gaze locked with his. "Don't stop fucking me."

"Wouldn't dream of it." He increased his strokes, slamming his cock into her core, his balls slapping against her pussy and their flesh smacking together.

Nicole went rigid and let out a scream like he'd never heard before.

"That's it, hon," he said as he continued his thrusts. "Ride it out."

Her body bucked against his, her eyes wide, and she kept making those sexy cries that drove him closer to the edge.

A few more thrusts and he gave his own cry of release. Black spots swam before his eyes, his climax was so powerful.

He continued working his cock in and out of her pussy until he was drained, then rolled onto his side, taking Nicole with him.

"We're all sweaty again. And sticky." Her breathing was still ragged. "And we smell like sex."

Kev tried to catch his own breath. "Hon, you better plan on plenty of sweat and sex when you're with me."

She grinned. "You've got a deal."

Chapter Seven

Come Sunday afternoon, Nicole truly was so sore she could hardly walk straight.

Even after Kev finished fixing her car, for some crazy reason she found herself procrastinating. She should have been heading back to Bisbee and to her bed-and-breakfast first thing that morning, but she and Kev had gone another round, this time in the hayloft. Over the weekend they'd used every position she could think of, and a few she'd never imagined.

But when it came down to it, she knew she needed to keep her distance from the man. She was not about to get seriously involved with anyone. Sex and sex only—that was it. For one month.

And what a wild month it promised to be.

After showering and dressing again in Kev's shirt and jeans, and grabbing her purse, they headed out to her 'vette, now parked outside the front yard of the ranch house.

She was barefoot, her spiked heels and dress fragments already stowed in the trunk, thanks to Kev somehow managing to get her keys out. He walked her to the car and caught her by the arm before she could slide behind the wheel. She almost dropped her purse in a puddle of water beside them.

"Hey." His tone was low and husky as his hazel eyes met hers. "Dinner tomorrow night. You pick the place."

Nicole tossed her long hair over her shoulder and gave him an appraising look. "You just want another good fuck."

He raised his hand and brushed his knuckles across her cheek. She shivered at the intensity in his gaze. Not a look of lust, but a look of caring. A look that scared her absolutely to death.

"Seven. I'll pick you up."

Even as she started to shake her head, words spilled through her lips she didn't intend to say. "We'll eat in. My B&B."

His hand moved from her cheek to cup the back of her head. Their lips met in such a slow and completely sensual kiss that it literally stole her breath away. They'd never seemed to be able to slow things down between them and their sex had been wild and rough, the way she liked it.

But that kiss…it thrilled her. She couldn't help but wonder what it would be like if he took it slow and easy with her.

When he broke the kiss, her breathing was shallow and uneven. She couldn't take her eyes from his. "Don't be late."

He ran his thumb along her lower lip. "Never."

It took a lot to tear herself away from that touch and to slide into her car. Kev waited until she started the engine, and then he shut the driver's side door and stepped back. He hooked his thumbs in his belt loops and watched her, a serious expression on his face. As she drove away she checked the rearview mirror to see him striding away, back into his house.

She must be going out of her mind.

Nicole braced her hands on the vanity dresser in her bedroom and counted to ten.

She was *not* nervous, and she was *not* thinking anything but carnal, lustful thoughts about Kev Grand. This was all about sex for a month, and no strings attached. She was Nicole Landford, the woman who did not get seriously attached to any man, the woman who enjoyed sex for the sake of sex, and was unapologetic about it. She got a kick out of men, loved everything about them, but she never had a problem separating sex from emotion.

Then why hadn't she been able to get the man off her mind from the time she left him until now, fifteen minutes before he was supposed to arrive? She kept getting lost in thoughts of what they'd shared this weekend. That day she'd managed to screw up a reservation, put double the amount of coffee beans in the grinder, water a fake plant, and put sugar instead of salt in the omelet she made for one of the B&B's guests.

And here she was, dinner set up on the round table in her huge bedroom, with enough food to feed all the B&B's guests, including herself and Kev. She'd cooked and baked all day. She had settled for more traditional fare, rather than anything too fancy. For appetizers she'd made extra-spicy hot wings, and stuffed jalapeños, since she'd learned Kev loved hot foods. For dinner there were barbequed baby-back ribs with her own spicy sauce, her special creamy mashed potatoes, fresh corn on the cob, hot corn muffins straight out of the oven, and a huge salad. For dessert there was her famous death-by-chocolate cake that everyone in Bisbee raved about.

She only hoped she hadn't used salt instead of sugar in that recipe.

Nicole rolled her eyes to the ceiling of her bedroom. She really was losing her mind.

Today she'd e-mailed her cousins Bri and Lily to tell them how things were going on her part of the bargain. All she'd written them was she had found someone to have a real good time with. One thing she wasn't about to tell them was how she kept thinking about Kev, after just one weekend. Instead, she'd been her usual flippant self. Of course she mentioned that she still didn't think Lily would hold up her end of the deal. That girl was seriously in need of some good fucking. She was way too uptight.

When she couldn't put it off any longer, Nicole smoothed her hands over her red thigh-length skirt then adjusted the matching button-up blouse that had a princess neckline. It was another favorite outfit and she hoped Kev wasn't going to ruin it, too.

The mere thought of Kev ripping her blouse off shot a thrill from her belly to her pussy. She really should wear something else.

Nicole took a deep breath and headed down the stairs to the quaint reception area.

Kev stood just inside the doorway, his gaze focused on her as she made her way down the staircase. He looked so good in his western denim shirt, Wranglers, boots and his straw Stetson. Damn but the man was built. And those strong, calloused hands, she could just imagine him touching her everywhere with them.

Her belly flipped. Why was she nervous? This wasn't like her at all. She raised her chin, determined that this man wasn't going to get to her.

When she reached him, Nicole tossed her hair over her shoulder and gave him a teasing grin. "About time you made it—" was all she managed to get out before he cupped the back of her head and brought her to him for a rough and wild kiss. His masculine scent of male musk, sun and wind filled her senses, and his taste drove her crazy with need. She slipped her fingers up his chest and leaned into him, thrusting her tongue into his mouth. His body was so hard and muscular against her softness and she could feel the outline of a growing erection against her belly.

When he finally raised his head, Nicole's head was spinning. All she could say was, "Wow."

Kev gave her a sexy grin that about made her melt. "I've been dying to do that all day."

"Dinner's waiting upstairs." She let her fingers slide down his chest to his waistband. "Don't want it to get cold."

"'Cole's been cooking up a storm," came Joshua's voice from behind the old-fashioned registration desk.

Nicole startled—she hadn't even noticed him when she came down the stairs, she'd been so intent on Kev. She tried not to glare at the ponytailed clerk as she tossed him a look over her shoulder. "I wouldn't exactly say that."

"You two enjoy that, er, death-by-chocolate," Joshua added with a mischievous grin.

Kev raised an eyebrow and the corner of his mouth quirked. "Sounds interesting."

"Come on up." Nicole gave Joshua a look that said *you'll pay later* and headed up the stairs. She felt the heat of Kev's gaze on her backside, and she wondered if he could see up that short skirt she was wearing. Her nipples tingled and her pussy grew moister. She wasn't wearing any panties, and if she got any hotter, her juices would slide down the inside of her thighs.

When she reached the top of the stairs, she paused to wait for him.

"A private dining room, I hope?" he said as they started to walk side-by-side down the hallway.

Nicole gave him what she hoped was a sultry smile. "You could say that."

When they reached her room, she let him in and the door closed behind them.

Kev's gaze landed on the four-poster, canopied bed first. "I think I'm gonna enjoy this dinner."

Those damn butterflies went berserk in her belly again. *Argh!*

When he saw the spread she had laid out on the mahogany table, he said, "Damn, woman. You know how to feed a man."

Kev's stomach growled so loud Nicole could hear it and she couldn't help but grin.

After he took off his Stetson and set it on her bureau, he settled in one of the mahogany high-backed chairs and dug into the meal like he hadn't eaten in ages.

A strange warmth settled in Nicole's belly as she watched the man eat. She felt unbelievably comfortable sharing a meal with him, chatting and arguing so easily. It had to be because she had known him forever. Not any other reason.

Kev managed to put away two racks of ribs, three cornbread muffins, a hefty helping of mashed potatoes, a couple of ears of corn on the cob, and a good portion of salad. You couldn't help but like a man who showed so much appreciation for a good meal.

"I have a question for you." Nicole laid her fork on the table beside her plate, her gaze fixed on Kev. "Why did you deck Ryan when he was my date for the prom?"

Kev paused as he was about to bite into a cornbread muffin. "You really want to know?"

She nodded. She sure as hell did. "Yeah."

He set the muffin down and eyed her straight on. "Ryan bragged to all the guys about how he had fucked you all night."

Hot fury washed over Nicole and her spine went ramrod straight. "That bastard. I never screwed around in high school, especially with him."

"I had a thing for you since the moment I met you." Kev's hazel eyes were dead serious. "I wanted to kill the sonofabitch."

"Wow." Nicole picked up her fork and pushed her food around her plate without looking up at him, but then glanced up. "I don't know what to say."

With a shrug he bit into his muffin, then finished clearing his plate. They chatted more, but she couldn't believe he'd done that for her, all that time ago. She'd never given Kev the time of day, no matter how many times he'd teased her and had asked her out. She'd always thought he was just trying to rile her up.

"You are one hell of a cook, Nicole Landford." Kev brushed his lips with a napkin then tossed it aside before meeting her gaze. "I'm really looking forward to some after- dinner sweets."

That damn fluttering sensation in her belly wouldn't go away. She reached out her hand and ran her finger over his mouth. "You missed a crumb or two."

Kev slipped his lips over her finger and sucked. Nicole caught her breath and her nipples and pussy ached at the promise in his eyes.

When he let her finger slide from his mouth, he murmured, "Let's try some of that dessert."

Kev's cock hardened at the thought of what he planned to do with whatever chocolate dessert Nicole had come up with. He tossed his napkin onto the table and pushed back his chair. He folded his arms across his chest, his gaze focused on her.

"Strip."

Her eyes widened slightly and then a sensual smile curved those sexy lips of hers. "Dessert coming up." With a little wiggle of her hips, she stood, a few inches away from him.

"Your blouse first," he commanded.

Eyes focused on Kev, Nicole reached for the top button of her blouse and paused. He narrowed his gaze and she bit her lower lip. With slow, torturous movements, she unbuttoned the blouse, revealing a matching red bra. Her large breasts strained against the lace and he could see a hint of her nipples.

She paused after the last button. "What now, cowboy?"

Kev held back a groan and resisted rubbing his aching cock through his jeans. But he couldn't help the huskiness in his voice. "Drop your blouse."

Nicole let the red material slide down her arms to land around her red high heels. Kev could already picture her in nothing but those heels, her ankles around his neck.

He cleared his throat. "Pull your bra down, and leave it under your tits."

With movements so slow that he knew she was trying to drive him out of his mind, Nicole pushed down one strap of her bra and then the other. When the straps were off her arms, she brought her hands up to the lacy cups and pulled down, her breasts spilling out into her palms.

Kev bit the inside of his cheek. Hard. "Play with your nipples."

Nicole's tongue darted out and she slowly ran it over her lips. She pinched and pulled her nipples at the same time.

"Suck them," he nearly whispered.

Never hesitating, Nicole pushed up the large pale globes of her breasts and flicked her tongue from one nipple to the other.

It was all Kev could do not to reach across the few inches that separated them, yank up her skirt and fuck her right then and there.

He cleared his throat. "Are you wet, hon?"

Nicole raised her head but kept playing with her nipples, pinching and pulling them. "I'm so wet I can hardly wait until you fuck me."

Shit. He couldn't either. "Drop your skirt."

She released her breasts and moved her hands behind her. He heard the soft sound of a zipper and then the skirt slid over her hips and landed at her feet.

Nicole wasn't wearing any panties. Her curls glistened with her juices and her pussy lips begged for his mouth.

And his jeans were so tight now they were nearly strangling his cock. "Finger your pussy for me. Nice and slow at first, then faster as you go."

Nicole widened her stance and he caught a glimpse of her sweet pink folds. Never taking her eyes from him, she slipped her finger into her pussy and began rubbing her clit. "Like this?"

Kev clenched his hands so tight his knuckles ached. "Yeah." He swallowed and watched her finger making slow, deliberate circles around her clit. "Make yourself come."

She brought her free hand to one breast and rolled her nipple between her thumb and forefinger while she stroked her pussy. Her blue-green eyes were dark and her lips slightly parted as she watched him. A flush spread over her fair skin and she began pumping her hips against her hand.

God, she was going to kill him. "That's it, hon. Imagine I'm fucking you."

Nicole gave a sharp cry and trembled against her hand. She continued to finger her clit, riding out the orgasm, as she pinched one nipple. She looked so damn beautiful. Her face flushed, her eyes heavy-lidded, only wearing her bra beneath her breasts, and her high heels.

Kev motioned to her. "Come here."

Nicole slipped her hand from her pussy and stepped away from the skirt and blouse she'd dropped around her feet. When she'd closed the few inches between them he took her hand, slipped her finger into his mouth and licked at her juices and drank in her scent.

Her breathing was still rapid and shallow as she said, "Ready for that dessert?"

He gave a single nod. "Bring it here."

Nicole turned and bent over the table, her legs wide enough that he could see her beautiful pussy.

Kev groaned. "Hon, you are just about to do me in."

She moved the chocolate dessert to the edge of the table and turned back to him with a sexy little grin. "Would you like me to serve it to you?"

He shook his head. "Straddle me."

She eased onto his lap until her large breasts, raised up even higher by the bra beneath them, were practically in his face. Her wet pussy was pressed to the cock that was dying to get past the denim and drive into her.

Nicole's squirmed on Kev's lap, enjoying the feel of his jeans between her thighs and against her folds. She rubbed her pussy along his erection and almost smiled at the pained expression on Kev's strong features.

He reached out to the decadent chocolate dessert and scooped some on his finger. Nicole shivered as he wiped the chocolate on one of her nipples.

He grasped her breast, trailing more chocolate over the firm flesh and brought the nipple to his mouth. Nicole moaned as he darted his tongue out and lapped up every bit of the chocolate, including what was left on his finger.

"Damn, that's good." He dipped his finger into the dessert again. "I'll say it again. You're one hell of a cook."

"Thanks." Nicole lifted her other breast high and offered it to him. "I must say I enjoy being your serving platter."

Kev spread chocolate over her other nipple and swirled his tongue around the areola and then sucked it away. Nicole's pussy ached so badly and her clit was so swollen that she could almost swear she'd come just by him sucking her nipples and her rubbing herself against his cock.

"Kiss me." He moved his mouth to hers as he grasped her hips in his large hands.

Her dessert had never tasted better than it did on Kev's tongue. He slipped his finger between her folds as he kissed her, and she braced her hands on his shoulders to steady herself. God did this man know how to kiss. Why in the world had she put him off for so long?

He withdrew his finger from her pussy and pulled back from their kiss long enough to slip that finger into her mouth. She tasted herself mixed with the dessert, and smelled her juices and chocolate on his hand.

Nicole couldn't take much more of this. She pulled away from his hand, letting his finger slide from her mouth. "Fuck me. I want you to ride me, cowboy."

He shook his head. "I'm not finished with dessert." He gestured toward the bed. "Take that chocolate and set it on the nightstand."

She did as he told her, but added an extra sway to her hips as she moved. She obediently set the dessert on the nightstand. Behind her she heard the thunk of Kev's boots as he kicked them off. She turned to face him as he tugged off his socks. Then in the space of a second, he stood just a breath away from her.

He brought her hands to his chest. "Undress me the rest of the way."

Without hesitating, Nicole grabbed his shirt and pulled apart the snaps, straight down to his belt buckle. She took a moment to rub her hands over his muscled chest and taut abs before reaching for his buckle.

Massage oil. She definitely needed to get some massage oil to rub all over his muscular body the next time she had her way with him.

"Have I ever told you what a killer bod you have?" She undid his belt and pulled it out of the loops. "I just want to eat you up."

He gave a low chuckle and tweaked one of her nipples. "Hon, that's just what I'm counting on."

With a grin, Nicole unfastened his Wranglers and pushed them over his lean hips, along with his underwear. Her breath caught at the sight of the dark hair that curled down and surrounded the base of his shaft. She pushed the denim all the way down to the floor so that she was on her knees before him, looking up.

"I sure love the way you look on your knees." He stepped out of his pants and kicked them aside. "Why don't you sample some of the dessert?"

"Can't wait." Nicole scooped some of the death-by-chocolate with her fingers and began coating his erection with it from balls to tip and back. She added more until the thick chocolate began rolling down into the tight curls at the base.

Kev clenched his fist in her hair and guided her mouth to his erection. "Are you just going to play with my cock or eat it?"

Nicole laughed and flicked her tongue around the head of his huge erection. His wonderfully male taste blended with the chocolate in a most decadent way. The recipe had turned out perfectly if she did say so herself.

She licked and sucked him, smearing chocolate on her cheeks, all over her lips, and throughout the hair around his cock. When she had cleaned off most the chocolate from his erection with her mouth, she went down on him in earnest.

Kev groaned as she worked one hand up and down his shaft while sucking his length. "That's it, babe. Damn but I love your mouth on me."

He grasped his hand tighter in her hair and thrust his hips back and forth. "I'm about to come."

Nicole moaned around his cock, and that simple vibration was all it took. Kev's hips jerked against her face and his come spurted into her mouth. It tasted of chocolate and cream and went down oh-so good.

"Damn, Nicole." He drew her up when he finished his climax, and kissed chocolate from her lips. "We have a hell of a lot more dessert and I'm going to be too exhausted to get back to the ranch and get any work done tomorrow."

Nicole kissed him back. "I plan on working you out real good, so you'd better be ready."

"I'm ready." Kev grabbed the bed covers and tossed them aside, leaving only the bottom sheet. "The question is, are you?"

She ran one chocolate-coated finger down his chest. "You betcha."

His voice was a near growl when he said, "Lie on the bed and spread your legs."

Nicole shivered at his tone. The way he dominated her sometimes so totally turned her on. She didn't hesitate to obey him, praying that he intended to hurry up and fuck her.

But instead he dipped his hands into more of the chocolate dessert and began painting her body with it, from the ankle straps of her high heels, up the inside of her thighs, and completely coating her pussy. He seemed to take great pleasure in using her as a canvas. He painted a flower on her belly, then, skimming over her bra beneath her breasts, he circled each of her nipples and topped them off, as if they were targets.

And then he slowly began to lick it all off.

Perspiration coated Nicole's body and she squirmed with the need to come. When he finally had licked all the chocolate off, with the exception of what coated her pussy, she was ready to scream.

Kev licked the crease of her thigh, avoiding her pussy and driving her even crazier.

"Kev!" Nicole couldn't help the pleading tone of her voice.

His lips hovered above her folds as his eyes met hers. "Tell me what you want, hon."

Begging, demanding, pouting, whatever it took, she was way past caring what she had to do to get him to finish the job. "Lick my pussy, *please*."

Kev buried his mouth against her folds and she screamed. Her cry reverberated through the room, and probably throughout her entire B&B. But all she cared about was his hot mouth devouring her, the spasms shaking her body, the waves of her climax that just wouldn't quit. No matter how much she begged him to stop, and her hips bucked against his face, he kept a tight grip on her thighs and wouldn't give up until he had licked all the chocolate from her pussy.

As she lay panting, trying to get her bearings, he nuzzled her curls. "I hope you don't mind a little chocolate on your sheets."

Nicole sighed with satisfaction. "Not when it means dessert in bed."

Kev rose up, grabbed her hand, and took her with him. "Come on. Let's take a shower and wash off some of this mess."

Nicole could barely walk after that orgasm, and leaned into him as he put an arm around her shoulders and walked her to the bathroom. She gave a pleased sigh. "Most fun making a mess that I've ever had."

As Kev got the shower going at a comfortable temperature, Nicole stripped off her bra and heels. They climbed in through the sliding glass doors and under the warm spray. First, Kev soaped her from head to toe, paying extra attention to her breasts and pussy. When it was her turn, Nicole took great pains to stroke and fondle his cock while she soaped the hair around the base of the shaft.

When neither of them could take it any longer, Kev backed up against the glass shower doors and grabbed Nicole by the waist. "Wrap your legs around me, hon."

Those now familiar thrills whirled through her belly as she climbed him. She braced her hands on his shoulders and wrapped her legs around his waist as he positioned his erection at the entrance to her channel.

Warm water continued to spray on their bodies and their faces as Kev brought her down on his cock, hard. Nicole gasped at the sudden feel of him deep inside her. It had only been yesterday since he'd fucked her last, and it already seemed like too long.

Kev backed her up against the cool tile and began fucking her deep and hard. His balls slapped against her pussy and their flesh smacked together with every thrust. He fucked her harder and harder and her climax built up so high she knew it was going to be incredible.

When she finally reached that peak, she let loose with a scream. Kev shouted and she felt his pulsing release inside her core.

As she came down from the high of her climax, Kev held her close and brushed his lips over hers. "Nicole Landford, you are one hell of a woman."

Chapter Eight

Kev held Nicole close as they swayed to a slow song in the middle of the crowded dancehall, and she snuggled against his chest. She felt so comfortable with him and he smelled damn good, of male musk and freshly laundered shirt.

He stroked one hand through her hair as they danced, and rested his chin on her head. She liked how that felt. Maybe too much.

It had been almost four weeks since the day her car had broken down at Kev's ranch. Almost four weeks of great sex and feelings building up inside her that scared her shitless. She'd never been serious about any man, and she wasn't about to start. Damn it, she was single and happy and intended to stay that way. Her parents had a good marriage and Nicole really didn't have anything against serious relationships, except for herself. She loved her freedom.

Kev's hips molded to hers as they swayed to the music, and her pussy tingled as she felt the firm outline of his erection through the thin material of her skirt. She liked that she had that power over him, that he desired her so much all the time. But what worried her was the way he seemed to be taking this sex thing way too seriously — he had from the start. It was good the month was almost up. She didn't want him getting too attached to her. They would just have to be good friends.

She bit her lower lip. Could they go back to being friends after all they'd shared this month?

Country western music throbbed through the dimly lit dancehall that smelled of cigarettes and the yeasty odor of beer. Nicole had been in the mood for dancing, so Kev had taken her to the dance put on by one of the local clubs. But as they swayed to the music, she found herself wanting to be alone with him again.

The past few weeks their sex had been wild and passionate, but there were times when it had been slow and sensual. She'd never fucked one man so much, or for so long, and no other man had even come close to comparing to Kev when it came to sex. When it came to anything else…like emotions, maybe…she wasn't even going to go there.

"What are you thinking about, hon?" came his low husky voice.

She tilted her head so that she could reach his ear. "Fucking your brains out."

Kev stilled for only a second, them grabbed her by her hips and held her so tight against him she could feel his belt buckle digging into her belly along with his powerful erection.

He gave a low groan. "You say the sweetest things."

Nicole laughed. She wrapped her arms around his neck and flicked her tongue in his ear. "I want you *now*, cowboy."

Kev growled, a low throaty sound that told her how much she turned him on. He released her only long enough to grasp her hand and lead her through the crowd, and out the front entrance of the dancehall.

She expected him to take her to his truck, to go find themselves a deserted road, but instead, he yanked her around the corner of the hall and into the darkness. All she could see was Kev outlined by a pulsing blue neon light. A loud country western tune pulsed through the night in time with the pulsating sensation in her pussy.

With a quick movement that caught her off guard, Kev pinned her up against the wall. Nicole gasped as he pushed up her shirt. She wasn't wearing a bra, and when he palmed her bare breasts, and tweaked her nipples, it caused her to cry out with excitement. He caught her mouth with his in a frenzied kiss that she matched with her own fervor. Her hands found his belt buckle, and in two seconds flat she had his incredible erection in her hands.

"God you turn me on, woman." He grabbed her ass, hiked her legs up about his hips, pushing her skirt up around her waist. He pressed her tighter against the wall. Her nipples hardened even more in the cool night air, and her bare pussy was wide and exposed.

"Fuck me, Kev." She squirmed as he took his erection in hand and brought it to her folds.

He drove his cock into her. Nicole barely kept from screaming at the intensity of the sensation of him thrusting into her, knowing they could be seen at any moment.

She gripped his shoulders as he fucked her hard and deep. She couldn't help the sounds that escaped her, each cry blending into the night with the throbbing country western tune.

"I'm gonna come, hon," he said close to her ear.

But she was already there. Kev barely captured her mouth in time to swallow her scream. She couldn't have held it back if she'd tried. He groaned as his body jerked against hers and she felt the spasms of his cock deep inside her channel.

While they both fought to catch their breath, Kev held her tight.

"You're all mine, you wild woman," he murmured. "And I'm not about to let you go."

Nicole wiggled out of his grasp and tugged down her shirt and her skirt. "You've got to stop that possessive crap." She pushed her hair out of her face and eyed him squarely. "How many times do I have to tell you that you don't own me?"

His mouth quirked into that sexy grin that always made her knees weak. "Doesn't matter how many times you say it. You're already mine."

Nicole rolled her eyes and started to turn away, but Kev caught her in his arms. This time his kiss was oh-so slow, causing her head to spin and her brain to short-circuit.

When he pulled away his look was more than possessive. No use arguing with him tonight. She'd be his—for a day or two more, and that was it.

* * * * *

"Nicole's Bed-and-Breakfast," Nicole answered the phone at the reception desk, barely holding back a sigh. It was the day after her night with Kev at the dancehall, and she found herself feeling down for some reason. Usually she felt pretty up after seeing him.

"It's Trace. You okay?"

Nicole did her best to sound a little perkier to her best friend. "Sure. Great. What's up?"

"Just thought I'd call and see how you're doing." Trace paused. "It's been almost a month now, hasn't it?"

Nicole almost sighed again. "Yup. Gotta break it to Kev today or tomorrow."

"Did you tell him?"

"What, about the fact that I bet my cousins I would see one and only one man for a month?" Nicole shook her head, even though she knew her friend couldn't see her. "One month of all-out sex, and that's exactly what I did."

Trace sounded hesitant as she asked, "So…you haven't developed any feelings for Kev?"

"Of course not." Nicole tossed her hair over her shoulder and rolled her eyes. "As if. I like my freedom. No man is going to take that away from me."

"Being married doesn't take your freedom away from you." Trace had a determined note to her voice. "If anything, it's *more* freeing. You have someone you love, who you know loves you. It should be unconditional and it shouldn't change who you are or what you do. It's just…wonderful having someone there for you, someone who really cares about you." She gave a little laugh and added, "Plus sex all the time is an added benefit."

"Yeah. Well." Nicole ran her finger over the old-fashioned telephone that was part of the B&B's charm. "Serious relationships aren't for me. If it wasn't for the damn bet, I'm sure I would never have lasted this long with Kev, anyway. In fact—"

A shadow fell over the telephone and Nicole jerked her head up to find Kev watching her. His jaw was set and anger darkened his hazel eyes.

"Nicole?" came Trace's voice over the phone line, but Nicole barely heard her.

"Hang up." Kev's voice was tight, his mouth a thin line. "Now."

Nicole hesitated only a second. She had to face this, had to get it over with.

"Listen, Trace," she said as calmly as she could. "I've got to run."

"Everything okay?"

"Fine. Sorry to run, but I've got a guest waiting."

When Nicole finally hung up the phone, she took a deep breath and met Kev's gaze head-on.

"A bet." Kev's thumbs were hooked through his belt loops, but his knuckles were almost white. "You fucked me because of a bet."

Nicole's cheeks heated. "I never lied to you, Kev. You've known from the start that I was only in it for the sex. The fact that we had a lot of good times is just that. Good times. Fabulous sex and fun. That's what it was all about."

Kev stepped behind the reception desk, caught her wrist, and jerked her toward him. "I don't believe you," he said, his mouth barely above hers. "I don't believe I mean nothing more to you than another good fuck."

Nicole's heart pounded like crazy. "I'm not into serious relationships." She tried to shake her head but he slipped his hand into her hair and clenched it tight, keeping her from moving. "I never have been."

"You are now," he said the fraction of a second before his lips came down on hers in a truly punishing kiss. It was hard and angry, a completely dominating kiss that sent her mind whirling and made her body weak.

She couldn't help how her nipples tightened and her pussy grew wet. She couldn't help how her pulse raced and her senses swam. Her body knew him, wanted him, and she was completely helpless to fight it.

He tore away from her, his eyes still angry, a harsh cut to his mouth. "I love you, Nicole Landford. When you get it through your thick head that you're in love with me, too, then you know where to find me."

Kev released her, turned on his booted heel and strode out the door, then shut it behind him. Hard.

Nicole's hands started trembling and she clenched them into fists.

Kev Grand was in love with her?

No. That couldn't be.

A strange sense of euphoria overwhelmed her, like she could almost burst with happiness.

God, she was losing her mind. She tried to stuff it down, to push it far away. "It would never work." She clenched her hands tighter, her eyes still focused on the door.

Nicole closed her eyes tight. "Freedom. I need my freedom."

Yet Kev had never crowded her the entire month they'd been dating. Yes, he was possessive when they were alone, but he never acted jealous about her past history. He had appeared to be confident in their relationship and in her as a person. He always asked her about work, enjoyed her B&B, and expressed how much he liked that she was an entrepreneur. He never questioned her need for time alone, never expected her to report in to him on where she was going, or insisted on going with her everywhere she went.

She had all the freedom she needed.

As she kept her eyes shut tight, she could see only images from her month with Kev, and even images from all the years they'd known each other.

This month they'd had dinner, went dancing, helped one another out with their respective occupations, and even went shopping together. They'd laughed, they'd talked, and they'd argued like crazy. And they'd made love countless times. Wild, hot, animalistic sex, and slow, sensual lovemaking.

"Made love," Nicole whispered as she opened her eyes and stared at the door that Kev had just walked through. "We made love."

No, it wasn't that.

Maybe it was?

Wait, it was all about the sex.

Nicole sighed. She finally had to admit it to herself—it hadn't been all sex after all. She'd known it, she just hadn't been able to face it.

Well, when Nicole Landford wanted something, she went after it. And this time she knew exactly what she wanted.

Chapter Nine

Thunder rolled across the valley as Nicole kicked the flat tire of her 'vette. "You have perfect timing, you know that?"

Her features softened as she trailed her fingers through the dust on the corvette's fender. "But if it wasn't for you....all this—Kev—never would have happened. I owe you."

Nicole looked off into the dusk in the direction of Kev's ranch. "If he'll forgive me." She rubbed her damp palms on her white jean skirt and set her mouth in a determined line. "He damn well better."

She leaned in the driver's side window to snatch the keys out of the ignition, then headed to the trunk. This time after unlocking the trunk, she stuffed the keys into her skirt pocket before leaning in to grab the tire iron and the jack. She carried both to the front of the car before returning for the spare. When she finally managed to drag it out, the tire slipped against her chest, down the front of her white blouse and her white denim skirt, and landed on her sandaled foot.

"Shit." Nicole grimaced and held her breath for a moment until the throbbing in her big toe lessened.

Great. Now she had a flat tire *and* she was filthy.

She cast a glance at the stormy sky and almost laughed. At least she should end up getting a good shower.

With fierce determination, she wrangled the tire around to the front of the car. She knew the routine for this old thing. Set the brake, place rocks in front of and behind each tire, just to make sure it didn't roll down the slope, and then jack up the car.

This part was the most fun, she thought as she slipped her torso beneath the car and placed the jack under the frame. *Not.*

When she slid out from beneath the 'vette, her skirt hiked up to her waist, and one of her buttons caught on the car and popped off.

Nicole groaned as she got to her knees and rearranged her clothing. Lovely. She now had dirt in her hair and on her backside, black down the front of her skirt and blouse from the tire, and her hands were black from everything she had come in contact with.

Raindrops splattered her face in big fat drops. And then it started pouring.

Nicole snorted. A small giggle escaped. The next thing she knew she was laughing so hard tears rolled down her face, mingling with the rain. She slid down the side of the car so that her knees were bent and her back against the driver's side door, laughing until her sides ached.

She wiped tears and rain from her cheeks with her palms and realized she'd just spread the black from her hands all over her face.

Nicole burst into giggles again. She buried her face in her hands, her shoulders shaking with laughter as rain pelted her, soaking her clothing and her hair.

Two large hands grabbed her wrists and pulled her arms down to her sides.

She jerked her head up—

To see the man she'd fallen in love with. "Kev."

"Now, hon," he said with a grin as he released her. "Aren't you getting to be a little old for mud pies?"

She clenched both fists in the wet earth beside her and gave him a devious smile. "Not even close." She brought her hands up and wiped mud down each of his cheeks. "I've wanted to do that since elementary school. Now we're even."

Kev growled and jerked her to a stand. He pressed her up against the 'vette, capturing her legs between his. "You've been a very bad girl, Nicole Landford."

She tilted her head back, mindless of the rain pounding down on them both. "Whatcha going to do about it?"

Kev gripped his hand in her hair, dragged her to him and kissed her. Their mouths met with all the fire and passion they'd known since the first time they met. She gripped his shirt tight in her fists, and felt the mud from his cheeks slide onto her own. His tongue probed the depths of her mouth and she tasted him, wanted more of him.

"Now," she said when they broke apart, "I want you now."

Kev couldn't argue. He wanted her just as badly. He picked her up and she wrapped her arms around his neck, and her legs around his hips, as he carried her to the rear of the car. He freed one hand long enough to slam the trunk shut, then set her on it and moved between her thighs.

Rain plastered her clothing to her skin. Her blouse gaped where she'd lost a button, and he didn't hesitate to lose the rest of them for her. He ripped the blouse open and then yanked down her bra. Her big, beautiful breasts spilled out onto his palms, and she gave one of her sexy little cries as he pinched her nipples.

Kev shoved up her skirt and tore off her thong. In mere seconds he freed his erection and plunged into her tight pussy.

Nicole cried out at the feel of Kev pounding his cock into her at the same time rain pounded down on them. She felt so wild and free as he fucked her out on his ranchland. Anyone could drive by, or a cowboy could ride up, and they'd see Kev thrusting into her. But she didn't care. All she cared about was Kev and how he filled her — mind, body and soul.

When she came, it was with a scream that tore across the valley. Her body spasmed as her climax and raindrops washed over her body in one incredible sensation.

Kev thrust hard and then he braced his hands on the trunk as he came with a growl. When his cock stopped pulsing in her core, he held her tight to him. "Tell me who you belong to, Nicole."

She sighed and kissed his wet lips. "You, Kev Grand. I belong to you."

* * * * *

Nicole snuggled up to Kev in his bed, and studied his tanned features. They'd just taken a warm shower together, and had toweled one another off before slipping into bed.

While he slowly stroked the line of her jaw, he studied her like he couldn't get enough of her.

She touched his stubbled cheek with her fingers. "You were right, you know."

His thumb caressed her jawline to her ear. "Yeah?"

Nicole took a deep breath. "I love you, Kev."

He moved his thumb to her lower lip. "Took you long enough to figure that out."

She smiled. That hadn't been hard at all. "You are one cocky SOB."

"Can't argue with you there." He feathered his thumb along her cheek. "Don't you think we need to buy you more reliable transportation?"

"We?" She cocked an eyebrow at him. "And what's wrong with my 'vette?"

Kev slipped his hand into her hair. "I can't see you driving that unreliable piece of—" At Nicole's dirty look, he grinned and said, "That vintage beauty, all the way to Bisbee and back when you're working your B&B."

Nicole stilled. "Just what are you trying to say, cowboy?"

He stroked the back of her head, a slow massage that made her shiver. "When we're married, I don't want to have to worry about you breaking down on your way to your B&B, or on your way home."

Nicole's eyes widened and she pushed herself up so that she was above Kev.

"Marriage?" She punched at his chest with one finger. "You really are cocky."

"As if you ever thought otherwise." He pulled her into his arms so that she sprawled across his chest. "I love you, Nicole, and that's all there is to it."

"But marriage. Wow." He looked so damn sexy she wanted to jump him. Wanted to say yes to anything. But she wasn't sure she was ready for that step. "Why don't you let me get used to the idea first, and then we'll talk about it."

"Fair enough." He placed his hands at her waist and moved her so that she was straddling him. "How about Vegas?"

Nicole had to laugh. She leaned forward so that her nipples brushed his chest. "*If* I say yes to marrying you, Las Vegas will be perfect."

Kev rolled them over in a fast movement, putting her beneath him. His cock nudged her pussy and she moaned.

"*When*," he said as he moved the head of his erection to her core.

"*If.*" She raised her hips trying to take him deeper, but he held back.

His eyes darkened and then moved his lips down just above hers. "*When* you marry me, we'll do it in Vegas."

"Okay," she whispered and then slipped into oblivion as he entered her.

He drove his cock in and out of her pussy, taking her to that place they had been together so many times before. But this time her heart and eyes were wide open. This was the man she loved, the man she would spend the rest of her days with. And nothing had ever felt more perfect than that very thought, than that very moment.

She rode the wave that overtook her, flowing with it higher and higher until she broke above the surface.

Kev came with her, his shout echoing her own.

When they both slid down from that perfect place, into the bed they shared, Kev held her tight to his chest and said, "How soon, hon?"

Nicole smiled. "Vegas, here we come."

About the author:

Cheyenne McCray is a thirty-something wild thing at heart, with a passion for sensual romance and a happily-ever-after...but always with a twist. A University of Arizona alumnus, Chey has been writing ever since she can remember, back to her kindergarten days when she penned her first poem. She always knew that one day she would write novels, and with her love of fantasy and romance, combined with her passionate nature, erotic romance is a perfect genre for her. In addition to her adult work, Chey is also published in young adult literary fiction under another name. Chey enjoys spending time with her husband and three sons, traveling, working out at the health club, playing racquetball, and of course writing, writing, writing.

Cheyenne welcomes mail from readers. You can write to her c/o Ellora's Cave Publishing at 1056 Home Avenue, Akron OH 44310-3502.

Also by Cheyenne McCray:

Branded Hearts

Nelissa Donovan

Chapter One

"I can't believe they talked me into wearing this," Lily muttered as she wriggled in the airline seat, the satin thong slipping even further up her rear. Who ever heard of wearing a micromini on a three-hour plane flight?

Insanity. Total and absolute insanity.

She eyed the middle-aged businessman next to her. Immaculate and comfortable in his sensible gray suit, Lily envied him. And, despite her I'm-an-available-whore attire, he'd been a perfect gentleman.

Which proved the point she'd made to Nic and Bri. It didn't matter how they dressed her up or, more appropriately, slutted her down, Lily Whitman just didn't exude sex appeal.

As to that ridiculous bet...

Lily flicked another glance at Mr. Perfect Suit. Nope. No vibes. No "trigger tripping", as Bri would have put it. Thank God. How many times had she promised her cousins that she wouldn't welch on their wager? Ten, at least. Maybe more.

"No welching, Lil," Bri had said with that I'll-make-you-pay-if-you-flake-out look. "If you get cold feet, call us and we'll set those beautiful tootsies back on the path of lust and self-gratification; got it?"

Self-gratification, right. Lily was perfectly gratified by her job as Southwestern Artifacts Curator at the Bisbee Museum. Sure, cleaning up, cataloging and presenting early southwestern artifacts wasn't the most glamorous job but it had its perks. Lily was always keen to travel locales across the western United States to analyze finds and, in some cases, purchase them for the museum. And then there was the fact that she was simply passionate about early American history. Especially Native American history.

"Not trustworthy," Lily grumbled to herself as the pilot finally announced their stop, which earned her a glance from Mr. Suit. She gave him a quick smile before squeezing past him. "Excuse me," Lily murmured. He smiled and moved into the aisle as she reached overhead for her laptop, the four inch heels Nicole had strapped her in wobbling like crazy. Finally wrenching the laptop free of the other briefcases crammed into the small space, Lily turned.

Only to find Mr. Suit had been staring, all googlie-eyed, at her legs and ass.

As his eyes finally made the trek to her face, he flashed an oily smile. Lily's first thought was to curl her lip and push past the asshole but her cousins' disapproving faces filled her mind. Reacting in her normal fashion wasn't part of the deal and, if she wasn't going to follow through, why come at all?

So, instead of the snarl, Lily forced a smile, showing a bit of her even white teeth as she moved in closer. "Oh, well, excuse me," she purred. "These aisles are so darn tight."

She almost laughed at the look of surprise on his average-guy face. He grinned even wider and leaned in. It took all Lily's self-control not to shove his leering mug away.

"Here, let me help you with that." He took the laptop and ushered her into the aisle ahead of him.

I can't believe I'm doing this, Lily thought, feeling his eyes glued to her backside as she stumbled her way to the front of the plane. She exited the plane and stomped off down the much-patched tarmac toward a modest, glass-paned terminal to her left. Her face flamed, and she knew her complexion was as pink as her Lycra top.

Damn it. Lily caught a reflection of herself in the terminal's golden windows. Short, cream, fringed skirt. Body-hugging fuchsia top and four-inch strappy heels.

Hell, she *did* look like a girl out for a good time.

Realizing that she was indeed on her own in unfamiliar territory, Lily stopped to view the countryside. Rolling fields of waving, golden grass were broken up by thick stands of pine. Lily breathed deep. Definitely pine, with a hint of cedar.

She looked up, her lips parting. The heavens were rapidly darkening to a striated burnt sienna. Hues of pale gold and crimson teased at the edges of a seemingly endless sky.

As she pushed through the double doors of the terminal and stepped inside, Lily grudgingly admitted it was one of the most spectacular sunsets she'd seen — and she'd witnessed some stunners. She'd traveled so much as a kid, following her military father from base to base, she'd had ample opportunities to observe Mother Nature in all her glory and fury.

Thinking Lily incapable of following through with the wager if left in her "familiar" environment, Sabrina and Nicole had pooled their resources and purchased a two-week vacation for her at a working "dude" ranch in Wolf Springs, Montana.

And for some crazy, out-of-control reason, Lily had agreed to go.

Why did I? Lily wondered as she smoothed her hand over the supple suede of the mini.

Because you're in a rut, girl. And if you don't break out now, it's likely to last well into your lonely old age. Lily sighed and brushed Aunt Viv's voice from her mind.

One person's rut was another's furrowed field —

"Miss Whitman?"

Lily stopped and looked up. A slender, rough-looking cowboy dressed in tight jeans and an equally tight flannel button-down long sleeve shirt walked toward her, fawn-colored Stetson in hand. He smiled, the attractive creases in his sun-browned face deepening as he thrust out a hand. "Howdy. I'm Darrell Donleavy."

Lily held out her hand. Calluses brushed her smooth palm. "Hello, Mr. Donleavy. You can call me Lily."

He raised brows the color of damp sand and fought to keep his pale blue eyes off her cleavage. "Well, if it's all the same to you, I think I'll stick with Miss Whitman." He cleared his throat and took her suitcase. "We're a professional team at Red Bear Ranch and I hope you get it on well with the guys." His face flushed crimson. "Uh, I mean, I hope you get something out of your dude ranch experience."

Lily stifled a giggle and followed the red-faced Darrell Donleavy through the tiny lobby and out the front doors into the parking lot.

Clearly uncomfortable with her attire, the whip-thin cowboy managed to look everywhere but *at* her as he led her to a green Chevy four wheel drive truck and opened the door. Lily couldn't blame him. She was an embarrassment. A slutty train-wreck of a woman. It was a wonder he was being polite to her at all.

What had her cousins been thinking, dressing her up like this? It certainly wasn't appropriate attire for a dude ranch. She'd take her books and antiques over sweaty men and horse shit any day.

Lily closed her door and tried to look less brazen by keeping her eyes fastened on the scenery outside the window as Darrell turned out onto the narrow, two-lane highway. At least this cowboy didn't dampen her panties. He was attractive, in a wiry sort of way, but nothing that made that rollercoaster dip in her abdomen.

"So, is the, uh…" Lily looked down at the computer printed brochure in her lap. "Red Bear Ranch far from the airport?"

She glanced over at Darrell. He shook his head. "Just the other side of town."

Town?

Lily gazed out the window and noticed a muted bank of lights in the distance as they rattled down the lonely road. In the last rays of sun before dusk, Lily could make out the shadowy shapes of old-fashioned clapboard style buildings. A sign on the roadway heralded Wolf Springs, Population 849.

In moments they were motoring down the main drag and, as Lily's gaze caught a street sign, she smiled to see it literally *was* Main Street. Butter yellow lights eked from open windows and a pang of homesickness hit Lily.

Her gaze went back to her bare legs. Then the ankle-twisting heels.

I can't do this. Panic bubbled in Lily's chest. *I can't show up at a ranch full of men — hard working men — acting and looking like a bitch in heat.*

Lily nearly placed a hand on Darrell's arm and demanded he take her back to the airport. The memory of her cousins' disapproving glares stopped her. Taking a deep breath, Lily looked out the window once more, the lights of the small town scrolling by.

Which was when she saw it.

A gold lasso encircled neon tubes on a sign that read "Last Chance Saloon."

"Stop!" Lily cried.

Startled, Darrell braked hard. "What? Did you forget a suitcase?"

She shook her head, her heart hammering with embarrassment. "I…I—" Swallowing, Lily glanced at Darrell while she opened the door and slipped out onto the darkening street, leaving her laptop and luggage behind. "I'm going to go inside for a little while. Uh, take the edge off from the long flight. Don't worry. I'll grab a cab out to the ranch." She forced a smile and, before Darrell could open his mouth, Lily scurried to the heavy oak door of the Last Chance Saloon and went inside.

Chapter Two

Smoke hit her as she sidled into the bar. Lily coughed, then squinted, letting her eyes adjust to the dim interior. Country music rocked from an old-fashioned style jukebox near the door. Tables were scattered throughout the room but few were occupied.

Cowboys leaned against the polished oak bar, their backs to her, while hoots and hollers erupted from the larger room to her right. Lily peered through the murk. Men reclined against a railing that squared off a space that housed a mechanical bull.

It was being wildly ridden by yet another weather-roughened cowboy. One hand held high, his body whipped and snapped with each jerky rotation of the bull. The crowd cheered and jeered, beers raised.

Wouldn't Susan just die if she could see me here, thought Lily. Her best friend from high school and college had been shocked when she'd heard about Lily's trip. She tried to convince her it would be more fun to spend the next few weeks with her in the sleepy Kansas farming town she'd abruptly moved to five months ago.

Taking one more sweeping look, Lily thought she might have been right.

Alcohol. *That's what I need.* Susan would agree with her under the circumstance. And if the cowboys got a little rowdy, Lily could always show them a little of the kung fu Susan taught her.

Smoke burned her eyes as Lily cursed her cousins and made for the bar. She'd be damned if she'd be the first one to bow out. She'd let one of *them* break the bet first...it was simply a matter of waiting them out. Then she could go home to her books and the storage room full of artifacts waiting to be catalogued.

A strange pang hit Lily and she sighed. Funny, but the prospect didn't fill her with the sense of comfort it should have.

Lily leaned against the bar, looking forward to numbing the fistful of butterflies in her gut. "Hello," she said to the bartender's back. He turned. A look of surprise, then cool appraisal flowed across his tan face.

"Didn't see you come in, ma'am."

Ma'am. Well, isn't that appropriate, Lily thought, feeling older than the hills.

The twenty-something shaggy blond looked around as if searching for who might have come in with her before leaning onto the bar. "What can I get you?"

Lily pulled her lower lip between her teeth. "I think I'd like a blue Long Island Iced Tea, please."

The bartender's brows peaked. "Sure thing."

With skill that comes from years of practice, the bartender flipped each bottle as he filled a large, 16 ounce glass to the brim. The blue Curaçao came last, coloring the potent mix of liquors. In went a straw before he slapped it onto the polished oak. "Wish I had a slice of lemon but we don't get much demand for them here."

He smiled warmly and Lily took the drink, returning the smile. "Thanks. This is fine." Her eyes closed as she took a long, cool sip.

"Well, where in the blazes did you blow in from, sugar?"

Lily released the straw, her gaze opening to meet the cool green eyes of a very bulky cowboy who'd sidled up on her left. Her face colored and she cleared her throat. "I just stopped in for a quick drink before heading for the, uh…" Lily fumbled for the brochure she'd crammed into her purse. "The Red Bear Ranch," she finished softly, reading from the crumpled trifold.

"Frank's place, er, I mean Shain's place, huh?" The cowboy tipped his hat up onto his square forehead and grinned so wide, Lily thought the creases in his face might split open. "Hey, boys!" he boomed. Heads turned, all male. All looking surprised, then predatory, as their eyes fastened on Lily at the bar. "We've got a visitor to Wolf Springs!"

The bulky cowboy turned back to Lily. "What did you say your name was, sugar?"

Lily's response usually would have been "I didn't say," but that wouldn't be appropriate. Especially in a room full of inebriated cowboys looking for a good time. "Take chances, Lily!" Nicole's voice filled her head. "What do you have to lose?"

Turning to face the other room, Lily held her glass up. "Howdy, boys! My name's Lil and it's my pleasure to make your acquaintance."

Big Boy slapped a hand to her shoulder, nearly sending her sprawling across the bar, her drink sloshing. "I think the pleasure is all ours, right, boys?"

Cheers erupted and, within seconds, Lily found herself surrounded by a herd of fine-looking cowboys, from big and hulking to small and wiry, their gazes fastened on every curve of bare flesh, their grins beyond huge.

Lily yanked the straw out of her drink, the plastic tube rolling to a stop next to a bowl of peanuts. In three big gulps, she drained her glass and smacked it down on the bar.

Her gaze found the bartender's. "I think I'm going to need another."

* * * * *

"Whaddya mean she jumped out of the truck?"

"I'm telling you, Shain, she was out so fast I didn't have time to try to convince her otherwise!"

Shain ran a hand through his dark, chestnut-streaked hair and tried to keep his temper in check. "Damn it, Darrell. How hard can it be to drive a client from the airport to the ranch?" His boots clomped heavily on the rough-hewn pine flooring as he made for the bunkhouse door. He threw another smoldering look his new foreman's way as he grabbed his black Stetson off the rack and smashed it onto his head. "I'll go get her myself. Where'd she bail out?"

"Well, uh, she went into *The Chance*, last I saw."

"What?" Shain roared. "Why the hell would she do a fool thing like that?"

"She, uh, well…she said she wanted a drink to burn off the jet lag. Said she'd grab a cab out to the ranch."

Shain laughed. "A cab? Where does she think she is? Billings?" He sobered as he thought of the mob that hung out of the Chance on Friday nights. Fresh from five days of backbreaking work, riding the bull and tossing back as many cold ones as their skimpy paychecks would allow was top billing for the week. Throw in a reasonably handsome gal, and it would be the highlight of their month. Even the bar fly regulars knew enough to avoid the rowdy saloon on a Friday night.

Shain's smoky brown eyes widened, then found, Darrell who was easing as far away from Shain as he could get. "And you *let* her go in there?"

Darrell sighed and held up his arms. "Look, Shain. I agreed to be your foreman, not a babysitter. That gal was lookin' for trouble. We'd be better off if she finds a cowboy to hook up with and forgets all about the Red Bear, you want my opinion."

Irritation and grudging respect for his foreman's plain speaking mixed in Shain's gut as he yanked the door open. "Might be that you're right, Darrell, but, if you want to get paid your foreman's wages, we need that broad, trouble or not, to pony up the cash for her 'ranch hand experience'. And she's not likely to pay if she's not here."

Shain strode across the wide front porch and down the granite steps to the flagstone drive. "Doesn't it fix to reason our first *client* would be some dumb, fool woman," he mumbled as he yanked his keys out of his pocket and headed for the 4x4.

He tried not to notice the yellowed grass of the lawn and the peeling paint on the sprawling house. Or the battered stock tanks or the rusting barbed wire that twisted its way across the rolling hills and flat plains of the Red Bear's six thousand acres.

Tossing his hat onto the seat, Shain eased his six-foot-five-inch frame inside the truck and gunned the engine. His sister's dark brown eyes and stern voice filled his head: "Don't you go and blow this opportunity, Shain. Our first customer will set the tone for other guests and tour book listings. We *need* this, Shain. We need *her.*"

Shain scrubbed a hand over his stubbled jaw. It didn't sit well with him, turning the ranch into a tourist attraction, but Nhya was convinced it was the only way to pay off the enormous balance due on the ranch's title by the end of summer. And after poring over his mother and stepfather's bills the past two weeks, Shain grudgingly conceded she might be right.

He slammed his palm onto the steering wheel. How in the hell had they managed to get so far behind? His mother had never said a word, but that was like her — never wanting to worry him or his sister. But now they were in a tighter spot than a rodeo clown in a barrel.

Shain sighed. As if dealing with the shock and grief of losing his mother and stepfather wasn't enough.

He recalled the cell phone call from Nhya four weeks ago to the day. His gaze cut to the green tinted dashboard clock. Almost to the hour. Her ragged, tear-clogged voice telling him he had to come home. That Mom and Frank were dead — killed instantly when their Cessna crashed somewhere in Wyoming. They'd been on their way back from a stock trade show — trying, Nhya suspected, to solicit help from friends to keep the ranch afloat.

Coming back and running the ranch wasn't something Shain wanted to do. In fact, he'd sworn to never get tied to the enormous commitment and thankless hours of work it took to run a ranch. He was well aware of the toll. He'd watched his mother and father build the ranch from the ground up on land willed to them by his Oglala grandmother after she passed. He'd been right there, even at a tender age, to muck stalls, mend fences and help herd and cut the cattle. Eventually Shain took to breaking the wild mustangs his father drove into Utah every summer.

But he'd also watched as the sun-up-to-sun-down, no-rest-for-the-weary lifestyle robbed more than just a few hours of recreation from his family. When his father died at the age of forty-three from, of all things, an untreated infection from a barbed wire cut to his knee, Shain swore he'd never tie himself to that way of life. He wasn't afraid of hard work. Far from it. He relied on mind-numbing labor to relieve the pressure cooker that built inside him in idle moments but he'd be damned if he'd marry himself to a piece of land and a family along with it.

Then there were the...other things about the ranch and the land. The whispered voices of their ancestors. Mostly his grandmother. The "feelings" his sister had always been sensitive to, even as a young child. Shain had gotten very good at ignoring the odd sensations, the prickling of intuition or guiding urges. But Nhya thrived on them. They were as natural to her as breathing. Shain had other opinions. Interfering. Unnerving. Unexplainable. He realized at an early age that it was something he'd rather escape than embrace.

And so he'd decided to do what he loved and leave the ranching to his new stepfather and mother. They seemed to thrive on it. He'd been relieved when his mother had remarried. Shain liked Frank well enough and his stepfather let him chase his passion for rodeo, driving him to compete in regional events. As soon as Shain turned nineteen, he hit the rodeo circuit full time, making a name for himself and having one hell of a good time while he was at it.

Twelve years later, Shain was one of the best bronc riders in the nation, spending over six months of the year traveling the circuit, competing and now training newer riders and wranglers. He'd become a legend as a hellion and vicious competitor, which was how Shain liked it. Despite his numerous injuries, he was still in the best shape of his life.

The muted lights of Wolf Springs split the night and Shain slowed. He pulled into the lot at the Last Chance Saloon and parked.

Not that it mattered now. He had "responsibilities", as his sister would put it. A duty to do what his mother and father would have wanted him to do—save the ranch. Nhya couldn't do it on her own...well, Shain thought with a wry smile, she probably could but she shouldn't have to.

His lips pressed into a hard line. Shain knew he was doing the right thing, but that didn't mean he had to like it. And the sooner he pulled the ranch out of debt, the sooner he could go back on the road, his only cares which stallion he'd be breaking before the day was over and which horny sweet little rodeo honey would be rubbing down his sore muscles, and other things, that same night.

He grabbed his hat and opened the door. Unfolding his tall, rock-solid body from the cab, he stood, his boots crunching on the limestone hard-pack of the parking lot. "All right, darlin'," he said quietly, before tossing back his hair, slapping on his hat and pulling the brim low. "Red Bear Ranch is waitin'. Time to get this show on the road and your money in my pocket."

Chapter Three

As Shain pushed his way through the back door, whistles and hollers hit his ears. It sounded like the party was in full swing. He rounded the corner and crunched to a halt on the peanut-strewn floor.

What the hell…

"That's it, sugar! Hold on tight!"

"Yer doin' great, darlin'!"

Bright, full laughter cut through the haze of cowboy hollers and Shain's gaze fastened on the tall, leggy blonde clamped onto the mechanical bull, which was rising and falling on the lowest speed, with no real twists and, even then, she was having a hard time holding on. The only thing keeping her from landing in a heap on the floor was the phenomenal grip of her bare thighs pressed against the worn leather.

Which brought on more laughter and shouts.

Shain took three strides forward then stopped. The closer he got, the stranger he felt. It was as if someone hefted a fifty-pound boulder and shoved it straight into his gut. Shain ignored the sensation as his gaze fastened on the honey's beautiful thighs, calves and lovely slim ankles. She was a looker, all right. And her outfit left nothing to the imagination. Her legs were longer than those of a quarter horse on steroids and her skin…a shade of sun-touched cream that left Shain with an absurd desire to seize that finely shaped ankle, pull it up, and run his tongue from the curve of her heel all the way to the tight flesh of her ass cheek.

Which was nearly as exposed as the rest of her body.

Darrell had been right. This one *was* trouble. Shain wet his suddenly parched lips and his gaze snapped to the rowdy regulars who had yet to notice him, their attention fully focused on Miss Thing.

With his fingers hooked in his belt loops, Shain made for the bull. The whooping quieted. Only the creak and twist of the mechanical springs could be heard and the lilting, nervous laughter of the woman—the *client*.

"Shut 'er down, Jimbo," Shain rumbled, his eyes drawn to the swell of the woman's breasts. Through the thin shirt and tight bra, he could see that her nipples tipped up, as if begging for a little extra attention. And with legs like that, Shain mused, it would take a lot for her other body parts to compete.

And then she looked up.

"Shit on a shingle," Shain murmured. Her eyes—green as freshly sprung pine needles—fastened on him.

"Oh," she whispered and Shain's gaze fell to her parted lips. He could just see the tips of her even white teeth. Out snaked a coral pink tongue to wet them and Shain's thoughts crashed to an image of that luscious tongue flicking across the head of his cock.

Damn...but her face would have no problem competing with her legs.

An impatient grumbling from the crowd brought Shain back to reality and he leaned in, placing his mouth next to her diminutive ear. "Let's go, darlin'. I think you've entertained the pack enough for one night."

The blonde stiffened and stared straight ahead, her teeth worrying her succulent lower lip. She mumbled something Shain couldn't understand and, from the high flush on her cheeks, Shain doubted even *she* knew what she was saying. "Come on. Fun's over," Shain said, reaching for her slender shoulder.

As his hand made contact, the woman gasped and then...of all things, whimpered like a lost kitten or mistreated puppy.

"Hey, Stevenson! What the hell?"

"Leave her alone, man! We were just havin' some fun!"

More hollers, and Shain felt the horde moving in. A familiar sizzle of cold seeped into the soles of his feet and he took a deep breath. Now wasn't the time to pound sense into a bunch of wasted cowboys.

What kind of game was she playing?

"Back off," Shain growled without turning his head. The disgruntled shouts faded to grumbling.

He leaned forward once more, bracing his hands on either side of her body, his palms touching warm leather. "Look, lady, I don't know what you're up to but, if I have to beat the hell out of this bunch of rock heads because of you, you can damn well kiss your ranch trip goodbye. We'll pack you onto the first flight out of Wolf Springs."

Of course, that wasn't what Shain *really* wanted to do with her. With his chest nearly touching her trembling back and her fresh, sultry scent of lilies and summer blooms wafting into his nose, all Shain wanted to do was tell her to hold on while he climbed up behind her and rammed his now pulsing cock into her sweet little pussy as she lay splayed out before him.

'Course, that wasn't an option—yet.

Shain realized that she was mumbling something. Ears straining, he picked up: "No, he can't be the one. He can't be..."

Shain grunted. He'd had enough. In one seamless move, he wrapped an arm under her waist and lifted her clear of the bull and turned her around, setting her onto her four-inch heels in front of him. She tottered forward and Shain was quick to hold her up, her pointy tits jammed against his chest. Shain repressed a groan, his focus captured by her upturned, dreamy-eyed gaze.

"Oh, my, God," she whispered. "You're my trigger tripper." And with that her angel face promptly fractured into tears.

Tears, for Godsakes.

Shain was quick to sling her over his shoulder, where she dangled, sobbing like a three year old that'd just been told her favorite horse had to be put down.

But it had to be done. He was gonna need his hands—and fists—free.

* * * * *

Dark, thick hair…full, demanding lips… chiseled jaw… and eyes the color of high-polished mahogany with a hint of a storm-touched sky.

Mine. All mine. Mine to tease, and suck and pump to distraction…

"Hmmm…"

A cool finger found her clit and Lily moaned, the sensation zinging straight through her abdomen and up into the pleasure centers at the top of her skull. She wanted him to do more than tease, though. She wanted to get a taste of those beautiful abs and feel his thick, luscious cock on her lips and tongue. Sample his essence. Know every ripple of flesh, muscle and bone.

The slamming of a door brought Lily upright.

She blinked. Rubbed her eyes.

I'm in bed…

Her bleary gaze tripped through the shadowed room. *Where the heck am I?*

Taking a deep breath, Lily looked down and gasped. She was perfectly naked. "Oh, lord," she muttered, pressing a hand to her throbbing head and pulling the sky blue sheets up to cover herself.

Fractured, half-formed pictures of the previous night came back to her. The drive from the airport. The bar…*ohmygod…the bar!* Lily remembered the attractive bartender, the blue Long Island Iced Tea and the cowboys. Who, if she was remembering correctly, had been pretty gentlemanly. But she hadn't stopped with that one drink. There'd been another and then she'd been persuaded to drink a couple shots of Jack D with the "boys."

What was I thinking?

I wasn't. That's the problem. This entire shindig had thrown Lily off track. Made her do things she wouldn't normally do.

That's the idea, cuz.

Nic and Bri's tandem voices sliced through the muck in Lily's brain and she groaned again.

But how had she ended up where she was now?

And, where exactly *was* she?

Lily forced her legs to one side of the four-poster pine bed and onto the cool hardwood floor. "There's no way I would have gone home with one of those guys last night. "

With the sheet wrapped loosely over her breasts, Lily made for the heavily draped window across the room. As she walked she realized the insides of her thighs were sore.

"Jesus, Joseph and Mary," Lily said, her stomach churning. "Nic and Bri, I'm going to rip every insane hair out of both your beautiful heads for this."

She made it to the window and, with a trembling hand, pulled the hunter green drapes aside. Early morning sunlight, pure and head-splittingly bright, flooded the room and hammered against Lily's squinting face. Closing her eyes, Lily let her body adjust to the laser-like pain, before forcing her lids open.

Her mouth gaped. The large window afforded her an unhindered view of a wide, uncluttered prairie grass lawn and, beyond that, a sprawling, sectioned corral. And barn. And sheds. Horses. Some milled in the pasture beyond the corral. Some in the corrals themselves. There were cows, too. Or steers. Whatever. Lily couldn't tell the difference and, besides, the lumpy black animals weren't what held her attention. It was the men. Five or six that she could see. All sun-browned and weather-toughened. Two were shirtless, their muscles flexing as they struggled with a fence post. The others were on horses, moving cattle toward some sort of long, narrow chute type thing. They were shouting. Motioning to one another.

"I woke up in *Bonanza*," Lily murmured, her eyes wide, one hand pressed to the window casing.

The unique scent of male musk and Old Spice tickled Lily's nostrils and prickles raced down the backs of her legs.

Lily stiffened as images crashed into her head. The smoky bar. The mechanical bull. Trying to hold on. Not feeling well. Wanting to get off. Find a dark corner. *Go home.*

And then *he* was standing there. An altogether different cowboy from the bar horde. Impossibly tall. With hair a rich shade of dark brown—lighter strands woven throughout the thick waves, and that masculine scent.

His eyes…warm, smoky…fastened on her, and it was clear as glass to Lily, even in her inebriated state, that this man was dangerous. Wild and uncultured. He'd spoken to her in that deep, rough voice but she hadn't understood a word he'd said. The only thing reacting to the stranger was her traitorous body. Instantly. Without shame or reservation, her vaginal muscles contracted, sending a nearly painful thread of longing rippling through her. Moisture warmed her nether lips, which were pressed against hot leather, and all Lily could think of was how much she wanted the dangerous-looking cowboy to rip her off the bull, push that tiny bit of skirt up around her waist before hooking his big thumbs into her G-string and pressing his powerful hips against her crotch.

And then he'd touched her.

Lily recalled the electricity that had flashed through her at the contact, which was when she knew. *He's the one.* The trigger tripper.

He'll chew me up and spit me out, Lily had thought.

Which is when she'd…

Ohmygod, Lily thought, her face burning, *I started crying.* "I acted just like one of the simpering *Bonanza* damsels in distress…"

"*Bonanza*'s a relic of the past, darlin'. The Red Bear is all about the here and now."

Lily gasped in surprise, nearly dropping the sheet as the sultry voice brushed the back of her neck.

She froze as two very large, tan and muscled forearms eased to either side of her, leaning on the windowsill. Heat, faintly damp and steamy, warmed her back and that scent again. Strong. Intoxicating.

Chest hairs tickled her shoulders and Lily bit her lower lip, her nipples tightening beneath the thin cotton.

"Like what you see out there, sweetness? Bet it's what you were comin' here for all along, hmmm?"

Remember your manners, Lily, and the wager. "Guess that's for me to know and you to find out," Lily managed to purr, wondering if she'd already done something in her drunken stupor to confirm his notion.

Lord.

His arms eased in tighter, hot flesh pressing against hers, his mouth directly above the curve of her ear. "I know all I need to know about you, sweetness. Seen your type in hundreds of different bars in a hundred different towns. The only difference between you and them is that you probably have the cash to legitimize your little games." Lily felt and heard him draw a deep breath, before blowing it out across the sensitive tips of her ears. She shivered. "That the way it is, darlin'?"

Panic seized Lily as that languid feeling seeped into her abdomen. That distinct sensation that preempted all rational thought with images of hot tongues, roving hands and thrusting hips.

"Uh," Lily mumbled, searching for an avenue of escape, redemption. "I—"

Before Lily could stumble through a sentence, a *slap* accompanied by a harsh sting made her jump and squeal.

He slapped my ass!

Lily spun, fury leaving her face a fine shade of crimson as she rubbed her stinging butt. "What in the he—"

Words stuck in her throat as she came face to face with her abuser. He was as she remembered him…tall…darkly handsome and built like a giant sequoia, slender in his hips but broad as a summer day is long, with muscles sculpted like iron, from his bulging calves to his rippling abs, on up to his full to bursting, crossed arms.

But it was his face that left her speechless—and alarmed. It was cold. His dark brown eyes fastened her with an intelligent and arrogant glare that made her want to shrink into a puff of dust and catch the first breeze out of town.

Then there was the little matter of the blue shiner and the hard red line of a cut beneath it. She was sure he hadn't had *that* last night in the bar.

It was at that moment Lily realized he was wearing only a white towel low around his strong hips. "Did, uh, we—"

He snorted and stalked to a chair near the bed. "Don't flatter yourself."

Without reservation, he dropped the towel and proceeded to dress. Lily burned with outrage at his words but, even so, her gaze feasted on his hard, chiseled ass, a shade lighter then his sienna colored skin.

What's wrong with me? Lily thought, turning away. The man just insulted me!

Lily realized with shock that it wasn't so much his insult that bothered her, as much as the fact that he didn't want her as her body obviously wanted him.

I've got to get out of here. Wager be damned…

"Hey."

Lily turned, only to be hit smack in the chest. She stumbled, her hands automatically grabbing at the bundle smashed against her tits, the sheet falling to the floor.

"Put those on. They're my sister's. Probably a little too short for you but, other than that, you're close to the same size."

Lily gritted her teeth and bent, trying to pull the sheet back up while holding onto the bundle at the same time.

"Look, I don't need someone else's clothes. Just give me back my—"

A snort. "Not a friggin' chance, lady. I agreed to let you stay since, according to my sister, you've already paid up but you're gonna follow my rules. And rule number one is you're wearing appropriate duds."

He raised a dark brow and Lily paused in her fumbling long enough to appreciate his outstandingly rugged and noble features. But there was that gleam in his eye. That flash that screamed 'caution!' 'danger!'

Then it hit her. "Wait a minute. Are you telling me I'm at the, uh, the…"

"Red Bear Ranch," he finished for her as he pulled on his deep blue shirt and fastened the snaps. He rolled the cuffs up to his elbows, then sat on the bed. With quick hands he shoved his feet into fawn-colored, well-worn boots, stood, then strode to the door. "You're gonna get what you paid for, darlin'." A smile stole across the hard planes of his face. "You're in for one hell of an authentic dude ranch experience."

He left, slamming the door behind him.

Chapter Four

Shain slammed the oak door with more force than he'd intended and gave a quick scan of the hall, before reaching down and shifting his painfully swollen cock in his jeans.

"Fuck me," Shain muttered. He wiped a hand over his face and walked to the balcony that looked down on the wide-open living room and entryway below. He could hear the bang and clash of pots from the kitchen where his sister was cleaning up. Damned if it hadn't taken all his restraint to not cup the leggy wench's nearly shaved, soft blonde mound and hang on.

She was one hot piece of ass. And now that he'd gotten a glimpse of her pussy, he knew she was a natural blonde, something completely unexpected. Her type was usually on intimate terms with peroxide and full of plastic to boot. His mind eased back to the delicious view he'd gotten of her tits. High and firm, with pale pink nipples pointing at him like come-hither fingers. No plastic there. Unique and distinctively delectable.

This was going to make it that much harder to keep his hands *off* her and his cock satisfied with thoughts of good fucks past. Closing his eyes, Shain wiped his mind free of images of *her* and focused on the workday ahead. It took a minute but his cock finally went back to a semi-comfortable size and Shain strode down the curving flight of stairs to the great room below.

He wouldn't have had to shower in her or, more accurately, *his* room if a pipe hadn't burst last night, rendering all the first floor bathrooms unusable. Nhya had made the last minute decision to put the unconscious woman in Shain's room on the second floor, which now had the only working shower except for those in the bunkhouse.

Shain had figured the broad would stay passed out until well after noon. Right. She'd been up at the window ogling the guys before she'd even gotten dressed. Seeing her staring at them in the thin sheet had made heat race to his head and all Shain could think of was how he wanted to bunch that sheet up in his fist and tie her to his naked body. Force her to wrap those long legs around his hips while he gripped her ass and ran his fingers across her moist slit.

At the hat rack Shain cursed. The bulge was back and even bigger now, if that was possible. He took another deep breath and slammed his hat onto his head. "Damned if this woman isn't going to get a lesson she's never gonna forget."

* * * * *

"What a prick," Lily muttered as she shoved her legs into the smooth, work worn jeans and buttoned them up. She'd searched for her luggage but only found her laptop, overnight case and unmentionables neatly folded in the armoire. Why the hell had he taken her clothes?

What had he said? Something about appropriate attire. "Oh, no," Lily said as it dawned on her that she'd left Nic and Bri alone with her luggage at the house for the entire day before her flight out while she wrapped things up at the museum.

"I bet they switched my wardrobe," Lily said to the sparkly dust motes dancing in front of her face.

But even if that *was* true…the *nerve* of that man to take them from her! What was this, a prison camp?

Lily found a pair of boots by the bed and pulled them on. The leather was supple and comfortable around her foot. She went to the wardrobe and took out her laptop. "I'm taking the first flight out of here."

A knock on the door nearly made Lily drop the case and, before she could answer, it swung inward, followed by a young woman, maybe twenty-five or twenty-six, bearing a huge smile and liquid brown chocolate eyes that instantly reminded Lily of the ethnic models she saw in magazines and on billboards.

"Good morning!" She walked over to Lily without hesitation and pumped her hand. "I'm Nhya. It's a pleasure!" Her gorgeous eyes did a quick appraisal, before rising once again to Lily's face. "I'm glad the clothes fit. Shain told me there'd been a problem with your suitcase and that you'd need some ranch duds while you're here."

Lily was at a loss. The woman exuded warmth and a strong aura of command. Sort of like —

"They're my sister's…"

The cowboy. His sister. Shain. *His name is Shain.*

Without missing a beat, the woman tucked Lily's laptop back into the armoire and grabbed her elbow. "You're up just in time for the last bit of breakfast. Come on down to the kitchen. You don't want to start your first day at the ranch on an empty stomach."

"Well, I —"

Lily never got to finish her sentence. Before she knew what was happening, they were out the door and headed down a grand set of rough hewn oak stairs to the impressive but homey ranch-style great room and then into the kitchen. The aroma of fresh bacon, fruit and coffee filled the air and Lily's mouth watered.

"Have a seat," Nhya said, waving to a stool at the long counter that faced the kitchen's massive prep area. Lily did, her mind whirring. She still hadn't had time to process all of last night's events but it was obvious from Shain's face that there'd been some sort of scuffle. She couldn't remember any of *that* but she had no doubt Shain had given more than he'd gotten, which was pretty amazing considering the size and number of cowboys who'd been there.

Shame colored Lily's cheeks and she glanced away from where Nhya was filling a plate at the stove to look out the large, picturesque windows at the Montana countryside. The grass seemed to stretch for miles but, in the distance Lily could see a thick line of trees and hills and, beyond that, mountains speared the clear blue sky.

Lily sucked on her lower lip as her thoughts tripped back to the moment she'd broken out into tears. *God...I never cry. What came over me?*

"Here ya go."

Turning, Lily smiled her thanks. The first thing she reached for was the cup of coffee. Anything to ease the ache between her eyes. As she sipped, Lily's brows knitted in surprise.

"Everything all right?"

Lily blinked at her hostess. "This coffee. It's just how I like it. Strong, with a hint of sugar and a generous amount of flavored creamer, which, if my taste buds aren't wonky from all the...er...well, anyway, it tastes like hazelnut. My favorite." Lily took another deep sip.

Nhya smiled and Lily was again stunned at her striking good looks. She could imagine her as an Aztec princess commanding her subjects. "I have a good sense for those things." She shrugged. "Besides, it's how I like it, too."

After a nod, Lily finished off the cup and asked for another while she dove into the fresh fruit. It was delicious and, despite her sensitive head, Lily found that she was famished. Must be the clean air, she thought. As she finished up, she exchanged pleasantries with Nhya, who was unfailingly polite and warm, but Lily sensed a measure of distance in the attractive young woman. A shadow of sadness. Lily was familiar with that shadow. She'd experienced enough tragedy in her life to recognize someone who'd suffered a recent loss. Not that she was about to ask her. It was none of her business.

While they chatted, Lily decided it might not be so bad to hang out at the ranch for a few days. At least until she could contact her cousins and ferret out who was closer to caving in. That weight lifted from Lily's shoulders, she began to look around with more interest.

"Ready for a quick tour?" Nhya asked as if reading Lily's mind.

Lily nodded and followed her under the carved lintel and into the great room. She'd never had much experience with a real, working ranch and Lily gave Nhya her full attention as the young woman spoke with obvious pride about how the home had been built by her parents and how special it was to them all. The house itself was beautiful, in a simple, elegant and functional way. The warm wood and rich stone on the fireplaces—Lily had seen three so far—gave it a distinct lodge type look, but with a unique flare. Native rugs graced the hardwood floors and hung in various locations on the walls, as well as pots, baskets and native art. Lily's trained eye identified them as authentic, some older in origin, some recent pieces of native craft from different nations.

Lily stopped at a built-in shelf in the library and gave a small "oh." She tapped a finger on the shelf. "This piece...it's Oglala, right?"

Nhya stood quietly for a moment before moving forward and picking up the clay pipe. "My grandfather's." Her gaze swept over Lily. "How did you know it was Oglala?"

"I'm a museum curator in southern Arizona. I've worked extensively with Native artifacts."

Nhya's patrician features hardened with doubt and Lily realized that, after last night, it was no wonder. Lily cleared her throat. "You have no reason to believe this but I hold a respectable job and, for the most part, I'm an extremely average woman."

There was another awkward moment of silence before Nhya's eyebrows rose. "Museum curator, huh?"

"That's right," Lily said, her gaze straying to other artifacts on the shelf. "These pipe bags are lovely, too. The bead and quillwork gives them away as Oglala. Beautiful." Lily longed to reach out and touch them, feel their history, but it wasn't done. Not without an invitation, which Nhya had not extended. Not that she could blame the woman. As far as she knew, Lily was some raving drunken slut who'd decided on a whim to while her time away at a dude ranch to shop for a husband.

Yeah. Right.

If she only knew...

Feeling her face flush with heat, Lily took a deep breath and turned toward the hallway. "Well, I don't want to keep you."

Nhya continued to appraise Lily with slightly suspicious eyes. "I think the boys have an itinerary all set for you. I'll show you outside."

The breeze was cool and the sun warm as Lily followed Nhya toward the enormous stable area. Nhya had given her a straw hat to wear that tied under her chin and Lily was grateful for the shade of the brim. Not to mention, if she tipped her head just so, she could scan the yard for Mr. Prick without it being too obvious.

The thought of seeing him again sent a delicious thrill through her abdomen and Lily wondered if this was the type of thing her cousins had been yapping about. That sexual energy that heightened every moment, punctuated every thought and action. Lily had only had two semi-serious relationships in the last ten years and, instead of a bang, each had started with gentle interest and ended with as much punch as a mild spring wind. No real entanglement. No messy commitments or emotions. Which is how Lily liked it. They had been...pleasant. Nice.

Booorrring...as Aunt Viv would say.

Lily curled her lip at the thought. She understood her aunt's point but Lily had learned early on it was easier not to make those deep connections. Not to hope for that unconditional love. Maybe it would have been different if her mother had been around to make up for her father's utter lack of warmth or compassion. Hell, even a small measure of affection from him would have been nice.

"Miss Whitman?"

Lily snapped out of her pity party long enough to meet the gaze of the very object of her torture. The throbbing pulse flooded back, low and fierce.

Get a hold of yourself, girl, Lily reprimanded herself, then was unable to contain a giggle,which earned her an instant scowl from Mr. Prick. She bit her lip and decided that she wouldn't let him get the best of her. He may not want her but damn if she'd give him the satisfaction of knowing she wanted him.

Lily squared her shoulders and tipped her chin. "You may call me Lily."

Shain snorted and Nhya stepped between them, hands raised. "Ooookay… I'll leave you in Shain's capable and," his sister threw a look over her shoulder. "*Professional* hands." Her focus returned to Lily, her gaze serious. "Remember to listen carefully, Lily, as a lot of the work the men do is dangerous. Do exactly as they say and you'll be fine. Before you know it, it'll be supper time and maybe it will be a good night to star gaze." Nhya smiled wide, then after giving her brother another pointed look, strode back to the house.

It wasn't until that moment, as she stared at her retreating back, did Lily realize Nhya wouldn't be staying with her. That she would be, for all intents and purposes, one of the guys for the day. *Crap.* How did Nic and Bri ever think she could do this?

"You done ogling my sister's ass?"

Lily's gaze snapped back to Shain. "*Excuse* me?"

Shain's full lips quirked as he fixed her with a cool look. "You can drop the Miss Priss act. You might have fooled my sister but she sees good even in me. It's just the way her heart's wired."

"You mean she *has* a heart, unlike her prick brother?" Lily said, anger burning in her chest even as her traitorous body longed to sidle closer to Shain. Smell his male scent. Taste his—

The smack of leather brought Lily's attention to his large hands where he'd slapped his gloves into his palm. Her thoughts went back to the moment in the room when that well-formed hand had landed on her ass.

Oh, you've got it bad, girl…

Get through the day, Lily thought, her face warm, her tits aching. *This man may not want me but there are many more afield.* Her gaze strayed to the other men scattered around the yard. She spotted Darrell saddling a dappled gray mare and lifted a hand to wave enthusiastically. Even from a distance, Lily could see Darrell's face color as he tipped his head her direction then went back to yanking the saddle straps tight.

A hot hand clamped onto her upper arm and Lily turned back to Shain. "Take your ha—"

After a quick shake, tall, dark and handsome leaned down, his spicy breath brushing the top of her head. "Stop it. As of right now, you'll keep your eyes, hands and intentions to yourself or, so help me God, I'll—"

In a moment of complete insanity, Lily pushed herself forward into Shain's chest. His male scent washed over her as she raised her face directly beneath his strong, stubbled chin. "Or you'll what?" she whispered against the sienna skin of his throat. "Spank me again?"

She felt the growl before she heard it and Lily squeaked in shock as she was propelled forward. Through the paddock gate. Across the dusty hard-pack and then, in one seamless move, tossed onto the back of the biggest black horse she had ever seen. Her hat tipped sideways, then fell to the ground as she settled across the girth of the saddle. The ebony equine rolled its eyes and snorted loudly. Lily gripped the pommel and yanked her legs away from the horse's twisting head. Not a horse. A monster. A huge, black monster with very big teeth that were bared in a lippy whinny that sounded more like its master's grunt than a horsy bray.

Before she could try to dismount, Shain swung up behind her, his thighs and broad chest pinning her in place. With his body pressed tight against her back and his arms encircling her, he took up the reins.

Shain wheeled the monster around with a jerk and, in seconds, they were riding through the gate and past the ranch hands that'd stopped working to stare. "I'm taking Miss Whitman on a quick tour, boys. We'll meet up with you later," Shain called out.

"Wait," Lily started, "where do you think you're taking—"

Shain heeled the stallion and the black devil launched himself into a run that slammed Lily against Shain's chest. She held on to the saddle horn for dear life, the landscape a blur as they sprinted through the waving grass toward a stand of trees north of the ranch. A peculiar mixture of horse, leather and Shain's intoxicating scent filled Lily's nose, and her heart beat triple time.

Where is he taking me? And why?

The 'why' part left Lily weak and she could already feel a dampening in her panties. It didn't help that she was pressed up tight against the saddle horn, her crotch rubbing with each pounding stride. In a matter of minutes they were across the open expanse and coming up on the tree line—fast. Shain gave a gentle pull on the reins and the black beast slowed to a canter, then a trot and, with a quick flick of his wrist, the stallion turned and slid right between the rough-barked pines into the shaded protection of the wood.

As her eyes adjusted, Lily was able to take in the breathtaking beauty. Ponderosa and short leaf pine rose in columns, tufts of green spreading beneath them like an organic carpet. The stallion picked his way between the trees, then down a slight embankment studded with granite boulders. As they descended, Lily heard the distinct chime of running water. In moments they passed through a thick wall of pine and underbrush into a secluded clearing. Lily barely had a chance to take in the fact that they'd arrived at a brook before Shain slid them both off the black beast's back and into the waving grass.

"Hey—"

Lily's breath left in a whoosh as she found herself upended over Shain's stocky thigh, his knee nearly pushing her breasts completely out of her blouse.

He wouldn't...

With her face only inches from the ground, the scent of rich loam filled her nose and Lily opened her mouth to demand Shain let her up. Instead a squeal popped out as a broad hand connected with her backside.

"What in the hell do you think you're do—"

Whack!

"Are you crazy?" screeched Lily, her ass smarting through the worn jeans, her heart up in her throat.

Whack!

"Stop it," Lily said breathlessly, wondering if she really wanted him to or not. The realization almost undid her and she cried out as his hand came down once more, this time landing on her right cheek with little force.

"Are you going to behave?" came Shain's guttural growl above her ear, his hand tightening ever-so-slightly on her ass cheek.

"I didn't do anything!"

Whack!

"Agggh!" yelled Lily as his hand smacked her for the fourth time. And despite the discomfort, a curl of desire lanced straight to her clit. Lily bit her lower lip and began to wriggle on his knee. "Let me go, you prick!"

"Such language."

As she tensed for another blow, Lily realized his hand hadn't left her butt. In fact, the fingers of his hand were lightly trailing the seam of her jeans down the middle of her ass.

She held her breath.

"Girls with your looks should have more class, don't you think?" he whispered.

Lily shuddered involuntarily as his questing fingers came to rest on the inside of her thigh directly beneath her throbbing slit. She couldn't think. Couldn't answer. Her mind was crowded with images of his long, thick fingers running flesh to flesh over her slick pussy, then sliding inside, finding that pulsating center and—

Whack!

There was no scream this time. The gentler spank sent trills of pleasure vibrating through her and it was all she could do not to cry out in bliss. Not to beg him to yank down her jeans and do it on her bare flesh.

Lily moaned. *I'm hopeless*, she thought. *I've become seriously depraved in only a matter of hours...*

Chapter Five

Control. He had it. She didn't and Shain was positive he could restrain himself—until she moaned. That throaty groan arrowed straight to his already swollen cock and any thought he had of simply scaring the little bitch out of her wits then letting her find her way back to the ranch on foot fled like raccoons from a spotlight.

By God, she liked it.

As his eyes fastened on his hand covering the gentle curve of her beautiful butt, Shain knew he had to have her. Tart or not, for this moment, she would be *his* tart. *His* gorgeous piece of ass.

And he wanted nothing more than to see her ass, bare and reddened by his hand. His breath a growl in his throat, Shain lifted her with one hand and set her on her feet, facing away from him. With one arm encircling her waist, he reached around with the other and ripped open the buttons of her fly. As he pushed the jeans past her hips, he heard her gasp and Shain's cock pressed so tight against his Levi's he had to undo his own fly to relieve some of the pressure.

As Shain sat back down on the smooth stump, he upended Lily over his knee once more. Her pants pooled around her ankles, leaving her luscious cheeks fully exposed. Shain's breath caught as he took in the pale perfection of her skin and the firm roundness of her slightly pinkened ass.

"God, you're beautiful," he heard himself say, then frowned. Shain had no intention of letting this little vixen know the effect she had on him but his brain seemed to be on vacation. He laid his hand softly onto the reddened flesh and felt her shudder at his touch. Shain slid a finger across her crack and down the roundness of her cheek stopping only a fraction away from the heat of her slit. He bent low across her back, the stimulating scent of lilies and summer blooms filling his nostrils. "So, are you going to behave now, *Lily*?" Shain allowed his finger to trace lightly around the outside of her steamy lips. "Or do I need to clip your stem?"

In response, Lily's legs spread and her back arched, causing Shain's hand to brush against her pussy. Heat and dampness coated his fingers and Shain hissed, his body gripped with a whip-tight tension that could be relieved only one way.

Shain lifted Lily and placed her on all fours on the grass in front of him. In moments he knelt behind her, pulling her jeans and panties all the way off. With quick hands he shed his own jeans and stifled a groan as his cock sprang free. He wanted to spread her cheeks and drive himself all the way to her core but that would be too quick. Too abrupt. A woman like this — a body like this — demanded attention. Shain wanted to taste her. Touch her. Know her, in every aspect. Possess her.

With blood pounding in his temples, Shain dropped to his knees and jerked her backward until his mouth connected with the small of her back. He laved his tongue across the flat area centered above her hips, relishing her salty taste. She was so small, his hands nearly touched on her flat abdomen where he gripped her. Controlled her.

His hold tightened. "Do you want me to taste your other places, Lily?" Shain murmured against her skin. He felt her quiver. Shain ran his tongue in a zigzag motion down one cheek, breathing warm on her exposed and glistening slit. "I didn't hear you, Lily... Do you want to me taste you?"

"Why?" she started, her voice husky and soft and, if Shain didn't know better, laced with insecurity. "Why are you doing this?"

Shain froze. *Why?* Wasn't it obvious? With all of her "I dare you to fuck me" performance, he was as randy as a stallion during a rut. He was only doing what *she* wanted. She should be happy about it. Overjoyed and ready to please him in any way he desired.

As his gaze eased over the luscious ass in front of him and then the pink, beautifully swollen lips aching for his tongue, Shain smiled. There was no doubt that she wanted him. It was just another game she was playing. A little head trip to keep him guessing.

Well, good luck messing with *his* head. She wanted to play games? Shain had a few she could sink her teeth into.

"I haven't done anything, yet, darlin'," Shain purred against her bare flesh. With deliberate slowness, he moved his hands lower around until they slipped inside her inner thighs. With the tips of his fingers, he spread the outside of her damp lips, exposing her crimson nub to his burning gaze.

"Beautiful," he breathed, his face even with her intimate areas, his groin throbbing with need. Unable to restrain himself, Shain dipped his mouth in for a taste. As his lips and tongue connected, he felt her buck, driving him deeper as he sampled her sweet essence. Seizing her tight, Shain controlled the depth of his thrusts by pulling her back into his ministrations, loving the feel of her bare, wet pussy slamming into his face and the sudden gasps of pleasure exploding from her tender mouth.

Sweet...so sweet... And even with just his tongue, Shain could sense how tight she was. How perfect she would feel around his cock. How friggin' amazing it would be to thrust into her over and over again while she begged him for more. Shain reached under her blouse and cupped a breast that had swung loose of its lacy bra. The nipple was crystal hard and, as Shain squeezed, Lily cried out and quivered against his still-twisting tongue. Shain grinned as he felt her orgasm take her and, with a guttural rumble, lapped up her creamy juices while lightly rubbing her pebbled nipple against his palm.

"Does this answer why, darlin'?" Shain said as he pulled away, his hands fastening on her hips long enough to spin her to face him.

Mistake.

Her deep green eyes were dark, her face flushed with passion, her pink lips parted and her breath coming fast.

She was the most beautiful thing Shain had ever seen. Anywhere. Horseflesh. Woman flesh. Land. Mountains. Nothing compared to what sat before him in that secluded glade. And he wanted her like he'd never wanted anyone or anything before.

"Fuck me," Shain whispered, knowing intuitively that life had just flung him airborne in a rodeo ring of very pissed off, horned bulls.

* * * * *

Lily couldn't catch her breath. Couldn't reconcile that she was sitting bare-assed in a fantastical Montana glade facing a rough, uncultured, drop-dead gorgeous cowboy who'd just given her the most amazing orgasm of her life.

Her eyes lowered. "Oh, wow," tumbled from her lips before she could slam them shut. *Naked* monster cowboy with the biggest cock she'd ever seen—not that she'd seen many— right in front of her. Standing at attention and so thick Lily thought maybe she was seeing things. A strange side effect from all the blood rushing from her head to other…parts.

Then his whispered words hit her. "Wh-what did you say?" she asked, her body trembling, even though it wasn't cold. Even though beads of sweat glistened on her breasts and back.

His gaze rose and Lily was captured by its smoldering intensity. He opened his mouth but no words came out. Until— "Shit."

She couldn't take her eyes off his face. Incredibly, he looked…*mad*. Pissed off. Like he had before he kidnapped her, took her to a deserted wood, whacked her butt, then… Lily's face colored. *What is wrong with this man? Does he want me or not? What kind of game is he playing?*

Lily began to cast around for her pants, embarrassment burning through her where, moments before, only passion had simmered. Scrambling to her feet, she made a beeline for the pile of clothes a few feet away. Tears burned and she scowled, forcing them away. *This mental prick isn't getting tears out of me again.*

As she grasped the faded jeans, Lily heard Nic's voice in the back of her mind. *What are you doing, Lil? This is what you're here for. Wasn't it fantastic? Didn't it feel great? Turn around. Turn around and look at him.* Lily's lip trembled but she took a deep breath and turned, the clothes clutched in her hand.

He was standing now. Six-feet-five-inches of beautiful male glory. His thick hair curled slightly where it rested on his neck and, even though his sculpted body was crisscrossed with scars, it screamed with an electric potency that stole her breath. Her eyes flicked downward—then widened. *Oh, God.* And he was still hard. His cock stood away from his pelvis as if it had a life all its own.

Moisture flooded Lily's already wet slit and she shuddered. Nic was right. What was she doing? She had this god of a man, rough and uncultured as he may be, in front of her. Naked. Horny. And even with an attitude, he was the finest looking man Lily had ever had the pleasure of standing naked in front of.

And regardless of what he *said*, his body sure as hell wanted her.

Lily dropped the clothes to the ground. There was no one here to judge her. And, by God, she wanted him. All of him.

And if he turns you down? Lily's green gaze narrowed and she smiled softly. *He won't. I'll make sure of it.*

With butterflies buzzing in her stomach, she stripped off her shirt, then her bra and cupped her breasts. Forcing her eyes to meet his, she began to trace circles around her nipples, teasing the pink buds to taut attention. The grass was cool beneath her feet, the air saturated with the scent of rich soil, water and green growing things. And then there was *his* unique aroma. Even from a distance, it enveloped Lily's senses, making every nerve tingle and jump.

"So," Lily said quietly. "You just spank 'em, lick 'em and leave 'em, is that it?"

His expression darkened and then, incredibly, he laughed. The deep rumble rippled through her and Lily almost let her fears get the better of her. It was amazing what kept coming out of her mouth. Things pre-Wolf Springs Lily Whitman would never *think* of saying.

He took an intimidating step forward. "I have to say, sweetheart, you've got a way about you."

With grim determination, Lily put one foot in front of the other, bringing her inches away from Shain's sculpted chest. The deep bronze of his skin looked warm and inviting under the bright morning sun and Lily knew she had to touch him. Feel the hard, broad length of him. As her eyes trailed his body, curiosity burned fresh. There was a freshly healed gash over his ribs. Older ones on his upper chest. More low on his hip. The telltale mark of stitches on his abdomen and on his shoulder.

"Pretty damn ugly, aren't they?"

Shain's harsh voice snapped her out of her dreamy perusal. She looked up into a once more hardened and closed expression. "No. Not ugly," Lily responded and she meant it. It was strange but the scars did nothing to detract from the man's charisma; in fact, they only added to his overall sense of magnetism. It was how he'd *received* all of the scars that left Lily with a healthy respect for his high tolerance for pain. "How—" Lily started. She raised a tentative hand and touched the slightly raised ridge of tissue on his ribs. His stomach muscles contracted at her touch and Lily went to pull away but Shain's warm hand covered hers, pinning it against his body.

"No. Don't pull away."

His voice was a rough whisper and confusion tickled Lily's already spinning head. "Does it still hurt?" She flattened her hand against his body, feeling the scar tissue and taut muscles underneath.

He made a sound close to a rumble and a thrill shot through Lily's abdomen, leaving her breathless.

Be brave, Lil, go for it!

Lily took a deep breath, nodded, then slowly ran her hand over his abs. "I wouldn't want to hurt you," she managed to get out, her heart thumping triple time. His hips shifting slightly to give her hand more freedom. Lily paused as her fingers brushed the tight curls near the base of his erection, her eyes riveted on the rigid, thick shaft. *God*, but he was huge. Lily's clit vibrated simply with the thought of what it would be like to have him inside her. Riding her…like she had ridden the mechanical bull at the bar.

Steeling her courage, she wrapped her hand fully around his length, the heat of his silken flesh warming her palm like a firebrand. She heard him suck in a breath, his entire body tightening. A chill chased its way up Lily's spine.

He's mine. For this moment. I'm the one in control.

The thought was incredibly titillating. Consumed with the sensation, Lily began to caress him, lightly at first, relishing the strong, yet soft feel. From base to stem, she pumped his staff with demanding strokes. The delicious, intimate act heightened Lily's already aroused state and her juices flowed freely, wetting the inside of her thighs. Shain moaned…a deep, animal sound as his hands fastened on Lily's shoulders.

"Darlin', I'm going to come if you keep that up," he said through gritted teeth.

Lily swallowed, her entire body tingling with longing. "That's the idea, isn't it?" As much as Lily wanted him to fuck her, she'd realized they didn't have any condoms out in the boonies, so it wasn't something they could do. He'd given her pleasure, she would return the favor.

Tit for tat, right?

Before she knew what was happening, her hand had been wrenched free of his pulsating shaft and Lily found herself pressed against the hard length of him, from shoulder to hip.

"Wrap your legs around me," came Shain's dark, demanding voice.

Lily did, her body shuddering as her pelvis met his rock-hard abs, her wetness pressing against his hot flesh. She gasped in surprise as Shain started to walk in long strides across the clearing. Lily twined her arms around the back of his neck. "What are you doing?"

He didn't answer, instead he gave a sharp whistle. Lily heard the unmistakable sound of trotting hooves and turned her head enough to see Shain's black beast approach from beyond the bend of the creek. What was he going to do? Stick her on the back of the horse buck naked?

The stallion came up alongside them and Lily could feel the heat simmering off the beast. With one hand holding her ass, Shain reached out with the other and wrenched open the saddlebag. Out came what looked like a towel, a small bag and something else he simply tossed onto the ground. Near the bottom of the bag, Shain smiled as he held up—

His wallet. With a wolfish grin, he flipped it open and with his teeth pulled out a small foil package.

Lily's jaw dropped. "You...you brought a condom?" she sputtered.

"Never know when the need might arise," Shain drawled, that canine grin still on his face.

It wasn't until Shain spun with her and began walking back to the lush patch of grass did Lily realize what finding the condom meant.

He's going to screw me.

Lily's eyes half-closed as she thought about Shain's rigid cock directly beneath her ass. *I'm doing it, Nic and Bri...I'm actually doing it.* Lily gazed up at Shain's strong jaw and smiled. *And you two were right, it's damn fun.*

Thoughts of her cousins were swept aside as Shain gripped Lily's butt and lifted her until they were face to face. Captivated by his smoldering gaze, Lily could only stare. So much passion. Fire. And a sense of strength that Lily had never encountered before.

"I'm going to fuck you, darlin'," Shain said matter-of-factly. "Any problem with that?"

His brazen words should have left her angry. Ashamed. To Lily's astonishment, they had the opposite effect. She ran her hands up either side of his corded neck and into the soft waves of his thick hair. "The only problem I have is that you're not already inside me, cowboy."

Lily found herself lifted above Shain's head, her breasts even with his face, and a hot tongue clamped around a nipple. She gasped, the sensation arrowing directly to her already swollen lips.

Wrapping her hands in his hair, Lily threw back her head. Blue sky filled her vision as the sound of Shain sucking and lapping at her breasts filled her ears. His mouth was hard, demanding, his hands squeezing her ass as he held her suspended. Lily's entire body quivered with need. Her nerves throbbed with desire.

"Please…"

Shain lifted his head and an eyebrow. "Please? Please what, Lily?"

Lily shifted against him, her breasts aching for his tongue. *I can't say it*, she thought. *I can't be as blunt as he —*

A warm, thick finger found her clit. He flicked the tip across her nub, then inserted it up to the first knuckle. Lily groaned and tried to lower herself onto the finger but Shain held her up. Refusing to let her impale herself. "Come on, sugar. Please, what?" He twisted his finger ever-so-slightly, putting gentle pressure on her throbbing center.

"Oh my," Lily moaned, biting her lower lip. "Please fuck me. Please…please."

Chapter Six

That did it.

If he waited one more second to bury himself within her, he'd explode. And it would be messy. Violent.

"Wrap your legs tight," Shain said gruffly.

She did.

"Tighter!"

Once he felt her heels lock behind his hips, Shain dropped his hands and ripped the condom open that he'd stowed in the spot between their sweat beaded bodies. He couldn't seem to get it out of the package fast enough. His chest heaved and his cock bucked as he palmed the sheath over his near-painful erection.

"Now unlock your legs."

Amazingly, Lily listened and loosened her legs on either side of his hips. No time for words. Or games. Shain needed this woman like a man dying of thirst needs water. With his hands on her hips, he leaned back, lifted the long legged goddess and brought her down one inch at a time onto his engorged rod. He paused, letting her adjust to his girth, gritting his teeth to keep himself from ramming it into her all at once.

"Friggin' goddamn," Shain exploded, the sensation of her slick, fiery hole almost making him come as he finally filled her to the hilt. Taking a deep breath, Shain fought for control. He held her still, her legs wrapped low on his hips, his cock buried deep within her.

And then she moved. Pushing out with her pelvis and driving him deeper, her hand twining behind his neck. Shain cursed again, his muscles cording in response to his need.

Determination raged and Shain lifted her free of his cock. She cried out in protest.

"Oh, you're gonna get what you want, darlin'…and maybe a little more."

Shain brought her down with force, his own body jerking along with hers at the pure pleasure of it. Damned if she was going to make him come this fast.

Again, Shain lifted her and again he pulled her down, her pussy smacking against his groin. His biceps bulged, his breath coming fast as he lifted her over and over, fucking her with every inch of his body, from leg to arm to grinding pelvis. Soft, then soul-deep moans fell from Lily's parted lips, driving Shain. Raising every sensation a hundred fold.

Fingers dug into his shoulders and back, an animal growl in her throat, and Shain looked down on her face as he rammed her up and down on his shaft. She opened her eyes and, as their gazes locked, Shain was utterly lost. It was as if they were outside of time. Beyond the everyday screw that felt good but was only another part of an ordinary day…

Her face was radiant, her eyes brilliant green under the summer sun.

"Damned if you aren't the finest woman I have ever seen," Shain whispered, not regretting his words. He was always honest. Even if it hurt. Even if it might come back to bite him in the ass later.

"You, too," Lily managed to choke out, her breath ragged, her pert breasts rubbing against his chest.

Shain grinned, his hands still yanking her up and down. "What? I'm the finest woman you've ever seen?"

Lily's glossy eyes popped wide and her mouth formed an "o". "What? No! No, I meant you're the finest looking man—"

Her words were cut short by a deep moan and Shain's expression darkened with passion. He pumped into her, striking her very core. "You take my breath away, woman."

"Oh, God," Lily cried, her legs wrapping tighter around Shain's hips. Two more thrusts and Shain felt her release. Her pussy contracted around his cock like a clamp. Shain gritted his teeth and fought the need to spill, right then and there. *Damn.* He'd never felt anything like that before.

Lily collapsed against his chest, her legs loosening.

Now it was time to get down to business.

Shain dropped to one knee, taking Lily down with him. He gently unwrapped her hands from behind his neck and laid her onto the grass. The air was cool on his still-throbbing erection. "Look at me, Lily."

She opened her sated eyes, their centers dark and sultry. Her gaze trailed him from chest to groin and Shain's need raged as her eyes rested on his cock. "You," Lily started. "I never thought a man could be…" She took a deep, shuddering breath. "So phenomenally large."

Shain slid between Lily's legs. "All the better to fuck you with, my dear," he growled. "Now spread your legs."

Lily's eyes widened. "You…aren't done?"

An eyebrow raised. What did she think he was, a total loser? "I'll tell you when I'm done. Now spread your legs."

After a blink or two, Lily shifted her thighs wider apart, her teeth worrying her succulent lower lip. Shain could sense her nervousness. He didn't understand it, coming from a woman with an obvious agenda, but he had to admit it was convincing and damn erotic.

"Touch yourself." It was almost a whisper but, after a slight hesitation, Lily responded by trailing her hand down her hip to her thigh and then through the narrow strip of hair above her slit. Shain's eyes fastened on her peach tipped fingers as they drew slow circles around the outside of her folds. He could almost taste her essence, feel her satiny lips.

Her fingers lightly teased her glistening slit, then slid inside. Lily gasped and Shain growled, his breath coming fast.

"That's it, darlin'. A little deeper." She plunged a finger inside her wetness and Shain nearly lost it as Lily cried out.

Yanking her hand free, Shain gripped her ass and buried his cock inside her creamy hole. The heat of her channel enveloped him and, with his knees digging into the turf, Shain rode her like an angry bull, driving every last ounce of his feverish need into her willing body.

She met his thrusts, her hips thundering against his, and for a moment, Shain worried she might break in two but that fear was pushed aside as he caught her whispered words: "Fuck me, Shain. Ohmygod, you feel so perfect."

Shain gritted his teeth and pulled her long, shapely legs up onto his shoulders, allowing his cock to delve even deeper. Lily's fist pounded the ground as Shain pounded into her welcoming center. She felt perfect around him. Hot, tight and, as Shain looked into her striking eyes, an electric sensation like nothing he'd ever experienced washed through him, from the top of his head past his heart and straight to his throbbing cock.

His thrusts were rhythmic and deep, his body wire-tight as he fought against release. Shain was consumed by the feel of her, the scent, and somehow his mind registered that sex with this amazing woman felt different than any other before. It was more than her gorgeous body. Her beautiful face. Her luscious mouth…

Shain groaned as his climax built like a wave rushing toward the shore and he was helpless to stop it. As the tip of his cock hit the apex of her womb, Shain exploded. He roared, his body pumping his seed into the condom. Shain prayed that it would hold.

His skin flushed, his heart nearly bursting with the force of the experience, Shain sucked in air and scooped Lily up, rolling them both onto their sides. He waited until his breathing was back to semi-normal before he reached down and pushed the condom off, relief washing through him when he realized it was still in one piece.

Listening to Lily's labored breathing, he wasn't so certain about his partner. He set the condom aside and focused his attention on the gorgeous, naked blonde in front of him. Shain ran a hand down her silky hair, stopping on her flushed cheek. What just happened? Sex. Just sex...so why did he feel so uneasy? Like how he used to feel when his grandmother caught him stealing bread fresh from the oven. It only took one look from her dark eyes to make him own up to his choices—

"So," Shain said, his hand stilling. "That was some action, darlin'."

Her eyes lifted and, if Shain didn't know better, he'd swear they were now smoky green with anger. "It's nice to get a little...action...every now and again, isn't it?"

Shain was quiet as he studied his gilded Lily's arresting face. *There's something a little off about this piece of work.* Shain sighed. No. He couldn't quite think of her as "a piece of work" anymore. The realization burned.

Keep it light, Shain...don't be a fool. Don't get caught with your hand in the oven.

"Right," Shain replied, sitting up. He ran a trembling hand over his chest, brushing away clinging blades of grass. "Gotta have some fun, now and again."

* * * * *

The man was a wolf. A beautiful one, but a dirty dog nonetheless. Lily sat up, irritation and embarrassment burning in her gut. What she'd just experienced...*God.* Incredible. She'd had no idea sex could be like that.

But it had been a game to him. A fun little romp.

Lily stood shakily and turned. Closing her eyes, she fought to regain her composure. A romp. That's exactly what she'd wanted, right? Exactly what the bet was all about. Finding a guy who turned you on and simply having the time of your life. No strings. No commitments. So why did she feel so infuriated? So let down?

Wiping a hand across her face, Lily took one more deep breath, then walked to where her clothes lay scattered across the grass.

I'm just not cut out for this.

The soft chime of the narrow river drew Lily's attention and she took a moment as she picked up her jeans to look around. Stunning. From the sparkling silver of the water and polished rock of the bed, to the thick green forest that lined it against the backdrop of jagged mountains spearing the clear blue sky.

It was the type of land that *could* grow a man like Shain Stevenson. Rugged. Hard yet mystical. Lily raised an eyebrow. Not that she'd seen a spiritual side of Shain yet.

Lily pulled her blouse over her head and, on the spur of the moment, walked to the creek, her jeans and panties draped over her shoulder. The water rippled with life and Lily knelt, dipping in a hand.

Cold. But clear. Before she could change her mind, she waded in and splashed her privates clean, goosebumps erupting up and down her calves.

"Darlin', you've got the nicest legs in the county, hands down."

Lily straightened, her breath catching in her throat at the sound of Shain so close behind her. Her heart thrummed at his compliment but she knew she couldn't get caught up in his flattery. Mistake it for affection.

Feeling brave, Lily turned to face him. Her nose nearly bumped his chest. Dang it. She hadn't thought he was *that* close. She sidestepped and forced a smile. "You're quite the flatterer, Mr. Stevenson."

Shain's eyebrows rose. "'Mr. Stevenson'? Honey, after that trip down pleasure lane, I'd think we'd at least be on a first name basis."

Trip down pleasure lane…now that *was* an adequate way to describe what happened.

Lily raised her chin. "All right, *Shain*...so, what now? Aren't you supposed to be taking me on a tour of the ranch?"

Sporting a wolfish grin, Shain waded right into the cold stream and, without so much as a shiver, dunked himself all the way under. He came up dripping, glistening diamonds of water. "Yup. Let's start here." He stood, water sluicing off the chiseled muscles of his chest and waist. "This," he said, opening his arms. "Is Wolf Creek, pleasant waterway in the summer, torrent stream come early spring."

Lily forced her eyes away from Shain's luscious body and, after shaking the water off her legs, stepped out and pulled on her panties and jeans. She cast around for her boots. She couldn't even remember taking them off, or Shain taking them off for her. Her face heated at the memory of what they'd just done.

Lord. I'd do it all again. Right now. Right here.

Shaking her head, Lily managed to roll her socks over her feet and sink them into the boots, knowing the longer she stayed undressed, the more her mind would be playing over other, intimate, possibilities.

Once fully clothed, Lily purposely ignored Shain and strolled down the creek toward a mound of upturned earth over a gentle rise. Anything to get her away from Shain. From smelling his heady scent. From thinking about sitting on that horse between his thighs...

She cleared the berm and, as Lily looked down, a tingle erupted across her shoulder blades. She sidestepped down the crumbling embankment, her eyes scanning the numerous depressions in the rocky riverbed soil. Stopping at a pile of fine grit, Lily knelt and plunged a hand into the chert, running it through her fingers.

"This is a dig," Lily said to herself. "Albeit a disorganized and messy one."

"What the hell..."

Lily stood and turned at the sound of Shain's gruff voice. He was standing above her bare-chested, hands on his powerful jean-clothed hips, a deep scowl on his face. "Goddamn them."

"Someone's been scrubbing for artifacts on your property," Lily said.

Shain crunched down the embankment, his smoldering gaze taking everything in. "Shit, these assholes don't know when to stop."

"What were they looking for?" Lily asked, her curiosity piqued, her professional outrage building.

Running a hand through his damp, thick hair, Shain let out a strained breath. "Like you said, artifacts. Native artifacts." Shain froze and his face hardened. "Why *did* you say that? How did you know that's what this was?"

A tickle of unease unfurled in Lily's abdomen. "It—it's what I do for a living."

Shain's eyes narrowed.

"Wait!" Lily held up a hand. "Not stealing. I'm a native artifacts curator for a museum. I travel all over to purchase things for our collection. *Legal* items," she added, alarm building in her gut at the stormy look on Shain's darkly handsome face.

He was silent, his face a study of mistrust and suspicion. Like his sister's earlier. Lily closed her eyes. *That's* why Nhya had reacted the way she had to Lily explaining her profession. They were embroiled in some sort of clash with treasure hunters. Lily knew the type. Some could be quite dangerous, depending on the value of the items they were after.

Shain crooked a finger. "Let's go."

Chapter Seven

Lily would have liked a *real* tour of the property but, as things stood now, Shain was in no mood to play tour guide. He was quiet as stone the entire way back to the ranch, and Lily resigned herself to the fact that, despite his current rosy disposition, Shain had helped her discover something truly surprising about herself: she liked sex. No, 'like' was too weak a word. She *loved* sex.

Her gaze strayed to Shain's strong arms on either side of her. More accurately, she loved sex with *Shain*. She frowned, trying to pull her thoughts away from such fantastical notions, like Shain feeling the same way about her. Wanting not just her body, but her smile, her laughter, her company.

Crap. Lily closed her eyes and breathed out through her nose. The sun was still high in the sky by the time they made it back to the paddock. Darrell opened the gate and they rode inside. Shain handed Lily down, before sliding off himself and giving the reins to one of the hands Lily had yet to meet.

"Ma'am," the red-headed cowboy said with a nod.

Lily tried to straighten her legs once she was on solid ground, wincing at the myriad of subtle aches between her thighs. "Hello," Lily responded, wondering if the young man could tell from her face alone what she'd been up to. Her cheeks colored, and she turned away, searching for Shain.

He was already through the gate and heading for the front door of the house.

Well, Lily thought with a scowl. *Goodbye to you too.*

She turned back to the redhead who was unfastening the saddle. "I'm Lily and you are…?"

Without looking at her, the cowboy said: "Peter, ma'am. Peter Owens."

Lily forced a smile. "Nice to meet you, Peter." Shain Stevenson be damned.

"Well, Peter. How about you show me how to remove the, er, tack, and how to rub this beast down?"

Peter stopped what he was doing and raised a coppery eyebrow. After a blink or two, he nodded. "All right. First thing you do is…"

* * * * *

Day one, and Lily had de-saddled her first horse, mucked his stall and portioned out feed to over twenty horses before helping rake and shovel the fouled bedding into a compost pile at the back of the barn. All this after a mind-blowing morning of sex-in-the-grass with the most gorgeous, work-toughened man she'd ever met.

Lily groaned silently, wiped a hand over her sleep-deprived face and forced herself out of bed. What had she been thinking yesterday? She hadn't been. She'd been feeling instead. Feeling all sorts of mixed up, fantastic, frightening emotions and sensations.

Her fingers gripped the oak frame, wood biting into the flesh beneath her nails. Shain. It still seemed so unreal.

Berating herself, Lily stood and stretched, grimacing at the myriad of aches and pains that assaulted her. She stared at her reddened palms. Darrell had handed her a pair of gloves halfway through the day, for which Lily was eternally grateful. The guys had told her more than once that she could knock off, take a rest, but Lily had refused.

She couldn't tell them that the work did wonders at keeping her mind off Shain, who'd stormed out of the house and driven off at top speed. And who was absent the entire day.

After spending a pleasant evening with Shain's sister, Lily had found she enjoyed the young woman's company and the atmosphere of the Red Bear immensely. As well as learning about her dangerous cowboy. Nhya talked about her brother with deep affection and respect. She told Lily about his fame as a circuit rodeo wrangler and all the many trophies and titles he'd earned, which explained the scars. Stories of him as a precocious, yet hardworking and focused child. Lily was beginning to think that maybe a week at the ranch wouldn't be so bad, *if* Shain didn't haunt her at every turn. *If* she could stop looking over her shoulder expecting—wanting to catch a glimpse of his smoky eyes and broad shoulders.

Unable to stop herself, Lily went to the window and yanked the curtains aside. She drew in a sharp breath. Shain's truck was parked in the drive. He must have come back sometime last night, or this morning. A thread of longing curled in her belly as she gripped the windowsill.

Calm down, girl...he might not even speak to you.

Dressing in a flash, Lily tripped down the stairs, trying to *not* look as if she was going to a five alarm fire. Hushed voices drifted out from the kitchen and Lily slowed, trying to settle her scattered thoughts.

"I don't trust her, Nhya."

A sigh. "Shain, you haven't given her a chance. I'm telling you, she's for real. I can sense it and—"

"Damn it, Nhya, we can't afford to rely on 'feelings' when it comes to the ranch. You need to let me take care of things..."

Lily pressed her back against the hallway and bit her lower lip. As quietly as possible, she sidled down the hall and made a beeline for the library. A quiet place to think. To escape. The muted light and dark wood welcomed her and she slipped into an overstuffed leather chaise at the back of the room.

He didn't trust her. Could she blame him? There was obviously something serious going on with the ranch both financially and personally with the looters. It *would* seem pretty coincidental to have a museum curator show up in the middle of all of that. Even so, Shain's words cut at her heart and left Lily empty, hollow.

"I need to leave." Lily said the words aloud, needing to hear something concrete to aid her conviction.

She was up the stairs nearly as quickly as she'd gone down. Lily grabbed her suitcase and began stuffing it with what few items of clothing and personal products she had. She looked down at the form-fitting jeans and worn, comfortable boots and shrugged. She'd have to mail the clothes back to Nhya once she got home.

You'll lose the bet.

Her cousins' voices chimed in tandem in her mind. Lily closed her eyes. Yeah, so what. She'd lose the bet. There were other, more pressing things she'd be losing. A friendship with Nhya. The experience and nearly magical atmosphere of the ranch. And Shain.

Lily roughly pushed hair out of her face. "He doesn't want you, Lily. Don't be a jerk."

"What in the hell do you think you're doing?"

She spun, suitcase in hand. Shain filled the doorway, his darkly handsome face thunderous. Lily's heart fell into her toes. Gripping the handle, she straightened and put on her best scowl. "I'm leaving."

Shain took a step forward, his bulk blocking the doorway. "Like hell you are." His hand shot out and gripped her suitcase. Shain yanked, Lily held on, which brought her stumbling forward within an inch of Shain's chest. Muscles rippled beneath the tight t-shirt. He obviously wasn't dressed for the day yet. Lily looked up. His hair, still damp from the shower, curled darkly against his neck. Lily could barely draw breath, her entire body electrified.

Forcing her gaze to meet his, Lily dug for courage. "I—I need to go."

Shain's brows rose. "One day of honest work and you're ready to throw in the towel, is that it?"

Lily's eyes narrowed. "What?" She released the suitcase and knotted her hands on her hips. "Absolutely not. I did fine yesterday, and if you'd been around, you would have noticed." As soon as the words left her mouth, Lily regretted them. Damn it. Why should she care if Shain was there to watch her work?

"That so?" With a flick of his wrist, Shain tossed the suitcase to the side. It landed on the bed with a plop. "Well, I'll be here today. Why don't you show me?"

Trapped. Lily bit her lower lip, her mind racing. Damn, damn, damn. She had to admit she hadn't wanted to leave anyway but the thought of working all day alongside Shain left her weak, breathless. Among other things…

But how could she refuse?

Lily took a deep breath and looked up. "Fine. But the first time you do something inappropriate, I'm gone. Got it?"

Shain's face fractured into that wicked grin. "You mean something like this?" Before Lily could react, Shain's hands were on her shoulders, pulling her in and up. His lips captured her in a bruising kiss and Lily's entire body shuddered with longing. She eased her lips further apart to take him in, a groan building in her throat, wetness dampening her panties.

Suddenly Lily found herself back on her feet, lips cool and swollen, her head spinning. Shain stepped outside the doorway, a confident, wry smile on his luscious lips. "Be downstairs and ready to work in fifteen minutes. If you're up to it."

For some absurd reason, Lily did as Shain demanded. Her heart thudded triple time as she made her way outside to the barn. Darrell was waiting for her, a strained expression on his face.

"Good morning, Darrell."

"Ma'am," Darrell replied, tipping his hat.

Lily studied the hardened cowboy, noting he looked as if he were about to deliver the worst news of the year. "What is it, Darrell?"

He cleared his throat. "Well, um, it seems as though we have a pretty full schedule this morning."

Lily's eyes narrowed. Shain. She scanned the barn and yard. "I imagine we do." Her gaze refocused on Darrell. "But I'm up to it." Lily slipped on her gloves. "Let's get started."

Eight hours later, Lily had helped mend two paddock fences, turn four huge, steaming piles of crap into the compost pile and curried every horse in the stable. Leaning against the water barrel near the pump, Lily groaned, her entire body screaming with fatigue.

And she'd done it all without catching as much as a glimpse of Shain. Her tormentor. Her nemesis. Damn him. Lily smacked her palm onto the dampened wood. Shain hadn't even been interested enough to hang around and see if she *could* manage the workload.

So why did you stay?

Lily squelched her little voice and stripped off her gloves. "Because I'm an idiot. A romantic, out-of-my-head fool."

Watching from the loft, Shain ground his teeth. Damn but the woman looked great, even after a back breaking day of hard labor. Even with her hair tangled around her flushed cheeks and stubborn chin. Shain's gaze cut to the front of her blouse that gaped from where she'd unfastened two buttons to cool off. His cock jumped at the mere thought of shoving his hand inside that small opening and cupping her pert breasts. Cursing under his breath, Shain sat back on his heels and closed his eyes. Eyes that had trailed her for an entire day...from afar. Shain knew when he'd stood in front of her in the house that morning, her lips red from his kiss, her green eyes flashing, that he'd never be able to work with her all day without throwing her over his shoulder and taking her into the nearest dark corner.

Without licking every inch of her delicious body. Twice.

Stifling a groan, Shain sidled to the open loft door, scanned the yard, then slipped down the rope to the hard-pack below.

He had to get away from the woman. From her rich, wildflower scent. From the deep longing that rattled him like a May tornado every time he saw her.

"You're a horny dumb ass, Shain," he mumbled to himself.

But he knew it was more than that. The whispered voices that were always present in his days growing up on the ranch had been pestering him since he'd stepped off the plane and onto home soil. Since Miss Whitman's arrival, they'd been practically screaming.

Pay attention! She's special.

"Shut up," Shain muttered as he walked around to the back of the house where he'd parked Nhya's truck. "Back to plan A."

Once inside, Shain took a deep breath and wiped a hand over his tired eyes. He'd spent all of last night riding range and keeping an eye on the house. Damned if he'd let the looters anywhere near his sister or Lily. He'd only been able to catnap in the loft, his thoughts and dreams tangled around a leggy, gorgeous blonde. Shain started the Toyota and pulled around to the front of the drive. Darrell stood just outside the barn. Their eyes met and he tipped his head. Shain returned the nod, then drove out. Only Darrell knew what Shain had been doing.

Shain couldn't imagine why the looters were still digging up random areas on the ranch. His jaw clenched and his hand tightened on the wheel. He'd gone into town yesterday and reported the trespass...again, getting nothing but a sigh and head shake from their seventy-something sheriff. Again, the sheriff said he didn't have the manpower to set up a sting operation out at the Red Bear. There were over six thousand acres. And there was no telling where they'd show up. Did Shain want him to call in the feds?

Hell no, had been Shain's heated response. He'd damn well take care of things himself. He'd stormed out, calling Darrell on his cell to tell him what he intended to do. And could he bring Windigo out to the culler's shack on Cragen Butte?

Darrell did what Shain asked but his foreman was none too happy with Shain insisting he search for the looters on his own. Shain made it quite clear that Darrell's job was to watch over the ranch and the women inside it. After much grumbling, Darrell had agreed and left Shain in the north pasture with his horse, a Winchester, food and water enough for four days and nights and curt instructions to not get himself killed.

But Shain couldn't resist coming back this morning. His rationale was that he needed to talk to Nhya, let her know what was going on. Truth was, he wanted...no, needed to see Lily. Touch her. Smell her. Find out if the intense feelings he had for her were a fluke.

They weren't. Seeing her that morning in her—*his*—room, getting ready to leave, had left him feeling as if someone had punched him in the gut, then jabbed him in the heart. The thought of her simply disappearing from his life before he had a chance to figure things out made him want to throw her suitcase out the window and toss *her* onto the bed.

But he couldn't. He needed time. Time to figure things out. Think. Plan. Investigate who Lily Whitman really was and what she meant to him and the ranch.

Which is what he was going to do. Shain pulled out his cell and punched in Lance's number.

Now.

* * * * *

It's none of your concern. Shain can come and go as he pleases. He made it quite clear he wasn't interested in a relationship, so who was she to anticipate more?

A damn fool, that's what she was.

To think she'd really wanted to prove something to that man. Lily slapped her soaked bandana over the clothes line and rubbed her tired back.

Peter and Darrell had turned out to be a font of information. They both talked about the Red Bear with obvious pride, as did the other hands. Lily learned that the Red Bear was one of the most respected cattle and horse ranches in the state. Their stock was quality, with both horse and bovine garnering top dollar.

But Lily detected unease at other moments. It didn't take a genius to figure out the ranch might be experiencing a financial crisis. There were lots of little clues. The weathered siding on both the house and the barn. A plumbing issue that she'd overheard Nhya ranting to Darrell about when she'd brought them out their lunch. Then there was the little matter of having not gotten their last paycheck. Lily knew Peter hadn't meant for her to overhear that when she'd rounded the corner. She pretended not to have heard.

And as Lily splashed cool water on her face from the trough outside the house, she began to realize *why* Shain and Nhya had kept her on as a boarder, despite her abhorrent behavior at the bar. They needed cash. Nic and Bri *had* said something about the Red Bear being a new dude ranch. But Lily had thought surely there would have been other guests.

That she wouldn't be the *only* one.

She sighed and dried her face on the towel hanging off the pump. Which is probably why Shain had given her that little speech this morning. That damn dare. And she'd fallen for it.

None of this is any of my business. Not their financial straits or the looters rooting up their land for native artifacts. Or the fact that the mere thought of Shain leaves me breathless with anticipation.

Even so, Lily kept thinking about the Oglala pieces inside the house, how beautiful and wild the ranch and its property was. And what a shame it would be for a family to lose such a home, such a history to thieves, whether it be a bank or looters.

"You're welcome to use the shower inside, Lily."

Lily turned at the sound of Nhya's voice, reassured by the friendly smile on her stunning face. "Oh, I will later, believe you me." Lily pushed straggles of hair away from her flushed cheeks. "It just that I can't fathom the thought of walking up those stairs at the moment."

Nhya smiled. "Come on. I've got a porch swing with your name on it."

On the wide veranda surrounding the ranch, Lily eased her aching bones onto the padded swing and took the glass of iced tea offered. "I know I said it before but you have a beautiful home. Great employees, too."

"Yes, we do," Nhya replied with a nod, her gaze fastened on the bunk house. "And it's my intention to see that things stay that way."

Lily started at the underlying thread of warning in Nhya's tone. "You think I'm somehow a threat to your ranch...to you?"

Nhya's chocolate eyes pinned Lily where she sat. "Are you?"

A fluttering filled Lily's abdomen and she swallowed around her sudden discomfort. "I'm going to be honest with you, Nhya. It wasn't my idea to come here." Lily took a deep breath and ran a hand through her now loose hair. "My cousins arranged everything." She smiled wryly, her cheeks flushing pink. "They think I'm too uptight and they figured tossing me outside my comfort zone would loosen me up, so to speak."

Lily's confession earned her a puzzled look from Nhya. She hoped she hadn't confused the poor girl even more but she'd felt a sudden intense need to be up front. Well, mostly up front. She liked Nhya, liked the Red Bear, and liked Sha—well, liked *parts* of him. They obviously had a lot going on with the ranch, and Lily had no intention of being a wrench in their works. She'd finish out her stay, they'd get their money and Lily would be happily on her way back to home soil.

"Well," Nhya said, a smile tugging at the corners of her mouth. "I'd say they succeeded, wouldn't you?"

A laugh popped out and Lily's face reddened even more as her thoughts zoomed back to her and Shain's escapade four days ago in the glade. "Uh, well...yes, I guess they did." Lily cleared her throat. "Seems as though I've been doing all sorts of things completely out of character."

Nhya placed a cool hand on Lily's arm. "When that happens, it's usually your inner spirit exerting some pretty serious influence." She dropped her hand and frowned. "Not that it's any of my business."

Lily appraised Nhya, a warmth building in her chest. "This is going to sound strange but I don't mind hearing that from you. It's as if..." Lily closed her eyes. "I don't know. I feel comfortable with you, Nhya, secure. I wish I could say the same of your brother." Opening her eyes, Lily cursed her loose tongue. *What is it about this girl that makes me want to spill my guts?*

"Shain's been going through a tough time lately." Lily sensed the pain behind her words. "We all have, actually. And as strong as he is, things are wearing on him. And you—" Nhya gazed at Lily again, her eyes hinting at something Lily couldn't quite put her finger on. "You've shaken big bro up a bit, I think." She grinned. "Which, in my opinion, is a good thing."

Relief washed through Lily. She couldn't imagine why. Shain had made it obvious a relationship was the last thing on his mind. She chewed her lower lip and grasped for something to steer their conversation down a different path. "Uh, I hope you don't think I'm prying but, when Shain and I were out earlier in the week, we stumbled upon an excavation site. Are you having problems with looters? I've had some experience in this area. Maybe there's something I can do to help?"

Nhya went ramrod straight.

"I'm sorry. I shouldn't have asked."

"No." Nhya raised a hand. "No, it's fine that you did." Her soft brown eyes fixed on Lily. "This entire incident has been infuriating. And after your find the other day, Shain, well, you saw him. He went ballistic. It makes us crazy that we can't protect our land better, from those..." Nhya's fists clenched and her jaw hardened as she swallowed the words she wanted to say. She flicked her long, straight hair back off her shoulder.

"This all started before my parents' plane crash. Of course we didn't know that until afterward."

Silence stretched and Lily knew Nhya was deciding how much to tell her.

Nhya leaned back in the swing, her fingers drumming on the painted wood. "Our mother and stepfather died in a crash a month ago but it wasn't until Shain and I started going through the books that we realized the ranch was in a financial bind. And that wasn't the only thing. There was a private collector who'd contacted Mom and Frank about doing some excavating on our land to look for a particular artifact he'd been researching. Of course they said no, which is when the trouble started."

"Can I ask what this collector's name is?"

A narrow gaze found Lily. "That's just it. We don't have a name, just a company, which turned out to be false. After Mom and Frank told him no, they started finding pieces of land torn up. In total these past five months, we've found ten separate areas," Nhya said with a growl. "Six of them since the funeral four and a half weeks ago."

Lily was quiet for moment, her mind ticking through various collectors, some of whom were known for not always being on the up and up. "Do you know what he's looking for?"

Nhya's shoulders tensed. "Maybe. Does it matter? These bastards have no right to it, whatever it is. This is *our* land. Our heritage."

"You're absolutely right." Lily met Nhya's unblinking stare. "But that won't stop them from searching for it. Whatever it is, it must be something big. Pipes, beads, bags, pottery...none of those things would be worth the risk he's taking." Lily's thoughts churned. "He's looking for some sort of native holy grail." She knew she'd hit the nail on the head when Nhya's olive face paled.

"You don't have to tell me, Nhya, but you need to realize that these types of characters are dangerous. And if you really do have this artifact, whatever it is, you need to take serious steps to protect it."

Her gaze snapped back to Lily and Lily was taken aback by the cool determination in the young woman's face. "What would you suggest?"

A tingle zagged up Lily's spine and she took a moment to process all that had been said — and not said. "First, I'd file police reports if you haven't already done so. Then I'd state very publicly that you've shipped this item off to whichever museum you think would best accommodate it." Lily paused. "Even if you don't."

Nhya was still for a moment, her face raised to catch the last brilliant rays of sun. "Why should he believe that?"

"Or she."

Lily's words earned her a stunned look. "I — I never thought it could be a woman."

"Oh, yes," Lily said, her gaze straying to the beginnings of a spectacular Montana sunset. "Some of the most passionate treasure hunters are women." Lily stared at Nhya. "As to why he or she will believe you. You show them the goods. Not them directly, but the local paper. Land yourself and the artifact on the news, and it becomes nearly untouchable. It makes it solid, real, and if it's a native artifact, going public gives ownership to an entire nation of people who will want to follow its fate."

Lily paused to sip her tea, the cool liquid washing away some of the dust. "Basically, you're making the risk too dire. Illegal collectors don't want to be noticed. They don't want to raise flags."

Her words seemed to hang in the air like lightning bugs, and Lily knew the young woman was dissecting her every word, motive and comment. Lily couldn't blame her. In fact, she admired her for it. She was also burning with curiosity over what the artifact might be and whether or not Nhya and Shain actually had it in their possession. The researcher and curator in her was intensely interested, while her practical side warned her to keep her distance — for more reasons than one.

"I'll think about what you said," Nhya finally responded.

Lily simply nodded, more words feeling out of place under the fire-red sky.

Chapter Eight

"That's it. Now tighten it one more notch. Rialda likes to hold her breath at the last minute."

Her face a study of concentration, Lily yanked as hard as she could on the saddle's leather strap, slipping the metal flange up. The mare blew out a heavy sigh and gave her a somber look. "Nice try, girl." Dropping the stirrups in place, she patted the dappled mare's neck and beamed at Darrell. "How'd I do?"

With a quick nod and a smile, Darrell flipped the reins over Rialda's neck onto the pommel. "Not bad for a first time." He motioned to Lily. "Up you go."

Since Rialda was several hands shorter than Shain's devilish beast, Lily mounted with ease and waited as Darrell adjusted the stirrups.

Shain.

Her gaze searched the yard for the hundredth time. No truck. It had been four days since her last encounter with Shain. She couldn't imagine where he was, what he was doing.

With another woman, most likely. A man like Shain would have his pick.

The thought made Lily's gut burn and her heart ache.

"Lily?"

Blinking, Lily looked down into Darrell's lean face. "I'm sorry, what?"

"I asked if you were ready to try some range riding."

Pushing Shain from her mind, Lily straightened and stared out at the open range. "Absolutely."

Darrell instructed her to walk Rialda around the corral for a few minutes, letting them get accustomed to one another while he and two of the other hands finished saddling their mounts and packing up the supplies they'd need to spend the entire day out on the range.

They were going to check fence lines, the free roaming herd and, from the under-breath conversations, Lily suspected they'd be looking for signs of the looters as well. As she urged the gentle Rialda in a circle, Lily's thoughts wandered. She and Nhya had spent the past four evenings chatting and looking at the wide expanse of stars that exploded across the Montana sky. Lily found Nhya so easy to talk to, confide in. Lily had talked about her life back in Bisbee, and in Tucson before that. About her distant father and her mother, who had died when she was only eight. She'd even related stories about her gorgeous cousins and her college days at Stanford with her best friend, Susan.

It was nice to look back and see that, despite the tragedies of her childhood, she'd had good times, made strong female connections and developed a solid love for history and the items that told the story of their past. She hoped that had come across to Nhya. Lily was disturbed by the thought that Shain and Nhya might still hold her in suspicion. Nhya's behavior didn't indicate that she did but the beautiful young woman maintained a level of reserve despite her warmth.

And deep worry.

Nhya took to looking out the window for Shain almost as often as Lily. And as Lily leaned down to pat Rialda's neck, she found a coal of anger smoldering in her gut. Who did Shain think he was, making his sister worry like that? Didn't she have enough to stress about?

When she saw him she'd give him a piece of her mind, attitude be damned. He needed to be here to support his sister. And if they *did* have that artifact somewhere on their property, be it in the house or secured somewhere else on the property, Nhya was at risk. They all were, actually.

A cool breeze rich with the perfume of sage, pine and mountain air stirred the wisps of golden hair that had already escaped the pins holding it up. Lily breathed deep and shivered as an electric tingle zagged down her spine. She'd felt that before, out in the glade with Shain near the dig, and again with Nhya as they'd talked about the artifact. It left Lily feeling dislocated, adrift, as if she were on the edge of something significant.

A sharp whistle shattered the moment and Lily twisted in the saddle to see Darrell waving from the gate. They were ready to go. With a cluck of her tongue, Rialda headed for the opening, her steps quickening when she realized they were on their way out.

"We're going to start in the east pasture, Miss Whitman," Darrell said, tipping his head her direction as Rialda trotted alongside his gray stallion.

"Sounds good," Lily responded, trying to push thoughts of Shain, Nhya and the ranch's issues out of her mind. The brief instant message chat that she'd had with Bri and Nic last night had done nothing to erase her unease. She had feelings for Shain. Feelings that had nothing to do with simply having a good time and being done with it at the end of the month. Sure, she was good at giving relationship advice to Bri but could she heed her own counsel?

Lily gazed over to where Shain's truck was usually parked and frowned. Not likely.

Interrupting her frazzled thoughts, Darrell introduced the other two hands. "Luke and Curt have been here the past month helping us catch up on jobs before fall sets in."

Lily gave them both warm smiles, which they returned. Luke and Curt looked similar enough to be brothers. Both had hair the color of raven's wings and, while Curt's was cropped short, Luke's hung in a tight braid all the way to the middle of his back. With their high cheekbones and midnight eyes, the pair were striking in a dark, brooding way.

"Heeyaw," cried Curt. He dug in his heels and his pale roan leapt forward, followed by Luke on his brown sugar pinto.

"Miss Whitman," Darrell said, his pale blue gaze all business. "Just follow us and don't ride any faster than you're comfortable."

Lily pushed the soft, tan wide-brimmed hat Nhya had given her low on her head. "Lead the way."

* * * * *

Shain grunted. Nothing. Nothing but an aching ass and hard-on number three from his thoughts wandering back to a tall, leggy blonde with full lips and a face and body that wouldn't quit.

He pushed his Stetson up on his forehead and tossed the piece of sweetgrass he'd been chewing. He winced as he flexed his left arm. Every part of him had stiffened during his fourth long night in the saddle but it was his cock that was intent on driving him mad with need.

"Shit," Shain murmured rubbing a hand over his stubbled face. He'd spent the past four nights roaming their acreage watching for looters, and each day spying on the ranch and trailing Lily's education with jealousy simmering in his gut. Lily had continued to throw herself into the experience with gusto and, as each hour passed, his respect grew. It didn't matter how difficult or dirty the job was, Lily did it without complaint.

As far as Shain could tell, Lily hadn't latched onto any other cowboy in his absence. Which thrilled and troubled him all in the same breath. He knew it was twisted but, if Lily went after someone else, it would release him from the overwhelming connection he felt for her.

Flicking Windigo's reins, he urged the stallion toward the hilly rise studded with old cedar and pine. If it had just been sex, why did he feel so different? Keyed up. On edge. All things that he needed *not* to be right now.

"Damn it," Shain muttered for the thousandth time. With powerful strides, Windigo climbed the hillside, his master leaning slightly in the saddle to provide the horse better traction. "What a mess."

He was still waiting on a call back from his buddy Lance, an FBI agent who worked out of Billings. He'd asked him to run a background check on Miss Lily Whitman. Lance had been keen to know what had prompted Shain to ask that type of favor, something his longtime friend never did. But Shain had been mute. "Just check it, would you, Lance?"

Of course his friend had agreed, with a promise to get back to Shain within seventy-two hours. Which was today.

On the hill, Shain paused to search the valley below. He fished out his binocs and scanned the treeline to the east. Nothing. Wait. Horses cresting the rise. He recognized Curt's roan, then his cousin Luke on the pinto close behind.

More movement in the distance. Another horse and rider. Shain's gut clenched. He'd recognize that blonde head and straight posture anywhere. *Lily*. On Rialda. And she was galloping hard, trying to catch up to Curt and Luke.

What in the hell was she doing out there with Curt and Luke? Where was—

Some of the fire in Shain's belly eased when he spotted Darrell's gray stallion at Rialda's flanks. Good man. He was tagging behind to make sure Lily didn't fall off and break her sweet little neck. Shain took a deep breath and went back to observing his gilded Lily. Damn, but she looked good in a saddle. Good enough to eat.

Shain grinned, his cock responding eagerly to the idea. Just as quickly, a band of protectiveness tightened around his chest. He should be the one riding with his ranch-hand trainee. Not Darrell. Or God forbid, Curt or Luke. Shain heeled Windigo into action and started down the hill. It would take him a while to head them off but it was only a matter of time. He knew they were on their way to the east pasture to check the fence line. He'd meet them there and take over Miss Lily's range riding *education*.

* * * * *

"Buffalo roamed freely here once. The herds numbered in the thousands."

As Lily's gaze trailed the vast expanse of waving prairie, she could well imagine the great herds of dark, shaggy beasts dotting the majestic landscape. What a sight it must have been.

"Have you lived in the area your entire life?" Lily asked Luke as their horses plodded the fence line. Darrell and Curt had ridden ahead to check the gate. They were on their way to join them.

He nodded, his braid slipping off his shoulder.

Luke wasn't much of a talker and, despite her best efforts, she'd learned zip about the handsome young man. Something about him struck her as familiar but she couldn't quite place what it might be. Even so, she felt comfortable with him. Safe. It was disconcerting how much she was relying on *feelings* and *instincts* since she'd been at the ranch. Where was the practical, sensible Lily Whitman? She hadn't even e-mailed her cousins last night like she'd planned. She gotten halfway through her message, then saved it to the drafts folder for later revision or deletion.

What was she going to say? That she'd dived into the bet headfirst and was so deep now she wasn't sure if she even *wanted* to go back to her old life? The thought left Lily feeling slightly ill and lightheaded. It was true. Lily couldn't imagine getting on a plane bound for Tucson in less than five days and melting back into her old life in Bisbee. How could she leave never knowing the outcome of the Red Bear? Nhya? And then there was Shain.

Stop thinking about him, Lily…

"Whoa."

Luke's soft call brought Lily's head up. The cowboy's deep eyes were focused on something in the treeline several yards away.

"What is it?" Lily asked softly, pulling Rialda to a halt.

"Something…in the trees," Luke said quietly, his shoulders tense.

That electrical tingle flowed through Lily once more, and she straightened, her gaze fastened on the gently waving pines. She could hear rustling underbrush. Something was moving in there. Something big.

Lily gasped, her hand flinging out to grab Luke's arm, which was stiff as a piece of petrified wood.

A massive, rust red bear emerged from the pines into the clearing. Even from a distance, Lily knew instinctively that bears weren't supposed to be *that* big. Or red as faded maple leaves before a frost.

Her heart hammered, her breath shallow, and, as the bear's massive head swung in their direction, Lily knew there was an unnatural intelligence behind those deep eyes.

That's crazy. Right? Crazy…

The bear sat on his haunches and chuffed so loudly Lily imagined she could feel the force of it from twenty yards away. *What was it doing?* With her blood thrumming, Lily turned to Luke. His gaze was still frozen on the bear, his body like granite. Lily squeezed his arm. "Luke," she whispered, "what do we do?"

After a second Luke responded: "We do nothing. For now. We stay still."

Which was when it hit Lily. Why weren't the horses freaking out? In every movie Lily had seen, when a predator showed up, horses went wild. *Their* mounts seemed totally unconcerned. Rialda was yanking out tufts of grass along the fenceposts and Luke's pinto was standing still but relaxed, its brown eyes blinking lazily.

"I thought you were supposed to scream and make yourself as big as possible if you encountered a bear," Lily murmured.

Luke didn't respond and Lily kept quiet, her entire body quaking. If Luke thought it safe for them to wait the bear out, then that's what they'd do. And wow…when would she ever get a chance to see such a creature? The beast was majestic, larger than life. And despite her fear, Lily felt a strange draw to the creature.

They sat in silence for a time, the soft breeze teasing at their exposed skin, hinting that fall was around the corner. As the light played across the bear's shining fur, Lily detected numerous colors in the animal's thick coat. It reflected the sun in shimmering waves, making it seem as if the beast actually glowed.

The bear's massive head swung her direction. It seemed to be staring straight at her! Tingles raced across her shoulder blades and down her spine as a low rumble reached her ears. It was coming from the bear! The sound reverberated through Lily's chest and her heart raced.

"Luke, are you hearing what—"

The unmistakable drone of hoof-beats shattered the moment and Lily and Luke turned in their saddles.

Shain!

He was thundering across the plain toward them; his stallion's neck stretched as its stride lengthened. Lily wanted to call out, stop Shain from ruining the moment, strange as it was. But Shain was riding as if the devil himself was on his heels. Sod churned as Shain pulled his horse up only feet away.

Lily couldn't help but appraise the impressive man in the saddle. He looked as if he'd been born to it and the hills. His strong jaw was flecked with a five o'clock shadow, which made him look even more dangerous, more weather-roughened. Lily's entire body vibrated as he pulled alongside, her heart hammering now for a different reason.

"Shain!" Lily called. "There's a—"

"Not anymore," came Luke's hoarse growl.

She looked back to the treeline. Gone! Lily scanned the area. There's no way something that big could have disappeared in a matter of seconds! "But, it was just there!"

"What in the hell are you—"

"A giant bear!" Lily exclaimed, her excitement getting the best of her. Making her forget how nervous she should be around Shain. How mad she was at him for running out on Nhya. And her.

Lily pointed to the trees. "There. It lumbered out and just sat and stared at us. I've never seen anything like it. It was red! Can you imagine such a thing? A rust red giant bear."

Shain's face went white, then whiter still as his gaze rested on Luke who nodded nearly imperceptibly in corroboration of Lily's story.

"It was probably a brown bear. Their fur can look reddish in the sunlight," Shain said gruffly.

Shaking her head, Lily urged Rialda forward. "No. It was red. And huge. Like, freakishly huge."

Shain grabbed her reins, pulling Rialda to a stop. "That's not possible."

Lily gazed at Shain's brown hand gripping her reins, then looked up. His expression was grim, indomitable…and something else. Fearful, perhaps? The realization sent that tingling careening down her spine again and Lily shivered as a sense of 'otherness' hit her.

"It's nothing. Just a bear." Smoky brown eyes crashed down on her with obvious irritation. "Weren't you told it was dangerous out here? Bears aren't the only predators."

Lily was speechless. He was *mad* at *her*? For going riding? What in the hell was the matter with this man? "Excuse me?" Her gaze went to Luke, who wasn't looking at either of them. "I was with *your* employees, Mr. Stevenson. Doing what I *paid* to do on the Red Bea—"

Ohmygod. Lily's hand went to her throat as her eyes cut back to the treeline. *The Red Bear Ranch.*

With a click from his tongue, Luke's pinto jumped forward. "I'm going to help Darrell and Curt." He tipped his hat Lily's direction, then gave a "Heeyaw!" propelling his mount from a side-stepping shuffle into a canter then a full gallop away from the fuming Shain and shell-shocked Lily.

Chapter Nine

Lily's attention snapped back to Shain, who sat frozen beside her, his hand gripping Rialda's reins. *We're alone. Again.* Lily's stomach flip-flopped and her mouth went dry. There was something not right about the whole business. The looters. Nhya and Shain's parents getting killed. The giant red bear.

Lily felt as if she'd landed in a Quentin Tarantino film. Uzi-toting killers were sure to spring out of the bushes at any moment, *while* she and Shain were having mind-blowing sex.

Wetness instantly flooded her pussy at the suggestion. *Ohmygod…I am depraved.* "Well," Lily stammered, pushing hair behind her ears. "I saw a giant red bear. You're not going to convince me otherwise."

Shain grunted and released her reins. "I suppose anything's possible."

She looked at Shain in surprise. The faraway, thoughtful expression on his face unnerved her. "Shain…your sister. We-uh-she's been worried about you."

Shain gave a ghost of a smile. "I called her the night before last. She's pissed but she'll get over it."

"Oh," Lily said, irritation pricking that she still had no idea where Shain had been or with whom. Jealousy flared and she flicked Rialda's reins. "We'd better catch up with the others."

She didn't get far. With a deep snort, Shain's stallion stepped forward, blocking her mount's path. Rialda bobbed her head against the black beast as the stallion nibbled her neck affectionately.

Lily sighed. Of course. Gentle, dappled Rialda and the muscled beast were mates.

"No."

"What?" Lily said, forgetting all about her anger as she stared at Shain's delicious lips, then his blazing brown eyes.

Dark eyebrows lifted. "I said, no, we're not catching up with the others." Shain pulled Rialda around. "Let's go."

"But, where are we going?" Lily asked, butterflies churning in her gut — and other areas.

Shain's smoky gaze glinted with deviousness. "A tour. I promised you one, didn't I?"

Remembering how their last 'tour' ended up, Lily's entire body cheered, with her mind quick to chastise. Shain cast one last glance at the woods before giving his stallion a nudge. Rialda jounced into action at the stallion's flank, taking Lily along for the ride. They cantered across the meadow toward the thick stand of trees north of the fence line. As they rode, Lily couldn't help but recall how erotic it had been to ride with Shain, the saddle rocking against her pussy, Shain's strong arms on either side of her, his lips above her ear.

This wasn't nearly as much fun but Lily consoled herself with the thought that it was probably a good thing. She was getting way too attached to a guy who thought it was normal as apple pie to stay out all night on a whim.

They rode in companionable silence for nearly an hour, skirting the fringe of the woods. Forest scents and sounds mingled with the steady pound of horses' hooves and soon Lily was immersed in the earthy rhythms. Her mind continued to trip over the bear sighting and Shain's strange reaction to it. She vowed to question him again at the first opportunity.

Suddenly Shain pulled up and Lily's mount followed suit, slowing to a trot, then a full stop. Shain stood in his stirrups and Lily frowned, wondering what he was looking for. With a quiet cluck of his tongue, the stallion bobbed his head, then side-stepped into the densely packed woodland.

"Wait!" Lily called, urging Rialda forward. Rialda didn't hesitate. She slipped past the low-hanging feathery pine boughs and into the shadowed forest. Once inside, Lily waited impatiently for her eyes to adjust and scanned for Shain. There! Only a few yards away, sitting straight in the saddle and staring at her with that unfathomable, polished mahogany gaze.

"What are we doing?" Lily asked, her heart up in her throat. "Is this part of the tour?"

Shain nodded. "There's something I want to show you." With a flick of his reins, he turned the stallion and started down what Lily realized was a faded trail weaving between dense, moss-covered trees. She and Rialda followed, Lily's curiosity piqued. A gentle breeze worked more hair loose from the knot she'd fashioned this morning before setting out. Lily felt her entire body relax as they traveled in slow silence, the calm, nearly supernatural ambiance of the forest cocooning her. Birds called softly overhead and Lily saw the occasional gray squirrel scurrying for a better vantage point to watch them pass.

The trail soon faded away to nothing and Lily watched in amazement as Shain picked out a path, leading them down a narrow, granite studded ravine, past a swift flowing brook and up the other side into woods so thick it seemed almost impossible that they would be able to pass through.

Shain seemed perfectly at home in the forest, his focus fastened on the nonexistent trail, leaving Lily plenty of opportunity to observe his powerful back and sun-streaked hair. Hmmm...she longed to touch her lips to the rich, sienna skin of his neck and kiss him in that tender spot between jaw and ear.

She shivered, desire raging through her at such a simple thought. The sky broke through the canopy overhead in sparkling slivers and Lily raised her face, taking a moment to quiet her raging hormones.

"Lily."

At Shain's deep rumble, Lily opened her eyes. "Oh," she said breathlessly as her gaze fell upon a small, secluded glade.

They'd stepped out into a clearing that was only a half acre or so, with grass so green it was nearly painful to look at. Blue sky crowned the picturesque scene and directly in the center of the clearing sat a log cabin, its weather-roughened logs warm and golden under the bright August sky. Wildflowers in blue were scattered throughout the lush meadow, competing with tiny white daisies that frosted the tops of hummocks.

It was amazing. Beautiful, in a desolate, wild way that left her breathless with anticipation. Of what, she wasn't sure but, as her gaze found Shain's, she realized that his eyes were dark with the same uncertainty.

Shain dismounted, gave his horse a pat on the rump, then walked over to Lily. He held up a hand and Lily took it, slipping off of Rialda, who, as soon as she was free of her rider, trotted to catch up with Shain's stallion. Shain's hand was hot against her palm and Lily breathed deep, trying to quell the burst of nerves tumbling inside her.

"What is this place? Does someone live here?"

"Not anymore." Shain raised a hand and pulled the pins free, allowing her hair to tumble free. His fingers trailed lightly against the side of her neck and Lily shivered, her lids heavy.

"Used to be my great-grandfather's place. Then my grandmother's."

Lily opened her eyes to view Shain's stubbled jaw only inches away, his lips at her temple where he placed a gentle kiss. Every nerve in her body sang at the sensation.

Shain pulled her forward. "He built it over a hundred years ago. Left the reservation to reclaim land that his family had lived on for the past four centuries."

They stopped in front of the weathered but solid door. "That would have been a big risk back then," Lily commented, understanding enough of the territory's history to know that just wasn't done—with much success.

Shain's mouth quirked into a grin. "Not such a risk. He didn't even tell his family where he was living until later."

His hand rested on the latch for a second before he opened the door and ushered Lily over the threshold. The tingling was back and she drew a deep breath as she stepped inside. Her gaze traveled the expanse of the modest room. It was clean, uncluttered and pleasantly cool. A large stone fireplace occupied one wall, shelves on another and, off to the right was a small, yet serviceable kitchen with an old-fashioned wood burning stove.

Light from a large plate glass window spilled across a sofa and two handmade chairs in the center of the living room. A single doorway led to a back area.

Lily looked up as Shain entered. "My great-grandfather, Hank, built everything by hand or dragged it up on horseback."

"He sounds amazing," Lily commented as she walked further in to stare at the beautiful woven blanket draped across the sofa. "Did he live here until he passed?"

Shain strode to the shelf and picked up a beaten silver frame. "He did. But it wasn't a long life." He handed her the picture. "I like to think it was a happy one. At least that's how our grandmother—his daughter—told it."

The frame was cool in her hand and Lily nearly gasped she stared at the yellowed photo. She gazed at Shain, her heart tripping. "You look so alike." Lily's finger traced the spitting image of her handsome cowboy. With longer hair and a few added years, they could be twins. And their eyes held the same intense, passionate gaze.

"You said he died young," Lily said softly as she handed the photo back to Shain. "What happened?"

"He was shot." Shain placed the photo back onto the shelf.

Lily moved in closer, trying to shake off the tingling that was back with a vengeance. "You mean, like murdered, or accidentally shot?"

Shain's expression hardened. "I mean assassinated. And by someone he trusted."

A cold knot tightened in Lily's abdomen. "But why?"

It wasn't quite a shrug but Lily was certain that Shain was suddenly uncomfortable with their subject matter. She wanted, no, *needed* to know why. "Shain, why would someone your great-grandfather trusted decide it would be a good idea to kill him?"

"Because the bastard wanted something he had no business having."

"What did he want?"

Shain's jaw clenched and Lily could feel the tension seeping off of him like steam escaping a pressure cooker. "It doesn't matter. The point is…" He turned to face her, his arms crossed, biceps bulging from beneath the rolled-up sleeves of his blue cotton shirt. "You can never be too careful. Too cautious about those you let in and those you keep out."

Lily leaned in, her head tilted to capture all of Shain's steely countenance. "So am I in?" She waved a hand. "Or would you like me to step back outside?"

The man didn't so much as blink but the nearly imperceptible twitch at the bottom of his jaw told Lily she'd struck a nerve. Her face colored as hot flesh fastened around her upper arms.

"Why don't you tell me, Lily?" He leaned in until his luscious lips were nearly even with hers. "Do you *want* to be in?"

"I-I…" Lily ran her tongue over her lips, imagining how it would feel to have his mouth fastened on her breast. His hand sliding across her damp slit. "Oh, hell." Collapsing into the startled cowboy, Lily pressed her lips to his. He was still for only a fraction of a second before he crushed her to him, his mouth welcoming hers with fervor. Fire spread to every limb as Lily deepened their kiss, her tongue snaking out to play along the even contours of his white teeth.

"Goddamn," Shain whispered into her mouth before lifting her entirely free of the floor and into his arms. Lily kept her arms wrapped tightly around Shain's neck, her face pressed into the male-scented flesh between cheek and ear. In three steps, they were inside the small bedroom. Lily looked down a second before she found herself on the raised bed. The handmade patchwork quilt was soft beneath her back, and as she gazed up at her startlingly handsome lover, she knew there was no going back. No pretending that her experiences at the Red Bear with Shain and his family could simply be a pleasant holiday memory. She had feelings for this bear of a man.

Feelings...

Shain made quick work of his buttons, shedding his shirt to expose the bronzed breadth of his sculpted chest, all the time feasting on Lily's face, drinking her in.

"Take off your shirt and shoes," Shain commanded.

Lily sat up, her hands moving on autopilot to do Shain's bidding, blisters and aches forgotten. She pulled off her boots, letting them *thunk* to the floor before slowly unbuttoning the white shirt. She slipped each arm free before tossing it into a corner, leaving her in her skintight cotton chemise. She hadn't worn a bra and her nipples were diamond-hard, thrusting against the thin cotton with direct intent.

Shain was motionless above her, his eyes hooded. "Now your pants."

With quick movements, Lily pushed the jeans past her hips and down each thigh until she was on the bed in only her low-rise lace underwear and top. Lily moved to her knees on the bed, putting her even with Shain's taut abdomen. She leaned in and pressed her lips to the scar above his right hip, then traced the ridge with her tongue. His skin was salty, warm — exactly as Lily knew it would taste. Delicious. Perfect.

Raising her hands she rested them on Shain's hips, then hooked her fingers into his belt loops and pulled the cowboy closer to her demanding mouth. "So beautiful," Lily whispered, repeating Shain's words to her in their first explosion of lovemaking. She felt his hands move to her shoulders where they pushed the thin straps of the chemise down onto the curve of her arm, exposing the tops of her breasts.

Smiling, Lily allowed her tongue to trail over the rippled muscles of his abdomen, lapping gently at the scar near his hip and stopping at the top button of his jeans. Moving her hands past his hips, she slid them across the denim to the button fly. Lily took a deep breath and worked each silver button free. Seeing and feeling the massive bulge pressing against her fingers, Lily's heart hammered and goosebumps shivered across her back and shoulders. Sitting up, she pushed his jeans over his powerful hips, sucking in a breath as his engorged cock sprang free.

Shain leaned back slightly, his hands tightening on her shoulders as his breath rasped out. Desire raged through Lily and, with quick hands, she shoved his jeans down into a pile at his ankles before kneeling lower and breathing out across his member. Bringing up a hand she cupped his testes, entranced by the weight of them on her palm. The spicy, male scent of him filled her senses and Lily used her other hand to grip the base of his cock. "I need to taste you," Lily whispered before flicking out a tongue to lap the pearly bead at its tip.

Shain's throaty growl spurred her on and Lily wrapped her mouth eagerly around his cock, twirling her tongue over the firm curve of molded flesh, sucking him in deeper as her hand worked along his length.

She was rewarded with an almost painful moan. His pelvis rocked into her mouth, his hands gripping her shoulders. Lily took him in, loving the feel of him inside her mouth, unable to control her own moans around his cock.

"Woman, you'd better find something else for your lips to do before I—"

Lily gripped his ass and worked into a fierce rhythm that gave no quarter and asked none. With a roar, Shain bucked against her, spilling himself into her mouth. Lily drank him in, using her hand to milk him dry before releasing him and sitting back on her heels.

Looking up, she smiled, feeling wanton and not giving a damn.

* * * * *

"Stand up, woman," Shain ordered, every fiber of his body whipcord tight.

Lily moved to her feet to stand on the bed, her toes sinking into the soft quilt. Her breasts were now even with his face, the tiny camisole top barely concealing the high, pale globes and their hard-tipped nipples.

One look...one thought of her going down on him like she just had, and Shain was hard again. So goddamn hard he wondered if the woman didn't possess some kind of magic.

Magic...the power of spirit.

Shain shook his grandmother's voice out of his head and refocused on the outstanding woman in front of him. Damn, she was a goddess in more ways than one and Shain realized that he could no longer think of her as a needy little manhunter. Shain had been intimate with enough women to know the difference between a woman wanting to please and a woman wanting to love. There was more than simple lust in her actions.

Miss Lily Whitman was loving his body, not fucking it. And as Shain's eyes drank in every delicious inch of her, stopping at her flushed face and swollen lips, he wondered if she realized it herself. Their eyes met and he was lost in the ocean-deep green.

As long as she keeps loving me, I don't care what she thinks she believes.

Shain knew that couldn't be true, not with all that was at stake, but at the moment it was the only reality he cared about. He lifted a finger and drew it down the side of her cheek. "Take off your shirt."

She hesitated only a moment before pulling the camisole over her head with both arms and tossing it aside. Her breasts were taut with anticipation, the pink buds hard enough to cut glass. Shain longed to crush her to his mouth but that wasn't how he wanted things to go—yet. She needed to understand that he was the one in control. That he was the master of what happened here on the ranch. This was *his* world and, if she wanted to play in it, she had to follow his rules, his lead.

With his hands in fists at his side, Shain leaned next to her ear. "Turn around and take off your panties. Bend over when you do it, so I can see your firm ass."

He pulled back and smiled at the startled look on Lily's face.

"Now," Shain said with a flick of his wrist. He had to force himself to stay motionless as she turned and, with slow movements, hooked her fingers into the narrow straps of her panties.

Sweat beaded on Shain's forehead at the erotic sight of her easing the panties down inch by slow inch. When she reached mid-thigh, she bent at the waist and Shain wrapped a hand around his throbbing erection in an attempt to restrain himself from plunging into her wet core. As she bent lower, she exposed a glimpse of her glistening lips and Shain's grip tightened on his cock. When her panties were finally over her feet, Lily paused and stepped out, her body quivering.

"What now?" came her low purr.

Shain could tell she was still uncertain, but trusting enough to play along, which only heightened his intense craving.

"Turn around and face me," Shain said firmly.

Lily did, her lips parted, her eyes dark. His gaze fell to her beautiful, upturned breasts. "Play with your breasts," Shain said.

After a slight hesitation, Lily's hands moved to cup the soft globes. She closed her eyes as her fingers found the pebbled tips.

"Open your eyes," Shain growled. "I want to see your desire and I want you to see the effect you have on me."

Lily's gaze dropped to where Shain was palming his erection and her eyes widened. She licked her lips, then pinched and rolled her nipples, a moan escaping. "That's it, my gilded Lily. Imagine my tongue on your breasts, sucking, moving from one to the other."

Shain swore under his breath. He had to touch her. Had to feel her writhing beneath him. Shain placed a hand on her thigh and Lily gasped. "Don't stop," Shain said. "Feel yourself, Lily. Understand how perfect you are."

She did and Shain was able to turn his attention to her creamy inner thigh. With her standing before him, her hands plucking at her nipples, Shain stroked her like a cat, moving his hand higher and higher until it brushed the soft strip of hair above her clit. Her knees nearly buckled but, with a sharp command, she stayed upright. Shain eased his fingers across her damp outer lips, his breath strained as he fought for control.

Lily moaned and Shain moved in closer until he could smell the freshness of her skin.. "Open your thighs wider for me, Lily."

She did, her hands still circling her breast. "Shain…please…"

"Are you saying I'm not pleasing you?" Shain asked softly before he delved a finger up to the knuckle into her creamy slit.

Lily cried out and fell against Shain's neck and chest. He held her up with one hand, the other still deep within her. With a steady rhythm, Shain thrust in and out. One finger, two…bending them to stimulate her red hot core.

"Oh," Lily said breathlessly, her silky hair brushing Shain's chest, sending tingles racing across his shoulders and into his already burning groin.

"Keep touching your tits, woman," Shain said gruffly, his own need near choking him. "And tell me what else you want me to do."

Lily gasped, her pelvis moving on his hand demandingly.

Shain increased the speed of his thrusts, feeling her close, knowing she was on the edge of climax.

"What else do you want me to do, Lily?"

She moaned and threw back her head, exposing the graceful lines of her neck and the sensitive hollow at its base.

With one hand on her ass, Shain lifted Lily a bit higher until his head was once again even with her tits. He blew across the red, puckered tips. "Tell me, Lily. What do you want?"

"Shain, damn it," Lily stammered, moaning again as he flicked her clit. "I want you to fuck me, lick me, do whatever in the hell you want to with me, as long as you do it. As long as— Oh!"

Shain wrapped his mouth around one pink nipple, his tongue dancing across the hardened tip. He withdrew and Lily cried out again. "As long as what, Lily?"

Lily's fingers found his head, pulling him toward her breast, but he resisted, his gaze finding hers. "As long as what?"

She gave a quiet sob, her lip quivering. "As long as you don't break my heart, you big prick!" she finished with a shout.

Shain went still, his finger still deep inside her, his mouth next to her perfect tits. Her words echoed inside him. *Does she mean them?* Hurt and uncertainty lurked in her forest green eyes and Shain recognized a measure of fear. The vulnerability that comes from letting someone in. Giving them space in your life, in your heart.

Crap.

One minute his whole attention was focused on saving the ranch so he can get the hell out and back on the road and, in the next, his thoughts and feelings were so tangled up in a woman, it was all he could do to function.

Feeling a push at his chest, Shain looked up. "Get off," Lily said and Shain realized she was on the verge of tears. "Damn it, let me go!"

"Lily," Shain started, only to get a smack on his chest.

"I mean it!"

He released her and watched as she scrambled backward on the bed, her breath coming fast, her head low. "Where are my clothes?"

Shain took a deep breath as his gaze followed her every movement. "Lily…"

Her head snapped up. "Look, it's no big deal if you don't want me." With a trembling hand she pushed hair away from her face. Trying to seem unconcerned. Trying to pretend she wasn't feeling like someone had just punched her in the gut. "But why do you keep asking me things like that? First you dare me to stay, then disappear for four days, then you bring me to a place like this… What kind of game are you playing?"

Anger sparked, then simmered in Shain's chest. "Games? You want to talk about games?" He leaned in and yanked Lily off the bed and onto her feet in front of him. Irritation mixed with desire and his own deep fear blurred his thoughts, skewing everything he'd always felt to be true. "How about you tell me what type of woman makes a bet to fuck the first man that 'trips her trigger'?" Heat spread through Shain like wildfire. "What about *that* game, *Miss* Whitman?"

Lily's mouth fell open and she froze. "Wh-what did you just say?"

Shain dropped his hands and crossed his arms. "You heard me."

She spun, putting him at her back. Shain could imagine the thoughts going through her head but, damn it, the little minx deserved to be made accountable for her actions. If he hadn't spoken to Nhya, then gotten the call from Lance less than an hour ago, he never would have known about the silly bet or the fact that Lily was, in fact, exactly who she said she was—a straight-laced museum curator with a nominal sex life and a passionate love for her job and family.

It was incredible, really, that she'd followed through on the wager and, from the tone of the e-mail Nhya had intercepted while snooping through Lily's laptop, both Lily *and* her cousins seriously doubted she'd make any attempt at all.

But damned if she didn't. Shain's cock was still rock-hard as he stared at her gently curved back and long, kill-you-with-one-look, legs. Shain wasn't certain if he should be pleased that she'd jumped into the bet with both feet or not.

Memories of their lovemaking wiped any doubt from his mind. Damn straight he was pleased...and doubly lucky that it was *him* she fell for.

Shit. Shain ran a hand through his hair, his entire body screaming with need and his heart tripping with feelings he hadn't dealt with for a very long time. If ever. There was no doubt, bet or not, Shain Stevenson was head-over-heels for this gorgeous, generous and passionate woman. And it wasn't just the sex. When he looked at her, it was as if he'd known her forever. Her smile. Her laugh.

Her spirit.

Shain sighed, accepting his grandmother's wise words. While he'd known he could never completely escape those odd moments where time seemed to stand still, where he heard gentle voices giving direction, advising, being away from the ranch for extended periods of time *had* lessened them. It was one of the reasons he'd been so keen to leave. It had been...different, to not be haunted by things he didn't understand, didn't want to understand.

Unlike Nhya who'd embraced it. Treated it as their heritage. Not something to fear, but something to treasure. To cultivate.

So who was the true fake here? Shain's gut twisted with guilt and a decision made. He stepped forward and placed a hand on Lily's shoulder, the smooth texture of her skin sinking into his belly like a slow drink of Jack D. "Lily, damn it, talk to me."

She shivered beneath his palm. "How—how could you possibly have found out about the bet?"

Shain shook his head. "It doesn't matter."

"It does!" Lily turned, her sumptuous bare chest rising and falling with the force of her breath. "There's no way for you to know about that unless you talked to my cousins and they told you, which wouldn't happen, or you—" Her deep green eyes widened, then narrowed. "My laptop!"

Shain frowned. This wasn't going the way he'd planned at all. *He* should be the one pissed as hell.

Nostrils flaring, he stepped closer, giving her his most intimidating glare. "Stop it."

Lily raised a fist and shook it. "Stop what? Being furious that you felt you had the right to go through my personal items? To snoop into my life where you had no business being?"

The strength of her words bounced off his chest and Shain was silent in the face of her distress. Her words were nearly the same ones he'd spoken earlier about his great-grandfather's murderer. And as gorgeous as she was with her fist raised and her eyes blazing, it wasn't really anger wafting off of Miss Whitman…it was hurt. Pain. Fear.

He knew her emotions for what they were, because he was feeling them too. They weren't so different, really. Classy, smoothly perfect Lily Whitman and rough, scarred Shain Stevenson. At their hearts, they were the same. Both desperate for a deeper connection but terrified about finding it.

And *had* they found it?

Shain captured her small fist in his much larger hand, holding her there as their gazes locked. "Stop it, Lily. No more covering up. No more lies. It's just you and me. Tell me…" Shain paused, a tingling rushing through his gut all the way to the top of his head. He swallowed, feeling a glimmer of rightness, a foot at the crossroads, as his grandmother would say. There was no going back. "Tell me what you want. With us, Lily. What do you want?"

After a moment of frozen stillness, she started to tremble. From her gorgeous legs, past her flat belly and up to her flushed cheeks. But her eyes stayed locked with his. Searching. Trying to decide if she should step up to the crossroads, too…and cross over.

"Shain," Lily murmured. "God help me... I want to be with you." She shook her head, silky hair swishing around her face in glimmering waves of gold. "I don't even know, really, exactly what that means. Being with you." She looked up once more and Shain's breath caught in his throat. She looked unreal, head tilted, her eyes wide, her barriers down. "You tell me, what does that mean, Shain?"

Shain tightened his grip on her fist and stepped in until she was directly beneath him, their clasped hands locked against his chest. "I'm not sure either, sugar, but I can't imagine starting another morning where you're not there to see it with me." He lifted his other hand and brushed strands of gold behind her delicate ear. "You're in my blood, woman. Last night all I could think about was you. Being with you. Loving you." Shain grinned wolfishly. "Fucking you."

Lily frowned.

He raised an eyebrow. "Honesty, remember?"

She sighed, a slight smile tugging at the corners of her mouth. "Since we're being honest, I spent the past four nights thinking of that, too. And how I was going to kill you the next time I saw you for abandoning me and Nhya like that." She paused, then chewed her lower lip before blurting: "I thought you were messing around with some other woman!"

It had never occurred to Shain that Lily would be worried or even take the time to be jealous. The realization made his chest warm and his cock throb and he pulled her in closer, the fresh, sweet scent of her going straight to his head. "Darlin', you had nothing to worry about. I spent every night in the saddle making sure those looters didn't get a leg up on me or anywhere close to you girls. I was supposed to stay out there from day one." Shain nuzzled her graceful neck, desire simmering in his belly like an over-fed furnace. Shain felt Lily relax into him, her high, firm breasts pressing against his chest, her legs tangled with his as they stood holding one another. "I knew it was a mistake to come back that morning. I couldn't think of anything else but you, so I had to leave. Get out. Clear my head and focus on the ranch."

"Did it work?" Lily asked softly.

Shain growled. "What do you think?"

He felt her smile against his chest and heat filled every pore of his body. "Fuck this," Shain muttered as he swept Lily off her feet and into his arms. He tossed her gently onto the bed, following her down, pressing her into the mattress. "No more talk, woman. We've established parameters." He dipped his head and caught Lily's nipple between his teeth. She arched against him. One lick, then two before he blew cool air across the beaded tip. Shain looked up, every muscle in his body taut with longing—a soul-deep need. "I want all of you. You want all of me. Neither of us is sure where that will lead but we're going to walk the path and find out, right?"

"Right," Lily said breathlessly. "Now make love to me, Shain, before I lose my mind."

Chapter Ten

Shain's attention went back to her nipple, his teeth grazing the sensitive tip. Lily screamed, unable to control the wild need surging within her. His tongue felt rough, hot and magical as it wound around her areola, sucking, teasing until she thought she would lose her mind.

With her fingers digging into his forearms, Shain released the sensitive bud and leaned back, dark hair falling over his forehead. "I've never felt skin so soft." He slid a hand beneath her upper thigh and lifted slightly. "That night in the bar, when I saw you hugging that bull between your long, beautiful legs, all I could think of was taking that delicate foot…" Shain ran his hand down the back of her leg, his eyes feasting on every inch. "And kissing your ankle." Which he did, slowly, tenderly, in that soft spot on the inside of her foot. His eyes lifted, his lips next to her skin. "Then taking my tongue…" He flicked once, the cool of his tongue sending shivers all the way to Lily's spine. "And running it up the back of those heart-stopping legs…"

Which Shain did with methodical, loving attention. Past the gentle swell of her calf, his hand holding her leg by the ankle, his head poised beneath it. He placed warm kisses behind her knee, then continued upward. His tongue painting spirals all the way to mid-thigh, where he paused. Lily's breath fell out in ragged pants, her body quaking, her juices soaking the velvet folds of her slit.

"And here," Shain whispered roughly. "Here is where I lick all the way up your ass cheek and bury my face into your hot pussy." As good as his word, Shain's head dipped back to the back of her leg, where he laved across the crest of her butt, stopping only when he was buried in her slick folds.

Lily cried out and bucked against his face, her hands digging into the bed. *His tongue...Ohmygod...* It darted in and out of her creamy hole and Lily felt the orgasm build like a tidal wave. The stubble on his checks rubbed against her sensitive lips and Lily gyrated against him, moans falling from her lips with abandon.

"Come for me," Shain whispered against her and, with shocking force, Lily's body complied. She screamed as her orgasm tore through her, her thighs vibrating on either side of Shain's head, her heart slamming against her ribs.

For a moment, Lily literally saw stars. She sighed in pure contentment and fascination, each nerve in her body firing pleasure signals.

Lily felt warm hands under her hips and, a moment later, she was flipped onto her stomach then pulled up to her knees.

"Now," came a deep rumble behind her ear. "We fuck."

Lily drew in a startled breath, instantly burning with anticipation as Shain's callused hands palmed her hips and drew her firmly back. She heard the telltale rip of foil, and loved him all the more for wanting to protect them both. Within seconds, the tip of his engorged cock stopped at her steamy entrance and she felt the warmth of his body as he bent low. His spice-and-leather scent enveloped her and she knew she would forever associate it with this powerful, beautiful man.

"Are you ready for me, Lily?" he whispered near her ear. His tongue snaked out and tickled the delicate outer rim and Lily shivered, her breasts tightening.

"I've been ready for you forever, cowboy. Give me all of—"

Lily cried out as Shain yanked on her hips, driving his thick rod past her slick opening and deep into her core. There was no stopping this time. No giving her pause to adjust to his girth and length. With one hand on the top of her ass, the other gripping her slender hip, Shain thrust rhythmically, each shift driving him full force into her center. Panting, Lily flattened her upper body against the bed, allowing him greater access, her hands gripping the quilt, her thighs meeting his diving plunges.

"Beautiful," she heard him growl as his hand caressed her ass, his testes bouncing against her slit.

Shain's palm flattened against the lower curve of her back and he leaned forward while pulling back on her hips with the other. The penetration was deep and Lily shuddered as another orgasm rocked through her.

Moaning, her hands dug into the quilt until they hurt, her head spinning. Shain didn't break his rhythm but she could hear his ragged breath, his deep murmurs of passion. Each plunge brought her closer to the edge once more but Lily had little time to be amazed. It felt too good. Too perfect. Too heavenly to analyze.

"Shain," she whispered, the slapping sound and musky scent of their lovemaking only heightening the erotic sensations.

"Jesus, Lily," Shain groaned. "You feel so goddamn perfect, I'm gonna explode, darlin'."

Lily smiled at the almost pain-filled tone of his voice. "Then do it. Come inside me, Shain. I asked for all of you...are you going to deny me?"

With an animal growl, Shain pulled her hard against his groin, driving his cock all the way to the tip of her womb. Lily cried out and gasped as Shain plunged into her at near manic speed, each stroke finding her center, each thrust forcing wild sounds from her throat and lips.

Shain literally roared as his rod contracted within her and Lily felt her own body respond, clamping around his cock. It was all she could do to breathe as the sensations washed through her and, within seconds, she felt herself doing the unexpected—crying. Tears poured down her flushed cheeks and she drew in a shaky breath.

Feeling Shain's hot, slick chest connect with her back, Lily tried desperately to curtail her bizarre reaction to the most amazing experience she had ever had, but it was no use. The tears kept coming and, as Shain wrapped his muscled arm tight across her chest, withdrew, and gently turned her over to face him, she raised a hand to cover her face.

He stopped her and Lily bit her lower lip and closed her eyes.

"Lily," came Shain's husky tenor. "Open your eyes."

She did. She had a hard time denying Shain anything. His rough, beautiful face was tense with concern, his gorgeous smoky eyes laced with worry. "I'm sorry, darlin'. Did I hurt you? Are you all right?"

A strangled laugh-sob escaped as Lily tried to smile. She raised her free hand and placed it lovingly along Shain's strong jaw. "I know you won't believe this but I never cry." She hiccupped and laughed, feeling giddy. Shain still looked deeply concerned—like she might have popped a cork. She ran her hand across his stubbled chin to his full lips. "Shain, I'm fine. Well, maybe not fine, but so satisfied, I'm a little punch drunk, I think."

She grinned and Shain raised a dark eyebrow before chuckling lowly. The sound made the hairs on the back of Lily's neck tingle and she curled into Shain as he relaxed onto the bed, pulling her tight to his chest. "Woman, you are going to make my life damn interesting—among other things." He nuzzled her neck and Lily nearly purred, feeling a tingle of need unfurl inside her once more.

How could I want him again so soon after what we just did? Lily kissed the side of his cheek and was rewarded with a deep rumble not unlike the red bear in the woods.

Thoughts of the bear brought back the tingling and a sense of knowing filled Lily. Driving her words. Directing her thoughts. "The bear," she murmured. "He's connected to this land. To the ranch." She drew back slightly so she could see Shain's face. "To you and Nhya. Tell me why, Shain. Please. I need to know."

Shain's face was awash with emotions. Consternation. Disquiet. Pride. Fear. Then finally resignation. "You'll never believe it."

"Try me." Lily kissed the edge of Shain's jaw, then rested her head in the cup of her hand.

His expression softened and he pulled the blanket up to cover their legs. "There's a legend in our family that tells about one of our ancestors. He lived in the long ago time—" Shain paused, as if embarrassed by his storytelling tenor.

Lily ran a finger over the back of his hand. "Tell it how your grandmother told it. I won't judge you, Shain."

Shain's gaze snapped to Lily. "How did you know Grandmother told me this story?"

She smiled warmly. "Nhya. She told me a few things about your grandmother. It was a good guess."

After a deep breath Shain continued. "His tribe followed the buffalo to these lands when the sun was high and the days warm. Even as a child, it was clear he was a *pejula wacasa*—medicine man. At the age of naming, he earned the title of *Mato Luta*, or Red Bear, because wherever the young warrior went, there were sightings of a giant red bear watching and sometimes warning The People of trouble or danger. Most believed the bear to be Mato Luta's totem animal but close family knew better, for he was more than a medicine man. Red Bear was an ancient shaman reborn, blessed by *Wakan Tanka* to be a spiritual warrior and guardian of his people. The bear was Mato Luta himself."

Shain ran a hand through his hair, the muscles in his chest rippling. "Mato Luta grew strong, married and stayed in the tribe for many years, fathering three children—my direct relatives—and helping The People to stay healthy and prosperous. His time away from the tribe became greater and greater as years passed. One time he came back with a single, fist-long crimson bear claw strung around his neck. Any who were sensitive to the ways of spirit knew the claw was an object of high magic. A power token. The People began calling him

Red Claw, in respect for this new, unknown power he held, and every time he went away and came back, there was another claw added to the necklace."

Shain's gaze held Lily's. "While his wife and children aged, Red Claw stayed the same, virile, strong young warrior he always was. His family accepted this but the rest of the tribe was frightened by this unnatural thing.

"Relations between his family and the tribe deteriorated and, after his wife's death, he made the decision to leave the tribe to preserve his children's connection within it. They were saddened but understood and respected his choice. On the seventh day of the seventh month, Red Claw held ceremony, promising them that he would continue to watch over the tribe and the earth he loved. After kissing each of his children and grandchildren, he took one of the claws from his necklace and held it up while saying words of power. A 'circle of light' opened before him and he handed the claw to my great-, great-, great-grandfather before stepping into the circle of light. He was never seen again—in human form."

The tale at its end, Shain leaned back and closed his eyes. The room hummed with an electrical charge and Lily rolled over on her stomach, her mind tripping with images of the shaman, his people, his life. It was unbelievable. A family myth, surely. A beautiful one, but—

"My great grandfather was killed because an acquaintance of his believed he had the pendant. When he couldn't convince Hank to turn it over, he shot him."

"That's terrible. Did they catch—"

Shain shook his head. "Hell, no. He disappeared, leaving my grandmother, who was only five, to find the body when they got home from town."

"Oh, Shain, how awful for her."

"She survived. As did the rest of the legend, which says that through the next three centuries, our family has been helped, saved or assisted by our ancestor—always in the form of a great red bear." He paused, his face grim. "I always wondered where in the hell the bear was when my great-grandfather was murdered."

The tingling was back as a memory of the beast filled her mind. Of its eyes...its otherworldly presence. "But," Lily said breathlessly. "I'm not a family member. And what would he be saving me from when Luke and I saw him?"

Shain grunted. "I don't know. And I didn't say *I* believe the stories."

Her gaze traveled back to her lover's stormy face and Lily was quick to recognize the thread of indecision in Shain's eyes. He wanted to believe—but could he?

Do I?

Lily shivered. "Shain. Have *you* ever seen the bear?"

He was silent for a time, the steady tick-tock of the clock over the mantel filling the room like a low heartbeat. "No. But Nhya—" He paused, his expression grim. "My sister says she has seen him in his spirit form from early childhood."

Shain looked decidedly uncomfortable with the path his words were taking them down and Lily couldn't blame him. She was pragmatic herself but in the short time she'd spent with Nhya, she'd sensed how different Shain's sister was. How...special.

In the same way that Lily had always felt her friend Susan was special.

Lily sat up, her heart thrumming. "Shain, I know this sounds crazy, but I believe that bear I saw today *is* something more than ordinary. I can't tell you why, but if you had seen it...felt it, you would too. I know it."

After a second Shain nodded curtly. "Well, if that's true, then I'd have to wonder why he showed up now and what he was trying to—" Shain's bronze face paled and he sat up, nearly bouncing Lily off the bed.

He stood and reached for his clothes. "There's something I have to check on."

"I'll come with you."

Shain spun. "No! You have to stay here."

Bristling from his tone, Lily stood, hands on her hips. Her mouth opened, but, before she could give him an earful, Shain pulled her against his bare chest and kissed her so hard it stole any convincing argument she might have had.

His dark gaze caressed her face as he pulled back. "I need to do this on my own. Stay here. I'll be back inside of an hour. I promise."

Lily chewed her lower lip, tasting him there. Needing him more than anything else in her life. "But I might be able to help, to—"

"Please, Lily," Shain said quietly. "Trust me."

After a moment, she sighed in resignation. He released her, his thoughts already far away, his stride purposeful as he made for the door, pulling his shirt on as he went. He slammed his Stetson onto his head and turned to her. "Stay inside. Keep the door locked."

Fingers of ice itched across Lily's shoulders.

Shain leveled a no-nonsense stare her way as he pulled his gloves from his back pocket and slid them on. "I mean it, Lily. Do as I say."

Unable to speak, she nodded and watched as her lover strode from the cabin.

* * * * *

Nhya's mare Keeta whinnied a greeting as he and Windigo slowed to a trot then pulled up. Dismounting, Shain's feet hit the earth with a muffled thump and he tied Windigo loosely next to Keeta before starting up the mountain slope.

The climb was steep and blood surged through his thighs as he crested the jagged rise. As always, the stunning view of the valley stole his breath and the strange, intoxicating energy that permeated the peak seeped into his bones and made his head fuzzy.

He spotted Nhya on the smooth, saucer-shaped boulder hanging at the edge of the rim. Her back was straight, her dark, silky hair lifting softly in the breeze, her face tipped to catch the last rays of yellow sun. As he walked over, a warm, slightly numbing sensation started in his toes then moved on up to his head.

Shain stopped a few feet away, his breath coming fast. He rubbed his eyes but it didn't lessen the glow emanating from his sister's still form. Blues and purples wafted from her in shimmering waves and Shain closed his eyes.

"Brother, it's okay. Open your eyes and sit with me."

Nhya's soft voice eased some of the strangeness and Shain did as she asked, happy to see the colors had dissipated. They looked out at the valley.

"So, tell me, Shain. How was it being away from the Red Bear? To not feel the land beneath your feet. To not smell the clean scent of the pine. To not touch the rich soil?"

Shain grunted and flexed. "Like I was missing my right arm."

Nhya smiled. "For me, it would be like not having a heart." She studied him and, after a moment, her gaze narrowed, then widened. "Shain...something is different. You—Lily," she finished with conviction.

A joyful laugh trilled through the air and Shain raised an eyebrow. "You approve?"

Nhya placed a hand on his arm. "I more than approve. I give you my blessing and a warning." Shain frowned at the look of gravity on his sister's striking face. "If you mess this up, Shain, I'll beat you silly."

Shain grinned wolfishly and Nhya raised finely arched brows. "I mean it. This is a good thing. The right thing. It's time to stop running."

Her words arrowed straight to his heart. "I know," Shain murmured, his attention captivated by an image of his blonde goddess's ethereal face. Her stunning body. Her pure heart...

"Nhya, how do I make this work?"

She took his hand, her palm cool and dry. "By thinking and speaking from here." She jabbed him lightly over his heart and smiled. "It won't lead you astray."

Shain gripped his sister's hand and cleared his throat. "Today, Lily and Luke say they saw—"

"Red Claw," Nhya finished for him.

"Luke told you?"

She shook her head, her gaze dreamy. "I felt him and I came here where his presence is strongest." Their eyes met and Shain knew he had to put aside his doubts, his suspicions of the old ways. Because his sister—his little Nhya—was connected in the way of his grandmother and her father before her. It was there in her dark eyes, that amber glint, that flare of knowing.

His chest felt warm, his head light, and Shain took a deep breath. "Is it real, Nhya? Do we actually have the pendant of the Red Bear?"

Her look said it all and Shain had a hard time swallowing past the knot in his throat. "When? Where?"

Nhya squeezed his hand. "I've dreamt about it for years but the dreams never revealed where—until today. And he said—he said that there would come a time where I would need to use the pendant. That I would know when that time was. Until then, I'm to protect it. Keep it hidden."

Anger sizzled in Shain's gut. "What? How can Red Claw expect that?" Shain stood and paced. "If this thing really *can* do what Grandmother said, it's fucking dangerous!"

Nhya stood. "Listen…"

Shain threw up his hands. "We have to get this thing and lock it up. Somewhere off the property and away from—"

"Shain!"

He stopped, blood heavy in his ears, and looked at his sister. She stood straight and regal on the top of the boulder, her hair streaming as if held up by invisible fingers. His anger drained away as if someone had pulled a plug.

"Brother," Nhya said, her voice lilting with an inner music that played softly in Shain's ear. "I am capable of this. Meant for this, as you were meant for other things." Her voice deepened, her words reverberating through his chest. "It is beginning now, with Lily, and others you will soon meet. Do not let your fear and anger blind you. It's time to let go, Shain. It's time to embrace your heritage and your destiny."

It was true. He knew it and, while he still wasn't comfortable with it, the idea no longer filled Shain with dread. In fact, the suggestion of a future with Lily filled him with elation. A sense of purpose — the promise of things to come.

Shain and Nhya locked eyes. "Where is it, Nhya? And what do we do?"

Nhya smiled. "It's hidden and protected by a spell of our great grandfather's design. That's why they haven't been able to find it."

Shain's heart stopped and he stepped forward on wooden legs. "Where, Nhya? *Where is it hidden?*"

Her smiled faltered. "I — it's at the old cabin. Set behind a spelled stone in the fireplace... Shain! What's wrong?"

Shain was already striding toward the path, every muscle in his body screaming for him to go faster, move quicker.

"Shain!" Nhya called from behind.

"Lily's at the cabin," Shain growled as he scrambled down the cliff, shale rippling in a wave at his descent.

Chapter Eleven

"Any time now, Shain," Lily murmured. The hour was almost up. She'd tried to busy herself by inspecting every inch of the cabin but, within thirty minutes all she wanted to do was see Shain and find out why he had to leave so abruptly. If she hadn't promised him she'd stay inside with the door barred, she could have at least gone out and explored the glade.

And why *had* he insisted she lock the door?

Lily crossed to the fireplace, admiring the smooth river stones that ran the width and breadth of the chimney and hearth. The mantel was lined with carved woodland creatures. Elk, wolf, trout, rabbit, but no bear. "Curious," Lily said aloud, reaching out to touch the wolf, admiring the fine detail and life-like essence of the carving.

A knock at the door made her jump. She set the wolf down and ran to the window. She couldn't see who it was and her heart raced. Shain wouldn't have knocked…

"Who is it?" Lily called.

"It's me, Miss Whitman."

Lily's eyes widened in surprise and she pulled the old fashioned bar lock off and opened the door. "Darrell. What are you doing here?"

"May I come in?" he asked, holding his hat in front of him like a shield.

"Sure." Lily stepped aside, then closed the door behind him. "So, what brings you here? I hope you weren't worried about me. Luke was supposed to tell you that Shain and I had—" Lily stopped and lowered her gaze, hoping it wasn't totally obvious what she and Shain had been doing.

"He did."

Darrell's edgy tone brought Lily's head up. A jolt shot through her. His expression was tense, almost feverish-looking.

"Where is it?"

"What?" Lily asked, taking a step back, her palms suddenly clammy. "Where's what?"

Darrell's hand clamped onto her upper arm. "Don't play games with me. *Where is it?*"

Lily stared at his fingers in shock. "Darrell, I don't understand."

In an instant he flung her aside. Spinning out of control, Lily struck the hutch on the far wall. Pain shot through her lower back. Dishes rattled. Glass exploded in a shower around her elbow.

There wasn't time to scream. Think.

"Never mind. I'll find it myself." Darrell paced the room. "Amazing that the glade and cabin were so well protected." He smirked. "Primitive magic. But effective. It wasn't until Luke mentioned in his native tongue that Shain had likely taken you here did I realize what I'd been overlooking. Of course he thought I wouldn't understand. Fool."

Lily tried to collect herself, tried to breathe through the pain as she forced herself to stand upright. To track the cowboy she thought she knew as he walked the room in an ever-widening circle, his once kind face vacant.

"I know it's here. I can feel it…"

His words washed over Lily like ice water, snapping her out of her shock. "You!" She stumbled forward, her face flaming. "*You're* the one looking for the artifact! Digging up Shain and Nhya's property. How *could* you?"

His eyes swiveled in her direction and Lily gasped. They were no longer the pale blue of an early morning sky, but rather the shocking turquoise of a robin's egg. And they burned with an unnatural glow that confirmed to Lily that what she'd always taken for reality was about to shift. Forever.

He stepped toward her. Lily stepped back. "How very astute of you, *Lily*. Did you figure that out on your own?"

Darrell's sarcasm didn't bother her. It was the disgust behind it that set the hairs on the back of Lily's neck on end. *He's insane.* And something else. Something beyond Lily's reckoning.

Shain. Where was Shain?

Lily itched to glance at her watch. But she couldn't. He promised he'd be back in an hour. She had to keep Darrell calm. Pacify him. Give Shain a chance to get there. Stop him from finding…what exactly *was* he looking for?

The pendant. The claw that could potentially open a doorway into another dimension.

Ludicrous. Outrageous.

But as Lily took in Darrell's fixed, hungry expression, she knew he believed it with every fiber in his body.

Oh, God…

"Darrell," Lily started, speaking slowly, calmly. "It's only a legend. A story. Surely you can't—"

"Quiet!" He didn't even look at her, just continued to walk the room, palms open. "Come out, come out wherever you are."

Think, Lily!

As he moved toward the fireplace, his lips curved into a disturbing smile. "I'm getting warmer."

The tingling was back and Lily knew she had to do something. *But what?*

"I know where it is," Lily blurted.

Darrell froze.

"Shain let it slip today, while we were…intimate."

In slow motion Darrell dropped his hand and turned to face her. Doubt tightened his features. "Oh?"

"I—I can take you to it."

Sandy eyebrows rose. "No. Tell me."

Lily shook her head, her heart pounding. "It's in the woods at a spot Shain took me to. I couldn't tell you where that is but I know I can show you."

"You're lying," Darrell said softly.

"I'm not," Lily replied, raising her chin. "What do I care about some stupid, worthless adornment? I've seen so many, it hardly seems worth all the effort you've gone through, but to each his own." She flipped hair off her shoulder and walked toward the door. "If showing you where it is will get you out of my hair, then I'm all for it."

"Step back and face me."

Lily froze, then did as he said, working hard to keep her expression self-involved and neutral.

He was smiling and, for a second, he looked like the handsome, unassuming cowboy she first met at the Wolf Springs airpark. But the grin melted into a bone-chilling sneer, leaving a hollow, tremulous knot in her chest. *He's not buying it...*

A laugh, deep and startlingly inhuman, crawled across her skin. "That was a decent effort but you broadcast your feelings like a spotlight." His expression turned thoughtful. "You didn't, when you first arrived. You were a closed book. Something I found interesting, which is why I stayed close—to get a better read. But now that you've opened your heart, you're as transparent as all the other fools."

His words made Lily's face flame and her mind spin. *How could he sense such a thing?* "What *are* you?" Lily said.

Flicking a hand he turned back to the fireplace. "Something beyond your understanding, Lily. Now be a good girl, shut your mouth and let me finish."

Lily's eyes darted, looking for something, *anything* she might use to stop him.

Darrell's left hand gripped one of the mortared rocks. "What a wonderful vibration you put off." He reached into a pouch at his hip, dipped his fingers inside, then wiped a wide blue streak across the stone. Darrell—or whoever...*whatever* he was—stepped back and began chanting a string of guttural words.

Electricity filled the room and Lily pressed a hand to her chest, her breath shallow, her face cold. As his voice rose in pitch, the blue streaks began to glow and, before her eyes, *the rocks dissolved*, gray running down the face of the fireplace to reveal a dark hollow.

That's not possible, Lily thought. Rocks don't just melt!

Darrell gave a shout of success and reached in, only to whip his hand back with a growl. Faint tendrils of smoke drifted off the tips of his fingers and he affixed Lily with a cold stare. "Come here."

She shook her head.

"I said, *come here*, Lily." Darrell raised a hand and twisted it in the air. Pain exploded in her abdomen. Lily clutched her stomach and, even though nearly doubled over, she couldn't take her eyes off his expressionless eyes and curving grin. "Don't you think you'd better do as I say?"

She felt her head nod as she staggered forward, her breath falling out in rasps.

"Now," came Darrell's voice near her left ear. "Reach in and pull it out."

Coolness brushed her, an unnatural, blistering cold that burrowed under her skin and into her bones. Sweat popped out on her neck, chest and brow and instinctively she knew it was from Darrell. From whatever power he held. Images flashed through Lily's mind. Fractured pictures of desert vistas, rolling hills, then waving fields of wheat.

"Pull it out, Lily," he whispered, his breath icy hot against her neck.

Lily wanted to resist, to refuse, but her hand lifted. As her fingers entered, a rush of cold bit into her. She gasped and tried to pull out but Darrell grabbed her forearm, holding her there.

"Keep going," he whispered.

Lily could see no other way and perhaps…perhaps she could find a way to keep it from him once she did. Fight. Run.

Swallowing, Lily forced herself to find a sense of calm. "Let go of my arm," she stated. Surprisingly, he did. Lily took a deep breath and plunged her hand to the back of the recess. A fraction before her fingers connected, Lily felt a warmth swelling in her chest then, as her fingers closed around the soft object, the tingling. It started in her gut and spread in a wave that left her breathless, detached, unafraid. As she had been in the meadow when watching the bear.

Gripping it tightly, Lily stepped back. Darrell's face twisted in a triumphant smile as it focused on the leather pouch clutched in her hand.

"Perfect." He held out a bandana. "Give it to me."

She shook her head, her body primed, her spirit knowing it was something she could never do.

His eyes snapped to her face, fury burning behind the bright blue irises. Before Lily could blink, his hand snapped out and fastened around her throat, her scream choked off as Darrell lifted her free of the floor and walked her to the opposite wall. Slamming her against it, he leaned in, his lips thinned into a gruesome slash. "I have searched for this for years, sacrificed, all the time working toward a single, ultimate goal and *you*…" His face dipped closer, teeth bared. "You…*nothing of a creature*…think you can stand in my way?" He reached down with his other hand and wrenched her arm up over her head. "Release it," he hissed.

Lily tried to move, to kick like Susan had taught her, but it was no use. She was losing ground every second air was denied her. Despite her terror, despite knowing that her decision may well doom her, Lily choked out, "Not on your life."

A snarl blasted into her as his hand tightened, crushing her airway, denying her any hope that this would end with anything other than her violent death.

I'm sorry, Shain…Nhya…

Chapter Twelve

Windigo ran like the wind, bending to his master's will with iron resolve. Shain pressed himself tight to the stallion's sweat-drenched neck, urging him on.

Finally the line of pine and cedars loomed ahead. Shain slowed Windigo to a gallop until they located the opening and crashed through. Windigo plunged down the twining trail, smashing branches, leveling shrubs.

Shain rubbed his heaving side, encouraging him. As they careened down the rocky embankment, the stallion stumbled and Shain pulled him up, barely keeping his feet under him.

"Whoa, boy."

They'd have to walk the rest of the way. It was too treacherous for Shain to demand the horse take it at speed.

"I'm sorry, Shain…Nhya…"

"Lily!" Shain shouted. Her honeyed voice echoed in his mind. So close. *So real…*

Shain dismounted, whispering quick words to Windigo before forging ahead at a dead run. Past the brook, up the other side. Pounding down the trail, around tree and rock, and finally through the thick tangle of vegetation and out into the sunny clearing.

A gray stallion looked up from where it grazed with Rialda at the far end of the glade.

Storm.

What was Darrell's horse doing here?

Cold seeped into Shain's chest. "Son of a bitch."

* * * * *

Pinpricks of light danced behind Lily's eyes, black lurking at the edges. She knew he was waiting for her to pass out and drop the pouch. Why he couldn't just *take* it was beyond her.

"Stubborn bitch, drop it!" he shouted inches from her face.

Lily ignored him, her mind spinning free. She closed her eyes as a subtle sensation of warmth filled her palm and spread up her arm and into her chest. It was pleasant, comforting and something else.

A promise...

Of what?

"Let her go, Darrell."

Lily's eyes flew open as the pressure on her neck eased. She gasped, dragging air into her tortured lungs and down her bruised windpipe.

Shain... He stood near the couch, the door open behind him. His hands were in fists at his side, his handsome face thunderous and his smoky brown eyes nearly black as he gazed at Darrell. "Get your hands off her."

Darrell complied and Lily barely caught herself as she hit the ground. She collapsed against the wall, hand to her aching throat.

"Why, if it's not my good buddy, Shain."

Lily's eyes watered as she fought for air, her throat burning, her chest aching. Looking down she realized that she still held the pouch and *it was glowing*. A gentle, golden-red glow of autumn leaves, a summer sunset, a mountain lake at winter dawn. And it seemed to shift in her hand — tug — as if wanting to move toward —

Her eyes rose, meeting Shain's around Darrell's coiled form. She recognized the fear for her safety in his gaze...and something else. A red-hot, formidable rage.

"Why?" came Shain's deep rumble.

She couldn't see Darrell's grin but Lily could feel it like a choking breath of deep winter. "You wouldn't understand,

Shain old boy, and I don't have the time or inclination to explain it to you. I had hoped to locate the pendant with you and your lovely sister none the wiser but your stubborn parents saw to it that I wasn't going to get to it in a…non-violent way." Darrell smirked and cold seeped into every inch of Lily's spirit. Her gaze cut to Shain, who was frozen, pain and fury burning in his eyes.

Darrell sighed. "Unfortunately, I also underestimated the ability of your great-grandfather to protect the amulet." He laughed. "So you see, we were both fools of a sort. Yet…" He paused and turned slightly to gaze at Lily. The manic gleam in his eye brought Lily straight, every nerve set on defying him any way possible. "I don't intend to be the dead fool."

With his gaze still on her, Darrell's hand shot in Shain's direction and Lily watched in horror as Shain doubled over. Darrell closed his hand into a fist one finger at a time in midair, and Shain's body twisted with it, slamming into the hardwood floor with a thud that made Lily cry out.

"Lily, love, would you like to hand me the pendant *now*?"

Without thought, she fell to the floor and kicked out with both legs at Darrell's knees. Susan's self defense class had taught her to go the floor and use her legs, the most powerful part of a woman's body, and, by the screech and twist of rage on Darrell's face, she was pretty sure the method was sound.

Before Lily could scrabble far enough away, Darrell gripped her ankle and yanked, sliding her across the floor and into his arms. She only had a moment…

"Shain!" she called as he rose like a great bear from a deep slumber. Lily lifted her arm and threw the pouch.

It sailed through the air as if borne by an invisible breeze. Time froze. All eyes watched its descent. Lily felt Darrell release her, his body readying to spring.

Shain stood to his full height and lifted an arm, the pouch landing squarely in his open palm. Lily scrambled to her feet and ran to Shain's side. His left arm engulfed her and Lily pressed her cheek into his sweat-dampened shirt, the leather and spice scent of him filling her lungs.

With unhurried hands, Shain looped the thong of the pouch over his head, letting it rest against his chest. Only inches away, Lily was startled yet comforted by the power wafting from the amulet. Darrell jumped to his feet and Lily gripped Shain's arm in warning.

"So be it. I'll simply kill you both," he said calmly, raising his hands in their direction.

"No you won't."

Lily and Shain twisted to see Nhya standing in the doorway, rifle leveled at Darrell's chest. She walked forward to stand beside them. "Move on or die here."

The surety in Nhya's voice chilled Lily and she found herself holding her breath as Darrell's lip curled into a snarl. "Too many unforeseens." He snorted. "No matter. There is another way." His turquoise gaze fastened on Lily and she felt Shain tighten his hold, his body primed for action.

He whistled softly, his eyes never leaving Lily's face. "Waving wheat, crackling dry." Darrell tipped his head her direction.

* * * * *

Shain didn't care what he was. He'd rip his leering eyes right out of —

Before he could move, Darrell sprinted across the room and leapt through the plate glass window. Shards exploded outward, catching the light like glittering crystals. Shain spun Lily aside and lunged forward.

"No!"

Nhya's shout and arm on his shoulder brought him up short. Brother and sister stared at one another. "Let him go, Shain."

He shook her off. "I'm going to smash that bastard into a million…"

The expression on his sister's face stopped his words. Her eyes were glowing again, and the pouch was getting warmer on his chest, tugging, *moving*…

"It is not his time. And if we kill him here, which, by the way, would be exceptionally difficult, here he would remain. For a very long time," Nhya finished, emphasizing the word long.

"Fuck," Shain muttered, understanding what Nhya was getting at. The freak would become a shade, a bad spirit, wreaking havoc on the ranch for God knows how long. Shain raked a hand through his hair and stared out the shattered window. "We can't just let him go. That son of a bitch is bad-ass dangerous."

"Yes," Nhya said with a sigh, moving forward to engulf Lily in a hug. "He is."

Gritting his teeth, Shain moved back to Lily's side. She left his sister's arms and fell into his. "He's not a normal man, Shain. You don't know…" Her words faded and Shain tipped her chin to get a better look at her neck. Bands of red were still visible and Shain knew she'd have an ugly bruise within the hour.

Fury burned in his gut and the anger threatened to overwhelm his good senses. He stepped back, fighting to control his temper. "What the hell happened here?" Shain growled. "Darrell…shit. And his comment about our parents."

Shain stared at Nhya, raw pain evident. "Do you think that crazy asshole had something to do with the plane crash?"

As the steady pounding of hooves receded in the distance Nhya wiped her eyes and lowered the rifle. "I don't know. Maybe. God help us."

With a roar, Shain slammed his fist into the ceramic lamp, shattering it much like the window.

Nhya placed a calming hand on his arm. "He fooled all of us, Shain. Even Curt and Luke who have a nose for magic."

"Curt and Luke?" Lily asked, perplexed.

"Our cousins," Nhya replied. "They came down last month from Billings to help us keep an eye on things. Darrell had worked here for about a year and Shain promoted him to foreman after our parents died. We needed someone. I was busy handling the books and he seemed so stable…"

Lily's eyes widened as Nhya's words sunk in. "Cousins. That's why I kept thinking Luke looked familiar. And the bear! So he *was* warning family. Luke. Luke is family."

Shain kissed the top of Lily's head, his nerves still pinging with adrenaline over the thought of losing her. "He is."

Nhya checked Lily's neck, her lips pursed in concern. "You're family now, too, Lily."

The thought mixed in Shain's gut like an explosive cocktail and the words fell out before he could stop to think. "She will be, once she agrees to marry me."

Lily gasped. "Did—did you just…" She affixed him with a firm stare. "I can't believe you said that. What happened to traveling the path to see where it takes us?"

Taking Lily's hands, he knelt and pulled her onto his knee. "Fuck that. No more waiting. Life's too damn short. I may have lost my friggin mind in the last forty-eight hours but I'd rather lose it with you than anyone else, darlin'."

Nhya snorted. "Well, if that wasn't the lousiest proposal I've ever heard. You'll be lucky if she agrees to spend another night at the Red Bear, you big lunk head."

Lily grinned and relief washed through Shain. His heart had been up in his throat as soon as the words left his mouth. Shain took Lily's hand and turned it over, running his finger across the pale skin of her palm to her ring finger. "Nhya's right. Shithead might be a better word for me on most occasions and I know we probably need some time but, by God, Lily, I know this is the right thing. At least tell me you'll stay on for a while. Give us some time, even if you don't want to decide right now…"

Before Shain could finish he found Lily flush to his chest, her face even with his, her forest green eyes gazing into his with a depth of sincerity that stole his breath. "Listen, lunk head, time's probably a good idea but damned if I want to wait either." She took his hand and pressed it to her chest, her lower lip trembling. "I've been waiting my whole life for someone to warm up to. You've branded my heart, Shain Stevenson."

Joy swelled in Shain's gut and he crushed Lily to him as they stood. "I think we branded each other, darlin'. And I wouldn't have it any other way."

Chapter Thirteen

Shain handed Nhya the pouch as soon as he had a hand free. "This belongs to you, sis."

Lily watched in fascination as Nhya reached out a mocha-colored, trembling hand. The pendant seemed to jump into her open palm and she gasped as the ancient leather made contact. "All this time. It was here. Waiting," she whispered, a single tear rolling down one cheek as her fingers closed.

They stood in silence for a time and Lily welcomed the odd tingle, knowing that this time, everyone felt it. "Will you open it?" she asked, her curiosity banked only by the significant nature of Nhya and Shain's inheritance.

Nhya shook her head. "Not now. Not yet. There will be a time."

Lily stepped forward. "We'll be here for you, Nhya, when that time comes. We'll help you protect it."

Shain joined her, his expression fierce. "Damn straight. And if Darrell, or whoever he is, comes back I'll break his legs and drive him into Billings before I strangle him."

Nhya looked up, her entire body radiating a subtle light that washed warm across Lily's soul. "He won't be back. But there might be others — we'll have to be vigilant."

"What *was* he, Nhya?" Lily asked, taking Shain's hand.

She shook her head. "I don't know for sure. He's a man who has captured power. I don't know how, or why, but he'll continue to use it for ill."

"Shit," Shain murmured disgustedly. "You should have let me break his neck."

Nhya sighed and tucked the pouch under her shirt. "There are others who will deal with him."

Shain raised one brow. "Do you know something that we don't?"

"Yes. No." Nhya laughed fitfully. "Maybe. This is all new to me...these feelings, these thoughts I have. As I child, they were always about ordinary things. My family. A pet that needed help or attention. A sick horse. An uncle who needed to see a doctor. Knowing when it would rain, or snow, or when to bring the herd in from the range. But now—" She paused and walked to stand at the front door looking out. "Now the feelings, impressions are stronger and wide reaching. But it's not always easy to interpret their message."

She turned. "Red Claw appearing to you and Luke. I have to think it was a warning of the menace in our midst. Unfortunately, I didn't read the signs well enough to realize Lily was in danger. I'm sorry."

Nhya's words wrenched at Lily's heart and she took her hands. "That's silly. There's no way you could have known that." She gazed at Shain. "Nor could you, so don't even *think* about beating yourself up over it. As a matter of fact, if I hadn't been here...if I'd left with Shain like I'd wanted, Darrell would have the pendant now."

The reality of her words hit everyone like a wall of cold water and their gazes intersected each others' with shocked realization. "She's right," Nhya whispered, her hand pressed against the pouch beneath her blouse. She stared at Lily. "Maybe his presence wasn't so much a warning, as it was a promise, Lily. A promise that by opening your heart and allowing it to lead you, you would find the strength to protect more than the road to your own future. There is no telling exactly how many lives, or even worlds, your actions shielded tonight."

Lily gaped, the thought so overwhelming her mind simply refused to contemplate it. "I—I don't even know what to say to that."

Shain squeezed her shoulder. "You don't have to say anything. I'm about done trying to understand all this friggin'' mumbo jumbo. Let's just leave it at what Nhya said and get the hell out of here and back to the ranch. I've got a goddamn foreman to replace and I think you've got some phone calls to make, Lily."

"Phone calls?" Lily said as she rubbed her forehead.

Shain leaned down and captured her lips with his. As need wicked through her belly, he pulled back slightly, a wolfish twinkle in his gaze. "Always make good on your bets, darlin'. Especially when you win."

Epilogue

"Do you think she chickened out, Bri? She should be here by now."

Sabrina rolled her eyes and grabbed her cousin's sun-browned hand, pulling her away from the window. "Relax, Lily. She'll be here. If there's one thing Nicole would never miss, it's a party." She raised gracefully arched brows and smiled. "Especially one in her — *our* — honor."

Lily sighed and hugged Bri before reclining against the sideboard and chewing her lower lip. "I know, I know. It's just that she sounded so mysterious on her cell phone when we called her yesterday to make the arrangements for the shower. Then there were all those buzzes and dings we heard in the background. It sounded like she was in an arcade!"

Crossing her arms, Lily started pacing again, her blonde hair, past her shoulders now that she'd been letting it grow, swishing back and forth wildly. "Do you think Nic's being straight with us? What if things didn't work out for her like they have for us?"

The question hung in the air between the two cousins like a rain-swollen cloud, eager to dump dreariness on an otherwise perfect day.

Each took a moment to contemplate what that would mean for them all. Thirty days ago, almost to the hour, they'd been in the very same room of the bed-and-breakfast, making a silly pact that would end up changing their lives in a drastic way.

A wonderful way.

Lily couldn't help the sugary grin that spread across her face at the thought of Shain, her soon-to-be husband.

Husband.

What a concept. One she still hadn't gotten completely used to but she had a few more weeks to let it sink in completely. Nhya was planning everything, with input from Nicole and Sabrina, who she'd been on the phone with plenty of times since their announcement last week. Surprise, surprise, Bri had made her announcement too, confirming what Lily had suspected all along.

She'd miss having Sabrina close by but she knew marrying Josh and moving to Texas was what her cousin wanted to do. They'd just have to make a concentrated effort to get together at least a couple times a year.

Then there was Nicole.

She was obviously enjoying her *man*. The only name Lily and Bri knew him by, as Nicole had yet to reveal his identity. After nearly an hour of browbeating, Nic had finally 'fessed up to the fact that she was indeed in love and committed.

Which had sparked the idea for them all, including Aunt Viv, to meet at the bed-and-breakfast, then hustle over to the Copper Queen Hotel to celebrate their good fortune. They had so many things to share. Bri was talking marriage in another month or so, once she settled in her new satellite 'home' office in Texas. And while Lily's had informed everyone that her pending ceremony was to be held at the ranch in Montana, Nic was mum on her plans.

Which had Lily worried.

She'd said she was committed, but that could mean anything. Maybe they'd be living together, rather than marrying, which would be so like Nicole.

"Well," Bri said, running a hand over the smooth, rich red silk of her miniskirt. "Since this is close to our last night of freedom, I think we need to stop worrying about our wayward cousin and go out and enjoy ourselves."

"But—" Lily started.

Sabrina pressed a finger to her cousin's lips. "No buts. It's what Nic would want us to do, Lily, and you know it. She can meet us there if she's coming. No more worrying."

Sighing, Lily nodded. "Okay. You're right." She straightened the silk blouse that outlined her slender form to perfection. "Let's go drink ourselves blind, cuz."

A throaty laugh filled the room. "Now *that's* the spirit."

Lily and Sabrina's attention twisted to the doorway. "Nicole!"

They were in each other's arms in less than a second, all three talking and laughing at once.

"Look at your hair, Bri," Nicole said, lifting the now shoulder length black tresses with a look of surprise on her face.

Bri smiled as she ran her fingers through the shorter locks. "Yeah, I knew I was due for a cut. I just wish it had been my idea as to how much," she said in a dry tone.

Nicole hugged her tight saying, "I was scared shitless when Lily told me what happened to you. Thank God for Josh's quick reflexes!"

Bri grinned at her cousins. "Yep, now that I've got my very own rescue hero, I'm good to go. As for my new haircut... Josh brushes my hair every night. I think he's hoping to stimulate the roots for faster growth," she finished with a chuckle.

Once their laughter died down, Lily stepped back to scan Nic's shining face. "And you! I was so worried! Is everything...are you...?"

"Single and miserable again?" Nic said, one eyebrow peaked.

Lily's mouth opened then closed. Sabrina took Nic's hand. "That's not what she meant, Nicole. Besides, I don't think you were *ever* miserable being single."

"True. I've always had plenty of good times and have always enjoyed my freedom." Nicole laughed, her eyes sparkling mischievously. "Now as far as you two go, I can tell just by looking at your shit-eating grins that you've both been getting the best sex of your lives and then some."

Bri laughed and Lily's face flushed red but neither of them contradicted Nicole. Lily crossed her arms and focused her narrowed gaze on her vivacious cousin. "Well?"

"Well, what?" Nic asked, all innocence, left hand pressed against her generous cleavage.

"*Are* you single and miserable and, er, free again?"

"Lily!" Bri said, shooting a surprised look at her normally politically correct cousin.

"Well…" Nicole started, her gaze falling to the floor.

"Oh, no!" Lily said, her expression crumbling.

"Nic, what happened?"

Nicole's head snapped up and her wide grin stopped Bri and Lily cold. "Ah, hell. I can't keep this up any longer."

With that Nic thrust out her left hand, turning it just so. "Watch the drool, girls."

"Oh…my…God…"

Squeals split the silence as Sabrina and Lily took turns grabbing Nicole's hand and exclaiming over the modest but beautiful diamond and aquamarine that graced her ring finger.

"You're engaged!" Bri said with a look of shock on her face. "It's beautiful, honey. The aquamarine matches the color of your eyes perfectly."

Nicole shook her head, that sly grin on her face. "Well, I'm not exactly engaged…"

Bri's jaw dropped. "What—"

"Tell me you didn't do this without us, Nic!" cried Lily, not truly upset, just shocked and thrilled all in the same breath. "You eloped!"

"Did we ever." Nicole quickly explained how they'd decided not to wait, and jetted to Vegas over a week ago. They'd spent a blissful seven days at the luxury hotel, eating, drinking and sunning themselves poolside between episodes of mind-blowing lovemaking. They'd tied the knot on the seventh day at a small chapel.

"Better to get it out of the way, was our thinking," Nicole said as the three cousins plopped onto the sofa. "We'd both waited way too long—and I was just too stubborn to see that he was the man for me." Nic turned the ring to catch the firelight and sighed. "I've found my man, ladies. You're not angry, are you?" she asked, not sounding the least bit remorseful.

They both leaned in to hug Nicole. "Not at all, Nic," Bri said.

Lily nodded in agreement. "I just wish we'd been there to see you in your dress."

Nic laughed and pointed to the tight, white leather mini that hugged her every curve. "You're looking at it, girls."

"You didn't," Lily said.

Bri giggled. "You bet she did. I can only imagine what your man wore."

"Speaking of which," said Lily, "When do we get to meet this mystery man?"

"How about now?"

The familiar, deep male voice brought all three heads up. Nicole was off the couch in an instant and into Kev Grand's arms.

Lily stood, her mouth hanging open. "Kev Grand?"

Bri joined her. "I'll be double damned," she whispered. "Kev freakin' Grand."

"Am I missing something here?" Lily's hands went to her hips. "Didn't you two hate each other a month ago?"

Kev wrapped a muscled arm around Nicole's waist and drew her in tight. "Hate's a mite strong, don't you think, hon?"

Nic snorted and poked Kev's shoulder. "It was more of a 'we could never see eye-to-eye' thing." She kissed the bottom of

Kev's chin then looked at her cousins. "As you can see, a lot has changed."

Lily approached the couple, green eyes narrowed. She leveled a finger at Kev's chest. "I'm thrilled for Nic, *and* you, Kev, but if you do so much as one dumb- ass thing to hurt my cousin I'll—"

"You'll what, Lily?"

Lily spun and gasped. "What in the hell?"

"Now what have I told you about that mouth of yours, woman?"

"Hubba, hubba," Nic said under her breath, staring with admiration at the cowboy that filled the room.

"Shain!" Lily plowed past Kev and Nic and proceeded to wrap herself around the hulking wrangler. "What are you doing here? I thought you were going stay at the ranch!"

Bri and Nic were forced to wait while the dark cowboy stole a deep kiss from Lily before making introductions.

Shain tipped his head at each of the women and shook Kev's hand. "I do believe my fiancée meant what she said, Grand."

Kev laughed. "I have no doubt." He tapped the end of Nic's nose. "You have nothing to worry about, Lily. I'd cut off my own arm before I'd hurt a hair on this beautiful woman's—my wife's—head."

"Well this is just perfect," grouched Sabrina, as she walked to the liquor cabinet. "Here we are getting ready to head out to our wedding shower and one of us already hitched." She shook the crystal stopper at Nic and then Lily. "And both of you with your trigger trippers by your side." She sighed and poured herself a full shotglass. "Guess it's just me, my thoughts of Josh and good ol' Jack D. tonight."

Before she could throw back the shot, Kev stopped her hand. "Not so fast, Bri."

Bri lowered the drink. Nic and Lily's expressions mirrored her puzzled look.

"You might want to keep a clear head. There's been a small change of plans."

Nic looked at Kev through lowered lashes. "Kev Grand, what are you up to?"

"You starting without me, darlin'?" The double doors to the salon slammed closed, the lock clicking in place.

"Josh!" Sabrina's shout nearly deafened them all. Even the folded table the sexy firefighter had lugged into the room didn't stop Bri from launching herself at him. He caught her with one arm, holding her against his side and burying his stubbled jaw into the cleft of her neck.

"It's only been a few days, darlin', but damned if it didn't feel like forever."

Nic and Lily sighed as the striking couple kissed, Bri's sleek, exotic beauty perfectly complementing the firefighter's wholesome good looks.

"Okay, this entire scenario is *way* too coincidental." Lily laid a hand on Shain's chest. "Spill."

Josh unfolded his burden, revealing a hunter green poker table. "What's the matter, ladies? Afraid of a friendly game?"

Kev reached into his front pocket and pulled out a new deck. He ripped the plastic with his teeth, liberating the shiny cards. After inspection, he tossed it on the table and pulled over nearby chairs. "Fresh deck. No bent corners."

Shain guided Lily to the table as Kev and Josh did the same, patting a bottom or stealing a kiss in the process.

Once each of the women was seated, Shain leaned in. "The game is strip poker." He grinned wolfishly as he fanned the cards out face up. "The doors stay locked and the lights stay low until the deck's played out."

Nic chuckled as she looked down at hers, and then Lily and Bri's, limited attire. "Seems as though you have us at a disadvantage, gentlemen."

Kev leaned across and nipped at Nic's ear. "Sorta like you gals had *us* at a disadvantage, hmmm?"

Nicole purred under Kev's teasing lips.

"It's only fair that we even up the odds, eh?" Josh said before stripping off his shirt, his pecs rippling. Bri hissed, unable to keep her hands to herself.

Shain and Kev followed suit, until all three men sat bare-chested in only blue jeans and boots.

"What I want to know," Lily said as she trailed a finger down Shain's bronze biceps. "Is how you three got together to plan this little rendezvous?"

The men shared a knowing smile.

"Oh, come on now." Bri tugged gently on a strand of Josh's golden hair. "You want us to believe you three just *happened* to find each other's phone numbers and decided wrangling us out of our clothes would be the perfect get-even plan?"

"It's not about gettin' even," Kev drawled as he draped an arm protectively around his wife's shoulders. "It's about learnin' to weigh the risk against the gain…"

"Before you make a play," Josh picked up where Kev trailed off, while he gathered up the deck and gave it a shuffle.

"Then layin' down your hand without looking back," Shain finished with a soft growl. "No regrets."

Lily huffed. "Oh! You all sound just like—"

Three pairs of eyes met across the table. "Aunt Viv!"

"I can't believe it!" Bri said.

Nic's full lips quirked into a grin. "I can."

"We should have known something was up when she cancelled on us with that lame excuse about needing to prune her roses!" Lily said, wiping tears of laughter off her flushed cheeks.

"Just one rule, ladies." Shain cut the deck then handed it back to Josh, his stormy gaze touching on each of the women in turn. "Hearts are wild."

About the author:

Romantica writer, reading enthusiast, and obsessive webmistress, Nelissa Donovan has always had an insatiable curiosity for all things mystical and supernatural. It's not unusual for her to whip out a set of tarot cards on a dark, stormy night and poke around in the playground of the paranormal. Fortunately, Nelissa is grounded by a strong passion for her family, friends and work, and floats back to reality long enough to pen her wickedly virile elves, magic-wielding heroines, luscious cowboys and naughty nymphs.

Nelissa welcomes mail from readers. You can write to her c/o Ellora's Cave Publishing at 1056 Home Avenue, Akron OH 44310-3502.

Also by Nelissa Donovan:

Night Elves: Dangerous Obsession
Night Elves: Wicked Pleasures

Why an electronic book?

We live in the Information Age—an exciting time in the history of human civilization in which technology rules supreme and continues to progress in leaps and bounds every minute of every hour of every day. For a multitude of reasons, more and more avid literary fans are opting to purchase e-books instead of paperbacks. The question to those not yet initiated to the world of electronic reading is simply: *why?*

1. *Price.* An electronic title at Ellora's Cave Publishing and Cerridwen Press runs anywhere from 40-75% less than the cover price of the <u>exact same title</u> in paperback format. Why? Cold mathematics. It is less expensive to publish an e-book than it is to publish a paperback, so the savings are passed along to the consumer.

2. *Space.* Running out of room to house your paperback books? That is one worry you will never have with electronic novels. For a low one-time cost, you can purchase a handheld computer designed specifically for e-reading purposes. Many e-readers are larger than the average handheld, giving you plenty of screen room. Better yet, hundreds of titles can be stored within your new library—a single microchip. (Please note that Ellora's Cave and Cerridwen Press does not endorse any specific brands. You can check our website at www.ellorascave.com or

www.cerridwenpress.com for customer recommendations we make available to new consumers.)

3. *Mobility.* Because your new library now consists of only a microchip, your entire cache of books can be taken with you wherever you go.

4. *Personal preferences are accounted for.* Are the words you are currently reading too small? Too large? Too...**ANNOYING**? Paperback books cannot be modified according to personal preferences, but e-books can.

5. *Instant gratification.* Is it the middle of the night and all the bookstores are closed? Are you tired of waiting days—sometimes weeks—for online and offline bookstores to ship the novels you bought? Ellora's Cave Publishing sells instantaneous downloads 24 hours a day, 7 days a week, 365 days a year. Our e-book delivery system is 100% automated, meaning your order is filled as soon as you pay for it.

Those are a few of the top reasons why electronic novels are displacing paperbacks for many an avid reader. As always, Ellora's Cave and Cerridwen Press welcomes your questions and comments. We invite you to email us at service@ellorascave.com, service@cerridwenpress.com or write to us directly at: 1056 Home Ave. Akron OH 44310-3502.

NEED A MORE EXCITING
WAY TO PLAN YOUR DAY?

ELLORA'S
CAVEMEN
2006 CALENDAR

COMING THIS FALL

Lady Jaided

The premier magazine for today's sensual woman

Lady Jaided magazine is devoted to exploring the sexuality and sensuality of women. While there are many similarities between the sexual experiences of men and women, there are just as many if not more differences. Our focus is on the female experience and on giving voice and credence to it. Lady Jaided will include everything from trends, politics, science and history to gossip, humor and celebrity interviews, but our focus will remain on female sexuality and sensuality.

A Sneak Peek at Upcoming Stories

Clan of the Cave Woman
Women's sexuality throughout history.

The Sarandon Syndrome
What's behind the attraction between older women and younger men.

The Last Taboo
Why some women – even feminists – have bondage fantasies

Girls' Eyes for Queer Guys
An in-depth look at the attraction between straight women and gay men

Available Spring 2005

www.LadyJaided.com

Lady *Jaided* Regular Features

Jaid's Tirade

Jaid Black's erotic romance novels sell throughout the world, and her publishing company Ellora's Cave is one of the largest and most successful e-book publishers in the world. What is less well known about Jaid Black, a.k.a. Tina Engler is her long record as a political activist. Whether she's discussing sex or politics (or both), expect to see her get up on her soapbox and do what she does best: offend the greedy, the holier-than-thous, and the apathetic! Don't miss out on her monthly column.

Devilish Dot's G-Spot

Married to the same man for 20 years, Dorothy Araiza still basks in a sex life to be envied. What Dot loves just as much as achieving the Big O is helping other women realize their full sexual potential. Dot gives talks and advice on everything from which sex toys to buy (or not to buy) to which positions give you the best climax.

On the Road with Lady K

Publisher, author, world traveler and Lady of Barrow, Kathryn Falk shares insider information on the most romantic places in the world.

Kandidly Kay

This Lois Lane cum Dave Barry is a domestic goddess by day and a hard-hitting sexual deviancy reporter by night. Adored for her stunning wit and knack for delivering one-liners, this Rodney Dangerfield of reporting will leave no stone unturned in her search for the bizarre truth.

A Model World

CJ Hollenbach returns to his roots. The blond heartthrob from Ohio has twice been seen in Playgirl magazine and countless other publications. He has appeared on several national TV shows including The Jerry Springer Show (God help him!) and has been interviewed for Entertainment Tonight, CNN and The Today Show. He has been involved in the romance industry for the past 12 years, appearing on dozens of romance novel covers and calendars. CJ's specialty is personal interviews, in which people have a tendency to tell him everything.

Hot Mama Cooks

Sex is her food, and food is her sex. Hot Mama gives aphrodisiac a whole new meaning. Join her every month for her latest sensual adventure -- with bonus recipe!

Empress on the Mount

Brash, outrageous, and undeniably irreverent, this advice columnist from down under will either leave you in stitches or recovering from hang-jaw as you gawk at her answers to reader questions on relationships and life.

Erotic Fiction from Ellora's Cave

The debut issue will feature part one of "Ferocious," a three-part erotic serial written especially for Lady Jaided by the popular Sherri L. King.

Discover for yourself why readers can't get enough of the multiple award-winning publisher Ellora's Cave. Whether you prefer e-books or paperbacks, be sure to visit EC on the web at www.ellorascave.com for an erotic reading experience that will leave you breathless.

www.ellorascave.com